RECKONING

BOOK 2
IN THE *ASHES* SERIES

KELLY COZY

ISBN: 978-0985123482

ACKNOWLEDGMENTS

The list of people I need to thank just gets longer with every book. Funny, that.

Thanks, first of all, to the Constant Reader Brigade: Erik Hoard, Gerry Hoard, Alyca Tanner, Albert Muller, and Karen Girard. Your advice, encouragement, and enthusiasm have made it all possible.

A big helping of gratitude goes to all the usual suspects: Mom and Dad, Loa Allebach, Lauren Baratz-Logsted, Andrew Farrell, Meg Gerzeske, Gary Glass, Richard and Aljean Harmetz, Barrett Keller, Billie Martin, Faith Martin, Elizabeth McCullough, Diane Molberg, Speer Morgan, Alan Natale, Linda Palkovic, Jim Reilly, Aimee Richardson, Pete Stefansky, Hannibal Tabu, Stanley and Janice Thompson, and Emily Thompson.

Very special thanks to all the readers who've come along for the ride with these characters. I hope you like the people you'll meet and the places you'll go to in this book. And my thanks go to the fans, friends, and followers who make this all possible.

Much love to Scott and Alex, for putting up with all those nights I spent hunched over the laptop, typing frantically and muttering to myself.

A shout-out to some of the indie bookstores who've been so supportive: The Book Loft in Solvang, CA; Vroman's Bookstore in Pasadena, CA; and Pegasus Books in Berkeley and Oakland, CA.

Book cover design by GoOnWrite.com. Smite Publications logo by alanNdesign. Copyediting services provided by Hannibal Tabu.

"I never saw a brute I hated so;
He must be wicked to deserve such pain.
I shut my eyes and turn'd them on my heart.
As a man calls for wine before he fights,
I ask'd one draught of earlier, happier sights,
Ere fitly I could hope to play my part.
Think first, fight afterwards—the soldier's art:
One taste of the old time sets all to rights."
— Robert Browning

"A man will reap only what he sows. If he sows in the field of the flesh, he will reap a harvest of corruption."
— Galatians 6: 7-8

"Though she be but little, she is fierce."
— William Shakespeare

Part One

Chapter One

The maple trees lining the walkway seemed to glow with a dim fire. The trees were beautiful at every time of the year, but to Father John Reilly the autumnal colors were a benediction, a reminder of God's goodness. It would have been easy for God to shape beauty into only the rarest things, but to put beauty into such a commonplace thing as a tree spoke of a great love for His creation.

This thought came to Father John every morning on his walk to the church — mostly, he understood with a wry amusement, because it was only his second autumn here in Indiana. Before, he had lived in sun-kissed California; his trees had been ficus and palm and eucalyptus. Either perpetual green, or nature decided to give color a miss and go straight from green to dead brown. Boring. Given another few years in Indiana, he might find the maples' fiery beauty boring. He hoped not.

Father John pushed open the door of the church, stepped inside, blessed himself and stood for a moment, waiting for his eyes to adjust to the dimness. First service had come and gone, as had the celebrants; only a few penitents sat in the pews, waiting. Saint Stephen's held reconciliation twice a week. Saturdays were always busy, with lines of working parents and high school students. Wednesday mornings were quieter, and the penitents were retirees, women mostly, or a few weary-looking men on their way home from third shift. Father John made his way down the aisle toward the confessional, absently taking note of the few attendees. His path took him past the alcove with its statue of the Virgin Mary. The lights in the alcove had not been turned on — lit only by candles, it was dim and, at first glance, unoccupied. A second look found a solitary person in the alcove, a vague male shape.

He was pleased with the assignment of Wednesday Reconciliation. He liked the still beauty of the church on these quiet mornings. There was a peace to it he found soothing, that helped him believe that people did leave the sacrament not only having received absolution, but feeling absolved as well.

The morning passed. Two doors in to his room, one for face-to-face confessions, the other for anonymous ones. On Saturdays most were face-to-face. Wednesdays was the day for voices behind the screen; his other senses sharpened and by the end of a Wednesday morning his nose and ears were as finely attuned as a blind person's. He heard the penitents' feet on the floorboards and the passage of air as they stepped into the confessional, could have an idea of their gender and age by the smell of cigarettes or lavender sachet.

Twenty minutes left; there had been no penitents for some time now. Father John sat, thinking of maple trees and piles of leaves burning, when the voice said: "Bless me Father, for I have sinned."

Father John was startled, for he'd heard nothing. Not a creak of the floor, not a rustle of clothing. It was as if a ghost had slipped in, *sans* Jacob Marley's dragging chains. His nose should have alerted him. He'd been thinking of leaves burning, had mistaken the used-cigarette smell of the penitent for that. The voice was hoarse, as if the man had only recently recovered from a bad case of laryngitis. A slight quality of hesitation, not as if the man was nervous about confessing, Father John sensed, but as if it hurt to speak in that rasping voice.

Recovering, he said, "In the name of the Father, the Son, and the Holy Spirit. May the Lord help you find it in your heart to make a good confession."

Silence on the other side of the screen, a pause that stretched out for so long that the priest wondered if he'd imagined the voice. Then: "It's been ...

oh, it's been a *long* time since my last confession." A rusty sound that might have been a laugh.

"How long?"

On the other side of the screen Father John could see no more than a dim shape, yet he sensed the penitent looking at the screen, trying to see through it. "How long have you been here, Father? At Saint Stephen's?"

"This is my second year here."

"And before that? Where were you?"

"In California."

A sigh. The man seemed to relax a bit. "Good. You wouldn't know me. I grew up here. Never thought I would come back. It's not a place you come back to, is it?"

"I like it well enough," Father John said. "And you have come back."

"Just for this. If things had gone differently. If I knew that Robert ..." The man stopped.

Father John waited, breathing in the smell from the other side of the screen, cigarettes and liquor, spent adrenaline and stale clothing. He wanted to say *Go on,* or reassure the man that by virtue of being here he was halfway to forgiveness, but something held him back. He waited.

"It's been a long time since my last confession. More than thirty years, I'd say. A person does a lot in that time, God knows I did. Enough to keep you here all the rest of the day if I wanted to go into detail. But none of that matters. If it were just that I wouldn't be here.

"I've taken life, Father. I killed a woman. And her child."

Father John did not feel cold, or even numb, but his limbs seemed too heavy. Last Christmas his brother-in-law had jokingly asked, "So, have any murderers shown up to confess yet?" Now one had.

Shocked, and somewhat sick, but not afraid. He got no sense of malice from the man. He found his voice, said, "The Lord can forgive any sin, even murder, if — "

"No!" This was followed by a cough and a hiss of what might have been pain. "No, it wasn't murder. I'd done murder before, I suppose that's what you'd call it. But this felt like murder.

"It's not making sense to you is it? That's all right. You see, right now you're in love with the pretty autumn leaves and all that. But I sat here so many years, waiting for something to happen. A lifetime of Friday night fish frys and Tuesday Rotary Club meetings might have been fine for my old man, but I was twitching like a finger on a trigger, I was that desperate to find something.

"You could say I found it. Once I left, you see, I went to work for the government. I was a spook."

"Spook?"

"You don't watch too many movies, Father? A spy. I started out during the Cold War, only it never seemed cold to me. I went places. Russia, Afghanistan, Nicaragua. Any place there was bad shit ... excuse me. Bad stuff going on. My specialty was deep cover, going in and pretending I was one of the bad guys so I could get close to them. It was the only way, most of the time. You have to earn their trust and become like a friend.

"I was good at it. I know I was good at it because the people who weren't and even some who were are all dead now. And five years ago the party was over. They gave me a nice chunk of money and shipped me off to Florida to mark time for the rest of my days. I could have started over, but I didn't. I waited for them to call me back.

"I guess something would have woken me up sooner or later. It was ... you said you're from California, right?"

"Yes," the priest replied. He'd forgotten he was hearing a confession. He was wondering who this man was and what turn his tale would take next.

"You remember the federal building bombing?"

"I wasn't there then, but yes, I remember."

"You saw the girl, the blonde woman who was in the picture that became so famous?"

"Yes."

A deep sigh, harsh like the wind rattling through dry leaves. "She's the one who woke me up. I wanted to help her. I even went back to the agency to see if they'd take me back and that rat bastard Halsey — sorry, Father — said no. Well I'd be damned if I was having any of that. I went to see Robert and he put me on the trail. It was a domestic group that set the bomb. I bet none of that ever made the evening news. I tracked them down to Wisconsin and worked my way in."

Another sigh. Father John wanted to ask who Robert was but before he could, the voice resumed, hoarser than ever.

"That's when it started to go wrong, Father. The agency sent someone after me, an agent I used to work with. I killed him. I had to, or he would have killed me. But it was how he died. Badly. If I'd just shot him, that would have been different. Robert told me at the start something wasn't right about what I wanted to do, but I thought killing Beatty would be the worst of it.

"The guy in charge of the group that set the bomb. His name was Richard and don't get me wrong, he was a bastard and what he'd done was wrong but I liked him all the same. He was honest in a way and he believed in his what he was doing. He was smart. If he'd been on our side he'd have been one of the best. It's funny. Betrayal is a part of the job and after a while you get to like it. You have to. But I almost didn't want to betray Richard, especially after he trusted me with her."

The priest felt his palms grow sweaty. Never had the small dimensions of the confessional closed in on him so. "What was her name?" he prompted gently.

"Anna." A long silence, followed by a gurgling sound and the scent of liquor. "Sorry, Father. Dutch courage. Anna was Richard's wife. She didn't know anything about his group. He wanted it that way. We all did. Even that rat bastard Steve did, I think. I didn't want to like her but I did. I couldn't help it. She was sweet and kind. I think she felt sorry for me. She thought I was this lonely divorced guy and she made me cookies and lasagna. Hell, she even wanted to set me up with her cousin. Sometimes I went over to their place not even thinking about the mission, I just wanted to be around her. I didn't have a thing for her, you understand, she was just … nice to be around.

"I killed her, Father."

He'd known this was coming but it was still a shock. Father John's ears were attuned to the nuances of emotion and he'd heard affection clearly. "How did it happen?"

"I came to the house. I won't go into details but my cover was blown. Richard and Anna still didn't know what I was. Anna was gone, and I was taking Richard away when she came home. Richard told her to leave, I did too. We wanted her safe. But she didn't go. She came after me, she was trying to keep me from Richard. I didn't want to hurt her, not for anything. I pushed her away from me, that's all I did, but I pushed her too hard. She fell and hit her head on the mantel. I think she was dead before she hit the floor. I can't stop hearing the sound her head made on the mantel, Father. The hand I pushed her with, it burns. It wasn't murder, but it feels like murder."

A silence. The priest broke it, saying, "You said you'd killed a woman and her child."

"Anna was pregnant. I didn't know at the time. Richard told me, after." A harsh, rasping laugh. "It was never murder before."

"Don't be so sure," the priest replied.

"Killing an arms dealer who specialized in chemical warfare isn't murder, it's a public service. It was never murder before because it was never innocent blood before. Anna and her baby ..." The man trailed off.

"What happened with Richard?"

"He nearly killed me. Caught me off guard and choked me. I don't blame him, I had that one coming. But I managed to conk him out. I had to get him out of there before someone came by. So I ... "

"What happened to Anna?"

A silence from behind the screen. Father John thought he could hear puzzlement in it. "There was nothing I could do for her. I put her on the sofa and put a blanket over her. I had to finish the mission, I had to take Richard to — "

"You just left her there?" Father John felt his well of compassion running dry, replaced by anger. He shouldn't feel that way, he knew, but the man left the woman's body to rot for who knew how long, until some unsuspecting person found it.

"Yes. It was all I could do."

Silence on both sides of the screen. The priest groped for the words he needed to say. His own feelings he could sort out later; right now he had to act in his role as confessor. "There is no sin that God cannot forgive — "

"I don't want forgiveness. Not now, anyway. Forgiveness now would be a charity. I don't want to be forgiven until I've paid for what I've done, and it's a long time before I'm paid in full. And I'm not even sure I believe in God. I need Anna to forgive me, not God."

"Then why are you here?"

"The only thing that's kept me going these last days is hoping I can tell Robert all this. He's my last friend. My only friend, really. We were in the agency together — I suppose you could call him my mentor. He helped me when this all started. He warned me, too, but I didn't listen. I need to tell him all this because he'll understand. But last I saw him, he'd been diagnosed with cancer. I haven't talked to him since. I don't even know if he's alive. And I thought, if he isn't ... I just thought ... someone should know what happened."

Silence again. After a few moments, the tolling of the church bell. A single bell — they'd been here a quarter hour past the time confessions usually ended. When the bell's sound faded, the priest asked, "What happened to Richard? And the woman you wanted to help, what about her?"

No answer came. His visitor had slipped out just as he'd entered, quiet as a ghost. Only the fading scent of cigarettes was a sign that the man had been here at all.

Father John resisted the urge to open the confessional door and get a glimpse of him. The man had chosen anonymity and the priest would let him keep that. Also, he needed to soothe his nerves, unraveled by the story. He used an old trick he'd learned in the seminary, reciting the Our Father in Latin; the unfamiliar language focused and settled his mind. When enough time had passed, he stepped out of the confessional.

He could not help giving a quick glance around the church. It was empty. As he walked toward the doors he passed the alcove. Recalling the vague male shape he'd seen there, he wondered if it had been his last penitent.

Something new was here in the alcove. Laid at the feet of the Virgin's statue was a flower. A white daisy. It hadn't been there when he'd first passed by the alcove, he was sure of it.

Father John picked up the daisy and walked along the fiery maple path to the rectory, the flower a jarring note of springtime in the autumn palette. Once inside, he found a small vase for the flower, then went to the shelves where in a dusty reference book he found what he was looking for. Daisy, symbol of innocence.

He went back to the church and left the flower in its vase by the Virgin's statue. Then he lit a candle and said a prayer— not that the man would be forgiven, but that he would get the chance to be forgiven. When that prayer was done, he started to leave, then lit another candle and said another prayer — this one to Saint Jude, the patron of lost causes.

Sean Kincaid sat in the van's driver's seat, wondering what to do next. After a little while the priest came out of the church; he was holding the daisy, Sean noticed. The priest walked to the rectory and went inside. He emerged a few minutes later with the daisy in a pretty blue vase, and went back into the church. A faint smile lit Sean's features for a moment, then vanished.

Confession was supposed to be good for the soul. He didn't feel any change; no weight had been lifted from his soul, if he even had one. If anything, he felt more heavily burdened for telling his tale to this priest, who seemed a kind, decent sort and so young. Barely out of seminary most likely, and too young to have to hear such things. One more thing to regret.

No, the talk had helped nothing. He was tired and his throat hurt. Sean rested his hands on the wheel, knowing he should drive to the highway and resume his eastward journey. What little he had seen of the town had not changed much in the last thirty years, and any changes were bad: Lander's pharmacy was gone, replaced by a Rite Aid. The empty fields west of town were now a Wal-Mart. Generic America was metastasizing into his home town.

He idly wondered if the house on Lincoln Street was still there. Who lived there now, and had they managed to breathe life into that house? For it had been nothing more than a way station between his childhood and the outside world since he was thirteen and his mother had died. After that it was just him and the old man; neither had understood the other and without his mother to bridge the gap, neither one cared to try. His only fond memories of that house were of the basement bomb shelter, which he had turned into a hideaway. His friends — all like Sean himself, bored by the town and their lives but too clever to drown their boredom in dissolution and petty crime — would come over and the basement room was a haven: Dave Brubeck music and a black-and-white TV showing creature features, dimmed lights and dancing with girlfriends. The taste of whiskey sours and the way Helen Karafilis' hair smelled like rosewater and honey from working in her parents' bakery. Helen had been his first lover and even now that rosewater-and-honey scent drove him mad. Maybe that's where it had all started, during those afternoons of sitting in the Karafilis bakery having baklava and outrageously strong coffee, watching Helen and her slightly exotic beauty as she boxed up pastries. Maybe that's when he knew that there was a life for him outside this town's borders, something outside of small-town provinciality. Perhaps he should stop by the bakery, see if Helen was still there. He wouldn't have to talk to her, didn't want her to recognize him. Just to see if she was still beautiful, have a little warmth and respite. He would do that. He would —

You just left her there.

The priest's question, now a statement. *You just left her there.* Sean's eyes closed, his hands went white-knuckle tight on the steering wheel. Yes, he'd just left Anna there, because taking Richard to Jennifer Thomson had been his mission. He'd gotten his quarry and escaped, and just left her there. Sweet Anna, who had been kind to him and whose only crime was to protect the husband she loved. He had left her there and who knew when she would be found, or what unlucky soul would find her.

In the agency days, cleaners had sometimes come to take the bodies. Even Richard had gotten a shallow grave. He could have given Anna that. Better yet, he could have not killed her.

You just left her there.

Sean opened his eyes, let out a sound somewhere between a gasp and a sigh. With shaking hands he turned the key in the van's ignition and started the engine. In a few minutes he was on the highway again, hoping he could reach Robert and confess to him, a confession that could give him some relief, if not absolution. Heading east, putting miles between himself and his unquiet ghosts.

Chapter Two

Deirdre Monahan tossed her purse and a bag full of dirty laundry onto the passenger seat of her truck, then sat down in the driver's seat. She'd had the truck since high school and it still ran well. The trick was getting it to run. You had to push the clutch in *just so*, give it precisely *this much* gas, and then — success.

"Good girl." Deirdre patted the dashboard. She was fond of the truck, faulty starter and all, and even more fond of it since the divorce had gone through. Her mother couldn't understand why she had let Randy have the Mustang; couldn't understand why Deirdre took as little of the things she and Randy had bought together as she could live without.

It was simple, really. She wanted to start over, on her own. Once her anger at Randy for putting them into a debt sinkhole and losing his job and cheating on her with that all-tits-and-no-brains floozy had subsided to a dull roar, once she was faced with legal papers and signatures to end the marriage, she'd found herself wondering what to do with her life. She'd said as much to her cousin Anna, who put things in perspective.

"You know what they say, Dee," Anna had said. "Everything happens for a reason. And when life closes a door, it opens a window as well. Did I miss any of the other clichés?"

"Every cloud has a silver lining."

"That too. Take your pick."

Deirdre liked the one about the door and the window best. So she had slammed the door (hoping to catch Randy's fingers in the jamb), and jumped out the window. She jumped out by herself, and that was why she'd kept the truck — she wanted to do this on her own, and she'd never been on her own before. After high school she'd lived with her folks, then with Randy, and now she was twenty-eight and had never had a life she could call hers alone.

So far it was working out all right. The job wasn't the best — she was a clerk at the new Wal-Mart over in Lakeside, but it paid the bills until she could find something she liked better. Likewise the apartment. It was threadbare and she was still living out of boxes, but she liked the freedom of eating whatever she wanted, cleaning up the house when or if she felt like it, and not having to share the TV remote with anyone.

Anna had offered her a room at their house. Deirdre hadn't known how to refuse without hurting Anna's feelings; Richard had come to her rescue. He'd seen her distress and said, "You need to sort things out and stand on your own feet for a while, don't you?"

Relieved, she'd replied that was true. They understood, but told her she was welcome at any time to stop by for a hot dinner, or use their washer and dryer, or go for a ride on one of the horses. It all sounded wonderful to Deirdre.

She had last talked to Anna on Sunday, nearly a week ago. Anna was glad to hear she was settling in. "Now that life's not too crazy you'll need to come by for dinner more often. Should we make it a standing date for Sunday?" Anna asked.

"That's not too much trouble, is it?"

"Of course not. Richard's always bringing his friends over, but they're all men. It'll be nice to have some female company for a change. Which reminds me, Dee. There's one of Richard's friends I think you should meet."

"I don't know if I'm up for meeting anyone new just yet."

"Just see if there's any sparks."

In spite of herself she was intrigued. Deirdre always felt weird going to restaurants or the movies by herself, and a date would be welcome. "Wait, it's not that Steve guy you told me about? He sounded like kind of a yo-yo."

"Have a little faith in me? His name's Sam, he's a very nice guy. A real gentleman."

"What's he look like?"

"Well, he's older than you, I'm not sure how much. Not too tall, not too short. Losing his hair."

"Sounds dreamy."

Anna never talked trash about people, and she didn't now, but she did say, "Handsome is as handsome does, Dee." Meaning that good-looking as Randy had been, as a husband he hadn't amounted to much.

"Touché."

"Not that I'm matchmaking or anything, but you need a steady guy. And he needs a nice girlfriend, not some slutbunny."

Deirdre laughed. "Nan! Do you kiss your mother with that mouth?"

Richard's voice boomed in the background. "Who's a slutbunny? Where can I meet her?"

"Oh stop!" giggled Anna. "Just think about it, that's all I'm asking. You'll see him at Thanksgiving, I'm sure, if not sooner. See how you feel about it then. You *will* be here for Thanksgiving?"

"Wouldn't miss it for anything."

"Good." Anna's voice dropped a bit. She sounded both shy and happy. "I may have some good news for you then."

Deirdre's heart had done a flip at these words. Anna wouldn't say what the news was, but Deirdre could make a good guess. Anna was expecting. Deirdre knew that Anna had wanted a child badly ever since she'd married Richard, but they'd had no luck yet. There had been two miscarriages that Deirdre knew of — she suspected there had been at least one more, judging by how unusually moody and silent Anna had been two Christmases ago. Deirdre was happier than ever that she'd moved close to Anna and Richard. If Anna was indeed pregnant, she'd need to get her rest, and what better way than for Deirdre to come by every Sunday to help with the housecleaning and errands, and whip up a batch of her famous Eggs McMonahan.

Now, thinking about all this, Deirdre put her truck into gear and began driving to Anna's house. It was a gloomy day, threatening to rain, but she didn't mind. It would be warm and cozy at Anna's house. It always was.

She opened the gate that led to Richard and Anna's Christmas tree farm, pausing to take a deep breath of the pine-scented air. Christmas was only a few months away; Deirdre had never been to the farm at the holidays. Anna said it was chaotic but fun, and another set of hands were always welcome. If cutting trees and tying them onto car roofs didn't suit her, there was always ringing up orders or running the snack stand.

After closing the gate behind her, she drove down the smooth dirt road to the house. Not for the first time, she felt an unwelcome twinge of envy. There was no resentment in it, no ill will. She just wondered why she couldn't have a life like Anna's — the farm, the pretty house, the husband who was not just handsome and charming but who clearly loved Anna more than anything else.

She was in luck. Richard's truck and Anna's station wagon were both in the driveway. She hated surprising them like this, but every time she'd called this week she'd gotten the answering machine. They hadn't called her cell; they must have been busy. She grabbed her purse and walked up to the front door.

The door had an intercom; a good safety precaution, Richard had told her, considering how many visitors they got with the tree farm. She pressed the intercom button and got no answer. She pressed again; although she knew her voice wouldn't carry, she called out anyway. "Anna? Richard? It's Deirdre."

No answer.

Deirdre was positive Anna had said they'd be home Sunday. Anna had even told her Richard might be able to look at the truck and see if he could fix the starter. Deirdre stepped off the porch and began to walk down the driveway, toward the back of the house. As she passed the stables a shrill whinny made her jump. Both horses were looking out of the stable windows at her. The palomino looked tired, almost ill, and the bay was tossing his head in agitation. Deirdre walked over to the stables, murmuring soothing noises to the horses. "Hey boys, hey pretty ponies," she sang as she got close to the horses. The bay whinnied again, and Deirdre looked inside the stables. She was shocked to see the feed bins empty, and the stable floor in need of a good cleaning. Still crooning to the horses, she found a basket of carrots outside the stables and put a half dozen in the feed bins; they were devoured in no time, and the horses looked at her expectantly. "Wait, guys, let me find Anna."

She headed back to the driveway, not quite running. Her spine felt crawly and she wiped her sweaty palms on her jeans. She stood indecisive in the driveway for a moment, then went to the back of the house, to the kitchen door. She banged on the door, called out Anna's name, and when there was no answer, tried the door. It was unlocked. Deirdre opened the door and stepped inside.

The smell hit her with the force of a slap. She stepped back, bumped into the door, and caught hold of the doorknob to steady herself. Deirdre pinched her nostrils shut and breathed through her mouth, but that didn't banish the smell — it was just lying in wait, pressing against her skin, waiting for her to relax her vigilance and breathe through her nose again. "Anna?" she called. Her voice seemed unnaturally loud. For the house was not just quiet. It was silent.

She blinked, her eyes adjusting to the dim light of the kitchen. After a moment she found the source of the smell: a whole chicken, taken out to thaw and left forgotten on the counter.

Her relief was short-lived. What was a rotten chicken doing left out in Anna's immaculate kitchen? Why were the horses unfed and their stables dirty? Where the hell were Anna and Richard?

Deirdre walked quickly out of the kitchen, into the hallway. The silence had a sound now, ringing in her ears. "Anna? Richard? Are you here? Please say something."

She went into the living room and stopped, staring. As she tried to make sense of what she was seeing, she forgot to plug her nose and the smell hit her harder than ever. She gagged and bit down on her arm to kill a scream. Plugging her nostrils, she looked around the room.

There wasn't much wrong with it at first glance. It was only if you knew Anna and what a good housekeeper she was that you'd know something had happened. Anna wouldn't leave dirty scuff marks on the floor, wouldn't leave the hearth rug bunched up and the fireplace pokers in a heap.

Then there was the afghan on the sofa, covering something. Covering someone.

Yes, someone, because there was a person-size shape under it. The afghan mercifully hid whatever lay under it, save for a pair of pink sneakers protruding from one end.

Deirdre swallowed hard, trying not to recall that she'd seen those sneakers on Anna's feet two weeks ago. She felt herself walking over to the sofa, saw her hand reaching out to that afghan. She didn't know why at first, and then understood. Because once she pulled it back and saw that it wasn't Anna after all, then the world would be OK again. There'd be an explanation somehow. Because it wasn't Anna here, it couldn't be. She just had to see for herself.

"Please," whispered Deirdre, and pulled back the afghan.

Chapter Three

Robert was waiting.

That was one of the worst things about cancer — the way it made you passive. You sat there while they bombarded you with radiation and dripped poison into your veins; you let them cut you open for surgery. You were laid low by fatigue and nausea. You were pain's bitch. Throughout all this, you waited — for the nausea to subside, for the next treatment, for the test results.

In the end, you waited for the doctor to tell you there was nothing more to be done.

Robert had suspected from the first diagnosis that he wouldn't win the fight. But he had fought regardless; he had been through too many battles and faced too many enemies to give in to this one easily. For a while it even looked as though he might win, as the first round of treatments pushed the rogue cells into remission. But after a few months' respite, they came back with renewed fury, as if their temporary defeat had made them eager to destroy their enemy. In the end, they won.

Robert had accepted the news of defeat calmly. The blow was not as heavy as it might have been. He had money for good nursing care and later, a hospice worker. He had no close relatives to subject to his slow dying; old colleagues got word and paid their respects. He ordered CDs and books by mail, and spent his days reading and listening to music. It was a curiously peaceful time for him — he was not in too much discomfort yet, and not as afraid of death as he would have thought.

He did fear dying, however, and if circumstances had been different, he might have spent a few weeks getting his affairs in order and enjoying the Maine summer, then shot himself before the inevitable pain set in. There was no dishonor in that, but he decided to wait it out as long as he could. Fighting the good fight had been only one reason he'd gone through the treatments. The other reason was that he was waiting to hear from Sean Kincaid.

He hadn't heard from Sean since right after the bombing of the Los Angeles federal building, when he'd put Sean on the path of an antigovernment group in the upper Midwest. Ordinarily the silence would not have bothered him. Robert had many old friends left, both in and out of the agency, and through them he'd heard that the agency had put Sean under surveillance after his bid to resume his duties was rejected. Sean had been one of Robert's prized pupils, and Robert was pleased that Sean had bided his time until the surveillance relaxed a bit, then slipped away so neatly that three days passed before they knew he'd gone.

Which meant Sean had been on his mission a year now — not too long, considering how little of a lead he'd had to go on. It was not uncommon for deep cover assignments like this to take months. But from the moment Sean had spoken of his plans, to find those responsible for the bombing and take them to the last survivor, that girl Jennifer — Robert felt a sense of deep unease. Not because of Sean's plans, which were, typically, daring and sensible at the same time. Not even because he'd heard that another former agent had been sent after Sean. Robert's unease was less definable, and therefore more troubling to him.

Now that the measure of his life was in mere months, he yearned for an end to the silence. Even a phone call to say *The mission's over. I'll be there soon.* But there was no phone call, and no news from his old grapevine. As every week went by the morphine dosages became a little stronger, and the time between them shorter. With every week his resolve not to use the gun hidden under his mattress weakened, but he would wait as long as he could.

He was waiting for Halsey as well, although he hadn't realized it until Halsey came to visit.

Halsey was their old boss, their last boss, the one who'd been brought in to keep things under budget and, to his credit, had done so. The cost had been compromised missions and replacing the best agents with spy satellites and other alluring technology. Whether the cost had been worth it depended on whom you talked to. Halsey was still employed, so he was in favor. For now.

Halsey came on a day that was beginning to show hints that fall was coming; a bit of a chill in the morning, the sun's light muted in the afternoon. Robert was fatigued — the pain and illness had taken a turn for the worse these last few days — and it must have shown. When Halsey saw Robert his eyes gleamed. "You look terrible," Halsey said with a faint but unmistakable smile that made him the poster boy for *schadenfreude*. He kept smiling as he watched Kumar, the hospice worker, help Robert onto the adjustable bed. "Get me something to drink, will you?" Halsey said, snapping his fingers at Kumar.

Kumar's demeanor, calm bordering on serene, didn't change. He ignored Halsey and asked, "Do you need anything, Robert?"

"Just some water for both of us, Kumar. Thank you." After Kumar left the room Robert said, "He's from hospice. He's not your manservant."

"I thought fetching me a Diet Coke would be a nice change of pace from bringing your pills and fluffing your pillows." Halsey sat down as far as he could get from Robert — as if he thought cancer might be contagious.

Halsey never did anything without a reason. If he was here, he wanted something. "Let's not waste time in false pleasantries," Robert said. "What do you want?"

"Where is Sean?"

"I don't know."

"Don't bullshit me," Halsey snapped. "I know he came up here to see you. What did he want?"

"He wanted to clean up the mess you let happen. I think you'd be grateful for that. You didn't even have to pay him. Less money out of your precious budget." Robert was enjoying himself for the first time in weeks.

"That is not the point," Halsey said. "He's completely unauthorized for this mission. I have — "

Robert smiled. "Unauthorized? Like the way you hired Beatty under the table and sent him to take out Sean?"

Halsey froze. "How could … You don't know that."

"Of course I do. We don't tell tales to outsiders, but among ourselves there are no secrets. Don't you know that by now? The management didn't want you to send anyone after Sean because that would be admitting they fucked up and let that incident happen in the first place. So you went under the table, and I am curious to know if management has found that out yet. How long did it take you to find someone? People weren't lining up for the job, were they?"

Halsey didn't answer. Kumar came in with two glasses of water. Halsey snatched one out of Kumar's hand and drank half of it down.

Robert resumed: "So you finally got a taker. Good old Beatty. When was the last time you heard from him?"

A grudging mutter. "Christmas."

"He's dead, then."

"You don't know that."

"It's the only thing that makes sense. The only other alternatives are that he decided to join Sean, which he was too loyal to do, or he gave up on the mission, which he would also never do, yes?"

"You don't know that."

Robert sat up despite the pain, feeling a distantly familiar sensation in his veins: anger. It was very welcome. "Sean was more right about you than I knew. You really don't understand us — any of us. You can't fathom why people would have set that bomb in Los Angeles to begin with. You don't know why Sean wanted back in or why he was so angry when you wouldn't let him. You can't understand why I helped him or why no one would go after him. Do you even know why Beatty took the job?"

"He needed the money."

Robert applauded. "At last, some insight. Bravo! Of course, the money. Dollars and cents, something you finally understand. And that's why Beatty's dead. Not because Sean was the better agent, although undoubtedly he was. But Beatty's heart wasn't in it. Why should it be? You threw us away when we were needed most, and you wonder why we don't do your bidding any longer."

Halsey jumped to his feet. "Shut up, for the love of God. It's not like it was any picnic being in charge of all of you. A bunch of whiny little brats, that's what you were." He sing-songed: "We need more time, more money, more this, more that. Boo hoo." He pointed at Robert. "Tell me where he is or I can make life very unpleasant for you."

Robert laughed. It hurt to laugh but at the same time it felt wonderful. "In case you've failed to notice, I've got terminal cancer. I have weeks if I'm lucky and months if I'm not. I've got all the unpleasantness I need, thank you."

"Fine. Maybe *she'll* tell me."

"Who's 'she'?" Robert asked.

"That lawyer. The one Kincaid used to bang."

"Which lawyer?"

"You know exactly who I mean. The brunette with the legs, Pavour or whatever her last name was."

"I don't remember anyone like that."

"I do. Maybe I'll pay her a little visit, find out what she knows."

"Go ahead. It's not as if I could stop you."

Halsey was silent for a moment, as if he'd been expecting a different reply. The voice that broke the silence was Kumar's, from the doorway. "Pardon me. I have to bring in some medication."

Kumar came in, bringing with him a glass of water and some pills. Robert accepted them gratefully. He'd been so focused on the conversation he hadn't noticed how tired he was, nor that the pain was starting to return. He swallowed the pills, ignoring Halsey's look of contempt. "You're going to end up a junkie," Halsey said.

"I'll donate my body to the Betty Ford Clinic, then," replied Robert. He had been more tired than he realized. Before he knew it, he was asleep.

He woke to find Halsey gone. Robert turned on the CD player. He listened to Beethoven's "Ghost" piano trio and pondered his next step.

He'd lied to Halsey, of course. He knew perfectly well who the brunette lawyer was; he'd even seen her and Sean once. He'd been walking past one of Georgetown's nicer bars, had glanced in the window and seen Sean and the brunette at the bar, drinking martinis and playing footsie. Sean had said something that amused her; she'd thrown her head back and laughed, a smoky-sweet laugh that made most of the men within earshot sit up and take notice. Robert even knew the brunette's first name, although Sean was more scrupulous than most about keeping his personal and his professional lives separate. He'd only slipped up once as far as Robert knew, on a particularly brutal mission in the dead of winter in Russia. They were half-frozen and had gone without rest for three days. Sleep would be fatal, so they'd kept it at bay by talking — about past missions, about women, about the ways they would exact revenge on the handler who'd left them to freeze. At one point Robert had asked, "What's the going rate for your soul?" and Sean had replied, "To close my eyes right now and wake up in Monique's bed."

Robert didn't know what Monique's life was like now, but she didn't deserve to have that bastard Halsey barge into her life without warning. Slowly, carefully, Robert hoisted himself out of bed and over to the computer. A few minutes on the internet, a few minutes typing in Microsoft Word, and the warning was there, in an envelope with no return address. Kumar posted it that day.

A few weeks later he knew he'd been right to warn Monique. Pain had attacked him in the night, left him vomiting and calling for Kumar's help in a voice made wretched by tears. Robert didn't know what was worse: the pain, the certain knowledge that there would only be more of it in the weeks to come, the way it had reduced him to weeping. No, the worst was the helplessness — he, who had helped changed the fate of nations, had to ask someone to bring him morphine and clean up vomit.

It was not death he feared but dying, and the prospect of weeks with this misery was intolerable. Once Kumar had left the room, Robert eased himself over to the side of the bed and carefully leaned over. The gun was hidden under the mattress, out of sight but well within reach. He'd made sure of that weeks ago. He'd selected the gun carefully; it was his father's gun, a .32 that would get the job done without leaving much of a mess for Kumar. Now he just had to hope Sean understood that he'd held out as long as he could. *I'm sorry, but I simply can't face weeks of this. Please try to —*

The gun was gone.

Robert leaned over further, swept his hand back and forth under the mattress. There was no question about it. Gone.

He lay staring up at the ceiling. Kumar knew about the gun, but would never have taken it. They had a tacit agreement that Robert wouldn't ask for Kumar's help with an early exit, but Kumar wouldn't stop Robert either.

Halsey had taken the gun. He must have done it when Robert fell asleep. There had been no other visitors recently, and even if there had been, his agency colleagues would never have taken it. They all knew the importance of saving the last bullet for one's self. He was now without an escape measure, but more disturbing was the surety that not only had he underestimated Halsey, but that Halsey disliked him enough to take the escape measure away.

Disliked him? No. Hated him.

Robert shivered. More than ever he was glad he'd sent Monique the note. More than ever he wished Sean would come back, so he could have fair warning as well.

Chapter Four

A corner office at the law firm of Beckman, Worth, and Spinnett. The woman sitting behind the large oak desk looked over her list of appointments for the day, toying with a lock of her dark hair. When the phone rang, she waited before answering — just enough for the phone to ring one more time. It was a hesitation invisible to any observer, who would have simply thought that she was giving her appointment calendar one last glance before answering. It was a pause to mentally prepare herself, to meet whatever came her way.

She picked up the phone. "This is Monique Pavour-Banks," she said, her voice betraying no concern.

"Good evening, madam. Have you ever considered the advantages of owning a really fine set of encyclopedias?"

Monique's smile spoke of pleasure tinged with relief. "Hey, sweetie," she said to Michael. "How's London?"

"Having a heat wave, actually. It's a whopping 80 degrees and people are flinging themselves into the Trafalgar Square fountains. It's quite a sight. Lots of pasty white people in Speedos. I'll email you some pictures."

"You're so thoughtful. Are you still due back Thursday?"

"Yes, should be in by 8. You'll be home?"

"Ready and waiting. Can you bring me back some tea from Fortnum and Mason's? Any kind will do."

"Consider it done. I'll see you Thursday, then."

"Fly safe. I love you."

Michael replied in kind and said goodbye. Monique hung up and sat for a moment, hands covering her eyes. Every phone call, every unexpected meeting, every knock at her door could be the one the note had warned her about. She almost longed for some Men In Black to show up and ask some questions, just so she could get it over with.

To take her mind off it, she looked at the framed picture of she and Michael. It had been taken last year, at his airline's Christmas party. In the picture she wore a red velvet dress; he wore a tux and a green elf hat. When they'd come home from the party, they'd strung up Christmas lights in the bedroom and made love under the twinkling lights.

They had met two years ago, not long after she'd joined Beckman, Worth, and Spinnett. Before that she had been with Schmidt and Montgomery, a big machine of a firm where sixty-hour workweeks were expected and constant fighting for more and better cases was the norm. The Marianas Trench had less pressure, and the price for the firm's prestige and monetary compensation was paid with ulcers, burnout, and broken marriages.

She had liked the prestige and the money, and for a while even throve in the driven atmosphere. Until one day she'd stopped into the office kitchen to get some coffee, and saw one of the other lawyers, Dennis Van Meer, slump against the water cooler, clutch his chest, and drop to the floor. She called 911 on her cell and ran over to see what she could for him. It was a mild attack — he hadn't needed CPR or the defibrillator the law office kept on hand. But when she'd gone to visit Dennis in the hospital, she knew how bad it really was. The man had a heart attack and he barely acknowledged it — he was too busy worrying about his caseload and whether this would jeopardize his chances to make partner next year. Monique had felt like stomping on the flowers she'd brought and yelling, *You had a heart attack, you nimrod! Get some rest and stop worrying about your clients. Lay off the quest for the big brass ring for a while or the next coronary might kill you.*

She'd gone home to her apartment, where she looked at the books she didn't have time to read, the movies she didn't have time to watch, the refrigerator full of take-out leftovers, and the bed that hadn't had a man in it since Sean left for Florida. She wondered why a law firm had its own defibrillator. That night she updated her resumé and the next day resigned.

Beckman, Worth, and Spinnett was a welcome change — so much of a change it took some getting used to. Somewhat less money, a good deal less prestige, and a great deal more sanity. There was the occasional long day or crazy week but no sixty-hour madness. She never once regretted joining the new firm, because working there helped her meet her husband.

She was meeting some of her coworkers for drinks and dinner one Friday evening, something unheard-of at Schmidt and Montgomery. Apparently most of the city had the same idea; the tavern was packed, and she had to wait outside for their reservation to be called. It was the first Friday in December and the trees were already twinkling with lights. The tavern, in an attempt to keep the waiting patrons occupied, was playing music over a loudspeaker. Monique was humming along to Dean Martin's "I've Got My Love To Keep Me Warm" when she spotted the dancing man.

He danced by himself in the parking lot, his arms held out to hold an invisible partner. The Christmas lights reflected off his glasses and gave an angelic glow to his unkempt blond hair. He danced in that clumsy but graceful way peculiar to men who've cheerfully adapted to having two left feet.

"Why are you dancing?" she asked.

He didn't miss a beat. "Why *aren't* you dancing?"

Before she could answer, Dean's song was over. It was Frank's turn next, his version of "The Christmas Waltz." The man bowed and extended a hand to her. "May I have this dance?"

She surprised herself by accepting, hoping those ballroom dancing lessons her mother had made her take when she was thirteen would finally pay off. They did.

Michael Banks only stepped on her foot once, but insisted on buying her dinner to make it up to her. He was an airline pilot, just back from a jaunt across the pond to England. It was a jaunt he'd made often enough for some Britishisms to creep into his language; when he'd stepped on her foot he'd sworn, "Bugger" and then apologized profusely. She had always thought a pilot would be stodgy — those uniforms, the responsibility for the passengers — but Michael was calm and confident, a little on the goofy side but after years of being around lawyers, goofy was a refreshing change.

They dated all the next year, neither caring to rush things. They adopted each others' pastimes with goodwill: he was a willing partner for karaoke, she obligingly dressed up for Renaissance Faire. His flights and her business trips gave them a chance to miss each other's company and appreciate reunions. They'd gotten married last year, choosing May 1 because (so said Monique) it would be easy to remember and (so said Michael) they could celebrate their anniversary and Beltane at the same time, and the only hitch in the whole day was her mother's repeated laments that her eldest daughter had waited until she was forty-six years old to get married. "Not only that, she robbed the cradle," Michael had laughed (he was forty-five).

With him she felt comfortable and loved, felt cared for in a way she hadn't since her early childhood. She touched the framed picture on her desk, her gesture part solace and part protectiveness. She could not let anything threaten Michael and the life they had together.

She'd gotten the note a couple weeks ago.

It was in a pile of mail that had arrived when she was on a business trip. A plain white envelope with no letterhead or even return address. The note itself was similarly unadorned, and without salutation or signature.

Sean is in trouble. People may come to talk to you. Be careful.

Monique had examined the note. Ordinary printer paper, as near as she could tell. Nothing about the font stood out either — it was Times New Roman, or something so close as to make no difference. The envelope was a standard business security one — you could buy huge boxes of them at any stationer's. The only clue was the Maine postmark. She knew no one in Maine; it was more than a bit unsettling to think that some person she'd never met knew enough about her to send her this note. It was almost as unsettling as the note itself.

Sean is in trouble.

Monique had met Sean halfway through her tenure at Schmidt and Montgomery, as she was coming off a year buried alive in work. The work had been an anodyne to her after a particularly ugly breakup, and it had worked well. Until one night when she'd been desperate to wear something that wasn't a lawyer's suit, to flirt a bit and see if she could still attract a man with her looks rather than her paycheck. To be perfectly blunt, she rather wanted to roll in the hay.

She'd met Sean, and he'd fit the bill perfectly. His looks didn't catch her eye immediately. In fact, her eyes went right past him at first. But before five minutes had gone she found herself drawn to his dark eyes and the dimple on one side of his face when he smiled. Oh yes, the smile.

As for what he was, that was part of the attraction. It was a safe thrill, like being on a rollercoaster, the illusion of danger with the knowledge that you would not be hurt. His hands were always gentle on her; as a passionate but tender and considerate lover, only Michael was his equal. But what he was had ensured that it would never last.

Part of it was her doing; she was caught up in her career and had no intention then of committing to a marriage. But mostly it was him and what he was, for how could she form any enduring attachment to a man whose past was a blank slate, whose work she could not know (and did not want to know) anything about, who might simply vanish one day?

They'd fought about it once, early on. He was due to leave the country one day and she'd left while he was in the shower, without saying goodbye. He'd called her from the airport. "I don't know when I'm going to be back. All you had to do was say goodbye. Is that so hard?" he'd asked.

"Yes, it is. I don't know when you'll be back. In fact, I don't know *if* you'll be back. What should I say? 'Thanks for a fun time, I'll see you whenever. Oh, and I hope you don't die or get horribly injured or see something that drives you insane.'"

He was silent for a moment. Then he said, "I'm sorry. This is new to me. Goodbyes were always easy because there was never anyone I wanted to come back to."

"I'm sorry, too, Flint," she said, using the nickname she'd given him. She *was* sorry, for him and for the lonely life he led.

"Don't be sorry. You don't have to say goodbye. Just kiss me next time."

"I will." Hoping there would be a next time. There was.

It had worked out well for the rest of their time together. He had always come back. Once he'd been gone for eight months and she'd been sure he was dead, but of course she had no way of knowing for sure. Then he'd shown up with no warning, looking perfectly chipper, with a present of Russian caviar for her.

It was when he was sent to Florida that she worried most about him. Forced retirement could do a man like him no good; what had his superiors been thinking? Surely they could have kept him on in some sort of advisory capacity instead of turning him out completely? Monique had seen it too often at Schmidt and Montgomery — retired lawyers showing up ostensibly to visit or have lunch, but really to revisit the times when their lives had meaning.

In the end, the note wasn't really a surprise — she'd always known Sean wouldn't go gently into the good night of retirement. The only surprise was that it had taken him so long to snap.

Thursday. When Monique came back from lunch, Lucy the administrative assistant flagged her down. "There's a man here to see you. He doesn't have an appointment but he said it was important. He said he was from the government."

Lucy did not seem perturbed. They were a corporate law office in Washington D.C. — governmental types were always in and out, needing something. But Monique was certain that one of those people who might come around asking about Sean had finally arrived. "Tell him I'll be there in just a minute. Thank you, Lucy."

She stepped into the women's restroom and looked at herself in the mirror. Calm and professional, as always. As it should be. She had nothing to hide. She didn't know where Sean was; in fact, had not heard from him in over a year, although that was troubling. He hadn't called her on New Year's or her birthday, and he always did that. She had no information on him, but that might not work in her favor. She had no doubt that people in Sean's profession could play rough. Look at Sean himself. The man had scars, for God's sake. Knowing nothing wouldn't necessarily save her. She could end up like the Dustin Hoffman character in *Marathon Man*, unable to tell people what they wanted no matter what they did.

Like hell I will. She kissed the Saint Christopher's medal Michael had given her not long after they met, then went to her office.

The man was tall and thin, expensively dressed. The suit looked tailor-made. He had a rodent's narrow, pointed face, and the coldest gray eyes she'd ever seen. He introduced himself as Frank Halsey, and they shook hands. His hand was surprisingly soft; she wondered if he went in for manicures.

As she moved to her chair, she noticed him looking at her legs none-too-surreptitiously. She was grateful to sit behind her desk, both for its solid oak barrier and because it kept her legs out of his view. "How can I help you?" she asked.

"I'm just here to ask a few questions, Ms. Pavour." Before she could correct him that it was Pavour-Banks he asked, "Pavour's a French name? Is your, uh, family background French?" He was playing good cop.

"Yes, but only on my mother's and father's sides," she replied.

The joke went right past him. Monique felt a fraction more at ease. Cunning he might be, witty he was not.

He apparently decided to leave repartee behind. "I'm here to ask some questions about a known acquaintance of yours," he said, and paused.

"Who is this known acquaintance?" she asked.

"Sean Kincaid."

Pretend it's a friendly inquiry. "Ah. How is Sean?"

"That's what I'm here to find out," he said. "When was the last time you saw him?"

"About four or five years ago. Right before he moved to Florida."

"Have you been in contact with him since then?"

"Oh yes. We'd talk on the phone sometimes. He'd always send me a card on my birthday."

"What did you talk about?"

"Movies we'd seen, how my job was going. That sort of thing."

He didn't frown, but his eyes got a shade darker. "Movies?"

"When he and I were dating, we liked going to the movies."

"Did you know him well?"

"Reasonably well."

"How would you describe your relationship with him?"

She had a brief urge to imitate Cloris Leachman's character in *Young Frankenstein*. *"Yes! Say it! He was my BOYFRIEND!"* "We dated, but it was very on-again, off-again. He was always traveling so much."

"Did he ever talk about his work?"

"I knew he worked for the government, but neither of us ever talked shop much." She leaned forward over the desk. "Is everything OK with Sean? Is that why you're here?"

He didn't answer. "When was the last time you talked with him, Ms. Pavour?"

"New Year's Eve." She saw a flicker of excitement in his eyes, then she clarified: "Not this past New Year's, the one before."

The flicker went out. "How can you be so sure of the date?"

"Sean always called me on New Year's. It was his favorite holiday."

"Why haven't you spoken to him since then?"

"Well, I told him that I was getting married. He seemed happy for me but perhaps he was upset about it. I called him a few months later to invite him to the wedding but all I got was his answering machine. To be honest, I've been so busy since then I haven't called him." She tried her best to look earnest. "Did he move? I sent him a Christmas card and it got sent back 'return to sender'. Is everything OK?"

He looked at her stony-faced for a moment, glanced at where her legs would be if the desk hadn't been in the way. "Everything's fine. This is just a routine questioning."

She hoped to God that Sean hadn't learned his interrogation techniques from this man. "I hope I've been able to help you," she said. "Is there anything else you need to know, Mr. Halsey? I have another appointment coming up soon, but we could always arrange to meet another time if you'd like."

"I'll keep in touch with you, Ms. Pavour. Thank you for your time." He got up. They shook hands and walked over to the reception area. He paused at the door, gave her a full once-over, and went out the door.

Monique went back to her office, where she closed the door and routed all her calls straight into voice mail. She fell into her chair and leaned her head back, eyes shut. It was over, for now. She'd won, she was sure of it. Monique smiled — surging through her was triumph so strong it was nearly primal. Only twice before had she felt that way: when she'd aced the bar exam, and the time she'd fought off an attacker in the Schmidt and Montgomery parking structure with the judo Sean had taught her and a dose of pepper spray.

In a way this had been easy. She didn't know anything; that was probably deliberate on Sean's part. Whatever he was up to, he didn't want her involved. *Be happy, Moni,* was the last thing he'd said to her.

Monique held on to her Saint Christopher's medal again. *Thank you for helping me through that. Bring Michael home to me. Safe passage to Sean, wherever he is.*

Michael Banks poured the last of the champagne into a glass, and they both took a sip. "Let me guess. It was a really good day, or a really bad day."

"A little of both," Monique said.

"Or you're just happy to see me."

"That too." She leaned against his shoulder, snuggled against him. She felt safe, but still a bit troubled by the way that Halsey fellow had been checking her out, something in his eyes. He reminded her of a guy from law school, who had stalked and raped his ex-girlfriend. Maybe it wasn't official business this Halsey fellow had been on. Maybe it was some weird personal thing against Sean. It might not be over, after all.

"You OK?" Michael asked. "You just seemed a bit faraway for a moment."

"I'm fine." She didn't add, *for now.*

Chapter Five

Deirdre was ten the summer of the family reunion. It was at her grandparents' summer house, a rambling two-story out in the Minnesota countryside. The Monahan family was the last to arrive and Deirdre, relegated to the middle of the back seat, her way blocked by four brothers and assorted bags and suitcases, was the last to get out of the car. When she finally scrambled out, she barely had time to take in the sight of the house and what seemed like a hundred relatives milling about before her mother said, "Here, make yourself useful," shoved a bag into her hands, and pointed in the direction of the house.

Deirdre didn't object; she didn't even mind. She was used to it. Four older brothers, a six-year gap between the youngest brother and her — you do the math. Her mother had been forty when Deirdre came along; weary after raising four wild boys on a tight budget, she hadn't welcomed the last-minute surprise. At least now that Deirdre was of an age to help with more of the household chores, her mother took notice of her, if only to tell her what to do.

All the people seemed to know each other, but Deirdre didn't know anyone besides her own family. This was the first year they'd been able to afford going to one of the reunions. She put things where people told her to and hung back on the edge, half hoping someone would take her hand and show her around, and half hoping that she could fade into the woodwork for the whole reunion. Maybe she could find some hidden bedroom or attic space and retreat up there with the books and comics she'd brought, lay in a supply of peanut butter sandwiches and spend the reunion with Scout and Jem and Dill, Taran the Assistant Pig-Keeper, and the X-Men instead of a bunch of people who didn't know her and wouldn't care if they did.

She might have looked forward to the reunion if she hadn't been in the throes of what she would later call "the ugly years" — that time between ages eight and thirteen, when her mirror showed her a freckled, carrot-topped, short and gawky thing, the freak in a tall and dark-haired family. "Lucky the Leprechaun" her brothers had taken to calling her. She just hoped no one at the reunion would hear about the nickname; if they did, she thought she might die.

The next morning she hid in her sleeping bag, glancing uneasily at her already dwindling supply of reading material and wondering if she could pilfer something from the shelves here without getting caught. Her brothers and a bunch of other boys came thundering in, pawing through their luggage for swim trunks and yelling about the cool swimming hole they were going to. Swimming. It sounded like fun. She couldn't get dressed until they left the room. Once they did she scrambled out of her PJs and into shorts and a blouse, but she wasn't fast enough — by the time she got to the porch the boys were well down the dirt road on their bikes or on their feet, and no one heard her pleas to come along or turned to see her standing on the porch.

She watched them go. It probably wouldn't have been much fun anyway. Surely her brothers wouldn't have missed an opportunity to tell the others about their sister the Leprechaun. It would be so nice to be invited somewhere, wanted for something, or so she supposed. It hadn't happened yet.

"Hi there," said a girl's voice.

Deirdre turned to look. The girl was older than her, a teenager. A redhead, like her, and although short, not a leprechaun. Pretty. Smiling. Deirdre looked around to see who the girl was talking to. Seeing no one, she realized the girl was talking to her. "Hi," she said.

"You OK?" The girl walked closer. She wore a paisley sundress and pink high-top sneakers with no socks.

"Yeah, no. They're going swimming and I wanted to go along but they didn't take me." Deirdre realized this was the most she'd said since they'd arrived.

"Did they say where they were going?"

Deirdre thought for a moment. "Cooper's Pond, I think."

The girl turned to look after the boys' dust trail. "Oh man," she said and shook her head. Then she grinned at Deirdre. "Don't feel bad that they left you behind. Cooper's Pond at this time of year? If the mosquitoes don't eat you alive the leeches will."

"Leeches! Oh my God." Deirdre found herself grinning back at the girl.

"You want to go on a picnic? Just you and me? I know a great place with no mosquitoes or leeches."

"Oh yes, please!" Deirdre tried not to seem too eager, but she couldn't help herself.

"Fabulous! Go get your bathing suit and anything else you need, and I'll get some food. You're Deirdre, right? Grandma told me all the names but there's so many I can't keep track."

"Yeah, I'm Deirdre. Who are you?"

"I'm Anna." She turned to head into the house. "Go get your stuff, we'll have a girl's day out."

Twenty minutes later they were on a wildflower-scented path behind the house. Deirdre had her bathing suit, sunglasses, and a few of her books and comics in a grocery bag. Anna pulled a red wagon loaded with a Styrofoam cooler, beach towels, and a cassette player; she wore a Minnesota Twins cap to keep the sun out of her eyes. The path ended where the trees began, but Anna knew the way. Soon they arrived at a large pond that was sheltered by trees but not gloomy. A tire swing hung from one branch, over the water. The ground was flat enough for them to spread a blanket and their towels. Anna loaded the cassette player with tapes and started the music playing.

Once they had their swimsuits on they took turns swinging out as far as they could, then leaping into the cool water. When they tired of swinging they opened the cooler and ate ham sandwiches and potato chips, drank ginger ale. They talked and told jokes and lay on their backs to watch the clouds scoot across the impossibly blue sky. They swam again, and finally in the mid-afternoon made their way back to the house. Deirdre steeled herself for Anna to grow tired of her company and dismiss her; instead, they relaxed in the hammock and read Deirdre's X-Men comics. When it got close to dinner, Anna stretched and stood up, and surely now would come the dismissal, Deirdre thought. But Anna asked, "Hey, Dee. Do you want to help me make some cupcakes for dessert tonight?"

She did.

When that week in Minnesota was over and Deirdre returned to the everyday world, she held on to the memory of those days. Just before school started, a package came for her in the mail. It contained a picture taken of her and Anna — by some miracle, she didn't look like a leprechaun, but pretty, like Anna. There was a pressed wildflower, and two cassette tapes with the songs she and Anna had listened to that week. There was a note that said: *Dee — Here's some souvenirs for you. Be sure to write to me and let me know how school goes. I miss you. See you next summer? Love, Nan.*

Deirdre didn't know how much a bus ticket to Anna's house would cost. Best to start saving now. She put all her money in a hiding place where even her brothers would never find it, and saved her X-Men comics to bring along. "See you next summer, Nan," she said.

Twenty years later, she still had the tapes Anna had made, but she didn't play them. She didn't have to. She knew them by heart, had the song order so ingrained that it sounded wrong to hear "Hey Bulldog" on the radio and it didn't segue into "Long Cool Woman In a Black Dress." The songs were in her head, a strange accompaniment to the days of grief and bewilderment, but they gave her an anchor. When evening came and she could no longer push things aside with work or by talking to relatives and police, she played the songs in her head, sometimes even sang. As long as she heard the songs she did not hear the dreadful silence that had been in Anna's house. She could replace the memory of finding the body with Anna on the tire swing, singing "Octopus's Garden."

It was getting harder, though. The funeral was tomorrow — there had been delays while they waited for the autopsy report. Tomorrow she would face the unavoidable reality of Anna being buried and the memories of that golden summer and the years since would be just that, memories.

Randy, of all people, had come to her rescue. He wouldn't be able to make it for the funeral, but yesterday he'd met her after she got off work at the Wal-Mart. They went to the Applebee's a block away and had dinner. Randy had dinner, actually. Deirdre sipped her Coke and poked her fork at her pasta. "I'm sorry about Anna," he said. "She was always really nice."

"Thanks," she said.

"Was it an accident or...?"

Deirdre shook her head. "They don't think it was an accident. Someone moved her and covered the body."

"Where's her husband? Richard, is that the guy's name?"

She nodded. "Yes, Richard. We don't know where he is. No one knows." Seeing the look on Randy's face, she said, "Richard didn't do this. I'd bet my life on that."

"Yeah, but where — "

"Stop. I can't talk about this any more."

"But — "

"Please."

"OK." He ate in silence for a while. "How you holding up?"

She shrugged.

He knew what that meant. Randy took a small envelope out of his pocket. "Here," he said. "You'll need these."

She took the envelope and peeked in. There were three joints. In spite of what a shit he was, she knew he was right. She'd need these. "Thank you."

Now, the night before the funeral, she lit the biggest of the joints and put on the tapes Anna had made. Mere memory wouldn't be enough tonight. She breathed deep of the sweet smoke as "Baker Street" started and the saxophone began its wail. The smoke made her eyes water but she did not cry. She had made a deal with herself. She would not cry until the funeral was over.

At the funeral and the reception following at Grace Methodist Church, Deirdre was reminded more than once of that long-ago family reunion. A huge crowd of people, most of whom she didn't know, gathered together. The difference was that this time, instead of being ignored, she was the center of attention. On the whole, she preferred being ignored.

The attention was not a welcome kind. There were the usual condolences from relatives. There were well-intentioned consolations from Anna's many friends in Du Lac. If that had been the end of it, she would have been fine.

It was the looks and whispers that wore her down, the covert glances and outright stares. By some trick of genetics Deirdre had outgrown her ugly years and looked enough like Anna for them to be mistaken for sisters. True, Deirdre was taller and Anna's hair had been a darker shade of red, but such minor details escaped most casual observers, who stared for a moment upon seeing a white-faced, black-clad, red-haired ghost in their midst. Whispered asides she caught as she made her way from chair to refreshment table to outside for a breath of air: "Deirdre, Deirdre was the one who found her. How awful for her."

Yes, how awful for me. Understatement of the fucking year. Deirdre walked outside, stood in the crisp fall air for a moment, then began walking back to the cemetery. It was nearly two miles and her new black pumps were not broken in — she was limping by the time she got there.

The grave, with its shiny new headstone and profusion of flowers, was easy to spot. Deirdre thought Anna would have wanted something much simpler, but funerals weren't about what the dead wanted. Deirdre sat down in the grass and took off her shoes; the autumn breeze was kind to her blistered feet. She sat looking at the stone, the dirt, the flowers. She waited to cry but no tears came.

She couldn't cry, but she could talk. "Nan?" she said, and stopped because there was no one to talk to. Anna was in the ground. The buried Anna wasn't the Anna she wanted — no, needed — to talk to, but it was all she was going to get.

"It wasn't supposed to be like this." When she spoke again, her voice was barely more than a whisper. "I don't know it was supposed to be, but not like this."

No agreement or disagreement. Just the wind, and the distant sound of cars on the road.

"What happened?" She'd asked it several times these last few days and had never gotten an answer. Not from the relatives and friends, who were clueless; not from the local law enforcement, who told her the investigation was ongoing. All those people, and no one knew what had happened? Not a single person? Deirdre didn't believe that.

"I'll find out what happened. I'll make things as right as I can," Deirdre said. She got to her feet, wincing. "I love you, Nan."

As she walked down the side of the road, carrying her shoes, carefully skirting pieces of trash and broken glass, the car pulled alongside. She glanced at it. The sheriff's car. The deputy's car, rather. He stopped and rolled down the window. "Ms. Monahan? Can I give you a ride?"

If he'd asked her if she was all right she would have gone on walking, because she most certainly was not all right, thank you very much, but he just offered the ride. She accepted, hoping to escape any further damage to her feet. "Just back to the church is fine," she said as she got in and shut the door. She tried to remember his name: Nick something. His last name was a blank — lots of things were.

"Do you need a hand getting home?" he asked as they neared the church hall. From the number of people outside, it seemed the reception was over.

"No, that's OK." Deirdre opened the door, put her shoes back on, and began to get out. "Thanks for the ride."

"Here," he said, and handed her a business card.

She didn't take it. "I already have the sheriff's phone number."

"It's mine. In case you want to talk."

"I've already told you everything I know."

"I didn't mean that. Just if you need anyone to talk to."

She looked at him. He had been kind during the interviews; talking to him had been much better than talking to the sheriff, who had a face like a clenched fist and a businesslike attitude. She took the card and saw that his name was Nick Eliot. "Thanks," she said.

"I'm very sorry for your loss." It seemed he was going to say something else, but instead he drove away.

That night she dreamed she was back in Minnesota, at the pond. She could hear someone crying, knew instinctively that the crying person was under the water. She dove and looked and surfaced over and over, but found nothing. When she woke, she was the person who was crying.

Chapter Six

There were different kinds of time, Robert had found. Back when he'd been an agent, he knew how long the minutes spent waiting for the quarry could seem, how fast hours in a raid could go by. Cancer had its own timelines as well. The agonizing minutes waiting for the morphine to kick in, the pleasant, hours-long haze of daydreaming once it did.

Today time had been particularly vague. The Maine coast had been shrouded in fog, and even the noon sunlight had been ghostly dim. Now it was near dusk, and it seemed the sun had finally found its way through the fog's armor, turning the light a murky orange. He looked out the window again, blinked to clear his vision. His sight had been playing tricks on him lately, whether it was from the drugs or the disease he did not know, and had no particular interest in finding out. It was a common enough thing to happen, the doctor had told him, but that was precious little consolation when Robert had found he could no longer read.

It was last week when he realized he'd been just staring at the page, unable to make out the words. If it had been a new book he might have realized it, but it was his old friend Hemingway, and it was some time before he understood that he had been staring at a single sentence and his mind, which had the stories memorized, had been fooled into thinking he was reading. He'd flung the book aside; if it had been a person who had done this to him he could have exacted revenge. Instead he methodically cursed the disease that had felled him and the drugs in case they had a hand in it, cursed Halsey for stealing the gun, cursed whoever had set that bomb in Los Angeles and set Sean off on his foolish quest, and cursed Sean for taking so damn long to come back. He cursed God and the Devil too, for good measure, and then reiterated all the curses in his native Czech, because they sounded more impressive in that language.

At Kumar's suggestion he'd tried audiobooks, but often he fell asleep and then woke, startled by hearing a strange voice. He'd had to stop listening to them; a pity, because perhaps they would have given some shape to this strange day. As the sun lowered and the light turned to twilight blue, Robert slipped into that half-doze so familiar now that his life was measured out with morphine doses rather than coffee spoons.

The voice woke him, made him wonder if he'd put one of the audiobooks back on by accident. But it was not in his room — he could hear it, an unfamiliar voice with a rasping undertone, in conversation with Kumar in the front room. Then came a heavy tread on the floorboards, and for a moment Robert remembered the tales his grandmother had told him of a troll who ate disobedient children and picked his teeth with rib bones. Here Robert was, as helpless as a child, and the troll was coming for him. He hooked his fingers into claws, ready to fight. It would not be much of a struggle and he would surely lose, but going out fighting was infinitely preferable to this slow decay.

A silhouette appeared in his doorway, not nearly as tall or broad as he would have imagined a troll to be. The shadow spoke: "Robert? Are you awake? It's Sean."

Robert blinked and shook his head to clear the confusion. Yes, it was Sean, he just hadn't recognized the voice, which was strangely hoarse, nor the tread, which was not a predator's light step but a heavy, burdened plod. "Yes, I'm awake. Let me put on the light."

He turned the light on. His eyes adjusted and the greeting he was about to speak died in his throat.

Never a heavy man, Sean was gaunt now. His cheeks were hollow and his clothes hung loose on him. There was more gray in his hair, and his throat was covered with fading bruises that were a sickly purplish-yellow. His eyes

56

were the worst — dark and haunted. Looking at Sean was like looking into a mirror, for he could see his own thoughts reflected precisely in Sean's eyes: *I knew things were bad with him. I didn't know they were this bad.*

Sean made the sign of the cross; Robert had never seen him do it before, didn't think Sean was even aware he was doing it. He walked over to the chair by Robert's bed and sat down. Neither said anything for a while, and Robert realized that both of them had been hoping the other one could help. Maybe it wasn't too late, maybe they could help each other, but first he had to help Sean, who seemed about to crack. "I'm glad you're back."

Sean got himself under control and smiled. Not his old, charming smile, just the ghost of it, but it was enough for now. "I'm glad you're still here."

Sean made coffee and brought it into the room. Robert sipped his gratefully. Kumar was a godsend, but a coffee-brewer he was not. Robert studied his old friend, noted the slight tremor in his hands as he held his cup, and wondered when was the last time Sean ate anything. "You still make excellent coffee," Robert said.

"I learned from the best," Sean replied, inclining his head toward Robert.

Robert waited, watched Sean closely. He could see Sean regaining his control, putting his emotions back behind a mask. It was like watching someone put on armor. "Tell me what happened," Robert asked.

"I found the group responsible, caught the ringleader, took him to Jennifer. He's dead," Sean replied.

"I don't have time for lies. Neither do you."

"You asked what happened, and I told you."

"There's a wealth of things you haven't told me."

"Things you don't need to know about," said Sean.

"I'm not going to judge you," Robert said. "And you don't need to protect me."

Sean was silent, staring down into his coffee. "All I wanted these last few days was to tell you everything. It's what kept me going. But now that I'm here ... I can't make myself feel better by shoving all this onto someone who's ..." He trailed off.

"Dying. You can say it." Robert hadn't actually said it himself, until now. "Sean, whatever happened is killing you, anyone can see it. If you outlive me it won't be for very long. It's too late to change what's gone wrong but maybe this will help you." Robert was quiet for a moment, turning a thought over in his mind. "Maybe we can help each other."

"How?"

Robert told him. It didn't take long. Sean thought it over for a moment and then nodded in agreement.

Finding the group responsible was easy. He made his way north from Florida to the Midwest and Great Lakes region, frequenting gun shows and town meetings, keeping eyes and ears alert. He found a spear-carrier for the group in Indiana, interrogated the man to find out what he knew, and dumped the body in a quarry. From Indiana he went north again, to Du Lac, Wisconsin; he ingratiated himself with the group's recruiter and its leader's right-hand man, a mostly decent sort named Doug MacReady, whom he would later kill after learning MacReady had been the trigger man in the Los Angeles bombing. He didn't accept the group's invitation to join right away; he hung back at first, taking the opportunity to do surveillance. It was during surveillance of the group's New Year's Day gathering at a lakeside lodge that Beatty found him. Their fight took them out onto the frozen lake. Sean knew the ice was weak, Beatty did not. Sean caused Beatty to fall through the ice, watched his old comrade struggle futilely and heard him scream Sean's name as he drowned. There were regrets on that score, plenty, but no time for them; soon after he was brought into the group and met its leader, Richard. Clever Richard, capable Richard, who took the vague dissatisfaction of local men and turned it into a force for violence against their government and those unlucky enough to hold federal jobs. Richard had trusted Sean completely. Even after Doug MacReady had gone missing Richard had trusted Sean, had even asked him to look after Anna while he was away. Sean should have known it could not end well, but he'd kept on and then Anna was dead, and so was the child she was pregnant with. He fled with his quarry, fled to a town called Haven Cove in British Columbia. That was where Jennifer Thomson, survivor of the Los Angeles federal building, had gone to begin her life anew. She'd made a quiet life for herself in a pretty little house, and he'd broken into her house and stolen her away to the safe house so she could have revenge on Richard. But she hadn't wanted revenge, she only wanted to live her life peacefully. In the end, she gave Richard a chance; she took three bullets out of the revolver Sean had given her, alternating empty and full chambers, and spun the chamber three times. She pulled the trigger, and the click of the empty chamber was louder than any gunshot, it seemed. For a moment they were all frozen: Jennifer with the gun in her hand, Richard bound to a chair and waiting for death, and Sean wondering where the lost girl he had pitied had gone. Jennifer put the gun down, crossed her arms as if she wanted to avoid the temptation of picking up the gun again, turned away from the men, and in that moment he knew she was stronger than he or Richard. She said in a clear voice, "Mr. Kincaid, take me home now." He tried to talk to her during that drive from the safe house back to Haven Cove, but she always held up a hand to ward off his words. She sat as far away from him as she could, pressed against the passenger door of his van as if she thought she might have to make a quick escape at any moment. She asked, "What will you do to him?" and before he could answer said, "No, don't tell me. I don't want to know." When they were back at her house she leaped out of the van before it had even stopped moving; he expected her to flee but instead she turned and looked at him for a very long moment. "Don't ever come near me again," she said. "I don't want you in my life." He saw anger and fear in her eyes but most of all he saw pity. She turned and ran, not to her own house but to the neighbor's house next door, where she banged on the door until a pajama-clad woman opened it. The door shut behind them and he was out of her life. He returned to the safe house to find Richard still there, having made no attempt to escape. Sean was not surprised. The loss of his friends and the death of his wife and unborn child had broken Richard. If Jennifer's gun had gone off, she would have been killing a dead man. "I can understand why you did this for her," Richard said. "Is she home safe?" "Yes," Sean replied. "Will she get over what we've done to her?" Richard asked. Sean didn't protest. He'd done as much damage to Jennifer's life as Richard had. "I hope so," he said, and started to speak again but Richard cut him off. "I know you're sorry about Anna. Don't say it again. It doesn't change anything." So instead Sean stood behind Richard, unholstered his gun and aimed it at Richard. "Ready?" he asked. Richard nodded. Sean pulled the trigger. There was no victory in it, no sense of justice done, no sense of revenge fulfilled. He hauled the body out to just beyond the safe house property line and buried it in the woods, digging a shallow grave with his hands while his mind chanted an idiotic mantra of Let the dead bury the dead. *It was over.*

Sean's damaged voice fell silent. Robert wished he could turn back the clock to last year, to the March day when Sean had come to him for advice and told him of his plan. Despite his misgivings he hadn't done much to dissuade Sean, for he admired Sean for taking on this quest and throwing off the dead weight of exile Halsey had consigned them to. "Sean," he said, "forgive me."

"What for?" Genuine surprise in the reply.

For helping make you what you are. If he said that, Sean might agree and despise him. Instead he said, "When I told you I had a bad feeling about this I just thought you might get hurt, or be in over your head."

"That's what I thought, too." Sean's voice was soft, uninflected. "You couldn't have stopped me. Don't worry about it."

"What will you do now?"

Sean settled into his chair, as if he was about to fall asleep. But his eyes were open, gleaming in the room's dim light. His face was expressionless. It had been that way all through his confession. He'd wept when he'd told Robert about Anna, but his face had not changed. It had been like watching a stone weep. "I haven't given it any thought," he said.

"I'm leaving you the house. And everything in it."

"Thank you."

"You should stay away for a while. Lie low."

"All right."

It was like talking to a mask. "Halsey's looking for you," Robert said.

Sean nodded.

He isn't listening. Robert wished he could have the unstrung Sean who'd first arrived rather than this placid one. At least the earlier Sean had been listening to him. "He's in trouble at the agency and I think he blames you. You slipped out from under his nose, so he hired Beatty under the table to go after you. And when Beatty didn't come back, his wife was pestering everyone to find out where — "

Sean looked up startled. His mask cracked. "His wife?"

Robert cursed himself. He hadn't meant to let that information slip. It was the fatigue and the drugs making him loose-tongued. He nodded. "That's why he took the job. He needed the money."

"I see." Sean closed his eyes for a moment. When he opened them, his face was calm again.

"You need to listen to me. Halsey wants to find you. He said he was going to talk to Monique."

That got Sean's attention, although not as much as Robert would have liked. "I'd put my money on Monique any day."

"Don't be so sure," Robert said. "Halsey hates you, and hatred brings out the inventiveness in people. I sent her a note, warning her that people might come around asking about you."

Sean smiled. "Thank you. Thank you so much."

"It was the least I could do. I saw her once, she seemed a fine woman."

"She is."

"You should go see her, make sure she's all right."

"I don't want to go near her."

Robert started to ask why but Sean cut him off. "I killed Anna, I probably ruined Jennifer's life, and I made Beatty's wife a widow. You think I wouldn't give anything to see Monique again? I called her from the road but I couldn't bring myself to talk to her. She has a life without me in it and it's better for her that way, believe me." Sean sighed, as if speaking had exhausted him. "I'm sorry. I should have ... Has it been bad for very long?"

"No."

"Are you lying to me?"

Robert nodded.

"Thought so."

Robert looked out the window, hoping for a glimpse of moon or stars. There was nothing, just the black fog night. Robert felt saddened in a way he couldn't recall experiencing before. Here they were, he and Sean, their lives twisted paths with wreckage in their wake. When had the wrong path been chosen? Years ago, decades ago — did it even matter, when there was no way to retrace their steps and find another path? They'd made the choice freely, no fooling themselves otherwise, and now had nothing to show for it save their last favors to each other. He heard Sean's confession, left him his house, and gave him fair warning. As for Sean's favor ...

He turned. Sean was looking at him. "Is it time?" Sean asked.

Robert told Sean where the pills were kept. From the kitchen Robert could hear the grinding of the mortar and pestle, the refrigerator and freezer doors opening and closing, the whir of the blender. Sean came back with a tall glass full of a purple-red smoothie. He sat down and began to hand the glass to Robert, then pulled it back abruptly. "Are you sure you want to do this?" asked Sean.

"I've been sure for a long time." He noticed that Sean looked oddly troubled. "What is it?"

Sean hesitated. "When Richard choked me, after … after Anna. It was close, another thirty seconds and he'd have killed me. Toward the end, there was this … "

"What was it?"

"It was *nothing*, Robert. Just this awful emptiness that went on forever. You can't go there."

The prospect of oblivion did not frighten him as much as it should have. There would be nothing, yes, but there would also be no pain. No wretched slow decay. To be truthful, he was tired. Exhausted. His life had been scheming and violence and constant watching and waiting. Never knowing if the next mission might be his last, he filled his time with more books, more wine, more music, more women. Never any rest. No, oblivion might not be so awful. Besides, it was too late to choose a different path and meet a different end.

"I'll find what's waiting for me," he said gently. "And meet it the best I know how."

Sean nodded. "That's all any of us can do, I suppose."

He handed the glass to Robert, who took it, and drank. It was sweet, with no hint of bitterness. For months food had been mere sustenance to him, but this drink was finer than any wine. "It's good."

"I put in honey to make it sweeter."

Robert drank down the last of the smoothie and gave the empty glass to Sean, who put it on the table. Robert reached out and Sean took his hand. "Be seeing you," Robert said.

"Be seeing you," Sean replied.

Robert didn't know how much time passed before he began to feel the effects — time no longer meant anything. What mattered was that the pain was gone, and soon he could not feel anything save for Sean's hand holding on to his. Waves of darkness came and went across his vision. The tide was coming in, each wave taking longer to sweep over him, and before long there would be a final wave that would take him out to whatever sea was waiting for him. There was no escaping it now and no chance left to change what destination would be his.

There was still time for Sean to change it. Time and opportunity, as long as he was alive. Did Sean know that, or did he number himself among the damned already? One look into Sean's eyes told him the truth. He tried to speak, tried to tell Sean that it wasn't too late to make amends, or at least to try. He was never certain how much he was able to say, or how much Sean understood. It would have to do.

The final wave swept over him. He let go of Sean's hand and, almost gratefully, let the wave take him.

Sean held on to Robert's hand. He held on as Robert's eyes closed and his breathing became slow and deep. When Robert said Sean's name and then something he could not understand, he squeezed Robert's hand and nodded, said, "Yes, of course" in as reassuring a voice as he could. He held on as the breathing became slower, the pauses between inhalation and exhalation longer, until the breathing stopped. He held on until Robert's hand lost its heat, cooled noticeably; then he let go.

Sean stood up, his limbs sluggish and his joints aching. He knew he should cover Robert's face — he owed Robert that gesture of respect — but could not bring himself to do it. He started to walk out of the room, then paused and looked back at Robert. The wasted, still figure there wasn't really Robert, just as the body he'd picked up off the floor and covered with a knitted blanket hadn't really been Anna. Both were gone, and he was left here.

He walked into the kitchen. As he did, his eyes moved unseeing over the house and belongings Robert had left to him. Very appropriate, for Robert was more his father than his biological parent had been. He was grieved at Robert's passing. As for Bruce Kincaid, he had died of a stroke while his son was on a mission in Turkey, and was two months in the ground before Sean returned to the States and was informed of his father's death. Sean had never gotten around to going home and paying his respects.

Sean went to the front door, put on his coat, and walked outside, wanting to be away from this house where his friend had suffered through these last months. For most of that lonely drive from Haven Cove he had told himself not to get his hopes up, that Robert was long gone. Only at the very end, during the last hours of his drive, did he allow himself to hope that Robert was alive, and the closer he got the more absurd his hope became. He'd hoped that Robert was not just alive, but well, and would not just hear his confession but tell him what to do next, because for the first time in his life, he didn't know what course to take.

Of course, hope had been false and he had to see his oldest and best friend reduced to that state. Adding to his freight of guilt was not helping Robert die but that Robert had held on so long, waiting.

The Maine night was foggy still, and cold. He walked the several blocks to the beach and climbed over the seawall to the rocky shore. The fog hid both moon and stars, the streetlights were behind him, and he stumbled a bit, unable to see his footing. He found a flat rock and sat down, looking out at the sea. The tide kissed the shore some ten yards away — whether the tide was high or low he had no idea. He wished the fog would lift, wished the moon or stars would light up this beach and give him something to look at besides the dimmest phosphorescence. With nothing to look at, his mind offered up all sorts of images. Robert in pain and wasted by disease, looking like one of those mummies in the Mexican catacombs, yellowish skin stretched tight over bones. Jennifer Thomson sitting pressed against the passenger door of his van as if she might have to escape him at a second's notice. Anna dead on her hearth, blood in her pretty red hair.

He pressed his hands against his eyes, trying to make the images go away. They didn't, and now he heard something. That young priest back at Saint Stephen's, saying *You just left her there.*

Sean opened his eyes, hoping for a glimpse of the moon. It was still hidden by the fog. No matter. "Be seeing you," he whispered to Robert.

He took the gun from its shoulder holster. His movements were smooth, without hesitation. He put the barrel into his mouth, angled it slightly upward, then flicked off the safety and pulled the trigger.

Nothing.

He squeezed the trigger again. Nothing happened.

He took the gun out of his mouth, tasting oil and metal, staring incredulously at the weapon. The safety was off, the magazine loaded and in place. He could count on one hand the number of times this weapon had misfired. Never had he owned a more reliable gun, and now, *now*, when he needed it most, the fucking thing jammed.

Words failed him. He laughed. It was just a giggle at first but soon it was wild laughter that echoed up and down the empty beach. When his hilarity had subsided a bit, he stood up and flung the betraying weapon away, hearing it clatter on the rocks and then land in some water with an anticlimactic splash. He drew in breath and released it not in a laugh but in a scream that brought pain roaring back in his damaged throat and now the oil and metal taste was mingled with blood.

The scream's echo died and it was silent on the beach save for the tide. The gun wouldn't do. He'd have to find the damn thing first, then take it down and reassemble it, and he didn't have the patience left for that, not when there was a cold ocean offering up all the oblivion he could ask for.

That's what he wanted, oblivion, wanted it more than he had desired any woman, hungered for it more than he had craved any food. An unpleasant death, to be sure, but it would give he and Beatty something to commiserate about when they met up in Hell.

Sean managed three steps toward the ocean, and then his legs gave way and he fell to the ground. He lay on his side, watching the waves roll in and recede, over and over. Tired. He was so tired. He would get up in a minute and finish things, but first he had to rest. Just for a minute. The coarse sand was cold against his cheek; his breath steamed in the fog. He watched the waves and rested. Just for a moment.

Chapter Seven

Sheriff Leo Sorensen stared at his brother. He thought about what Walt had just told him, and then pronounced judgment: "You stupid, dumbshit, God damn motherfucker."

Walt Sorensen said nothing, definitely the wise course of action. He'd seen Leo in moods like this, and you sure as hell kept your mouth shut. You waited until he got it out of his system and cooled down before you talked to him again.

Leo glanced at the door to make sure it was closed. The last thing he wanted was for the rest of the Silas County Sheriff's Department to hear any of this. He didn't know what enraged him more: that his brother had gotten mixed up in some antigovernment group, that this group couldn't be content to just piss and moan and had actually blown up a federal building, or that Walt had confessed to him only now. Probably the last was what angered him the most — that Walt had chickened out not before the bombing, but after, and only because half the group seemed to be dead or missing and Walt wanted to save his own hide.

"Now's a fine time to come to me with all this," Leo said.

"I'm sorry — "

"You're not sorry, you're scared. What was that, three hundred people you guys killed? And *now* you're sorry? Was there another one in the works?" Leo stopped, held up a hand. "No, never mind. I don't want to know. I'm not sure I care. I'm going to clean up the mess. And you're going to help me."

"Thanks, Leo."

"Don't thank me. Run through it again. The names and when was the last time you saw them."

Walt told him. Doug MacReady, missing since September, had been found a week ago. The body had been stashed in the trunk of his car, in the long-term parking lot at Green Bay airport. Some kid looking for stuff to steal had jimmied the trunk open — if he ever got out of the psych ward, his days of thievery were surely over, Leo thought with grim amusement. The body was so far gone that positive ID hadn't been made until today.

Other members were missing, had been for three weeks now — since about the time Anna Blaine had been killed. Steve and Eddie Wickersham, Sam Lewis, and of course Richard Blaine, the leader of the group and wanted for questioning in the death of his wife. Leo rubbed his temples — he knew most of the names. They were local people, upright citizens for the most part. None had so much as a parking ticket except for the Wickersham brothers, who had racked up a couple of misdemeanors back in the day, but that was years ago and there'd been no trouble since. There was only one name he didn't recognize. "Who's this Sam Lewis guy?"

"He joined the group in January. Nice guy. Real smart. He and Richard really hit it off. He had lots of good ideas."

"Details, Walt. Where did he work, how old is he, what's he look like?"

Walt squirmed uncomfortably. "I'd say he was maybe in his fifties. Black or dark brown hair, going bald in front."

"Big guy? Little guy?"

"Sort of in between."

"Give me something definite here. Eyes? Brown or blue?"

"Brown," said Walt. "I think."

"Where did he work?"

"I don't know."

"Where was he from?"

Walt shrugged.

Leo turned away and stared at the wall, counting to ten. It was deliberate, of course. The less the members knew about each other the less they could tell if they got caught and questioned. He took a shot in the dark: "Do you think this Sam fellow might have killed Anna?"

Walt looked shocked. "No way. He'd have never crossed Richard like that. Besides, he seemed sweet on Anna."

"'Sweet on her'? Did they have a thing going?"

"Sam would knock your block off if he heard you say that," Walt said seriously. "No, it was like those King Arthur stories. Like he would have been her champion or something."

Leo rolled his eyes. Some of the town's model citizens, a couple former ne'er-do-wells (his brother included), and some mysterious Sir Galahad involved in terrorist activities. It had all happened right under his nose, and what was this going to do for his chances to be re-elected sheriff? Or for that state assembly bid he had his eye on? Leo thought of the strongbox at home and all it contained: the money to grease political wheels, the dirt to throw in the machinery. No. He was not going to allow this bullshit to jeopardize his chances of getting out of this two-bit town. Damned if he would be the laughingstock of the nation for letting this happen on his watch.

"Then did Richard kill Anna?" When Walt shook his head Leo asked, "Was she going to blow the whistle on them?"

"Richard wouldn't have done it. She didn't know anything — we all kept it from her. That was part of the deal. I don't know who killed her. I wish I did. She was really nice."

"Who else is left from this group?"

"Just a few guys."

"Low on the totem pole?"

Walt nodded.

"OK. From now on you have no contact with them at all. If they contact you, tell them it's over, if they value their lives. Although if any more show up looking like Doug MacReady, that should be enough of a clue. We've got absolutely no trace on Richard. Nothing in the house was disturbed or stolen, bank accounts weren't touched. Besides the head injury, not a mark on Anna. But there was a third person there. She scratched someone and drew blood. It's O positive. Richard is B negative and Anna herself was A positive. It's not much to go on — O positive is common as dirt, but it's something. This is all confidential and if you breathe a word of this you'll get no more help from me.

"Anything you find out, anything you remember, you come to me. I'll look for this Sam fellow. You try and find Steve and Eddie Wickersham. Their mother has already filed a missing persons report but she couldn't give me any decent information. And not a word of this to anyone else, not even to the deputies. If you need to reach me, call me direct. Don't leave any messages. Got it?"

Walt nodded. He didn't look up at his brother. He knew Leo wasn't doing this to help him, but he didn't mind too much. He was too scared by what had happened to MacReady and shaken by what had happened to Anna to care about more than saving his hide. He'd go along with whatever Leo said, because if this all blew up in Leo's face, Walt would have to pull a disappearing act of his own.

After his brother left, Leo walked outside and smoked furiously for ten minutes. He kept trying to kick the habit, but every time he made up his mind to do it, something came up. He hadn't expected anything like this, though. Once all this was buried and forgotten, he would strangle his idiot brother. No, wait. He would thank him for telling him all this no matter how late in the day, and then strangle him.

When he walked back inside the station, Sharon called out to him. "Call for you, Leo. It's Deirdre Monahan. Again."

Again? Christ, that woman called every other day. How many times did he have to tell her there was no news and no leads and he'd let her know when he knew something? Not that he would, of course, the situation had changed, but it wasn't his fault her cousin got bashed in the head. "Put her through to Nick," he said.

Sharon shook her head, cracked her gum. "Nick's out on a call."

Leo debated having Sharon route the Monahan woman into his voice mail, but she'd only call back later and be even more annoying. Best to get it over with now. He went to his desk and Sharon put the call through. "This is Sheriff Sorensen."

"Hello, this is Deirdre Monahan." There was a lot of background noise on her end. Crying children and loudspeaker voices asking for price checks. She must be calling from work. "I just wanted to know if there had been any news."

"No, no news. I'm sorry. The investigation is ongoing. I'll let you know when there's been any further developments," he said.

"Yes, but — "

His nerves were too strained to go through this again. "I'll talk to you soon, Ms. Monahan. Goodbye." He hung up. Let Nick deal with her next time. Leo had other things to do.

Deputy Nick Eliot was on his way to Bill Marston's cabin on the shore of Deer's Head Lake. There had been a storm last night; the calm surface of the lake had turned to angry chop, and left an unpleasant surprise on the shore near Marston's cabin.

Bill Marston, a hale and hearty ninety-something, had seen it all before. His voice on the phone had been calm to the point of blandness when he told Nick a body had washed up on shore. "Pretty far gone, too," he'd said.

"Let me call Rose," Nick said. Rose Flynn was the county coroner.

"I already called Rose," Bill said. "I have her number, thought I'd save you the hassle."

"Thanks, Bill. I'll be there as soon as I can."

Marston's cabin was on the far side of the lake and there was little to no traffic, so Nick had time and opportunity to think. He was still new to the force, had been doing lots of traffic stops and breaking up domestic disputes. He didn't mind; was rather good at it. He had a knack for getting all but the most violent drunks to settle down. His quiet tone soothed distraught women and fooled abusive men into thinking he was on their side, until he snapped the cuffs on them. Silas County was quiet. You didn't see the sort of things here that you saw on the crime shows, and Nick was glad about that.

Things seemed to have changed, though, with Anna Blaine's death. He and Leo had arrived to find the cousin, Deirdre Monahan, sitting outside the house, rocking back and forth with her arms wrapped around herself. Nick had stayed outside with her, asking gentle questions, while Leo went inside. Then it was Nick's turn to go in and survey the scene. The signs of violence and the body itself were all the more awful for being in such pretty, peaceful surroundings. It left him with a sorrow he couldn't shake for some time, and Leo told him if he let things like that get to him, he'd never last.

As he neared Marston's cabin he thought this might be an opportunity to toughen himself up. Probably it was just some hunter, unlucky enough to venture onto a thin patch of ice while going after the goose he'd shot. It happened all the time.

Marston was waiting outside his cabin. The coroner's van was already there, but Nick didn't see Rose. Nick got out of the car and Bill walked over to him. They exchanged greetings and Nick asked when Bill had found the body.

"Just this morning. I was taking a walk to see what the storm did and found it. Can't tell much about it, except it's a man, got winter clothes on."

"Did you touch it or move it?"

"Are you kidding? I went straight back here and called you and Rose. It's a nasty piece of work." Bill pointed along the lake's west shore. "That way. Just before you get to the big oak. Rose is already there. Want me to put on some coffee for you?"

"Thanks, Bill, I'd appreciate that." Nick got his camera and evidence bags out of the car, then walked along the shore. He found Rose soon enough. She was sitting on a tree stump, smoking one of the fancy clove cigarettes she favored.

Rose waved. "Hi Nick. Fun way to start the day?"

"And how. Have you looked it over?"

She nodded. "I'll join you in a sec. Just needed a cig break before I took another look. It's not pretty."

Rose was right. It wasn't pretty. It lay in the muddy shallows, bobbing slightly with the lake's tiny wavelets. At first glance it looked like nothing human. It seemed a mass of what looked like grayish, congealed spaghetti, held together into a vaguely human shape by rotting clothes. Hair that might once have been blond clung to the skull here and there. The face was turned away from Nick, and he wasn't sure if that was a good thing or not. "Sweet Christmas, that's nasty," he whispered.

"That it is," said Rose, stepping up nearby him. Her round, cherubic face was sober. She pulled on a pair of latex gloves, then handed him a pair. "Let's take a closer look."

Nick walked closer to the body, trying to focus on one thing at a time. It was easier that way. The shoes were sturdy leather boots — Nick had two pairs just like those at home. He caught a glimpse of what looked like flannel lining on the pants. No blaze orange, but he'd seen few hunters who actually wore that. "He's got winter clothes on," said Nick. "You think a hunter."

"Very likely," said Rose. "Even if you know the ice, winters aren't as cold as they used to be. All it takes is one weak spot and down you go. Once that happens, nine times out of ten that's it. You get disoriented or panic and can't find the hole to climb back out. Sometimes it's the shock of the cold that kills you. My uncle Howard fell through the ice — his friends hauled him out before he barely got his head wet, but the shock gave him a heart attack right there. Still, I'll take that over drowning. That's not a fun way to go."

He tried not to think about how cold and terrifying it must have been. "If it happened in winter, why haven't we found him until now?"

Rose frowned. "This guy should have floated months ago. He probably got tangled up in something and the storm kicked him loose."

He could avoid looking at the corpse's face no longer. He stepped over to the other side of the body, and the sight was oddly reassuring. This, clearly, was human, the skull's empty eye sockets and lipless, grinning mouth. It might have been anyone.

Together, Nick and Rose turned the body over. Its humanity was no longer reassuring — without a face to give expression, the gaping mouth could have been open in a laugh or a scream. Probably just trying to breathe, the poor soul.

Rose, by contrast, was pleased with the sight. "Oh, good. He's got all his teeth. That'll help ID him if we need to."

Nick, gritting his teeth and breathing shallowly through his mouth, was helping Rose move the body into the van when he paused. "Wait."

"You notice something?"

In turning the corpse over, its coat had fallen open. What Nick saw was so familiar yet so out of place it took him a moment to place it. John Doe was wearing a shoulder holster. Since when did hunters wear those? The holster was empty, but on the man's belt was a speedloader. Nick examined the speedloader — it was full, the rounds were .38s.

"How soon will you do the autopsy?" Nick asked Rose after she'd shut the van doors.

"Today," she said. "Want to be there?"

"No, but call me if you find anything unusual. And let me know if you have to send out for dental records. I'll take a look in the missing person files and see if anything turns up."

She clapped him on the shoulder. "I know you're pretty new at this, Nick. But you did good."

He smiled faintly. After the van left he stared out at the lake for a moment. Hard to believe that under that glittering surface this horror had been lurking.

Nick spent the day looking through county missing person reports for the last year, but there were only two adult males in the reports, neither of them six-foot-tall blonds. Rose called him just as he was getting ready to head home. "Our John Doe didn't have any ID on him, so I'm sending out the dental records tonight."

"Thanks for doing that so quickly."

"Well frankly I'm curious, so we'll see what turns up. It's hard to tell with a body this far gone, but so far it looks like a conventional drowning. I'll let you know if I find anything else out."

Nick hadn't had a thing to eat all day. He'd had no appetite at lunchtime and now was ravenous. He found himself heading not to the nearest drive-through but over to the shopping center in Lakeside, where there were a variety of fast-food places, as well as the Wal-Mart where Deirdre Monahan worked. She'd never been far from his mind the last few weeks — he knew she'd been calling, and he knew there was nothing new for anyone to tell her.

He wanted to find out how she was doing but knew if he stopped by during the day it would look like an official visit, and get her hopes up.

He was looking for a place to park when he saw her come out of the Wal-Mart. She walked stiffly and had the set expression of someone trying not to cry. She got into her truck, slammed the door, and then let herself go. He could not hear her — he didn't have to. She slammed her fist against the dashboard, tilted her head back and he could see shining tracks of tears on her face.

He couldn't watch any longer. It felt like a violation, as if he was watching her do something terribly intimate. She would never have let herself grieve like this if she'd known he was watching. He drove away quickly.

There was a message from Rose asking him to call her when he arrived at the station the next morning. "Hi, Rose. You learn anything about John Doe?"

"Yes, and as Alice in Wonderland would say, it's curiouser and curiouser. I don't know what his real name is but those dental records came through mighty quick. When I got in this morning some suits were waiting for me. Had all the paperwork ready. Took the body and were gone before coffee break."

"What do you mean?" Nick asked.

"Federal guys. Damn scary, too. Dark suits and sticks up their asses, like those agents in *The Matrix*. I'm wondering if we found Jimmy Hoffa."

Nick was silent, thinking of that shoulder holster and speedloader. Flimsy things to go on, but they troubled him. "Maybe he was one of their own."

Rose laughed. "Nick! This is Silas County. Why would some CIA type be here? Looking for the Al Qaeda cow-tipping brigade?"

He ignored the joke. "Did they give a name? Anything?"

"No. Just waved their badges and signed the papers and took him away. I can laugh now, but they were creepy guys. There's something not right about this whole thing," she said.

As he hung up he knew Rose was correct. Something wasn't right. He just wished he knew what, or why.

Chapter Eight

Frank Halsey knew the call was coming. No one told him. No one had to. He ignored the glances he got as he walked down the agency halls, pretended he didn't hear the whisperings. He didn't sweat. Why should he? He'd done nothing wrong. Nothing any reasonable person wouldn't understand and forgive. Besides, all he had to do to cheer himself up was remember that Robert Dvorak was dead — all that fancy talk and smarty-pants stuff hadn't helped Dvorak in the end. He was still worm food, and one less thorn in Halsey's side.

The call came. The top brass's frosty secretary asked if he would kindly report to the ninth floor. Mr. Yates, Mr. Peters, and Ms. Freeman would like to speak with him.

Halsey began to sweat.

On his way to the elevator, someone stage-whispered, "Dead man walking!" Someone else giggled. He was alone in the elevator, and as he ascended he examined his reflection. The suit was sharp, as it should be, considering how much he'd paid for it. It covered the sweat nicely; as long as his forehead stayed dry no one would know. *And I've nothing to hide, anyway. Maybe I did a few things under the table, but it was all for the agency's benefit, and anyone else would have done the same.*

The secretary buzzed him in, and he entered the room. There was a single chair for him. Facing the chair, sitting at a large table, were Yates, Peters, and Freeman. They watched as he walked in. He tried to read their faces and couldn't. They didn't look happy, but they never looked happy. They looked as they always did. Yates with his nearly-bald head and his eyes shiny dark like teddy bear button eyes. Peters who looked like someone's grandfather.

Freeman's face like an Egyptian pharaoh mask. The secretary came in with a pitcher of ice water and glasses. Only three glasses, none for him.

"Please sit down," said Yates.

Halsey sat. He noticed that there was someone else in the room, an agent he didn't recognize. The agent was a nondescript fellow whose eyes never left Halsey, and when the agent shifted slightly there was the telltale bulge of a sidearm under his jacket. Halsey felt fresh sweat break out under his arms. He longed for a glass of water but damned if he would ask for it.

Peters began without preamble. "Three weeks after the Los Angeles federal building was bombed, you received a call from former agent Sean Kincaid, whom you had retired four years previously. You met with Kincaid and he asked to return to the agency, specifically to pursue the person or persons responsible for the Los Angeles bombing. You refused and you told him to return to his home in Florida."

"Which he did," said Halsey.

Peters gave him a look that said they wanted his corroboration only when they asked for it and not before then. "Before returning to Florida, Kincaid paid a visit to another former agent, Robert Dvorak. He had been Kincaid's mentor and the two stayed in contact after retirement. It can be reasonably assumed that Dvorak gave Kincaid encouragement, perhaps information."

Yates took up the reins. "You placed Kincaid under surveillance after he returned to Florida. Nevertheless, in September Kincaid disappeared and the surveillance team did not realize this for several days."

Halsey opened his mouth to protest that he'd had to reduce the surveillance team because they were needed on another job, and that Kincaid had rigged up his house with timers and paid his utility bills two months in advance so that no one would notice he'd gone. Peters gave him another look and Halsey shut his mouth with a snap.

Yates resumed: "A search of Kincaid's Florida home revealed no indication of where he planned to go or what his purpose was. However, it is presumed that he went after those who set the bomb in Los Angeles.

"In October, you asked for permission to send an agent after Kincaid to locate and terminate him. This request was denied. You then contacted a number of former agents to ask if they would locate and assassinate Kincaid. The agent who accepted the job would receive a substantial cash reward from you and the promise of reinstatement to the agency."

"To their credit, most of these agents refused," Peters said.

"However," said Yates, "a former agent named Dwight Beatty took you up on this offer. He went in pursuit of Kincaid. You last heard from him at Christmas of that year, when he told you he had found a strong lead. Beatty has not been heard from since then and is presumed dead. His wife, receiving no word for many months from Beatty or from you, found a phone number for the agency in Beatty's personal effects and has been calling repeatedly to find out more."

Peters spoke next. "I've been told that she had also been sending emails to her state representatives and senator. Only when she threatened to speak to the press did you placate her with money. However, she still wants to know where her husband is."

Halsey's hands clenched. Damn that idiot Beatty. He'd known that married agents weren't sent out into the field for missions like this. They stayed home and looked at satellite photos and pushed paper. That was why he hadn't mentioned until the last second that he'd found some woman dumb enough to marry him. "If I don't make it back for some reason, make sure the payment gets to my wife," Beatty had said. "Oh, didn't you know? I got married two years ago. And we've got a baby on the way."

"You got married?" Marriage had never agreed with Halsey — he had three ex-wives, all of them hateful money-grubbing bitches.

Beatty had gotten a moronic, in-love look on his face. "Yes, her name's Noelle. A sweetheart. Great cook, too," he'd said, patting his stomach. The moronic look had vanished and Beatty's voice, which had been genial and full of flattery, turned cold. "I'm doing this for her sake, not yours. So get that money to her if something goes wrong."

Yates tapped his pen on the table, calling Halsey back to the present. "Recently, in an attempt to locate Kincaid, you visited the workplace of a Washington lawyer named Monique Pavour-Banks, a known acquaintance of Kincaid. The fact that she did not know anything does not mitigate the fact that this interrogation was unauthorized and violated our procedures," said Yates.

"Kincaid's whereabouts have been unknown, until recently," said Peters.

Until recently? What the hell did that mean? Halsey tried to surreptitiously wipe his sweaty palms on his trousers.

"As you know, Robert Dvorak had been ill with terminal cancer. In fact, you paid him a visit a couple months ago asking if he knew Kincaid's whereabouts. Last week Mr. Dvorak died," said Peters

Halsey knew. He'd even gone to the local morgue to view the remains. He'd never been able to stand Dvorak, who was always quoting poems and saying things in other languages and generally acting like his shit didn't stink. If Dvorak had kept his big mouth shut, Kincaid wouldn't have gone off and Halsey wouldn't be in this jam.

"The toxicologist's report we received states that Dvorak's death was not from cancer but from a morphine overdose. A large number of morphine pills had been ground up, increasing their lethality, and given to Dvorak in a drink consisting of —" Peters paused to look at some papers. "Yogurt, blueberries, strawberries, orange juice, and honey."

Halsey couldn't keep silent. "Probably that hospice guy of his — "

Peters cut him off. "The hospice worker, Kumar Singh, said that a person matching Kincaid's description visited Dvorak that night. He made positive ID on a photo. Kincaid's fingerprints are also on the glass the drink was in and the blender used to make it. Unfortunately, Kincaid left Dvorak's house that night, and his whereabouts are once again unknown."

Freeman took a sip of water and spoke for the first time: "Mr. Halsey, in the decade you have held this position here, we've had the second-deadliest terrorist attack on U.S. soil, the perpetrators of which are still unknown and at large. When a highly skilled agent eminently qualified for the task asked to return to service and find those perpetrators, you denied his request without consulting us. You hired a former agent to terminate Kincaid. This also was unauthorized, and has resulted in considerable embarrassment and required a good deal of hush money. Kincaid not only escaped your surveillance in Florida, but he returned to Maine without your knowledge. You interrogated Kincaid's former girlfriend without authorization and in a manner violating agency procedure.

"There is a pattern of blatant disregard for procedure and authority, which could be overlooked if any of your actions had yielded results. But they have not, which leads me to conclude there is a second pattern of incompetence. You are to be placed on six months' paid suspension, after which you will return to the agency not in your current role but as financial administrator, which seems more attuned to your ... abilities."

Halsey's stomach plummeted, his breath seemed to stop. He'd never guessed it would be this bad. Six months' suspension? Demoted? Shame and rage boiled in his gut, and what he wouldn't give for some weapon that would blow all three of these smug bastards, Yates and Peters and Freeman, away.

He tried to keep his face still but some of it must have shown. The agent with the sidearm casually walked closer.

"You have the rest of the day to put your affairs in order. Thank you for your time," said Freeman.

Halsey wanted to make some witty remark but didn't trust himself to speak, afraid that all he would manage would be *Please* and *I'm sorry*, which would only deepen his humiliation. He nodded stiffly and kept calm until he was in the elevator. Between the seventh and sixth floors he hit the emergency stop button; he hammered his fists on the walls until he was panting and his hands were sore and bruised. It didn't help.

Most of what was in his office he would have to leave. Much would be given to his successor, whoever that might be. Whatever would be relevant to his demoted position would be sent to his new office and waiting there when he came crawling back with his tail between his legs six months from now.

He mechanically glanced through files to see if there was anything he should take with him. He already had a copy of the most important file at home — documentation of the Sean Kincaid matter dating back to when Kincaid had asked to come back, been refused, and had insulted him and stormed out. Halsey clenched his hands when he thought of it. Nearly everything Freeman had listed in her dressing-down had been Kincaid's fault. He had never liked Kincaid. Truthfully, he disliked all the agents — they thought they were so superior. Here he was trying to do the best this agency could with the budget cuts and political interference, and did he ever hear one word of thanks? No, they just looked down their noses at him because he didn't have to get shot at or slum around with dirty foreigners. Ungrateful and stuck-up, all of them, and Kincaid one of the worst. Everything was his fault — he probably sneaked back to Maine and gave Dvorak that morphine cocktail because he knew it would reflect badly on Halsey. Conniving, rotten bastard, so smug because he got to fuck that hot lawyer, and she sure as hell had known what was going on, Halsey was certain of it.

A tap at his door. "What?" he snapped. And smiled for the first time that day. Agent Larson stood in the doorway, looking deeply unhappy to be there. He'd caught Larson misappropriating funds several years ago, and the price for Halsey's silence was Larson bringing news to Halsey first.

Larson walked in and Halsey shut the door. Larson didn't sit down, although he was offered a chair. "They found Dwight Beatty," Larson said. "His dental records match with a John Doe pulled out of Deer's Head Lake in Silas County, Wisconsin. They're flying people out to pick up the body first thing in the morning. He's been dead for months." Larson turned and opened the door.

As he stepped out Halsey said, "Thank you." Something he'd never done before.

Larson nodded, smiled faintly, clearly hoping their arrangement was at an end.

It was. Before he left that day, Halsey sent a file with all his documentation of Larson's misappropriation to the top brass.

He thought about Larson's news. Wisconsin. Something to go on, along with the recent sighting in Maine. That evening he made a call from a pay phone, and spoke with Juliette.

It wasn't the first time he'd asked for Juliette's help. Back when he was first looking for someone to go after Kincaid, Juliette had been one of the top names on his list. But she'd merely laughed and hung up on him. Maybe this time it would be different.

"Juliette, it's Halsey."

"Hello, Francis. How's suspension treating you?"

Did these people do nothing but gossip? "I want to see you. I have a job for you."

"What sort of job?"

"It's better if I tell you in person. Can we meet for lunch?"

"Thursday I'm free. You're paying. And make it somewhere nice. I don't do drive-through."

He was a few minutes late getting to the restaurant, but Juliette wasn't there yet. He hoped she'd show. That would be like her, to go back on her promise to be there. He didn't know why the agency had put up with her for so long. Except that she was very good at her job, and nearly everyone in the agency was afraid of her.

Halsey was seated and well into his gin-and-tonic when Juliette arrived; he knew then why she was late. She had wanted to make an entrance. Halsey tried not to watch the show, but he couldn't help it. No one could. Juliette strode into the restaurant, clad in a suit that was conservatively gray but tailored to display her body and its long legs, slim waist, and full breasts. Crowning this perfection was the face of a queen, a goddess. Everyone looked, compelled as surely as if they'd had knives held to their throats. Like a queen, like a goddess, she recognized none of her adorers save to give a smile and a nod to the waiter who pulled her chair out for her.

She sat down. Halsey, who had started to rise from his chair, sat down as well. Juliette smiled. It was not a friendly smile. "Nice to see you, Francis."

Halsey nodded. He was having trouble speaking, still taken aback by the sight of Juliette and all her beauty sitting just across the table from him. Juliette had been an assassin for the agency; she'd always worked alone not simply because a lone assassin can more easily escape detection but because all the men in the agency were too awestruck in her presence to carry on a coherent conversation, let alone perform their duties. Even Agent Harris, who was stone queer, had been overheard saying that he could switch teams for Juliette. "Hello," he finally managed. As he spoke he unconsciously sat up straighter, restrained the urge to make sure his hair was in place.

She ordered a gin and tonic, then picked up the menu and studied it for a moment. She didn't speak until the waiter came to take their order. She picked the most expensive items; Halsey realized with a pang that he couldn't charge this meal to his expense account. She smiled that bright, unfriendly smile again. "So tell me about this job. Is it the same job you wanted me for last year?"

"In a way."

"My answer is still no."

"I can pay you."

"I don't need the money." Juliette gestured to her suit, her shoes, her handbag. "You think all this came from Goodwill? Why do you need me? Surely Beatty took out Kincaid?" Her look was wide-eyed innocence.

"You know perfectly well he didn't."

"You're right, I did know that. Silly me."

"Why won't you go after Kincaid?" he asked.

"Why should I? I respected his talent. He seemed pretty smart, for a man. Good manners, too. He would hold doors open for me. A lady appreciates that, in these boorish times."

He was about to say that Juliette wasn't his idea of a lady, but she continued: "Besides, I fancied him. He's kind of cute, in a nerdy sort of way."

"I don't know why you women like that beady-eyed bastard so much," he muttered, thinking of Kincaid's lawyer girlfriend. The bitch had been a tease just like Juliette. "He's going bald, for God's sake."

"I *like* bald men. It's a well-known fact that male pattern baldness indicates a higher testosterone level. Last bald guy I went to bed with, it was days before I could walk straight again."

The waiter, a balding young fellow, arrived with their food in time to hear this last bit of conversation. Though his ears flamed he didn't miss a beat while serving their food, and Juliette favored him with a smile that made her the star of his fantasy life for the next year.

Halsey didn't want to ask, because he didn't think he wanted the answer, but blurted it out anyway. "Did you ever sleep with Kincaid? Is that why you won't take the job?"

Juliette shook her head. "No, I don't go out with anyone in the agency. Too much potential for complications. Makes it messy if you have to terminate them. I made a couple mistakes like that early on. Definitely not worth the hassle."

She spoke of assassination as another person might speak of taking out the garbage. Halsey felt a bit of a chill as he watched Juliette blithely go from talking about murder to eating her lobster.

He still didn't have the answer. "Why wouldn't you go after him?"

"Because I had no reason to."

"I'm not asking this for me. Kincaid killed Beatty. They finally found the body. Beatty's widow deserves justice." He hoped she bought it.

She didn't. "How sentimental. You gave that same widow the run-around for months. Francis, the sooner you admit you've got a personal grudge against Kincaid the happier you'll be. If you want him so badly, find him yourself."

Halsey looked down at his food without seeing it. He'd suspected Juliette wouldn't take the job. But maybe she could help. "I'll go after him."

Juliette laughed, shook her head, and went back to her lobster.

He forced the words out of his mouth. The humiliation burned, but his hatred of Kincaid burned hotter. "Help me. Teach me how to find him. Tell me how to … terminate him."

"He'd eat you for breakfast."

"I'm serious."

"I know. You've got your hate on, anyone can see it. But it's not just about hate. Hate burns out." Juliette was serious. No mockery in her eyes now. "Do you have the will?"

"I do."

"Prove it. Tell me one thing you've done that shows me you've got the will. Or at least the brains."

Halsey took a breath. "I went to see Robert Dvorak a few months ago, to find out what he knew. He didn't tell me anything but after he nodded off, I found that he had a gun hidden under his mattress in case he wanted to check out early. I stole it."

Juliette regarded him coolly. "What a sneaky thing to do. Taking his only option out of a slow, painful death." She smiled, a shark's smile. "But it's *good*. Very cunning of you. I'll help you. For a price."

"What's the price?" he asked, thankful that he still drew a salary during his suspension.

The shark's smile widened. "You can afford it, don't fret. When the time comes to pay, I'll let you know."

"When do we start?"

"As soon as you're ready. But first, I'd like coffee and dessert."

Chapter Nine

Deirdre's alarm clock went off with a buzz. Already awake, she clicked it off and sat up, the roll-away bed creaking beneath her. She turned on the TV to one of the morning shows — it didn't matter which, she never paid attention. She just wanted the noise. Deirdre got up and walked into her bathroom, where she turned on the water in her coffin-size shower stall. After showering she dressed in khakis and a blouse and her comfortable sneakers. While the coffee brewed she made her bed, then walked about with coffee cup in hand, tidying things and moving objects around. The apartment was small and her possessions few but it made her feel better to be in motion and busy. As a result Deirdre, never known for her housekeeping, had the cleanest, neatest apartment in her complex. Even her mother might have been proud.

She put on her blue Wal-Mart vest and went downstairs to her truck. It was raining — a good thing, that meant she'd need to focus on her driving and on the road. She drove to work with exaggerated care, grateful for the truck's stick shift — it was familiar, it was solid, it was reliable. She could hold on to it.

When she got to work she paused a moment, setting her watch to beep when it was time for her break. She'd learned to do this or she might be so caught up in the monotony of scanning items, nodding at customers, and handing out receipts that she missed her break entirely and was more footsore than usual at lunch.

At break time she sat outside, watching the customers parade in and out, absently flexing her aching feet. A few coworkers passed by; a huddle of smokers stood in the overhang, hunched vulturelike over their cigarettes. One stomped her cigarette out and went back in, nodding at Deirdre as she did so.

Deirdre gave a nod back, said nothing. If she was lucky she could go an entire day without having to speak to anyone. That made things easier. Maybe she could pretend she had some exotic disease that robbed her of speech, so she'd have a good excuse. If she talked she would have to say how she was doing. If she talked it meant she could also cry, could scream, and she'd done that already and what had come of it? Not a thing. If she talked she could ask questions, and nothing had come of that either. The sheriff had gotten tired of telling her there was nothing new to report, and the last couple times she'd called she'd just gotten his voice mail. The last time she hadn't even bothered to leave a message.

Her break over, she went back to work until it was lunch. Her lunch eaten, she went back to work until the next break. That break over, she went back to work until it was time to go home.

This was the hard part.

Her shift ended at six, which meant there was still so much time left in the evening. Dinner wasn't a problem. She usually just heated a can of soup when she got home. Sometimes she'd get drive-through, ordering the kids' meal because she wasn't very hungry these days; she gave the toys to her coworker Yolanda, who had three kids. Yolanda had sorrowful eyes and a scar on her right cheek and seemed to understand Deirdre's need for muteness and routine. One day Deirdre meant to thank Yolanda for shushing the other employees who wanted to know what was up with Deirdre these days.

Once she was home and dinner was eaten and the few dishes washed, there was the rest of the night. She couldn't go to bed at eight. She'd tried and it was no good, she just lay awake and started thinking. She couldn't focus on books so she watched TV. She'd moved the TV into the bedroom because often she fell asleep watching it. If she didn't, she'd turn it off when she felt her eyes getting heavy. Deirdre would lie in bed, on the verge of sleep, and there was usually the thought, never consciously expressed, that she'd managed to go another day without thinking of Anna and what had happened to her.

Halloween was what did her in.

Not the holiday itself. That was almost two weeks gone, and she'd spent it with the lights off and hiding from trick-or-treaters because despite the Halloween displays at work and children nagging their parents to buy more candy and parents saying they would not buy that expensive costume, she'd forgotten the date and had bought no candy. Remembering the date would have meant remembering what her original plans for Halloween had been — to be at Anna's church, helping her and Richard put on a party for the kids in their parish.

The holiday was gone but the costumes weren't. Determined to squeeze every last dollar out of the holiday, the manager had put the unsold costumes on the clearance table. Today, after clocking out, Deirdre walked by and saw two girls goofing around with the costumes. Nothing worth noticing, except that one snatched up a wig — platinum blonde with the texture of cotton candy — put it on, struck a sultry pose, and began singing, "Happy birthday, Mr. President."

Deirdre hadn't stopped; she'd kept walking. But she'd stood outside her truck for several minutes, not noticing the drizzle. She wasn't seeing her truck or the parking lot, she was seeing a five-and-dime store in Minnesota, seeing herself and Anna goof off with Halloween costumes. Just like those girls. Nan and Dee swapping the wig back and forth and seeing who could do the best breathy Marilyn Monroe voice, until the store owner said he'd *give* them the wig if they would just be quiet.

The next morning, she started her usual routine for a weekend: turned on the TV and wondered what household chore she would tackle today. Then after a moment, turned off the TV. Silence, loud in the wake of the TV's chatter. She started to reach for the remote again, then pulled her hand away. What the hell was she doing? She had promised Anna she would find out what had happened, and what was she doing? Zombifying herself in front of the TV while the person who'd meant the most to her was dead and no one cared to do anything about it.

In less than twenty minutes she was showered, dressed, and in her truck, heading to Du Lac.

The gate to the Christmas tree farm had been locked with a new padlock. She climbed the chain-link fence, careful not to look down when she reached the top — she'd never had much of a head for heights.

Deirdre walked down the dirt road, trees on both sides of her. It was too soon for the farm to show signs of neglect, but there was something forlorn about these trees all the same. Soon she reached the house, and found visible signs of Anna's and Richard's absence. Weeds in the flowerbeds, the plants wilting for lack of water. No neighing from the barn; the horses had been taken away … where? She didn't know.

The front door had yellow "CRIME SCENE DO NOT CROSS" tape across it. She wouldn't have gone in that door anyway — that was the room where she'd found Anna and she couldn't go in there, not yet. Deirdre went around the side, trying every door and window. Everything was locked. Who had locked it, and who had the keys? Not her.

She couldn't get in. She could leave it at that, and go home. *Yeah, right.*

On the woodpile she found a good-size log that wasn't too big around but still had plenty of heft. She found a window low enough to climb into. Gritting her teeth and hoping whoever had locked the house hadn't also set the burglar alarm, she swung the log and broke the window. There was the sound of breaking glass, no alarm. Carefully she picked out the glass shards.

She put down the log, then for a reason she couldn't understand picked it up and tossed it into the house, through the open window. She hoisted herself up and wriggled through the window and into the house.

She had been most afraid of the smell; it was still there, because the house had been shut up, but it was not as bad as she had feared. Picking up the log, she held it tightly in one hand, and it comforted her. She couldn't bring herself to go into the living room yet, so she went to the other end of the house.

It was not a very large house. Down the hallway was a bathroom, a linen closet, a room that was both Anna's sewing room and a spare bedroom. Deirdre had stayed there once or twice. It was a nice enough room but she had once longed for the bed and the sewing machine to be taken out and for the room to be turned into a nursery, painted pink or blue. Pink. It would have been pink. The autopsy report said Anna had been pregnant with a daughter.

Deirdre bit her lip, clutched the log tighter. She wouldn't think about that now. She went down the hall, to the bedroom. It was neat and tidy, like the rest of the house. There was a night table on each side of the bed. The table on what had been Anna's side, presumably, had a bottle of Tums and a dog-eared copy of *What to Expect When You're Expecting*. She looked around, but there was no one to see. Feeling like she was trespassing, she opened the drawer of the night table. Nothing unusual: an old lipstick, a couple of fat paperbacks.

She turned away from the night table. Against the wall was Anna's desk, where she wrote letters — she had been the only person Deirdre knew who still handwrote letters on stationery — and did the household bills. Deirdre pulled the chair out and sat down at the desk. It was an old rolltop desk with half-a-dozen little drawers. If this had been Deirdre's desk those drawers would have been crammed with all sorts of junk, but this was Anna's desk, so it was no surprise to find the drawers neatly organized. One held letters and postcards Anna had received, another held her stationery and pens. One drawer held a variety of Altoid mints, Anna's guilty pleasure. In the last drawer was a packet of photos.

She picked up the packet. According to the envelope, the photos had been developed in late September. The words *Labor Day party!* were written across the envelope in what was clearly Anna's handwriting. Deirdre's eyes stung. She had wanted to be at that party, but had been too tied up with moving and getting the Wal-Mart job. She opened the envelope and took out the pictures.

They were color photos, and she guessed they had come from a disposable camera judging from the quality. She recalled Anna telling her that she was going to leave some disposable cameras at the party, let people take whatever pictures they fancied. "That way I might actually get in the pictures," she'd said, laughing. "Usually I'm never in them because I'm the photographer!"

The first photo was of Richard and Anna. They were hugging and smiling. Deirdre blinked hard. They were in love. Anyone could see it. Nine years of marriage and they could have been newlyweds. Richard had nothing to do with Anna's murder. No one looked at a woman like that and then killed her.

She looked at the back of the photo. *Hold hands, you lovebirds,* was written on the back in Anna's hand. Deirdre blinked again and bit her tongue, hard, until the tears went away. Now wasn't the time for bawling over pictures. She went through the rest of the photos. It must have been a big party — she only saw Richard in one other picture. The focus of the picture was the cake; Richard was off to the side, where he appeared to be talking with some men she didn't recognize. Richard looked intent, serious. She wondered what he was talking about. Deirdre had despaired of seeing Anna until she got to the last picture.

Anna stood with a plate of fruit salad in one hand and a glass of milk in the other. She was smiling, looking as if she was ready to laugh. Deirdre stared at the photo, looking not at her cousin but at the man Anna was smiling at. Because the man wasn't Richard. He was shorter than Richard, with dark, receding hair. His face was pleasant enough, nothing special. What caught her eye was his smile. He seemed to be telling a joke, anticipating Anna's laughter. His plate was heaped high with food, so he was obviously a fan of her cooking. Though both were smiling, it wasn't the same as in the photo of Anna and Richard. This was the smile of affection and friendship.

Deirdre turned the photo over. *Sam and me* was written there. Something rang a chord in Deirdre's memory. Where had she heard that name before? She slipped the photo, along with the one of Anna and Richard and the one with Richard talking to the group of men into her jacket pocket without thinking about why she was doing it, then put the rest of the photos back in their envelope, put the envelope back in its drawer.

As she pushed the drawer closed she thought she heard a noise. She listened, but heard nothing. It was enough to remind her that Anna's murderer was still out there somewhere. Holding the log in both hands, ready to give at least one good blow in defense of herself, she went back down the hall to the window she'd broken. The rest of the house could wait for another time.

She wriggled back out the window and jumped down into the back yard. There was no way to hide the damage to the window, but she pulled the curtains closed and hoped that would fool a casual observer. She tossed the log back onto the woodpile and headed for the front gate at a fast trot.

Too much time jockeying a cash register and not enough time exercising meant she was panting, sweaty, and had a stitch in her side by the time she got to the fence. After pausing a moment to rest, she climbed the fence again — it seemed to have gotten a lot taller — and made her way back down.

As her sneakered feet hit the ground she sighed with relief. Whatever that noise she'd heard in the house was, she'd escaped it. Probably just her imagination anyway. She walked to the clearing where she'd parked her truck, digging in her pocket for her keys.

"What are you doing here?"

The voice was low and harsh. And familiar. She looked up startled to see Sheriff Sorensen standing there, one hand on the butt of his gun, his face clenched tight and his mouth an angry line.

Before she could answer, he asked: "How did you get in?"

"I hopped the fence." For a second she regretted she hadn't lied, then realized she had no idea how long the sheriff had been here. He'd probably guess she hadn't just been hanging around the gate waiting for it to magically open.

"This is a crime scene. You're not supposed to be here."

"I just went to look at the horses, to see if they were still there," she said, hoping it sounded halfway plausible. "You think I *want* to go back in that house?"

He stood looking at her with stony eyes. "I know this is a difficult time for you," he said, "but I have to ask you to stay away from the house, and that includes the outside of it. You could inadvertently destroy evidence in the case and slow down the investigation."

Her anger surged, sudden and hot. She'd had no idea it was even there. "Yeah, right, because it's been going lightning fast until now. Have you made any progress, or were you saving it all up to surprise us?" Deirdre couldn't believe she was saying this but didn't much care. The bastard didn't even return her calls any more.

Sheriff Sorensen took a deep breath. He reminded Deirdre of her mother, counting to ten so she wouldn't haul off and start spanking. "Ms. Monahan, you should go home. You've been under a lot of strain. I'll let you know — "

"'If there's anything to report.' I heard it the first hundred times." Deirdre walked past the sheriff toward her car, the rage still lively inside her. As she passed the sheriff's car she saw another man, sitting in the passenger seat. At first she thought it might be that nice deputy, Nick Something. If so, she wanted to apologize for being rude. But it wasn't Nick. The man wasn't wearing a sheriff's uniform, and though he wasn't familiar the way he stared at her was. It wasn't until she was in her truck and on the road that she understood. The people at Anna's funeral had stared at her the same way. Whoever this man was, he'd known Anna.

Leo Sorensen waited until Deirdre's truck was out of sight. "I don't like it," he said to Walt as his brother got out of the car.

"She just wants to know what happened," said Walt.

"She's called my office nearly every day until this last week or so. She's getting obsessed. That plus pissed off is a bad combination. She could get us all into a lot of trouble." Leo drummed his fingers on the car's roof.

"You can't be serious. There's no way she can know anything. And if she wants to know, so what? She's not Sherlock Holmes."

Leo fixed his stony gaze on Walt, who squirmed uncomfortably beneath it. "You guys left enough pieces of the puzzle laying around for her to put something together. And even if she doesn't, I have to close this case or she's going to be complaining to the press and the attorney general and anyone else she can think of. I will not let that happen." Leo leaned close to Walt. "If it does, I will throw you to the wolves. Understand?"

Walt nodded.

"And another thing. Next time you see her, try not to act like you saw a ghost, OK?"

"Sorry," muttered Walt. "It's just that she looks like Anna. It freaked me out."

"Well, get used to it. I want you to keep an eye on her. Make sure she keeps her nose out of trouble."

"When the hell am I supposed to do that? I'm still trying to find out what happened to the Wickersham brothers and to Sam Lewis. What do you want me to do, quit my job for all this?"

"If you have to, yes," said Leo. "While we're here, let's look around." He reached into his pocket for the keys, and unlocked the padlock for the gate. "Where did you say the group met? The basement?"

"Yes," said Walt. "If Richard kept anything it'll be there."

"Think Deirdre would have looked down there?"

"She said she didn't go in the house."

"Walt, were you born an idiot or did you become one later in life?"

Walt shrugged. "I don't know."

"Well, let's find out." Leo opened the gate, and they drove down the dirt road to the Blaine house.

Chapter Ten

Hell wasn't at all the way he'd imagined it would be.

It was neither as hot nor as cold as he would have thought; in fact, it was rather comfortable. The air carried the scent of the ocean and wood smoke — and unmistakably, coffee.

Sean opened his eyes. He was on the beach in Maine. Someone had put two wool blankets over him, and there was a good-size campfire close by. On the other side of the campfire was, presumably, his benefactor. He was an older man, probably in his sixties, with a full beard. He wore a long wool coat and he appeared to be a large fellow, bulky but not fat. A travel-faded fedora shielded his eyes from the brightening mist. He took an enameled metal coffeepot from the fire, took off the lid, peered inside and nodded. Then he looked over at Sean. "I see you're among the living," he said.

The man's voice was low, melodious. Sean was reminded of Orson Welles, and of Robert. Sean sat up, tried to thank the man and ask his name, but his voice was gone. He was about to mime writing but the man reached into a knapsack and took out a small notebook and pen, gave them to Sean.

"Would you like some coffee?" the man asked as Sean fumbled with the pen and notebook. He asked this calmly, as if finding unconscious mutes on the beach was a commonplace occurrence.

Sean nodded. He opened the notebook, and wrote *Thank you.*

"You're welcome." The man handed Sean a mug of coffee. "I'm Pete, by the way."

Sean, he wrote and then put down the pen and notebook so he could take the coffee. It was hot and strong, it hurt his throat to drink it, and it was one of the best things he'd ever drunk in his life.

Pete reached into his knapsack and took out a small cast-iron skillet. It looked as if it had seen many years of use. Near the knapsack was a brown paper bag; he took out English muffins, bacon, and eggs. "While you were asleep I took the liberty of going up to the store and getting some breakfast things. Does this suit you?"

Sean's first impulse was to protest, write something like *No thank you, I'm fine,* but the mere thought of food brought on hunger so fierce it made him light-headed. He tried to remember the last time he'd eaten. It was before he'd crossed into Maine, he knew that much. He'd refused to stop for anything but gas once he'd crossed the state line, kept going by his need to see Robert. He nodded vigorously to Pete's suggestion of food, but Pete had already taken him up on it, was carefully angling the muffins close to the fire so they would toast, and heating the pan for the bacon and eggs.

Sean wondered briefly if it was permitted to make fires and cook food on this beach, but it didn't seem to matter. No other people were about, and the beach was still shrouded in mist. They seemed to be isolated from the world, outside of time. Fog still hid the sun.

Pete didn't speak. He was intent on his work, as if breakfast was a serious matter. Once he looked up at Sean, who felt Pete's gaze pierce through the fog. It was like being caught in a searchlight, and Sean instinctively went statue-still, something he felt sure was not lost on Pete. The man was not just some ordinary drifter, that was certain. There was the matter of the wool blankets. He hadn't just put them on Sean, he'd gotten them under Sean as well, keeping the cold ground from leaching out his body heat, and preventing death from hypothermia.

Not soon enough, breakfast was ready — bacon and eggs on English muffins, and although eating hurt his throat more than drinking the coffee did, Sean ate and began to feel less unreal. Things were coming back to him. Nothing he wanted — thoughts of Robert, of Anna, of Jennifer.

Pete offered another cup of coffee, which Sean accepted, then took out a pipe and lit it. "I'm sorry, but this is my only one, so I'm afraid I can't offer you a smoke. It's just as well. Smoking wouldn't be good for your throat, the shape it's in," Pete said. "Don't worry, I won't ask how you came by those bruises. You don't have to lie. Have you ever been to Kenya?"

The question was so unexpected Sean readily answered, shaking his head. He'd been to Libya and Morocco, but never Kenya.

"You should go, some time. Once when I was there, I stayed awake all night, just to watch the stars and listen to the night. It was very late, probably two or three in the morning. It had been quiet for a very long time. And then I heard them. Hyenas, laughing in the night. It's not the sort of thing you want to hear in the middle of the night. Their laughter is not sane.

"Last night I was getting ready to make camp when I heard what sounded like a hyena laughing. I don't mind telling you that I almost didn't investigate. You don't go to see what the hyenas are laughing at. But curiosity won out. Which led me to you.

"I don't know why you were here. I don't *want* to know much about you. Please don't take offense, but you don't seem entirely safe to yourself or to others."

You don't have to be afraid of me, Sean hastily scribbled.

"I'm not. You're in my debt and you know it. You aren't a mindless predator, no matter if you laugh like one. Predators feel no remorse. And even a blind man can see you've done something you're repenting. Am I right?"

Sean nodded.

Pete sighed. "To quote the Bard, 'But if the cause be not good, the king himself hath a heavy reckoning to make.' It will only get heavier, you know. It will end up killing you as surely as the cold would have killed you last night. Should I have let that happen?"

After a long time Sean wrote *Maybe so.*

Pete knocked the ashes out of his pipe. "Perhaps. But I didn't let that happen, and now here you are, and what are you going to do next?"

He'd meant what he'd said to Robert last night. He hadn't given it any thought. All his thoughts had been focused on getting to Maine and seeing Robert. Beyond that, nothing. He'd gotten what he wanted. Robert was there and heard his confession, but it was a temporary relief, no more a cure than Robert's morphine shots had been a cure for cancer. There was no cure, only the obliteration of pain. *There's nothing I can do,* he wrote.

Pete turned to look at him, and something about that look was familiar. "You could always make amends."

Oh yes, Sean thought but didn't write. *Tell me how to turn back time and resurrect the dead.*

His thoughts must have shown. "Of course you can't undo what's happened," Pete said. "I mean putting things right, as much as you can."

How? Sean wrote.

Pete smiled, began dousing the fire and breaking camp. "You'll figure it out. I have every confidence of that. By the way," he said, reaching into his knapsack again. "I think this belongs to you."

He took out Sean's gun and held it out to him. Sean took it, glad that Pete required no explanations. He wrote one last time in the notebook. *Thank you.*

"You're welcome," Pete said. In just a few moments he was packed and stood with his knapsack on and a stout walking stick in one hand. With the other hand he tipped his fedora. *"Vaya con Dios."*

Unable to reply in kind, Sean bowed a little. Pete turned and began walking south, down the beach. Sean wondered how far his wandering would take him. All the way to Florida? Would he continue and loop around the country, perhaps one day end up back at this rocky beach?

Pete disappeared into the fog. Sean looked around. There was no sign of anyone else, and no sound save for the ocean and the occasional screech of a gull. If not for the signs of the campfire, he might have imagined the whole thing. Maybe he was imagining it. Maybe he was back in Du Lac with Richard Blaine choking him, and the last two weeks were just a hypoxia-induced hallucination. No such luck. He was alone — he could fix the gun and use it, or walk into the sea. But he didn't.

He walked away from the beach, back up toward Robert's house. Only three blocks' distance but there was noticeably less fog here. He paused by his van and saw, parked outside Robert's house, an ambulance and the coroner's van. He stood watching as two men carried out Robert's body — hidden by a sheet, it was so small, so insubstantial.

Sean watched, feeling some awful sensation he couldn't recognize. Duller than fear, deeper than pain, it left him shaking so he had to sit down in the van's driver's seat and look away from Robert's house. It was grief, which he hadn't felt since his mother died over forty years ago. Mingled with the grief was guilt. Robert had hung on, waiting, knowing that he would be needed. What shamed Sean was that he would not have waited that long, had their roles been reversed.

It was bravery, he thought, glancing back in his mirror to see the body easily lifted into the van. Easily, for the disease had laid waste to Robert and reduced him to nothing. Not the charge into the hail of bullets — but was that gaudy bravery much better? Sean and Robert and their colleagues had shown that sort of bravery all their lives, and what had it gotten them? A pat on the head and a pension to live on. And the world was no better for their work. Probably was worse.

He thought of quiet bravery like Jennifer Thomson's. The woman he'd seen in British Columbia wasn't the frightened victim any more. She had beaten her demons and proved stronger. Strong enough to offer Richard a chance. Brave enough to tell Sean — not ask him — to leave her be, and able to let her last look at him not be one of fear.

As much as he did not want to think about Anna, he thought she might have been the bravest of them all. When faced with losing what she most cared about, she hadn't weighed chances of success or calculated the price of loss. She had fought for it. Died for it.

What was the course of courage for him now? To do what Pete had suggested, to do what he now felt sure Robert had been trying to tell him last night. To make amends. Putting a bullet in his brain only looked like bravery. It was the coward's way, and he'd never been a coward until now.

Just the thought of trying to put things right was daunting. He was exhausted in every way, and felt old for the first time in his life. He had no idea where to start or what was the right course to take. He was on his own, for the first time. Robert was gone, and could not give counsel. It would not be easy, but if he had wanted an easy life he would have stayed in Indiana and joined his father's insurance business.

He sat for some time after the ambulance and coroner's van had driven away, giving himself over to grief. He made no sound and shed no tears but mourned silently. After a time he mastered himself; not even grief could overcome his instincts, now that he had a purpose again. He needed to go to ground, and then decide his next step.

With the turn of the van's ignition key he started on the path, and never in all his years had he been on a more unfamiliar road.

Part Two

Chapter Eleven

Juliette's house was on a posh, tidy little street in Georgetown. The yard had the immaculate look of a place tended by not one person but an entire team — in fact the team was there, pulling weeds and edging the lawn to precision standards. The sound of the edger did not quite drown out the music blaring from the house. It was only nine but Halsey guessed few neighbors were brave enough to complain to Juliette about her music.

He straightened his tie and flicked some dust off his suit. The suit was one of his best, appropriate for an important occasion like this. He rang the doorbell and Juliette opened the door. She wore jeans and a velvet sweater, and her feet were bare. "Good Lord, Francis. Did you just come from your mother's funeral? Loosen that tie before you strangle yourself."

Halsey stalked in, following Juliette into her living room. She said something but he could barely hear her over the music. She took her time, shimmying across the floor to the stereo's beat, then turned off the music and sat down on the sofa. "Want some coffee?"

"Sure."

"It's in the kitchen," she said, waving in that direction.

He went and got a cup — it was midnight black. He wanted to ask if she had any decaf but knew she'd just make fun of him.

"OK," she said when he came back, "Give me the full details on the situation with our friend Sean."

He did, from the time just after the Los Angeles bombing to the news that Kincaid had been in Maine. Halsey thought he'd done a respectable job of things, considering he'd had no support from top brass. She said nothing throughout his story, just looked at him with a half-assessing, half-bored look. Finally he asked, "Well? What do you think?"

She smiled. "I think I should withdraw my offer. You were smart to tell me that sneaky business with stealing Robert Dvorak's gun. That's the only clever thing you've done in this whole affair."

"I suppose you'd have handled it differently?"

"Damn straight. First, I'd have thanked God on bended knee for Kincaid's offer to help with Los Angeles. That's the sort of job the man was made for. Don't you remember, they used to call him The Chameleon? So he went off on his own and did it. What's the harm in that? I wager the people behind it are all pushing up daisies now. But no, you had to send someone after him, and you had to send a married guy whose wife didn't know the full situation and got all screechy when hubby didn't come home. And then, in what I imagine was an act of desperation, you went to see Kincaid's old ladyfriend."

"She didn't know anything."

"She might have had him hiding under her desk but you wouldn't have found that out. You interrogated her in her office. That's her turf, that's where she's safe. You should have kidnapped her, smacked her around some, taken her to some basement in the middle of nowhere and left her without food or water for a day or two. Maybe pull out a couple fingernails while you were at it. That would have softened her up. But at her office, all she had to do if it didn't go well was buzz security and have you tossed out on your ass. I imagine she probably laughed her head off when you left."

Halsey could imagine it well.

"And then Kincaid made Dvorak that little cocktail out of the *Final Exit* cookbook. Enough morphine to kill an elephant, I heard. Good for Dvorak, I say. That's a fine way to check out."

Halsey blinked, confused. "I'm surprised you feel that way. The other day you said…"

Juliette laughed. "I admired your ingenuity. I had nothing against Dvorak. I liked him. Before he got sick he was rather attractive, in a librarian sort of way. He wrote me a sonnet once."

"A what?"

"A sonnet. A sixteen-line poem. Shakespeare wrote sonnets, perhaps you've heard of him? Anyway, Robert wrote me a sonnet once. He didn't sign it but I knew he wrote it."

Halsey got the subject back on track. "Kincaid hasn't been seen since Dvorak died. Dvorak left Kincaid his house in his will but I don't think he's been back there since."

Juliette rolled her lovely eyes. "Of course he hasn't, you ignoramus. Dvorak probably told Kincaid you were hot to find him, just in case Kincaid couldn't figure that out for himself. Probably even told Kincaid you questioned his ladyfriend and I bet that didn't go over well. It doesn't matter where Kincaid is, because even if we had him right here, you couldn't do anything about it."

"Why not?"

A quick blur of movement and Juliette had a gun pointed at him. Halsey's breath caught as he remembered what she was, and that she'd never liked him.

She laughed. "See how easy it is to die? I could have put a bullet in your head before you knew what was happening. Of course, I'm a bit faster than most because I specialize. Here, catch."

Juliette tossed the gun to him. He grabbed, fumbled, almost dropped it. She pointed to a door down the hallway, a paper target tacked to it. "Shoot. Now."

He aimed, trying to be steady but his hand was shaking. He pulled the trigger and nothing happened. Halsey looked at the gun quizzically, then at Juliette.

She leaned forward and grinned at him. He flushed with embarrassment and the realization that she wasn't wearing a bra. "The safety's on," she said.

He looked at the gun again.

"There, on the side."

He finally found it, moved the little switch. He aimed again at the target; nothing but a click and a jerk as the slide moved forward. "I think…"

"Yes?" The voice of a very patient teacher with a very stupid pupil.

"I think it's not loaded."

She applauded. "And here begins lesson one, Your Friend the Pistol. You'll spend today learning just how your friend works."

He spent that day assembling, taking down, and reassembling several of her pistols, over and over again. She waved off his suggestion of target shooting. "You think I'd trust you with live rounds? Besides, I don't have the broad side of a barn handy." He gritted his teeth and seethed with every snotty remark she made. He worked until his hands were greasy and aching, until he sported several blood blisters from getting his fingers pinched in the slide. She didn't offer him lunch. She sat watching him with that mocking smile. For a while she busied herself with painting her toenails, adding acetone to the oil and metal stink of the guns. By the time she said he was done for the day he had a raging headache and his hands were cramped and aching. Thank God his car was an automatic or he didn't know if he would have been able to drive home.

"Let me see your hands," she said, taking them in hers. He wanted to pull them back, afraid she might squeeze them. Instead, she did something worse. She leaned down and gave them a kiss; her hair tickled his wrists, her breath was warm on his palms. She was so close it made him dizzy. The scent of her hair, the heat radiating off her skin. That perfect body was within his reach; he burned to touch her but knew she would kill him if he did. He pulled his hands out of her grasp, stepped away from her.

She smiled, winked, then opened the door and pushed him outside. "See you tomorrow," she said. As the door closed Halsey could hear her laughter, and despite the pain his hands clenched into fists of impotent fury.

Chapter Twelve

The second letter Monique received that was postmarked Maine came on a Saturday morning. Indian summer had just said farewell to the East; it was the first day that felt autumnal. Monique and Michael were going to do some early Christmas shopping that day, for with their extended families, his coworkers and her clients, their list was a long one. Michael refused to go into malls or department stores after Thanksgiving, Monique refused to do all her shopping by catalog; an early shopping day, combined with lunch out and possibly a movie, was a fine solution for them both.

She heard the mail slide through the slot and land on the living room floor with a papery whisper and thump, but didn't get up to investigate. The mail was Michael's job; he was not as bad about letting it pile up. Besides, she was in the middle of yoga, trying to arch her back and lift her body entirely off the floor and stand crablike on her hands and feet. So far it wasn't going well.

Michael walked in and observed. "I saw that in *The Exorcist*."

She laughed, her strained stomach muscles cramped and she collapsed to the rug. "Bastard," she wheezed. "My Zen mood is completely gone now."

"No, not the Zen mood! Shower's all yours."

Wincing — her stomach muscles still hurt — she got up and headed for the shower. "Mail's here. Can you get it?" she asked Michael.

"Sure thing."

She showered, then dressed in a denim skirt and the jade-green sweater Michael had given her last Christmas — it was just festive enough for early holiday shopping. She went into her office to get the list of clients worthy of cards and presents that year, and saw the letter on her desk.

Monique's heart gave an unsteady thump. A little jolt of adrenaline went through her, making her fingertips tingle. She didn't have to pick the letter up to know whom it was from; she knew the handwriting well enough. Spiky and slanted, it gave the impression of having been written in a hurry but was always perfectly legible. No return address. A Maine postmark. Monique knew she should leave it here, let it wait until she got home. She would have done that, if it hadn't been for the other letter telling her that Sean was in trouble. If it hadn't been for that cold-eyed guy in the suit who came to talk to her. If she hadn't gotten that strange hang-up call, the one she felt sure was from Sean, for who else would call her from Montana at nearly midnight? She had to know.

She picked up the letter and the brass opener, and deftly slit the envelope. She sat down at her desk and read the letter — it was written on a single sheet of paper, yellow and lined.

Monique,

I'm taking a chance on this, but there's no other way for me to reach you. I don't know how much you know, so I'll tell you this much. I went off the rails a bit. The people I used to work for weren't happy about it. I've heard that someone came to talk to you. I hope nothing bad came of that. I never wanted that part of my life to touch yours. You're too good a person for that.

I've made a terrible mess of things and I need to put things right. I don't have the right to ask anything of you, but could you let me know if you're all right? You don't need to tell me if anyone came to talk to you or what you said. That doesn't matter. I just need to hear that you're OK. If you're not, please tell me that so I can try to make amends. You can send a letter in care of General Delivery, Green Bay, Wisconsin. I won't answer. You're safer that way.

It's best if you don't hear from me again. But I'll always care about you, and wish you the happiness you deserve.

He signed it with the old nickname she'd given him. *Flint.*

She managed to push the letter out of her mind for most of the day. It wasn't until she and Michael were sitting down to their late lunch, as she looked at the menu without really seeing it, that she thought about the letter. It wasn't anything the letter actually said that troubled her. Sean had gone off the rails; she'd suspected that would happen ever since they forced him into retirement. His bosses weren't happy; she had first-hand knowledge of that. The secrecy was no surprise either. What troubled her was the letter's tone of desperation and its undercurrent of need. That wasn't the Sean she knew.

"...and the liver-and-onions tartare for my lady here."

Michael's voice snapped her back to attention. She looked to see him smiling at her. The server was nowhere near, thankfully, and hadn't heard his awful joke of an order. "Just wanted to make sure I hadn't lost you," Michael said.

"I'm back. Sorry, I was woolgathering."

"Is that all?"

"What do you mean?"

His smile went away. "You looked like something was bothering you. Are you feeling OK?"

"I'm fine. Feeling fine, I mean." She had never liked lying and she couldn't now, certainly not to Michael. And yet she didn't know how much of the truth to tell him. It wasn't the past she wanted to hide. There was nothing to hide. *My last boyfriend was a spy,* she'd told him when they were courting. *Really? Cool! Like James Bond?* he'd asked. *Well, yes, only without the tux, or the Aston Martin, or the Walther PPK, or the cool gadgets from Q, or the fancy champagne, or the not-so-latent misogyny.* They'd both had a laugh over it. Michael wouldn't care that she'd gotten a letter from Sean. Hell, she could go have lunch with Sean and it wouldn't bother him. Michael was divorced himself, but the split had been an amicable one — Tania simply hadn't been able to deal with his pilot's schedule — and he and Tania had dinner once or twice a year when business took him to Boston.

It wasn't the past but the present she wanted to hide. Sean wanted to keep that part of his life separate from her. But now the wall had been breached and she had no idea what lay on the other side. Possibly nothing to worry about — she hadn't heard a thing or seen anything suspicious since that lame interrogation. But the tone of Sean's letter put her on edge. As did the fact that others knew of her connection to Sean — whoever had sent that anonymous note, for one. And the guy who had done the interrogation; he'd bungled his questioning of her but she still felt uneasy remembering his cold eyes and the way he kept checking out her legs. She appreciated male attention as much as the next woman, but there had been something covetous and predatory about that man's look.

Years ago her aunt Marguerite had told her about woman's intuition. Monique, just entering law school at that time and convinced as only a college student can be that she was right about everything, had scoffed. But now she thought aunt Marguerite had been right about that, at least. Monique felt sure for no reason she could pinpoint that this business with Sean and the interrogator wasn't over. It would touch her life again.

She just had to make sure it didn't touch Michael's life.

"I had some news from an old friend," she said. "It's been a long time since I heard from him and he's going through a bad patch now."

"Is there anything you can do to help?"

She shrugged. "Not much, unfortunately. Write him back and keep him in my thoughts, that's about it."

"Hold him in the light. That's what my Grandma used to say when someone was in trouble. 'I'll hold you in the light.'"

"It can't hurt, and it may help," she said.

"Exactly."

"Then that's what I'll do." That and write back to Sean, let him know she was fine. And hope that would mean an end to it.

Chapter Thirteen

"Did you find everything OK?" Deirdre asked, smiling at the woman as she swiped the purchases with her scanner.

"Yes, it was fine," replied the woman.

"Glad to hear it." As she scanned the items — toothpaste, vitamins, a box of Goldfish crackers, a sexy vampire novel — Deirdre looked over the woman. She seemed in a good mood. She wasn't accompanied by a sullen boyfriend or squalling children. She was polite enough to actually answer Deirdre instead of pretending her purchases were rung up by magic. Deirdre glanced around; her manager was nowhere in sight. He'd called her on the carpet twice in the last couple weeks, she couldn't risk much more trouble.

As she handed over the woman's receipt she asked, "Ma'am, could I ask you something?"

"OK," the woman said.

Deirdre held up the photo from Richard and Anna's birthday party, the photo of Anna and the guy named Sam. "I'm trying to find the man in this picture. Does he look at all familiar to you?"

The woman looked at the photo — really looked at it. Most of the people she asked ignored her request, those who did look usually just gave it a cursory glance. But this woman looked, and for a moment Deirdre's heart raced.

The woman shook her head. "I'm sorry, never seen him before."

"That's OK." Deirdre acted as if the matter was of no importance. "Thank you for shopping at Wal-Mart today," she said with a smile.

When her shift ended she didn't linger. Her manager was still skulking around and she didn't want to see him. Didn't want to hear him say that her job was to ring up purchases, not wave around pictures at customers, and what was the deal with that, anyway? She didn't care so much what her manager said; rather, she feared what she might say back. That surge of anger she'd felt when talking to Sheriff Sorensen had been no fluke. It was as if some alien thing had hatched and now lurked inside her. She never knew when it might rear its head again. It was growing with every day that she heard no news, every person who refused to look at her picture, every thing — and there were so many — that triggered memories of Anna.

She feared the anger because she had no idea what to do with it; she was not in control. When she tried to cry for her cousin and found herself wanting to break things instead, she worried that the alien rage was an evil twin that had killed its good sibling grief, the way a fetus can devour its twin in the womb.

Deirdre walked quickly out to her truck, hopped inside. She paused to lean her head back, let her facial muscles relax. She wasn't used to so much forced friendliness. The last few evenings, her face ached at the end of the day. It reminded her of the summer she'd worked at The Dells, having to smile at all those customers. She ran her hands through her hair and sighed, then started the truck. Tomorrow was her day off, which meant she could work on finding the man in the photograph, in a way a little less random than asking customers at the store.

She didn't go home straightaway. Instead she drove out to a roadhouse just outside Du Lac. Deirdre could never remember the place's name — its neon sign never worked — so she christened it The Stagger Inn. Going there had become a ritual on nights when her grief and loneliness and rage threatened to overwhelm her. She downed a meal of greasy bar food and danced. She never had a dance partner; she didn't need one. She didn't even need alcohol. The Stagger Inn had loud music that never stopped, and once she'd eaten, neither did she. She danced, losing herself in noise and motion, stopping only during the rare slow dances, when she would guzzle a glass of water and use the bathroom before returning to the dance floor. She danced, and never once realized that the reason no men ever tried to hit on her was not because they were gentlemen, but because when she danced her masks fell away and her sorrow and rage were there for all to see and frightening to anyone not blind drunk.

She had a list, culled from the phone book, of apartment complexes in the Lakeside and Du Lac area. List in hand, she drove to the apartments, asked to speak to the manager, and held up her photo. It wasn't much of a strategy — who knew if the guy even lived in an apartment? Maybe he lived in a trailer park (she'd get to those eventually, but not right now, she was sure they were full of serial killers). Maybe he lived in a house outside the county. But it was all she had to go on.

Saturday was the day for apartment complexes in Lakeside. Deirdre drove in her faithful truck, her legs and hips aching. Last night's playlist at The Stagger Inn had been heavy on old disco tunes. She drove from complex to complex with her photo. One manager wasn't in. Another was too busy to talk. Three said they'd never seen the man.

As she walked into the manager's office of the sixth place, she was about to speak when a man walked in, holding an envelope. "Here's the rent, Glen. Sorry it's late but yesterday was really hairy."

She recognized the voice first, probably because she'd never seen him out of his uniform before. He knew who she was right away, though.

"Ms. Monahan," Deputy Nick Eliot said, "how are you doing?"

Deirdre realized she had no idea if what she was doing was even legal. It wasn't much different from handing out flyers about a lost pet, was it? She decided to damn the torpedoes, he could arrest her if he felt like it.

"I'm OK," she said. "I need to ask Glen something."

Nick stepped out of the office. Deirdre went through her routine, showed the picture, and got another negative answer. She thanked the manager and walked out. Nick was there, leaning against a lamp post with his hands in his pockets, looking at her in a way she couldn't quite fathom.

"I was getting ready to head out to lunch," he said. "Would you like to come with me?" When she hesitated, he said, "It's not police business or anything. I just want to have lunch."

Grief said she should go on to other apartments. Rage said that the local law enforcement had done jack shit so far and why should Deputy Eliot waste her time. But loneliness shouted them down. "OK."

They sat in the diner's booth, saying nothing at first, neither sure how to break the awkward silence. Finally Nick spoke. "Can I see the picture? I'll give it back."

She gave him the photo. "Do you know who the guy is?"

He shook his head. "Never seen him. Why are you looking for him?"

Deirdre wasn't sure why she had latched onto this picture and this man. Probably it was because he and Anna both looked happy in each other's company, and yet she couldn't recall seeing this man at Anna's funeral. That had been part of it, but the clincher had been when she'd examined the other photo, the one of Richard with the group of men. This Sam fellow had been there too, standing close to Richard; he was off to the side so you missed him at first but he was there, clearly part of the conversation with Richard. From the serious look on Richard's face, she doubted they were talking about the Packers' chance of making it to the Super Bowl. This man had known Anna and Richard, maybe he could shed some light on why one was dead and the other missing.

She told Nick this. He nodded. "It can't hurt," he said. "But you should tell all this to Leo Sorensen. It's his case."

The suspicions she'd been repressing for weeks finally emerged. "Do you really think he'd do anything about it?"

Nick looked dismayed. "Deirdre, I know you're upset by what's happening…"

"Nothing is happening! It's been weeks and I'm supposed to believe Leo when he tells me there's no leads. Here," she said, and reached into her pocket for the picture of Richard with the group of men. "Has Leo talked to any of these guys?"

As she put the picture down she realized she had seen one of the men before. It was the man who'd been with Leo when he caught her climbing the fence at the tree farm. She pointed at the man. "I saw that guy with Leo a couple weeks ago. Any idea who … Nick? Are you OK?"

Nick was pale, his glass of iced tea was raised halfway to his lips. He leaned forward and stared hard at the picture, then sat back in his seat. His eyes met hers. "I don't think you should go asking about that guy, or any of these guys any more."

Deirdre laughed without mirth. "Screw that sideways, Deputy Eliot." She reached out to pick up her photos and leave, but he caught hold of her hand. She shook him off.

"I mean it, Deirdre. I think something bad is going on and you're going to get in over your head."

"Wow, first nothing is happening and now it's something too big and bad for little me," Deirdre snapped. "Such progress has been made and we haven't even had our food yet."

"Will you listen to me?" His voice was low and serious. Sparks flared in his eyes. "I could get in a lot of trouble for telling you this stuff. Losing my badge forever kind of trouble, so listen.

"I know who some of those guys in that picture are. This one here is Doug MacReady. That guy with the mullet is Steve Wickersham and I'm pretty sure the one next to him whose face you can't see is his brother Eddie. They were always joined at the hip."

"Can you question them?"

Nick shook his head. "They're dead. MacReady's body was in the trunk of his car at Green Bay airport. A hunter found Steve and Eddie Wickersham yesterday at an old cabin in the woods. We don't have an autopsy yet but they were pretty far gone. I wouldn't be surprised if they were killed the same time as..." Nick trailed off.

Their food arrived, but Deirdre wasn't hungry. Before she could ask what all this meant, Nick continued. "Something else. This guy here," he tapped the photo, "is Leo's brother Walt."

Deirdre felt her insides slither around as her anger and sorrow fed on all this new knowledge. "Did you question him?"

"He's on the record as knowing that group of people socially and that's it."

"It was more than that." Deirdre told him about going to Anna's house, realizing too late that she'd just confessed to breaking and entering. "Walt saw me, and he stared because I look like Anna."

"That doesn't necessarily mean anything bad, all we know for sure is that he knew what she looked like." Nick frowned. "If Leo was there on police business, Walt sure as hell shouldn't have been along." He picked up his burger, made as if to take a bite, then put it down. "I think you should leave all this alone for a while."

"I can't."

"Haven't you heard a word I've said?" His voice was a low, harsh mutter so it would not be overheard. "We've got four people dead in the last month. Your cousin's husband is missing and who knows who else may be. There's something else. We found a body in Deer's Head Lake a few weeks ago. Some FBI types from Washington took it away as soon as his dental records matched up with theirs. I don't know if it was coincidence or what. All I know is that some weird shit has been happening lately and I don't want you to get caught up in it. So leave it alone. Please."

Deirdre looked at Nick. He was kind. He cared. He could be tossing his career away to tell her these things. "I can't," she said. Before he could reply she held up a hand. "I know you want to help. But you have to understand. I loved Anna. She loved me. Sometimes I think she's the only person who loved me. Oh, I guess my folks did but not as much as I wanted. That happens when you're an 'oops'. My ex-husband was a cheating flake. There's no one else.

"It's not just that, though. Back in high school did you ever read *Hamlet*?"

He shook his head. "No, I got *Twelfth Night*."

She said, "I asked the teacher when we were reading *Hamlet*, why it was such a big deal for Hamlet to get revenge for his dad's murder. The teacher said that back in Shakespeare's day, some people believed that the soul of a person who'd been murdered couldn't rest until whoever committed the murder had been brought to justice." Deirdre shivered. "I've never forgotten that. It would hit me at weird times, you know, just when you read about somebody being killed and I'd think that if they never found who did it, the person who died could never be at peace."

After a moment Nick said, "That's not how it is. It's too unfair."

"How do you know? You *don't* know. *I* don't know. But every time I think I should let it go, all I can think of is Anna and…and…" Deirdre trailed off. She stared down at her food, then looked back up at Nick. "I know you want to help. But I can't wait for Leo to tell me things. I think he knows more than he's telling. I can't do anything about that. So I'm doing what I can."

She took the last photo, the one of Anna and Richard, out of her pocket and handed it to Nick. He smiled as he looked at it. "They look happy," he said.

"They were."

Nick gave her back all the photos, put his face in his hands. "I'm starting to hate this job." Looking up at her he asked, "Can you do two things for me? One, no more breaking and entering. And when we're done here can you come back to my place for a second?"

Nick's apartment was small, and tidier than she would have expected. He left her in the front room while he rummaged in another room. After a moment he came back with small yellow canister. "Here," he said. "It's pepper spray. I want you to carry it with you all the time."

She looked at the canister. It didn't look all that impressive, but she wasn't about to test it and find out for certain.

"I can't stop you from doing what you need to do. But please, please be careful. I'm out of the loop in the investigation. Leo's always been on the ball as far as I know so I don't think he's stonewalling. But there's something going on and I don't want anyone to be hurt." Nick paused, then blurted out, "Especially you."

Deirdre didn't know what to say other than to thank him. She left him and went back to her truck. For a while she sat there looking at the pepper spray, thinking about what Nick had told her. She should leave it alone. People had been murdered. It wasn't safe.

But she could not let it go. "I'm sorry, Nick," she said, and put her truck in gear.

Two days later she found some answers and more questions.

It was the second apartment complex of the day, a place called the Lakeview Terrace in Du Lac. The day was cold and blustery, the complex lot was full and she had to park two blocks over and down, so it was a relief once she stepped into the manager's office, which was nearly tropical in its heat. Deirdre had a hard time seeing the manager's desk, it was so covered in ferns and African violets. A fat gray tabby, who had been sleeping on a chair, looked up at her, regarded her with haughty yellow eyes, then dismissed her and went back to sleep.

"Hello?" called Deirdre.

"Hi!" said a cheerful voice from behind the plants. A woman, fortyish and plump, stood up. "I'm Tess. Looking for a place? I'll have a vacancy in a week or so."

"Oh, no thank you. I'm looking for a person, actually. I was wondering if you've seen this man."

Tess put on her glasses, looked at the photo and smiled. "That's Sam Lewis. I haven't seen him around lately, though. I wish he'd come by, I have a pie plate I need to give back to him. Why are you looking for him? If I see him I can tell him you stopped by."

Deirdre started by saying, "Oh, it's a long story," but was saved from further invention when a frantic-looking old lady rushed in.

"Tess," the old lady said, "you've got to help. Something went wrong with the dishwasher and there's water everywhere!"

Tess ducked behind her desk, and then emerged with a small metal toolbox. She went out with the tenant, calling over her shoulder to Deirdre, "I'm sorry, but I have to help with this. I'll be back as soon as I can."

"No problem." She watched as Tess and the old lady vanished around a corner of the building. No one was looking; the cat was asleep. Deirdre ambled about the small office, moving toward the manager's desk. She leaned on the desk's top, and peered down to see what she could see.

She told herself she wasn't looking for anything in particular. Just idly killing time while she waited for the manager to come back. But when she saw the wooden board with the keys hanging on it, and the list of tenants and apartments, she saw the name she was looking for and grabbed the passkey for room 233.

Deirdre resisted the temptation to run. She sauntered out, looking over the flowerbeds and the laundry room. No one saw her walk up the stairs to the corner unit. She knocked on the door. No answer. She pressed her ear against the door. Silence.

She gripped the passkey in her sweaty hand. What she was about to do was a less forgivable breaking and entering than she'd done at Anna and Richard's house. At least there she'd had some justification for her actions. What did she have here? A photo and gut instinct.

She'd gone this far. She might as well go all the way.

Deirdre steeled herself for any number of possibilities — a dead man, an insane killer, a man going about his business who simply hadn't heard her knock. She clutched the pepper spray in her left hand. In the right she wielded the passkey. The key in the lock, a twist, and she was inside the apartment.

It was empty. She knew that the instant the door shut behind her. No lights were on. The air had a stale, shuttered-room feel. No bodies would be found here. Putting the pepper spray and the passkey in her pocket, she decided she might as well look around.

In the front room was a wing chair that looked second-hand. In front of it, a TV that did not look second-hand, with a DVD player and a stack of movies. Most of the DVDs had price stickers that indicated they'd been bought from the used bins of the local rental places. Her curiosity piqued, Deirdre pushed the "Eject" button on the player. *Vertigo* popped out.

She walked into the kitchen. The dishes — just a plate and a pot and a handful of flatware — were done and stacked in the drainer. The refrigerator held soft drinks and a bottle of club soda, almost nothing else. Opening a freezer door revealed a stack of frozen entrees. The Galloping Gourmet this guy was not. No wonder he was so keen on Anna's cooking, Deirdre thought with a smile.

Wandering past the bathroom and into the bedroom, something nagged at her. There was something wrong about this apartment. There wasn't a bit of mess in the place. It was orderly and clean. She stopped. That was it. This place was like a hotel room, lacking any personality whatsoever. There were no pictures on the walls, no magazines laying about, no pile of mail waiting to be sorted. Even the book on the bedside table, the latest Stephen King paperback, might have been left here by anyone. It was like a prop in a play. The only sign that a real person had lived here was that pile of DVDs — a person choosing props wouldn't have selected things like *Romeo is Bleeding* and *Joe Versus the Volcano*.

Deirdre stood in the tidy bedroom, feeling deflated. There was nothing here for her. No clues leaped out at her. She'd have to start opening drawers. Probably she'd just been chasing a shadow. The camera had caught Anna and this Sam guy at the right moment, and he hadn't been around because he was job-hunting or visiting his ailing auntie or shacked up with some floozy.

A knock at the door sent Deirdre's heart hammering. The manager must have seen the missing passkey and come to investigate. Deirdre stood, unsure of what to do, and her heart hammered louder when she heard not the manager's voice but a male one call out, "Sam, you in there? It's Walt."

Walt. The sheriff's brother. He knocked again. Deirdre held herself still, making no movement or sound. Maybe he would go away.

Walt said something she couldn't make out. Then she heard a voice she knew well. "Well, *try* the fucking door, then. Do I have to do everything?" said Leo.

She heard the doorknob rattle and remembered with dawning fear that she hadn't locked the door behind her. Deirdre looked around for a place to hide. Not under the bed — it was a Murphy bed and anyone could see underneath it without trying. She opened the closet and got inside, tucked herself as deep inside as she could, putting some shirts and a leather jacket between herself and the door.

Walt and Leo were in the apartment now. Deirdre tried to remember if she'd moved anything out of place. She carefully felt her pocket — the passkey and the pepper spray were still there. Moving slowly, hoping she didn't bump some object in the dark closet and make a telltale sound, she got the pepper spray out of her pocket.

The men were walking around the apartment , touring it much as she'd done. She could not make out their words but the tones of the voices were clear. Walt sounded defensive; probably he was afraid of Leo. Leo's voice was tense but restrained. She thought of a cobra swaying with its hood raised, ready to strike.

They were in the bedroom now. Deirdre pressed herself against the closet wall. Her fear was not of being arrested if she was caught. Something else made her afraid — Leo's voice. Heard on its own, without his reassuring uniform and badge, its cold anger was revealed. It was unforgiving. It would not listen to her justifications. For the first time since she'd started her clumsy sleuthing, she was afraid for her safety.

She held herself still, barely breathing. Her heart seemed loud enough to give her away. Over its gallop she heard Walt say, "There isn't anything here."

"This Sam guy was one of the smart ones. Didn't write anything down. Just like Richard. Those two were cut from the same cloth."

Just like Richard. What did that mean?

"You guys did your work a little too well for my taste," Leo went on. His voice got closer and Deirdre realized he was heading for the closet. She pressed back harder against the wall but there was nowhere to go. If he opened it, the clothes and jacket might shield her.

Or they might not.

The closet door started to open. Deirdre held her breath.

"I found it!" Walt said.

Leo turned, walked away from the closet. Over the rapid fire of her heart Deirdre heard Walt say, "I've seen this rifle, he had it when we went hunting. You said Steve and Eddie were shot."

Leo sighed exasperatedly. "It wasn't with a rifle. Eddie got two nine-millimeter rounds in the back. Steve had a .22 round in his head but that was just a *coup de grace*. His windpipe was crushed, he'd have died anyway. Check that closet, will you? There's something I want to see over here."

Deirdre gripped the pepper spray, put her finger on the trigger. How many shots were in the canister? She had no idea. One good shot, that's all she needed. One good shot into Walt's eyes, then somehow get past Leo — that prospect made her shudder — and get the hell out of here. *I should have listened to Nick. God, please get me out of this one and I'll do…something. Anything.*

The closet door opened. She had a glimpse of Walt in perfect profile. He looked bullied and unhappy. He glanced around the closet, pushed half-heartedly at a few shirts, and shut the door. "Nothing," he said to Leo.

Their voices went on for a while, accompanied by the sound of drawers opening and closing. Eventually she heard the door open and close. She remained where she was, afraid they were lying in wait for her.

A throbbing pain in her gut — she desperately needed to pee — finally drove her from the closet. She stepped out cautiously. They were gone. She ran into the bathroom, used and flushed the toilet, hoping that they didn't hear.

She slipped out of the apartment unnoticed and went downstairs. There was no sign of the apartment manager in the office but Deirdre's nerves were in no shape to attempt putting back the passkey. She settled for putting the key into the mailbox, then ran to her truck and got on the road back to Lakeside as fast as she could. Only when she was in the safety of her own apartment did she give in to the shakes. Beneath the reaction to nearly getting caught was a deeper dread that Anna and Richard had stumbled onto something that had cost Anna her life. It was not just the things Walt and Leo had said, nor Nick's news of multiple murders, that troubled her. This Sam fellow was the guy Anna wanted to set her up with. She'd thought highly enough of him for that. So why was his apartment more like a set on a TV show? Why had he disappeared? It was as if he was some kind of ghost. Deirdre shivered, feeling afraid. Haunted.

Chapter Fourteen

He came back to Du Lac after midnight. It was a clear night, and cold. There would be frost in the morning. He drove through the empty streets to the Lakeview Terrace apartments. Nothing about the town seemed to have changed in his absence, but then he hadn't been gone for long. Two months, according to the calendar. By his own reckoning, longer. Much longer.

Back in Maine, Sean had found a small motel and decided that was as good a place to hole up as any. He stocked up on food and some other essentials at a nearby grocery store, feeling unreal and lightheaded the whole time. Upon returning to the motel, he hadn't bothered putting the groceries away, had just collapsed on the bed and slept for nearly twenty-four hours.

Sleep hadn't refreshed him, though. He woke to a headache and a racking cough, and it was clear his lightheadedness was not just from hunger and weariness but fever. Sean smiled mirthlessly. He couldn't remember the last time he'd been sick. No matter. He was in no hurry. A couple days with rest, and some chicken soup heated in the room's microwave, ought to put things right.

But after a day and night of shivering and sweating and coughing he knew he was seriously ill. Pneumonia, or something like it. People got it every day. Sometimes they died from it. At first the idea seemed ludicrous — over the years he'd been shot, stabbed, nearly blown up, had almost died of exposure in the Afghan desert, been choked — he'd even survived his own attempts on his life. As night fell and he still burned, he realized this fever might succeed, just as cancer had destroyed Robert.

He could have dragged himself to the emergency room, but remembered Robert's admonition to lie low. He had no idea of what to expect from his former employers. They could have had agents scouring the state for him once they learned Robert's real cause of death and got a positive ID from the hospice worker. They could have simply cut their losses and written him off — they did that sometimes. But if they were after him they would surely catch him and any chance to make amends was blown forever.

Sean waited as long as he dared, not knowing which was worse: the buildup of tightness in his lungs or the pain that ripped through him when a coughing fit struck. He waited until just after midnight, then slipped out of the room and made his way to a nearby pharmacy, a mom-and-pop affair that would have what he needed but that wouldn't have an extensive security system. He found a side door and set about jimmying the lock.

It had been years since he'd done this sort of thing. He was out of practice, his hands shook, and the fever made him dizzy. It seemed he could hear the fever, a high note like a theremin. Sean shivered, wiped off his sweaty palms, got to work on the lock again.

"Hey Irish," Beatty said. "When you get in there, see if they've got some brandy or something. Don't know about you but I'm fucking freezing here. You know I hate the cold."

Sean stopped, was very still. He listened. He didn't hear anything. There was nothing to hear. Just the fever talking. Not Beatty, who was months dead. Sean recalled the first mission when he'd killed someone. It had been necessary, of course. It always was necessary. Sometimes even regrettable. Still, that first time had shaken him a bit. He'd been sitting at the safe house afterward, remembering how the man he'd shot had just dropped to the ground without Hollywood dramatics, the life going out of his eyes even as he'd fallen. Sean had heard something behind him, had looked round startled to see Robert standing there, wearing a smile that came not from contempt but from understanding. "Don't worry," Robert had said. "They don't come back."

He went back to work on the lock. Beatty spoke up again: "Or some schnapps, that would work. Remember Berlin?"

"Be quiet," Sean rasped. "You're not there."

Beatty laughed the way he had whenever he'd finished telling one of his wretched jokes. "Don't fool yourself, Irish. I'm *always* here."

They don't come back. He ignored the voice, and it didn't speak again. Which was fine, but he still couldn't get this damned door open. Time to quit finessing it. He went to the other side of the building, picked up a rock and smashed in one of the plate glass windows. The burglar alarm's surprised whoop doubled his headache; he stepped through the hole and made his way to the pharmacy counter. He grabbed several kinds of antibiotics, figuring one of them had to do the trick, and then scrambled out and started back to his motel.

No one saw him. He was back in his room before he heard the first police siren. Sean sat down and with shaking hands pried the cap off a bottle. He chased the pill down with water; his instincts were returning, he had enough sense of self-preservation to note the time so he would know when to take the next pill. Still, it was humiliating to be reduced to robbing a pharmacy for medicine.

"It's a sad state of affairs, isn't it?" Richard Blaine said, commiseration and scorn in his voice.

"Damn right," Sean replied. He started to say something more but the sight of Richard with the back of his head blown away was unpleasant and he had to turn away. When he looked back, Richard was gone.

A spasm of coughing left Sean too weak to sit up, or even make his way over to the bed. He lay down on the floor, and either passed out or fell asleep. He woke when a cold voice of reason not touched by fever spoke in his mind, told him he couldn't wait for the antibiotic to bring the fever down.

Sean hauled himself into the bathroom. Without bothering to turn on the light, pausing only to take off his coat and his shoes and his gun, he crawled into the shower and turned on the water. It was barely cool but he was so hot it felt like icewater; he gritted his teeth and wrapped his arms around himself. It worked. After a while he felt more lucid. He saw nothing that shouldn't have been there and heard only one thing strange. He heard Monique singing in the shower. Lovely as her speaking voice was, she'd always been a terrible singer. Still, hearing her massacre "Bye Bye Blackbird" soothed him and he nodded off.

The antibiotics worked. After a couple days his fever was gone, and he was deeply relieved not just because it meant he was getting better, but because the voices and visions were gone as well. Hearing Monique's voice was one thing. Seeing Jennifer Thomson sitting at the table, not speaking but looking at him as if he might bite her was worse, but tolerable. Seeing Anna dead on the floor of his room was bad enough to make him wish he'd just let the illness take its course.

Though he was still sick, he at least knew what was real and what was not. He let his body decide how much rest it needed, didn't push himself. Sean spent his days channel-surfing for movies, a welcome distraction. It kept him from thinking, because when he thought his mind inevitably turned to Anna, to Jennifer, to Robert; to his ghosts, his phantoms living and dead. He would have to think about them soon enough, but wanted to wait until he was well again.

He didn't plan. There was nothing to plan for; he had no idea what he would do to make amends. He didn't worry about getting back into fighting shape. Even if the agency had asked him to come back, he would have refused. It was over. He'd lost his taste for the challenge of the mission, for the intrigue and violence. All he wanted to do was to pay his debt.

His convalescence lasted a month, and on a cold day when the last of the leaves blew off the trees and the world seemed to have turned gray and brown, he gathered his belongings together and made ready to leave.

Before he left he wrote to Monique. He had known for some time now that he would do this. Robert's news that Halsey had gone to see Monique troubled him more than he would have imagined. Halsey knew budgets and figures, not people, and had probably never interrogated someone in his life. Surely Monique could hold her own, but it wouldn't pay to underestimate Halsey as he'd underestimated Richard or Anna or Jennifer.

He waited until the last minute to write to Monique, and asked her to send her reply to Wisconsin. He knew that if she replied to him in Maine, and if her reply suggested that anything was amiss — admit it, even if she said she was perfectly fine — he did not trust himself to keep away from her. Even if he went to just see her, not make contact, it could be dangerous for her. He could not let that happen, ever; he could not get her into trouble just because she had been his lover.

As Sean left the motel room he paused a moment to look in the mirror. It had been a long time since he'd looked in a mirror other than to shave. He was surprised to see that his outward appearance, such as it was, seemed the same as always. The bruises had finally faded from his throat, and he was thinner. The real change was not apparent to him or to a casual observer. Perhaps only Robert or Monique would have seen that his eyes had changed — they were no longer part of the mask, the disguise. They showed emotion now always, not just when he wanted them to. But Robert was dead and Monique he kept at a distance, and neither was there to warn him.

On his way out of town he stopped by Robert's house. The gates were locked, the windows dark. Empty, abandoned. His house legally, he supposed, but even if his employers were not looking for him, Sean felt no right to claim it. Not yet. Maybe after his debt was paid he could come back here.

Sean had no idea where Robert was buried, or if he'd been cremated. It didn't matter; if Robert's spirit was lingering anywhere it would be here. "Wish me luck," Sean said. He would need all the luck and good intentions he could get. "Be seeing you."

He began the long drive back to Wisconsin. For some time he'd thought that he should go to British Columbia first, to see how Jennifer Thomson fared, but once more the words of that young priest in Indiana came to him: *You just left her there.*

That's where his duty lay, back in Du Lac. He had to find out what had happened and what he could do to pay the debt.

He parked not in the Lakeview Terrace's lot but a block away. He didn't want Tess the landlady to know he was back. Most of the important possessions were already stashed in his van, for he'd never known when he would have to leave town. All he wanted from his apartment were some clothes. Tess could keep everything else — no doubt she'd like that TV.

He slipped into the apartment, stood looking over the front room. Everything seemed to be just as he'd left it that day when Richard had called and asked him to meet, when Steve Wickersham had been waiting by his van with intentions to kill him, when Anna —

He forced the thought away. And noticed that everything was not quite as he'd left it. The DVD player was open. He never did that.

Someone had been here.

He wasn't aware of drawing the gun; it was simply there, in his hand. The instincts were still there. He prowled the apartment, looking for an intruder, looking for any other sign. He found nothing. Still, he was sure someone had been here. Looking for him. Tess was the most obvious candidate — she had the passkey — but he dismissed it. Tess was entirely too polite for skulking; she'd have left a note. Cops or one of the last members of Richard's group, he supposed. They hadn't found anything. There was nothing to find.

The thought of someone being here without his knowledge was disturbing. Someone had made a connection. He holstered the gun and quickly gathered the things he wanted: His clothes, a few books, his favorite leather jacket. Tess could keep the rest. He dashed off a quick note apologizing for his departure and telling her she could have everything here.

He was in and out of the apartment in less than fifteen minutes, then he was back in his van, looking for a place to hole up. Tomorrow or the next day he would start finding out what had happened while he'd been away, and plan his next move.

Chapter Fifteen

Frank Halsey had a new morning routine these days.

He got up, ate a large breakfast. Sometimes Juliette provided lunch, sometimes she did not. On the days she did not, when hunger and low blood sugar got the best of him and he snapped at her, she just laughed and invited him to find another person to help him out. After that he kept silent and made sure to eat well in the morning.

His clothes were ready and waiting — jeans and a casual shirt, not at all what he usually liked to wear. He looked and felt uncomfortable outside the confines of a suit, always had, but the suit he'd worn that first day had been ruined by gun grease, and he'd learned to wear things he didn't care about.

As the steam rose in the shower he thought of Juliette. Dancing about in that velvet sweater. The way she smoked, exhaling smoke and then sucking it back into her half-open mouth, seeming to caress the smoke with her lips and tongue. How she'd leaned her body against his the other day when showing him how to stand while holding the gun…and how she'd slapped him when he tried to lean back into her. He thought of Juliette and jerked off with rough efficiency. It was not about pleasure. It was a release — of anger, of lust, of humiliation — and a very necessary one. It took hardly any time at all.

He was ready for another day.

Though it was ten in the morning when he arrived, Juliette wasn't dressed yet. She wore a white silk robe embroidered with dragons. Her hair was down as she answered the door, and she looked almost angelic. Until she smiled. "Good morning, Francis."

Halsey went inside, and only then noticed that Juliette's robe was one of those short ones that was barely decent. He followed her into the kitchen —

she'd gotten him hooked on coffee, now he couldn't function without the damned stuff — and saw some tall blond guy, all big shoulders and big chin, standing shirtless in Juliette's kitchen as if he had a right to be there. Blondie took a bite of English muffin and cheerfully waved hello at Halsey.

Juliette snuggled up to Blondie. She said to Halsey, "Introduction time. This is Darren."

"Derek," said the blond.

"Good friend of the family," Juliette said with a wink. Turning to the blond she said, "That was my last muffin. Are you going to be a good boy and share?"

"If I don't, will you spank me?" he said with a big stupid grin.

Halsey looked away, trying to ignore the giggles and kissing sounds from the kitchen. He wanted to walk away but knew Juliette would tease him mercilessly if he did. They were going to the range today to do some actual shooting and he didn't want her to toss him out with no lesson.

Silence from the kitchen made him glance back; most unfortunate timing as he saw Darren-or-Derek with his hands all over Juliette's ass. Halsey turned away, unconsciously filing the image into his catalog for the morning shower routine, and once again cursed Sean Kincaid. It was all Kincaid's fault that Halsey had to put up with this shit from Juliette. What he wouldn't give to screw over the two of them royally, then they'd see he was no one to trifle with.

Finally Juliette shooed the blond studmuffin along. As Derek-or-Darren walked out the door he said to Halsey, "Nice meeting you."

Halsey lost it a bit. "Move it along, monkeyboy."

Blondie sneered and walked out, slamming the door behind him.

Juliette gave Halsey an icy look. "Kindly do not insult my man-whore. Just for that I ought to send you home for a week."

"No." He swallowed his pride and said, "Please."

This seemed to satisfy her. "I need to get dressed. Make us a pot of coffee. And put more beans in this time. That last one you made was weak tea."

The gun she gave him was tiny. Insultingly so. He glared at her and put the .22 back down on the table. "I'm not going plinking at beer cans. How about a real gun?"

"That is a real gun. The Mossad uses them for assassinations. You put long rifle rounds in there, then get the target up close, back of the head. The round penetrates the skull but doesn't have enough force for an exit wound."

"So?"

Juliette sighed. "So the bullet ping-pongs around in your skull a while. Turns your brain to mush. Great effect and very little mess. Do the job in a noisy, crowded place and no one hears a thing. Not ideal for your situation, though."

Once she'd described the effect he was intrigued. "Why not?"

"Because Kincaid would have to be comatose or already dead before you could get close enough for that. But this is a good gun to start learning with. Am I correct in thinking you've never shot before?"

He didn't answer.

"Francis?"

He nodded.

She set the target at ten yards. He stood the way she'd taught him, held the gun the way she'd taught him, and pulled the trigger. An unimpressive little pop. He tried not to think about that, tried to think about bullets ping-ponging in a skull.

A sterile click and the magazine was empty. Juliette brought the target in. "Nice shootin', Tex!"

He'd fired ten rounds and only one had hit the target. It hadn't even hit the man-shaped silhouette, but the outlying white space. He was glad the range was deserted and there was no one but Juliette to witness this.

She laid one graceful hand on his shoulder and squeezed, her grip painful. "Don't worry, Francis. We all have to begin somewhere, don't we? Reload and we'll go again. I've got all day."

He reloaded and shot, reloaded and shot. On the fourth set Juliette asked, "So why do you have such a bug up your ass about Kincaid, anyway?"

Halsey was still trying to figure out the sighting and he hated how this tiny gun felt in his hands, like it was just a toy. "Can we talk about this later? I'm trying to focus."

"If you're out in the field people aren't going to quiet down so you can concentrate. This is good training for you. And besides, I'm bored." Juliette sat down in a chair, propped her feet up. In the tight jeans and suede boots her legs looked a mile long. "What did he do to piss you off so badly?"

"He left the agency without my permission."

"I meant besides the obvious. What did he say to you?"

He pulled the trigger hard three times in quick succession, remembering. "He called me a bean counter." *You're nothing but a fucking bean counter* had been the exact words.

"That's all? Huh." Juliette sounded disappointed.

"You don't think that's insulting?"

"The truth's not an insult. And someone had to say it, I'm just surprised it was Kincaid. I like the grapevine's version better — he said he hoped your children would be born without eyes."

Halsey nearly dropped the gun. "What?"

"Just reporting what the grapevine says. That and he told you to fuck off in five different languages."

The magazine was empty. Juliette brought the target back. Four rounds had gone through the silhouette. "Much better. We'll keep going until you get all ten in the black."

"I need a break."

"Not now."

"I said I need a break."

"No. Now shut up and go again."

"Fucking cunt," he muttered under his breath.

Juliette was out of her chair instantly. Before Halsey knew what was happening she had made him drop the gun, had him on his knees and it felt like she was pulling his arm out of its socket. The pain was huge; it seemed to explode in his shoulder, shot down his torso, left him breathless and queasy.

"Look at me, Francis."

He was gasping for breath, couldn't raise his head. Below the shoulder his arm had gone numb. Her free hand grasped him under the chin and raised his head up until he looked her in the face.

She didn't look angry. There was no emotion in her face at all. "Listen, because I won't tell you this again." Her voice was a machine's, low and uninflected, the syllables carefully measured. "When you learn from me, you do what I ask, when I ask it. You do not touch me, and you do not call me names. Understand?"

"Yes," Halsey whispered.

"Good." She let go, and he gasped with relief as the pain eased and some feeling came back into his arm. "Now get up and reload that gun."

He did. Reloaded and fired, reloaded and fired. He stopped seeing the silhouette after a while — he saw faces ten yards away. He saw Kincaid and Dvorak; he saw Peters, Yates, and Freeman from the agency. Mostly he saw Juliette's face.

Finally Juliette looked at the target and saw ten holes punched in the black. There were only two head shots, the rest scattered over the torso. "Still, it's a start," she said, and called it a day.

They returned to her house where he found a ticket on the windshield of his car. She hadn't told him it was street-sweeping day. Halsey snatched the ticket and crumpled it up, shoved it into his pocket.

Juliette watched him. Her smile was back. "Put some ice on that shoulder joint tonight and take some ibuprofen or you'll shoot even worse tomorrow," she said, then went inside and slammed the door behind her.

That night Halsey sat with an ice pack on his aching shoulder. The TV was on but he wasn't watching it. He was watching a montage of memories. His high school graduation when he was passed over for valedictorian and that kiss-ass bitch Stephanie Jackson gave the speech. Having to beg and plead for money for the agency from a bunch of elected hicks. His first meeting with agents, having to tell them they'd have to do the job with half the budget, watching those two sons-of-bitches Kincaid and Dvorak roll their eyes at each other. Kincaid walking out on him, calling him a bean counter. Yates, Peters, and Freeman looking at him like he was some kind of bug. That lawyer bitch of Kincaid's thinking she was safe behind her law degrees — Halsey just *knew* she was still fucking Kincaid on the side, and what did she see in that beady-eyed bastard anyway?

Why could no one show him a little respect?

That was all he wanted. Respect. Why was it so hard to come by? His mother had respected his father, though he'd had to show her who was boss a few times. Well, more than a few. (He'd forgotten how afraid he'd been that his father would turn his fists on him; now he only remembered the look of fear that passed as respect in his mother's eyes, and the way she scrambled to do his father's will.) He wanted to be respected, to be obeyed, to have people not taunt him or walk away from him.

144

He wanted it. *I will have it.* No matter how much humiliation he had to take from Juliette, no matter how hard Kincaid was to find, he'd make them respect him. He'd bring that back to the agency when he returned, like a trophy.

Chapter Sixteen

Sheriff Leo Sorensen sat at his desk, shrouded in cigarette smoke, spinning lies.

He did not consider himself to be an especially duplicitous man, no more than most. Most of his lies in his role as sheriff had been more omissions than anything else, or putting a pleasant mask on ugly truth. The lies had grown as his role in law enforcement had; it was all part of the game. Let the mayor's son slide on those possession and assault charges, and there would be favors he could call in when he needed them…not to mention valuable campaign contributions from the mayor and all his relatives when Leo decided to make his bid for the state government. Things like that. Leo didn't see it as justice thwarted — who would benefit if the mayor's son spent some time behind bars? No one. A little duplicity on his part, and all of them would benefit.

What he pondered now in his smoke-reeking office was duplicity of a higher order than anything he'd attempted before. He needed to not simply come up with an explanation for the four recent killings, but to do so without drawing attention to the extracurricular activities of Richard Blaine and his band of merry men. Worse still, he didn't have the full story to work with. Just because Blaine and that Sam Lewis fellow were missing didn't mean they were responsible. Hell, they could be corpses just waiting to be found, waiting to screw up whatever story Leo concocted.

"What do you think happened?" Walt had asked him. Leo hadn't replied — he was too angry with Walt, who was completely useless in helping sort all this out. Besides, what Leo thought had happened was irrelevant. What mattered was finding a way to explain this — something that would make all the friends and relatives let things go. What mattered was getting things back to normal and next year, by God, Leo would be on his way to the capital and out of this backwater.

He needed to figure out something soon. The press was sniffing around. Steve and Eddie's mother was wailing to all and sundry about her poor dead boys. Deirdre Monahan had stopped calling but that only increased Leo's apprehension about her. There was something about Monahan he didn't like; she was volatile and smarter than she seemed. Most of all, she'd loved her cousin. No one but Steve and Eddie's mother gave a tin shit about the brothers, and Doug MacReady was the stereotypical loner divorced guy, estranged from his ex and from most of his family. They'd be forgotten in no time.

It would be easiest to say this was all the work of a random lunatic, some drifting serial killer who had made Du Lac his target for reasons unknown. One problem was that the time line was too strange — MacReady had been killed nearly a month before the others — and the cause of death was different for each person. The other problem was that there were too many weirdos out there who would get interested in the possibility of a serial killer. The tabloids and the regular news would be all over it, and Leo knew his lies wouldn't stand that level of scrutiny.

His other choice was somewhat distasteful but would work out best for all — a crime of passion. A love triangle of some sort, with revenge killings. There would be some scandal and some hen-clucking as people wondered how such a nice couple like the Blaines had turned out to be so sordid. A month at most and it would be forgotten by nearly everyone. Lust and jealousy were too commonplace to hold peoples' interest for long.

The more Leo thought about it, the more he liked it. That it would sully the reputation of a good woman bothered him not at all. His own reputation, should the truth come out, stood to suffer a great deal and he would not allow that.

Leo lit another cigarette. He had work to do. He would get Walt and maybe one other member of the group to go along with the crime of passion story. He'd start dropping hints into the answers he gave reporters. He would soon see an end to this, and then just had to hope that neither Richard nor that Sam guy turned up. He doubted they would. They were either dead or fled, and wouldn't be coming back to Du Lac any time soon.

The phone rang. "Rose Flynn for you from the coroner's office," said Sharon. "She says it's urgent."

Flaming shit on wheels, what now? he thought. "Thank you, Sharon, put her through," he said.

Leo could have gone to break the news to Deirdre on his own, but he brought Nick Eliot along. Nick was typing out a report, his fingers flying over the keys with a speed Leo found suspicious — fast typing was for women and admins, real cops did hunt-and-peck. "Can that wait a bit." Leo said it, did not ask it. "I need you to come with me." He brought Nick along because he wasn't sure how Deirdre would take the news; the two of them might be needed if she went ballistic. Besides, Nick had a soft spot for the girl, probably would give her a bunch of consoling hugs given the opportunity. Nick was a sucker for ladies in distress, lost kids, and kittens stuck in trees.

With Nick along, he could start sowing the seeds of his lies.

He didn't tell Nick what it was about until they were in the car and heading to the Wal-Mart in Lakeside. And he didn't tell him everything. "Rose Flynn called. A request for dental records came through on the wires, and they matched up with Richard Blaine's. A hiker found him in Canada. British Columbia, to be exact." *Buried in a shallow grave, still trussed up with duct tape.* "Cause of death was a gunshot to the head." *Back of the head, execution style.* "It's still sketchy. They think it might have been self-inflicted." *Let him believe that.*

Let them believe Richard killed the others, ran off, then got remorseful and turned the gun on himself. That'll bury this shit once and for all.

Nick said nothing for a moment. "Poor Deirdre," he said softly. "Do they have ballistics yet? Was it the same gun that killed Steve or Eddie Wickersham?"

"That'll be a while in coming. We'll just have to wait."

Neither spoke for the rest of the drive. That suited Leo fine. His mind was busy sorting things out, wondering how much misdirection he could get away with, if he could put any pressure on Rose to fudge with the rulings. Let Nick worry about Deirdre — it wasn't Leo's concern. If her cousin's husband hadn't gotten it into his head to blow up a federal building, none of this would be happening. Leo's only consolation was that someone had taken care of Richard Blaine for good and all. Now if he could just maintain a good cover story, none of it ever had to trouble anyone again.

Deirdre was working the register when they arrived. She was no fool; the moment she saw them she knew it was bad news. She paged for someone to take her place, then beckoned Leo and Nick to the back of the store, to a door that said *Employees only.*

The break room smelled of cheap coffee and burnt popcorn. Deirdre sat on the cracked vinyl couch and put her hands on her knees. "Tell me," she said, and after that said nothing while they told her. She squeezed her knees with her hands but made almost no movement. Strangely, she didn't look at Nick, who did a lot of the talking. She looked at Leo the whole time. Her face was a blank. Her eyes gave away nothing. Neither did his.

Finally she said, "Thank you for telling me." Leo and Nick got up to go, and she walked with them to the front of the store. As she headed for the register Nick went and spoke to her; Leo couldn't hear what Nick said or what Deirdre's reply was. Leo gazed out the window for a minute, thinking about his next move, and when he turned back he saw that Deirdre and Nick were both looking at him. Leo felt a nasty thump in his chest; there was an assessing quality in their eyes he didn't like. It was a look most suspects who visited the sheriff's station would have recognized. It was a look that wondered what Leo knew and how much of that he was telling.

Leo tipped his head toward the door, and Nick came along. Deirdre went back to her cash register. Just a glance, a fleeting moment. It might have been nothing, but Leo knew it wasn't. Not only did he have to be careful about Deirdre, he had to be careful about Nick too.

Deirdre thought she was handling it pretty well.

She didn't feel particularly upset after Nick and Sheriff Sorensen told her that Richard was dead. She didn't feel much of anything. For a couple days she went about her business, feeling muffled, as if she was wrapped in an invisible cocoon. She heard things, saw things, but none of it really affected her. She even went and danced at The Stagger Inn, but couldn't get into the music and went home early.

This cocoon, whatever it was, came in handy at work. It was December now and the shopping season was in full swing. Deirdre ran cart after cart of stuff over the scanner, no longer bothering to show around her photo of that Sam fellow or even to make any eye contact with the customers. What did it matter? Deirdre's only hope had been that somehow Richard would show up and help explain things. Now Richard was gone, too. Probably murdered by the same person. It made no sense, and Deirdre was tired of trying to make sense of it.

Today was biting cold, clouds creeping across the sky, and it would definitely snow in the next few days, Deirdre was sure of it. It was too cold to stand outside, so she took her break inside. She didn't go to the break room, for that was where her last hopes of getting life back to halfway normal had been dashed. So she went to the aisle where the artificial Christmas trees had been set up, and sat down on the floor. This was strictly against the rules, but Deirdre was, in the words of her ex-husband, half-past give-a-shit.

By some miracle, the aisle was not overrun with grumpy shoppers and squalling children. She was the only person here. She sat looking at the trees with their twinkling lights. Artificial trees had come a long way since the silver pipe-cleaner ones of her childhood. These almost looked real. There was no pine scent, but that was all right. They looked almost real, and that was enough. Christmas. How the hell was she going to be able to stand Christmas with Anna and Richard gone? She had no clue.

She sighed, shut her eyes. When she opened them, she wasn't alone in the aisle any more.

A little girl, no more than four years old, stood looking at the Christmas trees with an expression of wonder on her face. No matter, the Wal-Mart was filled with kids these days. No matter, except that this girl had red hair almost the same shade as Anna's. The girl's eyes were wide like Anna's, but their color was gray like Richard's. Could there be ghosts of people who had never been? Was this the ghost of Anna and Richard's daughter, visiting her? The girl looked at her and smiled, shyly waved hello.

Deirdre was frozen, not in fear but in wonder. This ghost was nothing to be afraid of. She wanted to embrace the child, ghost or not, take this one thing she could keep, this gift she had somehow been given. A glimpse of what might have been. She wanted to weep, and have the child pat her hair and tell her it was all right. She wanted to know that what she was seeing was real. She recalled the name Anna had always wanted to give her daughter, and said, "Tara? Is that you, Tara?"

"There you are, you little shit!"

A metallic rattle and bang as a shopping cart ran into the endcap. Before Deirdre or the girl could speak, a scrawny woman had snatched up the child in hands with cruelly tight fingers. As the girl wailed, the woman snarled,

"Haven't I told you to stay right by me? You pull this stunt again and I'll call Santa Claus and tell him you don't get anything this year." The woman stuffed the girl into the cart and before Deirdre could say anything, they were heading down the aisle to another part of the store.

She should do something. Go after them. Say something. Before she could, the manager came by and looked at Deirdre with his long-suffering expression. "Break's over, Deirdre."

She was back at her register when she saw them again. They were at the next register over, the woman grabbing things and putting them on the belt with one hand, holding a cell phone in the other. The girl sat in the cart. She was no longer crying, but she wasn't the smiling, enchanted child either. As Deirdre watched out of her peripheral vision, the girl reached down into the cart, picked up a bottle of shampoo, and handed it to her mother. Mom didn't say thank you, just grabbed the shampoo bottle out of the girl's hand and flung it onto the counter. The girl asked her mother something but Mom went right on yakking into her cell phone. "And then, then he says to me, he says Oh yeah? And I'm, like, Yeah." Then they had paid and gone and were out of Deirdre's life.

Except they weren't. Deirdre could see them through the windows, out in the parking lot. Could see the woman, still barking into her cell phone, haul the girl roughly out of the cart and almost throw her into her car seat.

Something clicked in Deirdre's mind. She didn't feel angry. She was calm, cool, in a way she couldn't recall ever feeling before. "Excuse me, I have some business to attend to," she said to her bewildered customer and started walking out to the parking lot. She was vaguely aware of customers and coworkers staring at her, of Yolanda's frantic whisper: "No, Deirdre, don't."

The woman was standing by the car, still talking on the phone. Deirdre plucked the phone from the woman's hand. The woman stared at her like she'd gone nuts. "What the hell are you doing?"

"I need your phone for a minute." Deirdre pushed the *End* button, then dialed a number she knew by heart, the Silas County Sheriff's Office. "Hi there. I think I have a case you guys can handle. I want to report a case of child abuse here at the Wal-Mart, 223 Granite Circle. Might want to send someone from Child Protection Services while you're at it —"

"You crazy bitch!" the woman yelled, trying to grab the phone back from Deirdre. It slipped from Deirdre's grasp and fell to the ground with a clatter. "You probably broke my phone!"

As the woman stooped to pick up her phone, Deirdre grabbed the woman's shirt and yanked her back upright. "If I ever see you yell at or manhandle that child again, I'll break more than your phone." She still felt calm, not at all angry. She just needed to make this woman understand that a child like that was a gift, something that had to be cherished. Anna would have given her soul to have a sweet girl like that, so would Richard. This woman couldn't appreciate that, and it wasn't fair. Not at all.

Nick was already on his way to the Wal-Mart when he got the dispatch. He was hoping to catch Deirdre on her lunch hour, maybe see if he could talk to her. Nick hadn't liked the way Deirdre reacted — or didn't react — to the news that her cousin's husband was dead. When the call went out on the radio about a disturbance at the Wal-Mart, Nick knew it was Deirdre, and wasn't at all surprised.

Once he got past the onlookers, he saw Deirdre hanging on to a woman by a handful of shirt. All Deirdre seemed to be doing was talking, so low he couldn't hear her; the woman, by contrast, was yelling and flailing. She seemed either afraid to hit Deirdre or had extremely bad aim. Deirdre's hair was mussed and she had a scratch on her neck but that was it.

"Hey there, hey there," he said in the soft, crooning voice he used for calming angry drunks and growling dogs. "Let's break it up."

"She started it! This crazy bitch took my phone!" screamed the woman.

Deirdre still had a fistful of the woman's shirt. Nick wrapped his hands around her fist. "Let's let go, Deirdre, OK? You don't want to hurt her."

Deirdre looked at him for the first time. "Hurt her? Like she hurt that little girl?"

In the end, Nick got it sorted out. The woman wouldn't press charges once the Wal-Mart manager told her Deirdre would be fired. Nick gave the woman back her cell phone, and suggested she might want to count to ten or something next time she got mad at her kid. (He was disgusted but not surprised that she seemed more concerned about her cell phone than her child, who had been watching the whole thing with saucer-wide eyes.) Once the woman left, he turned to talk to Deirdre, but she was already halfway across the parking lot. He called her name but she didn't acknowledge him; she tossed her purse and a small shopping bag into her truck and hopped in. The truck roared into life, the tires spun, and she was on her way. Before she exited the lot the driver-side window rolled down, and out flew a ball of blue wadded-up cloth. When he picked it up he saw it was her Wal-Mart vest, the name tag still attached.

After Nick got off duty he stopped by Deirdre's apartment. Her truck wasn't in the lot, so he sat in the car and waited for her. He sat for an hour, killed time by station-surfing on his radio and eating the Quarter Pounder meal he'd bought for himself. The meal he'd bought for her was stone cold by the time he got tired of waiting.

Nick knew he could drive all over the county and never find her. So he called up two of his friends in the department who had the night shift. Evans and Rodriguez both owed him favors, it was no trouble for them to keep an eye out for a green Ford pickup truck with an "I brake for redheads" bumper sticker. Two hours later he got a call from Rodriguez. She'd seen the green pickup at a roadhouse a few miles outside Du Lac. Nick relaxed — he knew the place. It wasn't the Four Seasons but it wasn't too disreputable either. Deirdre could keep out of trouble until he got there.

Nick heard the roadhouse before he saw it. Sound carried far on these cold winter nights, and he could hear a heavy bass thump before he turned into the lot. Sure enough, there was Deirdre's truck. Nick pushed open the door and was immediately greeted by a wave of sound and the quintessential scent of a bar — sweat, liquor, cigarette smoke, people. Even the music seemed to have its own scent, thick and insinuating. No, that wasn't the music, that was pot. Never mind that, he was off duty and even if he wasn't, he had better things to do.

He squinted in the dim lights, looking for Deirdre's telltale hair. He couldn't see her at the bar, and the dance floor was a jostle of people. Nick walked over to the bar, then changed direction and headed to the source of the music, because he recognized the DJ.

Jim saw Nick and waved hello, beckoned him over. Despite his worry over Deirdre Nick found himself smiling. Jim was an old buddy from high school; he'd been a gentle, dreamy pothead then, completely harmless, so sweet in his own befuddled way that he never lacked for a girlfriend, and teachers hated to fail him even though his schoolwork was abysmal. Nick himself had been straight-arrow as they come, yet he'd liked Jim and did what he could to help him skate by. After high school Jim had been his usual stoned, sweet self until a car accident wiped out most of his family. His parents dead and his sister needing years of therapy to recover, Jim had straightened up with a vengeance, quitting the drugs and getting a job to help pay for his sister's care and keep their family home. He now worked for a talk radio station in Green Bay, where the hosts were all to the right of Ghenghis Khan and whose rants sometimes scared Nick, no lefty himself. Several nights a week Jim did DJ work at places like this, not just for the extra income but to feed something in his soul. Blasting raucous music — right now it was

---

155

"Brand New Cadillac" by The Clash — made his day job much more tolerable.

Nick arrived at Jim's station just as "Brand New Cadillac" ended. "Hey Nick!" he said. "How's it goin'? You look good!"

"Thanks. How's Laurel?"

"Wait a sec." Jim cued up the next song: "Ball and Chain" by some band called Social Distortion. Nick had never heard of them. "Laurel's good. She wants to have a party for Christmas. Think you might want to come? She'd love to see you again."

"It sounds good. I'll let you know." Nick pulled up a chair and sat by Jim. "I'm not just here to say hi. I'm looking for someone."

"Business or pleasure?" Jim asked, and grinned.

"A little of both. I'm looking for a woman named Deirdre. Maybe 30 years old, about five-foot-four, red hair."

"You probably mean the Dancing Queen. That's what we call her. She shows up probably five nights out of seven. Has something to eat, hits the floor and only takes a break during the slow ones 'cause she has no one to dance with."

"She's alone?"

"Always." Jim looked into the crowd of dancers. "She leaves alone too. No one ever tries to pick up on her. She gets this scary kind of look on her face sometimes. Reminds me of the look Laurel would get when she was going through all the PT. The Dancing Queen — what did you say her name was, Deirdre? She's not doing this for fun. You can tell. One of us usually watches out for her when she leaves, makes sure she gets to her truck OK. Strange girl. Something broken about her."

Nick nodded. "You could say that."

"There she is."

Jim inclined his head toward the far end of the dance floor. Deirdre was dancing, had been for a while judging from the disarray of her hair and the Vs of sweat down her back and her chest. In one hand she held a glass with some dark liquid in it. "That's different," said Jim.

"What is?"

"I've never seen her drink anything but water before. Not so much as a Coke. That's why I've never worried about her getting home."

"Put on a slow song soon, I need to talk to her."

"Consider it done. Song after the next." Jim gave him a thumb's up.

"Thanks, Jim. I'll let you know about the Christmas party."

Nick made his way to Deirdre, weaving past the dancers. Deirdre was in the heart of the throng but separate from it too — the other dancers gave her a wide berth. Perhaps it was that aura of strangeness Jim had mentioned, or perhaps it was the way her drink sloshed about while she danced.

"Deirdre!" he called over the music. "Deirdre, you doing OK?"

She grinned at him. "Deputy Eliot, want to dance?"

"I'm not much of a dancer." On her breath and from her glass he caught the distinctive scent of rum and Coke. He forgot himself and slipped into cop-speak. "Is that an alcoholic beverage?"

"Why, do you want some?"

"I'd rather talk. Let's go outside."

"After this song. I like this one."

He nodded and headed for the patio, leaving her gyrating to Golden Earring's "Twilight Zone."

It was both quiet and cold outside on the patio. No snow yet, but he could tell it was coming. His breath steamed and the lake was sheeted with ice. Nick walked over to the railing and looked out at the lake; he thought about that poor soul who'd washed up on the shore of Deer's Head Lake and shuddered. Probably he had nothing to do with the general weirdness that had been happening, but that didn't soothe Nick's nerves. Neither did the spots he saw on the patio floor by the railing. Three dark spots the size of coins. They didn't fade when Nick scuffed at them with his toe. In the poor light from the strung lightbulbs the dark spots looked like blood.

The music faded down, and he heard some cheesy ballad. After a minute Deirdre walked out. She had a drink — a new one, some bright-colored concoction with lots of maraschino cherries — in one hand and her jacket in the other. "Wooh!" she said as the cold air slapped at her sweaty skin. "I bet it's going to snow tonight." She stood by him, set her drink on the rail and put her jacket on. "So what did you want to talk to me about?"

"I just wanted to find out how you were doing."

Deirdre laughed. "Well, let's see. My cousin's been murdered. So has her husband. No one knows or is telling me a thing. And I got fired today. Other than that, life kind of bites." She took a swig of her drink. "Ever had one of these? It's called a Pain Killer. I don't know what the hell's in it, but it's good, I think."

"That isn't going to help you," Nick said.

"I know. It's just nice not to have to think about stuff for a while. Thanks for helping out today, at the Wal-Mart."

He'd been worried that she would blame losing her job on him, but it was that or have assault charges filed against her. The Wal-Mart manager had told him privately that he wasn't surprised, given Deirdre's behavior. She was bound to get a pink slip sooner or later.

"You need any help finding another job?"

She waved dismissively. "Ernie said he'd fix my record so that the bad stuff wasn't in there. He said he knows what I've been through. Said there were mitigating circumstances. I'll find something."

They stood in silence, looking out at the lake. There was not a sound, just a slight change in the feel of the air, and then snow was falling. Nick reached up to catch a snowflake. He'd be sick of snow before long. It was certainly no fun to drive around in and he got tired of helping stranded motorists who insisted they'd never needed chains before, but the first snowfall of the season was always magical. "First snow, Deirdre."

His words died as he looked at her. She was staring out at the lake. Her hair was dusted with snow, a single tear track was on her cheek. She squeezed the glass in her hand, and after a second it broke. She didn't flinch, just put her hand over the railing and let the pieces of glass, ice cubes, and maraschino cherries fall onto the ice.

"Did you cut your hand?" he asked. "Here let me get some water—"

She didn't seem to have heard him. Deirdre casually examined her hand — it wasn't cut — wiped it off on her jeans. She said, "Where's Anna? She should be here. She should be getting the tree farm ready for Christmas. Where will people get their trees?"

"Deirdre…"

"Why is she dead? Why is Richard dead? Why can't one single God damn fucking person tell me why?" Deirdre's voice not loud, but low and savage. "I can't cry for her, Nick. I try but I can't. Not the way I need to. A sniffle here and there doesn't do it. I need to know why this happened and who did it. Then I can stop wondering. I'll have someone to be mad at. And then I can cry. Have you ever stayed awake for days on end? And at first you're OK. Then you just think you're OK. By the end sleep is all you can think about. It's all you want. All I want is to cry. I want to grieve for Anna. And Richard too. But I can't do that until I find out what happened, and why, and who did this."

Nick, like many decent men, was cursed with honesty. He yearned to lie to her, to tell her that of course they'd find out who did this, of course she'd get justice and…what was the word they used on TV? Closure. But if he lied to Deirdre he would gain only her contempt and lose everything else.

There was nothing he could give her. Leo had the case and all the files. If Nick let on about some of the things he'd told Deirdre or went snooping into it he could lose not just his job, but his career. He could protect her if he had the opportunity, but he could not stop her from trying to find out what had happened. "Whatever you need to do, Deirdre, just promise me you'll be careful. And remember that I'm here."

She turned away from the lake and looked at him. She smiled, sadly. "You're a good man, Nick. Too good to be around me." She moved over to him, leaned against him. They stood on the patio with snow falling on them. "You know what made me break that glass? It's awful and you'll hate me but I have to tell someone. I was thinking that if God gave me a choice of seeing Anna again or finding the man who killed her, I'd pick finding the killer." She stepped away from him, as if fearing she might taint him.

"What would you do if you found him?"

He knew the answer before she said it. He could chalk it up to liquor or the day's events but he knew it was the answer from her heart.

"Kill him."

Chapter Seventeen

Outside the world was monochrome. White ground, gray sky. Bleached of all color. But inside it was spring, all colors trying to catch the eye, flowers spilling their scents into the air, as if in a frantic bid for attention. *Pick me, pick me.*

Sean only had eyes for the daisies. *Gerbera daisies,* said the sign, and he chose two of every hue. Red, white, yellow, pink, orange, peach — a dozen daisies, and would the clerk make that into a nice bouquet for him? She certainly would. When he left the florist's shop and stepped into the snowy outdoors, cradling the bouquet in his arms, it was as if he held springtime itself.

His journey from Maine to Wisconsin had been uneventful. His first stop had been the main post office in Green Bay. He almost didn't go, was afraid to find out what Monique's reply was. If she'd replied at all — if she hadn't, he couldn't blame her. But there was a letter. He recognized the handwriting at once. Sean took the letter with him and sat in his van, wanting to open it but not daring to. Finally he scolded himself for his cowardice and opened it.

Flint,

Thank you for writing to me. I'd been worried about you.

Someone did come to talk to me — tall, thin, guy with a face like a rat's. Very well dressed. You probably know who I'm talking about. But he didn't ask me anything I couldn't handle, and I didn't have anything to tell him. I didn't like him, though. There was something not quite right about him. I think he's got a grudge against you. But you probably knew that too.

Someone sent me a warning that you were in trouble and that people might come around to ask about you. If you find out who sent that, please thank them for me.

I don't know what else to say, except that you shouldn't let me add to your troubles. I'm fine. Michael is fine. No one else has contacted me about you. I understand you can't answer. Just know that I'm holding you in the light.

I hope this letter finds you, and finds you well.

He folded the letter and put it back in the envelope. So Robert was right. Halsey had gone to talk to Monique. But she'd held her own, and it was true, she had nothing to tell. At least she was all right. He had that much on his side.

The letter and Monique's words soothed him during the drive from Green Bay to Du Lac, but once he reached the county line the warmth of her letter faded. Too many familiar sights, none of them pleasant. The turnoff to Deer's Head Lake. The road leading to the cabin where he'd killed and dumped the Wickersham brothers. The roadhouse where he'd knifed Doug MacReady.

He went out of his way to avoid driving past the Blaines' tree farm and house.

After getting his things from his apartment and realizing that someone, at least, had been looking for him, he drove out of Du Lac proper to the next town over, where he found a motel to hole up in. An apartment wasn't worth the hassle, and he sensed that he might not be staying here long. Things seemed very...temporary.

He spent the next day at the library, paging through newspapers, both the local and the *Green Bay Press Gazette*, and clicking through online stories. Everyone had been found: Anna, Doug, Steve, Eddie, Richard. All now present and accounted for, and it took him a few moments to understand why he felt so uneasy. The deaths and discoveries were duly noted, but aside from one human interest piece about the Blaines' tree farm being closed now because of the tragedy, there was almost nothing in the papers.

Sean was no expert in these things. Back in his agency days he almost never dealt with the aftermath of his work. Bodies were unceremoniously dumped or the cleaners were called, and he moved on to the next assignment. But in a sleepy area like Du Lac, surely there should have been some outcry over five unexplained deaths. There should have been speculations about serial killers, impassioned pleas from the local law enforcement for the community's help. Instead, there were only grudging details given, and the constant reassurances that the investigation was ongoing. Sean had heard that phrase many times over the years, when missions went wrong.

He steeled himself to look over the stories again from the beginning. Those first ones were the worst, for Anna had been the first one found. The reports about her death were the most detailed. It was with the second discovery, that of Doug MacReady, that details became sparse, interviews with the sheriff's department not forthcoming.

They were stonewalling. He was sure of it. The only question was why.

Sean put the papers aside and shut down the computer, then walked to the library's men's room to wash the newsprint smudges off his hands. He scrubbed at his hands for longer than was necessary; it was back, that burning sensation in his left hand, the hand that had pushed Anna. The other night he'd dreamed that the burning had stopped, that all sensation in the hand had stopped, and when he looked at the hand it was black with rot, bones showing here and there through the decaying flesh.

He knew what had happened while he was gone, but he was nowhere near an idea of what he should do next. Save for one thing — pay his respects.

The snow had started the night before last, had continued all through yesterday while he was at the library. He arrived at the cemetery with his bouquet of daisies to find that the place was nearly deserted. Only the parking lot had been plowed; a few tracks disturbed the snow but for the most part the cemetery was blanketed in pristine whiteness. Reluctant to mar the snow with his footprints, against his better judgment he went into the cemetery's office and asked where Anna Blaine's grave was.

He trudged through the snow, up a small hill that was crowned by a maple tree, leafless now. The snow was not deep enough to hide the names carved on the headstones, and he wasn't long in finding Anna's grave. People had been here not too long ago; standing sentry by the headstone were two pots of poinsettias, nearly buried in snow. He brushed the snow off the poinsettias but soon wished he hadn't, for they were dying in the cold and looked shrivelled. He laid his flowers down by the headstone and they looked too bright, too gaudy, and what had he been thinking when he bought them?

Anna Lynn Cleary Blaine. She had been thirty-four years old. She had always seemed younger to him. The first time he'd met her, she had seemed to be only just out of college. She had made him some brownies that night, as a gift to a new friend. Why had she done that? Why couldn't she have just ignored him the way most wives would ignore their husband's friends who came over to talk shop? Why did he let her befriend him? He could have been surly and uncommunicative like Steve Wickersham and it wouldn't have blown his cover. But she had been nice to him. And he had wanted to be her friend. He should have refused Anna's overtures of friendship but he was too weak, or sentimental, or stupid to do so. None of that mattered now. What mattered was that Anna had paid the price. Anna and her child.

He sat, gazing at the stone and at his flowers so bright against the snow, and said nothing. What could he say? *I'm sorry.* He'd said that a thousand times, and Richard had been right, it didn't change anything. He could say it had been an accident, and while that was true, it also didn't change anything. Sean thought of that joke Beatty had once told him. *You know what's the password at the gates of Hell? "But I didn't mean to!"*

He wanted to ask Anna for her forgiveness, but that was the most pointless of all. She wasn't there to answer, and even if she was, surely she could never forgive him for what he'd done. No one could.

He sat in the cold for a long while, then finally got to his feet. Sean noticed that his flowers were falling over. He knelt down and shaped a vase out of snow, stood the flowers upright. He stood up, took a step back to observe the effect. Good. That was much better. Sean turned and began to walk away from the grave.

A woman's voice called out: "Sam?"

He froze. Slowly turned to see who had spoken.

Anna was standing there, staring at him. He stared back. Knowing she would have found him sooner or later. Knowing this wasn't a fever-induced hallucination, that she was really here. "They don't come back," Robert had said. *Oh, but they do. She has.*

His head was full of a strange rushing sound. She said something but he couldn't hear her. He couldn't see her, because the world went gray, and then black.

Chapter Eighteen

Deirdre had forgotten what hangovers felt like. She hadn't had one since the early days of her marriage, when she'd learned the hard way that it was a mistake to match Randy drink-for-drink. The first day of her unemployment she spent huddled on the couch in her apartment, the TV volume low because the noise made her headache worse. The shades were drawn although it was snowing and the sun never once made an appearance, for even the dim light seemed to jab at her eyeballs. It wasn't until afternoon that she poked her head outside the apartment and saw the scruffy-looking but always polite teenager who lived two doors down — he seemed to have a crush on her, was always offering to bring in her mail or help carry out the trash. She gave him five dollars and asked him to go to the convenience store and get her a six-pack of ginger ale and a box of saltine crackers. He'd nodded sympathetically and come back with it all in record time.

As Deirdre cautiously nursed the first ginger ale, she tried to remember all of last night. She and Nick had talked a bit more, she knew that, then she'd gone back inside to dance and drink more. That's where things had gotten hazy. Deirdre wasn't entirely sure how she'd gotten home, but home she was, and her truck was parked down in the lot. She suspected it was a team effort by Nick and the DJ there at the Stagger Inn; now there came a fragment of memory, she in the passenger seat of her truck with Nick at the wheel, she singing bits and pieces of Christmas carols.

As the day went on her headache and nausea subsided, but she still felt wretched. How could she not? She'd admitted to a cop that she would happily murder whoever had killed Anna and Richard. She'd made a drunken ass of herself. She was unemployed, had lost her job for manhandling a customer, and despite her assurances to Nick she had no good prospects of employment. Most of all she felt ashamed. What must Nick think of her, after the things she'd said and done? What must Anna think of her?

By the time dusk fell, she was able to hoist herself off the couch and look out the window. Snow blanketed everything, turned even her dull street into a scene worthy of a Christmas card. Deirdre's eyes stung but she could not cry. As she stared out the window she saw the kid who'd gotten her the ginger ale and crackers. She waved to him, and opened her window. Then she tossed down twenty dollars she really couldn't spare and asked him to go out and buy the prettiest wreath he could find — a real one, no plastic crap. Though she cynically expected that he would pocket the money or at best come back with some spindly piece of greenery, in less than an hour he showed up at her door with a lush holly wreath trimmed with ivy and a red ribbon. Perfect.

Deirdre carried the wreath as she made her way to Anna's grave. She had only been here once since the funeral and the snow had changed the cemetery's landmarks. She had to retrace her steps, and more than once stumbled over headstones or mementoes buried under the snow. Finally she reached the small hill where Anna's grave was. She was glad she'd come. Some quiet time here was just what she needed, and because she was alone, she could talk to Anna if she felt like it.

Except she wasn't alone.

As she reached the top of the hill, a man stood up. Startled, Deirdre stopped where she was. He must have been kneeling by the grave, hidden by the headstone. He didn't look up, didn't see her. He was looking down at Anna's grave.

It was the man from the photo.

Deirdre couldn't speak. After all the time she'd spent looking for him, here he was, and everything she'd planned to say vanished from her brain. She understood now that hard as she'd looked, she hadn't really expected to find him. What if it wasn't him? What if she was mistaken?

The man turned to walk away, and she caught his profile — the same as it had been in the picture. Yes, it was him. She couldn't let him just leave.

"Sam!" she called out. He stopped, and slowly turned to look at her.

Deirdre was used to the stares, the double-takes. By now she expected them. But she didn't expect a reaction quite like this one.

He didn't say anything. He didn't even seem to be breathing. He stared at her, looking terrified at the sight of her and at the same time relieved, as if he'd been expecting her all along. His face drained of color, went not white but gray as the cloudy sky, and he swayed on his feet. Alarmed, she asked, "Are you all right?" but before she finished his eyes rolled back to whites and he collapsed to the ground.

Deirdre dropped the wreath and ran over to him, hoping that he hadn't bashed his head on anything when he fell. Hoping it was just a faint, not a heart attack or some kind of fit. She knelt beside him; he lay on his back in the snow, unconscious but breathing fine, no head injury as far as she could tell. She picked up one wrist and hunted for a pulse, found it. Deirdre was relieved. This she could handle. Anna had fainted once, the first time she was pregnant. They were at the county fair, she and Anna and Richard, and Anna had fainted in the line for the Ferris wheel. Richard had known what to do; he'd asked Deirdre to help shade Anna from the sun, and lifted Anna's feet up a bit, and in less than a minute she was conscious again.

Deirdre moved down by the man's feet. She knelt in the snow, sitting back on her ankles, and raised the man's feet up, resting them on her knees. While she waited she studied him carefully. He looked thinner than he'd been in the photo, and older as well. She wondered if he'd been ill. Glancing over at Anna's grave she saw a beautiful bouquet of daisies and wondered if he'd brought them. Maybe he was missing Anna as much as she was, and though

168

Deirdre wouldn't wish grief on anyone, it wouldn't be so bad if he was missing Anna; she could have someone to talk to, someone who would understand. What should she say to him when he woke? Apologize for her resemblance to Anna? Ask him what he knew?

He started to come out of it. She watched as his eyelids flickered, and his hands made vague swimming motions as if struggling his way back to consciousness. He muttered something and then his eyes opened. She lowered his feet to the ground. He didn't seem to know where he was or why he was on the ground.

"Sam?" she said. He looked at her and at first there was no recognition. The next second, he lunged away from her and knelt in the snow, watching her warily.

"Are you all right?" He didn't answer. She held up her hands to show him they were empty. "You thought I was Anna, didn't you?"

He didn't answer. His face was blank; it was as if he thought she was a predator that could smell fear, and if he showed none she would leave him be.

"I need to talk to you," she said, but he got to his feet and backed away from her. "Wait!" she called but he turned and was walking fast, back to the parking lot. "Wait, God damn you!" She ran after him.

He was surprisingly fast for an older guy who'd been in a faint just moments before, but she was fuelled by anger and her need to know. She caught up to him in the parking lot. He got into his van, was closing the door when she yanked it back open. "I need to — "

He held a gun, aimed at her face.

Deirdre froze. Her legs went hot, then cold, and she dimly realized that she'd wet her pants. The gun looked huge, just inches away and if he pulled the trigger there was no way he'd miss. Seconds passed, and he did not pull the trigger. She forced herself to look away from the gun, to look at his face instead. He seemed as frightened as she. Maybe even more so, and that gave her the courage to speak.

The courage but not the ability at first. Her lips felt numb, her tongue dry. She finally managed to get the words out. "My name's Deirdre Monahan. Anna was my cousin. I want to talk to you. That's all."

She looked in his eyes the whole time. In her peripheral vision she saw something move, and realized his hand — and the gun it held — was shaking. "I need to know what happened," she said.

He finally spoke. "Please," he said. "Let me go."

She held on to the van's door for the time it took to say, "I live in Lakeside at the Pinewood Court apartments. I just want to talk to you." She let go of the door.

He put the gun down, reached over and closed the door, then started up the van. Deirdre felt numb. All this time she'd been looking for him, and he stuck a gun in her face and was just going to drive away? Just like that. "You know something," she called over the sound of the van's engine. "Tell me what happened!" she yelled as he pulled out of the parking spot and drove away without a backward glance. "Please," she whispered as she watched the van disappear. She stood there for a long time, waiting for him to come back. Waited while her feet went numb and her legs burned with cold. Waited, and he did not come back.

Chapter Nineteen

It annoyed Halsey, the way Juliette drove. Like an old lady or a housewife, keeping to the speed limit, slowing down at yellow lights instead of blazing through them. He tapped his foot impatiently as she came to a full halt at a stop sign. "Can't you speed it up a bit?"

She didn't even glance his way. "A handy hint about undercover activity, Francis. Don't do things that call attention to yourself unnecessarily. If you keep to the small rules you can get away with breaking the big ones."

"Which means?"

"Which means that I'm not going to get a speeding ticket and risk having my car searched just because you're feeling low on testosterone this morning."

He kept his mouth shut after that. As they neared the freeway he opened his bag and took out one of his CDs. Even more irritating than the way Juliette drove was the awful music she played. If he was going to be captive in her car and suck up her insults, at least he could have something nice to listen to. Halsey waited until she was merging into traffic and started to put the disc into the player; Juliette's reflexes were good, though, even while she was driving. She snatched the CD out of his hand, looked at it. "Jesus H. Christ! What are you trying to do, make me crash?" Before he could take the disc back she had lowered the window and tossed the CD out onto the freeway.

Halsey fumed silently as he watched an SUV run over *The Essential Michael Bolton* and as he heard some singer who sounded like a cat in heat warble out of Juliette's stereo. No wonder the bitch was crazy, listening to crap like that all the time. "I'll take the cost of that CD out of your payment," he said. "When are you going to tell me what all this will cost?"

Juliette had her eyes on the road, didn't glance his way. "When the job is done. I learned that from my father, never give a price until the work is done."

"Sounds like a car mechanic."

"He was."

Halsey snorted. It amused him that for all her superior act Juliette was just a grease monkey's daughter. It also explained a lot, not just about Juliette but about the agents in general — blue collar like Juliette or Eurotrash like Robert Dvorak or lace-curtain Irish like Sean Kincaid. No wonder they were so flaky.

"What's funny?" asked Juliette.

"You. A car mechanic's kid. Funny, you don't seem like that."

She smiled. "And you don't seem like a trust fund brat whose Daddy was the politicians' professional cocksucker. I've been dying to know, Francis, did you kick in any of that trust fund to get the job with the agency, or was it a gift from Daddy?"

Halsey didn't see the need to dignify that with a reply. He looked out the window and wondered where they were going. She hadn't told him. She never did. He'd given up asking her what the plan was because all he ever got was her mockery. "You don't do this job by putting things in a Day Planner," she'd said. "Improvise. Work with what you have."

"Make it up as you go along?" he'd sneered.

"Exactly."

They went south, into Virginia, leaving the freeway and taking a zigzagging route he couldn't have retraced if his life had depended on it. They were on a deserted two-way road in the woods when Juliette took out a cell phone, dialed a number. "It's Juliette," she said to whoever answered. "Five minutes." A pause. Then she laughed, incongruously girlish laughter. "Oh, you're right about that. See you."

"Who's that?"

"Old friend," she replied.

They drove on, and soon came to a metal gate; as they approached it swung open and Juliette coasted through. They continued their drive, down a private road bordered by trees so tall their canopy hid the sky. They seemed to be going through a tunnel. Halsey looked up for a glimpse of sky but caught only bits of gray clouds. Uneasily he looked out at the woods and wondered if there were bears out there.

The woods opened up and in front of them was a small wood house, tucked in among the trees as if it had been forgotten there. Or not forgotten — the house seemed well kept — but hidden. Juliette parked, and they got out of the car. "Where are we? Who are we meeting?" Halsey asked. It gave him the creeps, out here in the boonies, and who knew what toothless yokel was lurking in that house. "What's going on?"

"Talkative, isn't he?" said a woman's voice. Halsey turned and saw an older woman. She wore riding boots, jodhpurs, and a black sweater, had her blonde-silver hair tied back in a black scarf. She carried herself with an elegance that seemed to belong more to an English hunt club than a house in the wilds of Virginia. "Is he always this way?"

"Most of the time," Juliette replied. "I've got my work cut out for me."

"That you do. You look good, J. Life treating you well?"

"Well enough." The women shook hands and Halsey saw something resembling real emotion flicker across Juliette's face.

"Everything's ready for you and Boy Wonder here," said the blonde woman.

Halsey's temper, never soothed by uncertainty, slipped its leash. "My name is Frank Halsey."

The woman glanced at him. Her eyes were blue and frosty, and when she smiled it was like Juliette's shark smile. "I remember you, Halsey. You gave me the axe your first week on the job."

He should remember, he knew. But he'd never been much good with names, and he'd usually let minions break the news to agents he fired. If the agent snapped and got violent, better someone else bear the brunt. "Ah, yes," he said.

"Ruby. Does that ring a bell?"

"Yes, it does." He wished it didn't. Ruby had helped train Juliette. "Been a long time," he said.

"You have no idea," Ruby said. Turning to Juliette, she said, "The guns are right inside there. Let me know when you're ready and I'll take you out. Don't be too long, I want to take Bree for a ride." She inclined her head back toward the house, where Halsey now saw a corral, and in the corral a white horse. As if it saw him looking, the horse snorted and lifted its upper lip in a look of equine contempt.

"We won't be long. Will we, Francis?" Without waiting for a reply, Juliette turned and strode toward the house. Halsey tagged along after her, and barely got in the door before Juliette came back outside. She thrust a bundle at him — Halsey fumbled it, undid the bundle. Goggles, a small knapsack, a pistol the likes of which he'd never seen. "Today we're going to play paintball," Juliette said.

She had to be kidding. "You've got to be kidding," he said. "I'm not paying you to —"

Pain, sharp and stinging, in his left shoulder. Halsey yelped and looked around. Ruby stood some distance away, a paintball gun in one hand and a smile on her face. "Now that was fun," she said, and walked away.

"As I said, today we're going to play paintball. In addition to being a hobby the whole family can enjoy, paintball offers a good way to see how well skills transition from the range to the field," Juliette said.

Halsey craned his head back, trying to look at his shoulder. A gaudy splatter of yellow paint marked his jacket. "This stuff washes out, right?"

Juliette ignored him. "You're halfway decent on the range now, most of the time. But the chances of Kincaid standing still long enough to play range target are somewhere between infinitesimal and nonexistent."

A laugh from inside the house, and Ruby emerged with a cup of coffee in one hand. "He's going to go after Kincaid? Sean Kincaid?"

"That he is."

"Oh, that's dandy. Buy me a ringside seat for that one, will you, J?"

Halsey and Juliette rode in the back of Ruby's jeep. Halsey tried to pay attention to where they were going, but it all looked like a blur to him, a winding dirt road through the woods with no landmarks that he could see. Instead he fumed about Juliette and Ruby, and wondered if this paint would come out of his jacket. Probably not, with his luck.

Ruby brought the jeep to a halt. Juliette hopped out. Halsey started to get out but Ruby started up the jeep again. "I thought — " he started.

"I'm taking you further down," she said. "The idea is that you both try to make it back to the house, and if you see each other along the way, that's what the paintball guns are for. There's a fence around the perimeter. Even you can't get lost."

Halsey wanted to ask if there were bears out here, but before he could, the jeep stopped. "Out," said Ruby.

He got out and stood, waiting for further instruction, words of encouragement, anything. Ruby just looked him up and down, smiled, and drove away.

Halsey stood, listening to the sound of Ruby's jeep driving away. It wasn't long before the sound vanished and all that was left was the quiet of the woods. He put on his goggles, loaded his paintball gun, and tried not to think about the quiet. It creeped him out, because mixed in with the quiet were sounds he couldn't identify — rustles and rattles and what he assumed were birds or animals of some sort, and who knew what else. Ruby was crazy. She had to be if she'd trained Juliette and if she wanted to live out here in this wilderness. She'd probably rigged up booby traps out here.

This was all a stupid idea anyway. Juliette was just doing it so she could find another way to make fun of him. He shouldn't play along. He should just stay put here and they could come pick him up when it got late. Halsey sat, and waited, but after a while the sun came out from behind the clouds, making it uncomfortably warm to sit out here in the open, and besides, he was getting bored. He got up and walked into the woods, hoping to find a cool, shady spot and perhaps take a quick nap.

The paint pellet hit him in the chest, a sharp, stinging blow that left him gasping. He jumped to his feet, wiped paint spatters off his goggles, and saw Juliette.

"Can't you at least make an effort?" she asked. "I swear, you are the single laziest person I've ever met. Head east, that'll put you in the right direction. Don't worry, I'll give you a good start. By the way, east is the direction of the big shiny yellow ball up in the sky."

Humiliation stinging worse than the paintball hit, he went east. Past tall pines and leafless oaks. Over emerald moss and brown leaves. He splashed through puddles, crushed a spray of woodland flowers underfoot. None of it he paid any mind. He'd almost stopped wondering if there were bears out here. He was sick of it, just wanted to get this exercise in stupidity over with and go home.

He'd been trudging steadily for an hour when the now-familiar sting of the paintball pellet hit him again, in the back this time. "That's cheating," he said when he got up again. "You're not supposed to shoot people in the back."

"Now's not the time for ethics," Juliette said. She regarded him for a moment, then said in a more serious tone: "You know, I might be going out on a limb here, but you don't seem like your heart's in it today." She walked over to him, her feet cat-silent even in the leaves. He remembered his own loud, blundering trek through the woods and felt the blood rise in his face. "Can it be true? Has Frank Halsey lost his thirst for vengeance? Doesn't he want to get even? Doesn't he want revenge to savor when he goes back to the agency?" She was very close to him now; her breath smelled like cinnamon, her hair stirred in the breeze. "Doesn't he want it?"

Before he could answer, she turned and walked away into the woods.

Yes, he wanted it. But did he want it enough? Was it worth the insults and taunts from Juliette? Was it worth the shameful knowledge that he wasn't very good at the things he needed to catch and kill Kincaid? Maybe it was all just a pipe dream — something to fantasize about but nothing he could make real.

He had been walking, trudging east for some time. The sun went behind a cloud and he paused, leaning against a tree, basking in the shade, taking off his goggles and letting the wind cool his sweaty face.

Something happened.

Some interior voice he had never heard before told him to look on the other side of the tree, to do it now. He did, and saw Juliette standing there, fifteen yards away. He watched as she raised a water bottle to her lips and drank. She stood unaware of him, as graceful and at home in the woods as a deer, and she had never seemed so beautiful to him.

The voice told him to lift the gun, reminded him how to aim, how to stand, how to squeeze the trigger gently. The crack and the recoil of the gun were sweet to him, sweeter still was the orange paint blotch that spread over Juliette's back, but sweetest of all was her look of surprise.

Halsey smiled. He did still want it, after all.

He felt content, encased in a cocoon of satisfaction. Nothing could faze him the rest of that day. Not Ruby's cool contempt. Not the giggles of the teenage girls who saw his paint-spattered clothes when he and Juliette stopped to get some food. Not Juliette's wretched music on the drive home. Not Juliette herself.

Halsey gazed out the window, not seeing the passing countryside. Instead he replayed over and over the sight of Juliette unaware of him, of the gaudy paint splash appearing on her, of her look of astonishment. Bitch didn't know he had it in him. He'd shown her, and soon he'd show Kincaid. Maybe show that lawyer girlfriend of Kincaid's while he was at it. Show them all.

When they got back to Georgetown, as he was getting into his car, Juliette said, "You did all right, Francis. But a word of advice for you."

"Sure," he said.

"Don't get cocky. It doesn't matter how good you get — and trust me, you're not nearly good enough — there's always someone better than you, or more careful. And then there's luck. A funny thing about luck. It runs out."

He nodded, smiled, only half listening to what she said.

"And now," she said, "I have a homework assignment for you. Find out where Kincaid is."

Halsey came back to earth. "What? How should I know where he is?"

"The pieces of the puzzle are all there. You have some. Other people have their own pieces. You can put it together if you try."

Like hell he'd do that. What was he paying her for? He'd pay her more and let her figure it out. To shut her up he said, "I'm on suspension. I can't go back and find out what people know. And if I ask, they won't tell me."

Juliette rolled her eyes. "Francis, Francis. If people don't want to tell you, then make them tell you."

He felt a cold queasiness at what she seemed to be saying. "You'd tell me how to do that?"

"Oh, I'll do better than that," she replied. "I'll show you."

Chapter Twenty

"Hit you again?" the bartender asked.

Sean considered for a moment: what he wanted was balance. Just enough liquor to ease the fear, not enough to make him reckless. Enough to get him to the Pinewood Court apartments ten blocks away, to help him ring the doorbell of Deirdre Monahan's place and tell her what she needed to know. Enough to face what might happen afterward. He nodded and the bartender poured another shot of Johnnie Walker.

Balance was the key. Too little and he would put it off as he had these last couple days. Too much and he would be panicked and paralyzed the way he'd been in the cemetery. Craven behavior, that, but seeing Anna standing there, calling his name, had shaken him as nothing else had in his life. When he came out of the faint, he knew it wasn't Anna because her features were a little different from Anna's, and because her voice wasn't Anna's, and because Robert had been right, they don't come back. He also knew that if it wasn't Anna herself it was a close friend or relative, someone he could never help, only harm, and if he stayed near her he would bring her to grief — never mind that he didn't want to, for he hadn't wanted to harm Anna and look how that had turned out — because that's what Hell was like. You were condemned to repeat your mistakes over and over again, and you never got to avoid it because the circumstances were always different, you didn't see it coming.

So he'd run, and when she wouldn't leave him alone he tried to frighten her away. She'd been afraid, but not enough because she'd been able to look away from the gun and look at him instead, to tell him her name and where she lived. Her name — that had been the key.

For Sean remembered the name. Deirdre. Remembered the Labor Day party, Anna offering him a refill on his Coke and asking if he wasn't seeing anyone, would he be at all interested in meeting her cousin Deirdre? She was recently divorced and starting over with life, could really use a nice, steady guy like Sam, and would he at least think it over? *After all,* she'd said, *you and Deirdre are two of my favorite people.*

He'd said he'd think it over, although of course he wouldn't. To tell the truth, he had entertained a passing hope that Anna's cousin might turn out to be a tall brunette (he had been a long time without female company). He had also been genuinely flattered.

But it had all gone wrong and there was Deirdre, looking like Anna but with a desperate anger and grief that he'd never seen in Anna. She had begged him to tell her what happened, and what had he done? His usual. Just left her there.

"Need another one?" the bartender asked.

He didn't. The balance had been achieved. One more and he would lose his nerve. Or visit Deirdre and make a mess of things. Or yield to the temptation to let that group of thugs at the end of the bar size him up as an easy mark and pick a fight, lose himself in simple physical violence. Sean shook his head and thanked the bartender, left a generous tip, and got up. As he walked out of the bar he heard the jukebox start up with the last of the songs he'd selected: Johnny Cash singing about how he'd shot cold, mean Delia.

The apartment building was a lot like his place in Du Lac. Perhaps a little less well-kept, but similar enough to make him wonder if these things were pre-fab from some factory. Lower middle class apartment housing, one each. He checked the mailbox. Monahan, room 303.

When he knocked on the door, he heard her voice almost immediately. "Who is it?" As if she'd been standing right next to the door, waiting this whole time for him to come knocking. Perhaps she had been.

"It's Sam," he said, using the alias she knew him by. Before he could say anything else the door opened to the width allowed by the safety chain. Sean knew from experience that such chains were scarcely better than nothing when it came to home security; he could have snapped it in seconds if he'd wanted to. More of a deterrent was what he could see in her hand: a small yellow canister that was either mace or pepper spray. "You don't need that," he said.

"You sure?" Deirdre asked. "Last time, you stuck a gun in my face."

"I'll give the gun to you," Sean said. "I just want to talk to you."

She regarded him silently for a moment, then shut the door. He heard the rattle of the chain being taken off, and she opened the door again. She was still not welcoming — she walked beside him to the front room, kept the canister aimed at his face the whole time. She gestured to an oval table in the front room, with a lumpy overstuffed chair at one end of the table. "Put the gun at that end," she said.

He took the gun from its holster and laid it down on the table, then sat down on the sofa, at the end of the table furthest from the gun. She sat down in the chair, laying the pepper spray down beside her. Her gaze danced from him to the gun and back again several times, then finally settled on him.

Sean studied her. She wasn't what he had expected. Now that the shock of her similarity to Anna had worn off, he found himself noticing the differences. Deirdre was taller, her features sharper, her hair a lighter shade of red, her eyes green instead of hazel. Most of all, it was her manner that was different. She seemed a not-quite-domesticated animal on a leash, and if the leash was released there was no telling what she might do. There was something familiar about that, and about the careful, assessing look in her eyes, but he didn't know why it was familiar — Anna had never looked like that. Deirdre was younger than Anna but seemed older; as if life, and not just her recent grief, had hardened her. Her apartment wasn't like Anna's house. Most of the furniture looked like hand-me-downs or secondhand stuff, and there were almost none of the pretty domestic touches Anna would have had.

He wasn't sure if these differences troubled him or eased his mind. She sat and looked at him and he realized she would wait days if that's what it took to get him to speak.

"My name isn't really Sam," he said finally, unsure of where to begin. "It's Sean Kincaid. Sam was a fake name. I used to work for the government, as a covert agent. I did what they call deep cover assignments."

She said nothing as he talked. He couldn't help remembering Jennifer Thomson back in Vancouver, how full of questions she'd been when he'd brought Richard to her. It had been clear what was in Jennifer's mind, her bewilderment and confusion. He'd known how she would react, or at least he'd thought he'd known. What Deirdre would do, he couldn't hazard a guess.

At one point Sean stopped, trying to decide how to proceed, but Deirdre was the one who spoke.

"You must think I'm really stupid," she said. "Don't feed me this bullshit story. Tell me what happened."

"This is what happened." It had never occurred to him that she might not believe him.

"I'm supposed to believe that Richard and his friends went 9/11? Why would he do that?"

"He thought that was the way to get his point across."

Deirdre shook her head. Sean could see that Deirdre had been a little in love with Richard, and would not want to believe the truth. "He was the idea man. His friends did the work and set the bomb off."

"I don't —"

"Doug MacReady, Steve Wickersham, Eddie Wickersham. Do any of those names sound familiar?"

They did. She was silent, then rallied the troops of disbelief. "You could have made a mistake."

"They were planning to do another building. An IRS one this time."

"How do you know that?"

"I joined the group. Richard trusted me. It was the only way I could get close to him. I know that he seemed like a good man. He —"

"Shut up," she said.

He could see the conclusion she was leaping to. "Anna didn't know anything about this. Richard kept it from her. We all did. She thought we were just discussing local business or politics. She didn't know." Until the end, he didn't add.

For a while she was silent. He could see her mulling it over, weighing her denial against his reasons for lying.

"Let's say I believe you," Deirdre finally said. "Let's just imagine that this is true. Even if Richard did do that, he never would have hurt Anna."

"Of course not!" Both of them were surprised by the vehemence in his voice. Sean almost forgot to be afraid of what he would have to say next.

"Then who killed her?" Deirdre asked.

He'd once had to pull shrapnel out of a wound in his leg. He steeled himself to say the next two words as he'd steeled himself to pull twisted metal out of his flesh and bone. "I did."

She was fast, so fast he was surprised. She snatched the gun off the table and pointed it at him; after a second she thumbed the safety off. Now he knew why she'd been looking at the gun so much when he first put it down, and some part of his mind that had never left the agency was impressed. *She's good.*

"Why?" she said. The gun jittered in hands that shook with rage, not fear. "Why? What did she ever do to you?"

"It was an accident." And told her how it had happened.

"You didn't even call an ambulance?" she asked.

"There wasn't... It was too late."

"You seem pretty sure about that."

He didn't answer. He knew death when he saw it but there was no good way of telling Deirdre that.

She laughed, a rusty, bitter sound. "All this time I was looking for you because I thought you were her friend."

"I wanted to be."

"So you left her behind like a piece of trash. Didn't want her to ruin your precious mission, did you? Never mind how fucking long it would be till someone found her."

"I knew that someone would —"

"I found her," Deirdre snarled. "She'd been there for days. She was *rotten*."

He could say nothing to that. He couldn't look at her any more. Sean looked down at his hands, wishing the earth would open up and swallow him, send him straight to Hell right now. Nothing else would do.

Cold metal against his forehead. "Look at me," Deirdre said.

She stood in front of him, pressing the muzzle of his own gun against his head. "What did you do to Richard?"

He told her.

She didn't react. Probably she was too numbed by it all. After a moment she asked, "Why are you here?"

"I hoped there was some way I could make amends for Anna." What a foolish, misguided hope it had been. Anna had been everything to her, anyone could see that. What could he possibly do to ease that pain? Had he even helped by telling her? Or just done more damage?

"You can't," she said.

She was right, of course. There was only one choice left for her to make and he knew what she'd choose. He wouldn't get a chance, like Richard had, but a chance was not what he wanted. Sean watched her finger tighten on the trigger and felt no fear, only relief.

Deirdre held on to the gun. It was the only solid thing in the world and she held on to it, for if she let go the world might fall to pieces and her with it. She couldn't take it all in, not now. Truth or not, his story didn't matter.

What mattered was that he had killed Anna. Even if it was not murder, Anna was still dead. Deirdre thought of that long-ago family reunion. Of all the years since that time, when no matter what paths their lives took, she and Anna always stayed close. The two redheads, Nan and Dee. She thought of not just what was gone, but what would never be. No Sunday dinners with Anna and Richard. No helping out at the Christmas tree farm. No chance to be a fun auntie to Anna's daughter. All that was gone. He'd taken it away and there was nothing he could do to give it back.

What would Nan want her to do? Deirdre felt certain Anna would not want her to kill him. But Nan was a better person than she; Nan probably had it in her to forgive. Deirdre just wanted him dead.

She looked into his eyes and saw it was what he wanted too. That made it the right thing to do, didn't it?

What would happen afterward? Not the immediate aftermath — surely she could make up some tale about a crazy prowler she'd had to shoot in the head — but then what? The rest of her life to miss Nan. Just the thought of all those years made her exhausted. Like facing a prison sentence. A life of grief with no possibility of parole.

No. She wouldn't be the only one to endure that.

Deirdre stepped back from Sean. "Get out," she said.

He shook his head a little, as if he hadn't quite understood what she'd said.

"You don't get off that easy. Live with it a while. I have to. You deserve to." She had to make him understand this wasn't mercy.

He stood up. "Deirdre." His voice was hesitant, as if he wasn't quite sure how to pronounce her name. "I'm sorry about Anna."

"Get out." She heard her voice shake and knew she was close to losing it. She had to get him out before that happened.

He walked to the door, opened it. Before he stepped out he turned to her. "If there's anything —"

"Go away. Just. Go." *Don't plead.* "Now."

He went. She heard his footsteps going down the hall, down the stairs. She heard a car start up and drive away. When she was sure he was gone she put the gun down on the table and then ran to the kitchen sink to wash her hands, which felt contaminated. When she felt sure her hands were clean again, she weaved to her sofa and fell onto it, picked up a pillow — needlepoint, a gift to her from Anna of course. She bit at the fabric, muffled her screams in it. She did that for a long time. The next morning she wondered if she'd imagined it all, until she saw the gun, an ugly, deadly-looking thing, on her table. Until she found the note in her mailbox. Just a phone number.

She stared at the note, wanting to burn it, or crumple it and toss it into the gutter. Instead she put it in her wallet, and did not ask herself why.

Chapter Twenty-one

Nick stood with a cup of coffee in one hand, his cell phone in the other, listening to Deirdre's phone ring. He hung up when it went into voice mail, trying not to feel worried. But he hadn't heard from or seen Deirdre since the night he'd taken her home when she was too inebriated to drive and that was over a week ago now. If he just hadn't been able to catch her on the phone, he wouldn't be concerned. But he hadn't seen her at the roadhouse. He'd driven by her apartment a couple times after his shift ended, knowing he was acting like a weirdo but too worried to let that stop him; he'd seen the bluish flicker of the TV screen but no other lights. Her windows were the only ones without Christmas lights. Last night he'd knocked on her door, and even though he knew her TV was on and her car was in the apartment's lot, she hadn't answered.

She was in trouble, anyone could see it. He couldn't predict her, had never seen anyone react as she did to grief. She wasn't like anyone in his family: not like his father's side, who closed up tight like clams and didn't let out so much as a sniffle; not like his mother's side, who wailed and held loud drunken Irish wakes. The closest he'd seen to Deirdre's reaction was his friend Jim's sister Laurel. Nick had been at Jim's house, helping to make the modifications for Laurel's wheelchair, when Jim brought Laurel home. Jim had pushed Laurel in her chair, up the ramp, and when Laurel saw Nick, she winked and sang, "Roll out the cripple..."

Nick had been shocked, yet in a way admiring. To take the grief that had wrecked your life and make gallows humor out of it was not his way, but it took a kind of strength he admired. Likewise, Deirdre's rage and her need to know what had happened to Anna — they would either carry her through this the way Laurel's jokes had carried her, or they would wear her out and break her. Nick hoped Deirdre's scarcity this last week didn't signify the latter.

The day was impossibly bright — cloudless skies and snowy ground. Even behind his sunglasses Nick squinted a bit, but he didn't miss Deirdre's green truck, parked in the cemetery's parking lot. He made a highly illegal U-turn and parked nearby her truck. Getting out of his car, he paused to take a deep breath of the wintry air, hope for the best, and then followed the footprints.

She was sitting by her cousin's grave, a miniature Christmas tree in a small pot in front of her. A few ornaments hung on the tree, and as Nick approached he saw Deirdre put a star on top. The star seemed a bit big for the tree, and for a moment Nick wondered if the tree might lean over like in the Charlie Brown Christmas show, but it stayed upright.

His feet made crunching sounds in the snow, and he meant to say hello but before he could, Deirdre started and whirled around. She was white-faced, thinner than when he'd seen her last, and it seemed she'd been expecting someone, but not him — she looked at him with puzzlement.

"I'm sorry if I scared you," he said. "I saw your truck and wanted to find out how you were doing."

She stared at him a moment longer, and for a moment he thought it had been a terrible mistake, coming to see her. Then she smiled. It was like the Christmas tree, a little off-kilter, but a smile nonetheless. "No, it's fine. I'm happy to see you. I just wasn't expecting you."

Nick knelt down beside her. The little tree gave off a sweet scent of pine. "It's pretty."

"The ornaments were a housewarming gift Anna and Richard gave me when Randy and I got married. This seems like the best place for them now. Do you think when spring comes I could plant the tree here?"

"Probably not."

"I guess you're right." She adjusted the star, then looked at him. "Were you worried about me?"

"Yes. I couldn't reach you on the phone."

"I know, and you came to my place too. I'm sorry, but I've just needed to be alone these few days. I've had a lot to think about."

Nick couldn't interpret the look on her face. Something had happened beyond her losses and being fired from her job, but he could tell that now was not the time to ask about it. He maneuvered into safer territory. "Any luck on the job front?"

She shook her head. "It's my fault, I haven't been looking too hard."

"My dentist's office needs someone. Just phones and filing, but at least you wouldn't be on your feet all day like at the Wal-Mart." He handed her a card from Dr. Foley's office. "If you're interested."

She took the card. "Thanks, Nick. One of these days when my head is more together I'll find a way to thank you for everything you've done for me."

Nick didn't know what to say. He'd done what he could, done what anyone should. It wasn't enough. "I should be going," he said.

"I'll come with you." She stood and brushed snow off her jeans. "I was nearly ready to go. My legs are half frozen."

They walked back to the parking lot, not speaking. As Deirdre was rummaging in her purse for her truck keys, Nick asked, "Are you busy this weekend?" Before she could answer he found himself blurting out, "My friend Jim, he's the DJ at the place you like to go dancing, he and his sister are having a Christmas party Saturday night, and I was wondering if you'd like to come with me."

Deirdre stopped, keys in hand, and gave him an odd sort of look. Nick realized that he'd just asked her out on what could be considered a date, and that he'd done so in the parking lot of a cemetery. "I'm sorry," he said. "Wrong time and place. That was weird."

"That's all right. It's not half as weird as what happened to me last time I was here."

"What happened?"

"I'll tell you some other time."

Nick turned to walk to his patrol car, and he heard Deirdre call his name.

"What time on Saturday?" she asked.

Deirdre stood up, walked over to the mirror. For the fifth time in the last twenty minutes she surveyed her reflection. *Casual,* Nick had said. *Nice but casual.* She supposed she fit the bill and looked reasonably festive in her forest-green jeans and a winter-white sweater. But it had been months since she'd done anything so normal as go to a party. It had been months but felt like years. Anna's death and everything that followed had taken over her life and Deirdre was hard pressed to remember what a normal person's evening out could be like.

She wondered again if she should call it off and stay home, but the last few days had left her desperate to get outside and to break the groove her thoughts had worn into. Ever since Sean had told her his story, it seemed she'd been made prisoner by what he'd told her. She lurked in her apartment, subsisting on ramen noodles and grilled cheese sandwiches, staring at the TV without seeing it, trying to make sense of everything and having no luck.

How *could* she make sense of it? How could she even believe it? That Richard had pulled an Oklahoma City and blown up a federal building. It was impossible. Only crazy people did stuff like that, and Richard wasn't crazy. No one in their right mind could do such a thing, kill over three hundred people just because he didn't like the way the powers that be were running things. Richard couldn't have done that. Deirdre thought of Richard and how much he'd wanted a child, how good he was with the kids at the family get-togethers. Would a man like that blow up a building that had a day care center in it? Of course not. This Sean guy was the one who was crazy, making up this bullshit story for no reason Deirdre could fathom, and why should she even try to understand. She wouldn't try to understand, because he'd killed Anna and that was what mattered, not the rest of it. Which she didn't believe anyway.

And yet.

Why would Sean make up a story like that? For what reason? If he was going to lie about Richard, wouldn't he have simply said that Richard killed Anna? But he hadn't. He could have pinned it on one of the other dead guys, that MacReady fellow or the Wickersham brothers. But he'd confessed to killing Anna, and he wasn't lying, Deirdre felt sure. No one could fake the remorse she'd seen in his eyes, nor the relief he'd shown when she put the gun to his head.

Unwillingly she'd found herself examining memories, picking them over like a gold miner examining his pan. Unwillingly she'd found things. Anna telling her about the men who came over to talk with Richard, down in his basement. Talks Anna wasn't privy to. Local business or politics, supposedly, but how much business could you talk about in a backwater place like Du Lac? Richard wasn't even on the city council; he was too busy with the farm. Richard dissuading her from staying at the Blaines' house while she got back on her feet. Had he been encouraging her independence, or had he not wanted another set of eyes in the house — eyes that might see something was amiss? She remembered how grateful she'd been to Richard, for she hadn't wanted to hurt Anna's feelings by refusing her offer of room and board.

And yet.

For days she had chased these thoughts round and round her brain, trying to make sense of everything. Sometimes she believed what Sean had told her, sometimes she didn't. Mostly she wasn't sure, and in a way this uncertainty was worse than knowing nothing at all.

Several times she'd taken the phone number out of her wallet. Once she even picked up the phone to talk to Sean, but rage took over — for all else aside, he had killed Anna. He might not have meant to, he might be half-crazy with remorse, but he had killed her, and she didn't trust herself with him. Deirdre had been able to let him walk away once. She doubted she could do it again.

When her exhausted mind would not let her think about it any more, she'd bought the small Christmas tree and taken it, along with her ornaments, to Anna's grave. She hadn't expected that to soothe her, but it had. Maybe because the one comforting thing Sean had told her was that Anna knew nothing of what Richard had supposedly done. She was innocent. Thank God. Deirdre felt sure she could not have endured it if she'd learned that Anna was somehow involved in that bombing.

Sitting by Anna's grave she'd felt strangely peaceful. Never mind that she still didn't know what to believe, or that she didn't know what to do about Sean. Never mind that she had no job and a rapidly dwindling supply of cash, and that soon it would be a choice between getting another job or ending up on the street or back home with her parents. (Deirdre almost preferred the idea of living on the street; she couldn't stand the thought of a week, let alone months, of her mother alternately chastising her for getting fired and treating Deirdre like a fragile glass thing and all without ever once mentioning Anna's death, because such things were so unpleasant. No thank you.) She'd felt peaceful until she'd heard the sound of footsteps in the snow and had been sure it was Sean come back to haunt her. As she'd whirled around she'd remembered with a sick jolt in her stomach that she'd left Sean's gun at her apartment and her pepper spray in the truck.

She'd been surprised at how relieved she was to see Nick. He looked so solid, so real standing there in the snow. Even in full deputy regalia, even with the aviator shades hiding his eyes, he didn't look like a cop.

When he'd asked her to the party, her first impulse had been to say no. But she was so tired, so lonely, that she found herself accepting his invitation.

Now she regretted it, because what would she do at the party? When was the last time she'd held a normal conversation with anyone? Could she have a nice time with a nice guy?

Probably not. Why take the chance? Besides, she looked like hell. Deirdre went to pick up the phone to let Nick know she wasn't feeling well, when there was a knock at the door.

For a moment she was sure it was Sean, back to tell her more things she wasn't sure she wanted to know. She opened the door and it was Nick, standing there with a pale pink rose in one hand and a shy smile on his face. "Merry Christmas," he said.

Nick's car was just as ordinary and quietly comforting as Nick himself. There was an air freshener tree hanging from the rear-view mirror, a McDonald's cup in one cup-holder and a Starbucks cup in the other, and a few empty CD cases littered the floor. A faint smell of Armor-All hung in the air, and Deirdre guessed he'd given the car a quick clean-up earlier that day. She felt strangely touched by that.

"Sorry I'm a bit late," he said as he put the car in gear. "They had the Santa ride tonight."

"The what?"

"The Santa ride. Mr. Polonsky dresses up like Santa and the fire department gives him a ride on one of the engines. They go to a couple neighborhoods and he greets the kids, hands out candy, that sort of thing. They always have a couple police cars as an escort and I had that duty."

She was about to ask Nick if he'd volunteered or had been pushed into it, but from the way he smiled she knew he'd volunteered. He would always volunteer for that. "By the way," she said, "Thank you for telling me about the opening at Dr. Foley's office. They're closed until after Christmas but they said I can come in for an interview the day after. Dr. Foley sounds like a nice guy."

"He is. Does a good job and he's not stingy with the goof gas either," he replied, and they both laughed.

Neither said much for the rest of the drive, but it was a relaxed quiet. He put the Charlie Brown Christmas music on the tape player; Vince Guaraldi's festive yet melancholy music suited her. She was content to watch the Christmas lights go by and to listen to Nick hum along with the music.

The house was off the highway between Lakeside and Du Lac, a ranch house on what Deirdre guessed to be a half acre or so. The driveway was already full of cars, so they parked half a block away. Snow was falling and it dusted their hair and jackets with white as they walked to the house.

By the mailbox a battery-powered plastic Christmas tree sang as they passed, its eyes winking unnervingly. "That was disturbing," said Nick.

"They had one of those at Wal-Mart," Deirdre said with a shudder. "Unemployment is no fun, but at least I don't have to listen to that damn thing every day."

Fortunately the tree was the only tacky thing about the party. Strings of lights bordered the walkway to the house, and lit the railings of the porch steps and the ramp leading to the front door. Seeing Deirdre's quizzical look, Nick said, "Laurel was in a bad car accident a few years back. She can walk but not very far or for very long, so she's usually in a wheelchair."

Before Nick could ring the bell the door was flung open. "Feliz Navidad!" sang out Jim. Deirdre recognized him from many nights at the Stagger Inn, and also remembered that he'd helped get her home that night she was too drunk to drive. Before she had a chance to be embarrassed, Jim gave her a hug. "I've known Nick longer but you're prettier, so you get the hugs first," said Jim.

"Gee, thanks," said Nick.

"Truth hurts, doesn't it Nicky-boy? Come on in, the both of you."

The room was so packed Deirdre couldn't tell much about the house, and Jim had to talk loud to be heard over the din of conversation and the Christmas music. "The eats are over there," Jim said, pointing. "And there's a couple ice chests of drinks in there too. And a few coolers outside too."

"Where's Laurel?" asked Nick.

"In the kitchen. Making eggnog, I think." The doorbell rang and Jim excused himself to go answer it.

Nick leaned down close to Deirdre so he didn't have to shout. "Mind if we go to the kitchen? I haven't seen Laurel in a while and want to say hi to her."

Deirdre nodded. After the last week of sitting alone in her apartment, she was feeling a bit overwhelmed by the crush of people and the noise. She tagged along after Nick as he pushed through the crowd.

Luckily the partygoers seemed to be concentrated in that front room. By welcome contrast, the kitchen was nearly empty: a few couples stood around chatting, and by the stove was a young woman in a wheelchair, fiddling with something "Gah! I'm being outsmarted by a nutmeg grinder!" she exclaimed, then looked over at the new arrivals. "Nick! Merry Christmas!"

Laurel spun her chair to face Nick and Deirdre. Nick leaned down to hug Laurel, then made introductions.

"Merry Christmas, and welcome to our house Deirdre." Laurel's prettiness was marred by a scar that ran down one side of her face, and Deirdre had seen other scars on her hands and arms when Laurel reached up to hug Nick, but her smile and the warmth in her eyes almost made the scars disappear. Deirdre felt she wanted to make some sort of connection, but felt too shy for a hug and a handshake seemed too formal. She reached out one hand, and felt awkward and stupid until Laurel clasped Deirdre's hand in hers for a moment.

Deirdre felt the last of her hesitation about coming to the party vanish. It seemed some weight had fallen off her. "Thank you," she said. "I'm glad I'm here."

Nick was having no luck with the nutmeg grinder. "Where's Jim? Maybe he can figure this thing out."

"He should," said Laurel with a laugh. "He used to *take* nutmeg."

Jim arrived in time to hear this. "Once! Just once! That shit was too nasty even for me." He took the grinder and in no time had it working and a fine dusting of nutmeg over the top of the eggnog.

"Jim's had a slightly checkered past," Nick told Deirdre.

"Haven't we all," she replied.

Laurel deftly filled four cups with eggnog and handed drinks out to Jim, Nick, and Deirdre; she raised hers in a toast. "Merry Christmas."

"And a happy new year," said Nick.

"God bless us every one," said Jim.

Deirdre didn't know what she would say until the words were out of her mouth. "To absent friends," she said, and felt sure it was the wrong thing.

To her relief, they were all still smiling. Laurel held her cup out, and they all clinked together.

Deirdre usually hated parties where she knew no one. So much of her life she'd felt like an outsider, standing apart from others: from her family, from the kids at school, from Randy's friends and after a while, from Randy himself. Tonight was different. She didn't belong, but she didn't mind the feeling of separation. Tonight it was enough to stand next to Nick, who never left her side, as he chatted with the partygoers. Most of them were people he'd known in high school, and she had nothing to say but stood half listening to the conversations, half absorbed in the blur of party chatter and holiday music. She was not ready to be a part of it all, yet, but it was a welcome, and healthy change from the isolation she'd been in for so long.

"Want to get something to eat?" Nick asked after a while.

"Yes, let's."

As they started to head toward the den, Jim's voice boomed above the party noise. "Make way, make way! There you are, Nick! They're playing your song!"

"Oh please, God, no," moaned Nick, but he let himself be dragged off by Jim. Deirdre followed, wondering what was going on.

In the den, not far from the food tables, was the TV. Stacked on top were DVDs and tapes of every Christmas special Deirdre had ever heard of and even some she hadn't. She recognized the image frozen on the screen — one of the Rankin-Bass puppet animation specials, but which one? *The Year Without a Santa Claus*, that was it.

Jim aimed the remote at the TV and pressed "play"; a human icicle began to dance. With a sigh, Nick clasped his hands behind his back, like a little boy at the school recital, and sang along with the Snow Miser, and by the time he finished and everyone applauded, his face was bright red.

"I take it there's a history behind that?" Deirdre asked.

"Middle school Christmas party at Jim's house, and none of us knew he'd spiked the punch. And that's all I'm saying. Will you be OK for a minute? I have to go beat up Jim."

"Do that. I'll get something to eat and watch the show."

As Nick vanished into the crowd, Deirdre made her way over to the food table. A good-size table, it seemed, should be plenty to choose from.

She stopped, and looked down at the table.

A punch bowl, full of steaming wassail, giving off the scent of apples and cloves and oranges. Chicken wings and stuffed mushrooms. Bacon-wrapped dates. Deviled eggs. She picked up one of the eggs, took a bite. Yes, of course. Anna's recipe. She'd know it anywhere. *You smush the yolks through a strainer*, Anna had said. *It makes them nice and smooth. Trust me, it'll make all the difference.* This spread of food might have been from one of Anna's Christmas parties.

The room seemed to have gotten quiet. She couldn't hear the TV's noise or the chatter of the guests. It all seemed far away, but she clearly heard Laurel's voice as she rolled up beside Deirdre. "Are you all right?" Laurel asked.

"Yes. It's just...memories."

Laurel said, "You're Anna Blaine's relative, aren't you?"

"Her cousin."

Laurel nodded. "You look very like her. My parents, God rest them, were members of Anna's church, and after the accident the church ladies would come by with their baskets of food, or offering to help. And you could tell with most of them that they just wanted to leave their casseroles and then take off. People get scared, they think stuff like this — " Laurel gestured to the wheelchair — "is catching or something. But Anna was different. She didn't just do her duty and run off. She cooked meals and helped clean up. She drove me out to Green Bay to do some shopping.

"That first Christmas after the accident Jim and I were missing our folks so much, and we weren't sure if we were going to be able to keep the house what with all the medical bills. A couple days before Christmas Anna came by with these plates of food — all finger foods. Not just some hot dish. For the first time, it felt like Christmas. She gave me the recipes and I make them every year." Laurel's look of reminiscence gave way to alarm. "Oh jeez, I'm so sorry. Here." She handed Deirdre a napkin.

Deirdre wondered what Laurel meant, and realized that she'd been crying. She hadn't realized it — there had been an ache in her chest and throat when Laurel started talking about Anna, and after that she was caught up in Laurel's words, did not notice that the ache had turned to tears. She didn't feel terrible, despite the tears. It was like letting go of a heavy load, one she'd been carrying so long she didn't notice the weight of it, nor the pain, nor how both had brought her low. Tempering the sadness was relief that she could grieve, could mourn her cousin like a normal person would. She could leave the rage behind and reminisce with someone who had known Anna and loved her, and who missed her too. This was the way it should be.

"It's OK," Deirdre said after she'd wiped her eyes and blown her nose. "Really it is. It's just the time of year. And no one talks about her to me. It's like they want to forget her. But I can't. I won't."

Laurel put her hand on Deirdre's. "Neither will I."

After a few moments, when her tears had dried, Deirdre piled high her plate and filled a cup with wassail. She sat down on the lumpy couch, and raised the glass in a toast. *To absent friends.* Soon Nick sat beside her, his plate piled even higher than hers. "Have you tried this?" he asked. "I usually hate deviled eggs but these are really good."

"Yes they are," she said.

Some time after midnight the partygoers decided it was time to make snow angels. Jim and Laurel led the way, and people fanned out onto the front lawn to stake out a patch of snow. Deirdre watched while Jim helped Laurel walk unsteadily from her chair to the snow. "OK, places everyone," Jim called out. "Ready? One. Two. Three. FLOP!"

At his command they all flopped down on their backs into the snow. Deirdre had snow in her hair and what felt like a croquet hoop poking into her back and a daffy grin on her face. She couldn't remember last time she'd made snow angels.

"Fly, angels, fly! Flap those wings! One, two! One, two!" Laurel's voice rang out. "Feel the burn. There are no flabby seraphim in my heavenly choir."

Deirdre and Nick laughed. They lay in the snow and watched the flakes dance and twirl on their way down; until Laurel announced that there was hot chocolate for anyone who wanted it. Nick got up, helped Deirdre to her feet, and they joined the crowd heading back into the house.

"I want to thank you," Deirdre said. "I would never have come here if you hadn't invited me. And it's been a really nice time."

He took her hand in his, squeezed it. "I'm glad."

Something caught her eye as they stood on the porch. "Hey, look. Mistletoe."

He looked up at the mistletoe, then down at her. "So it is."

It was like a high school kiss — awkward and sweet. Strange that it should be that way when both of them were years away from high school, but it seemed fitting, and very sweet.

They sat on the porch glider with their near-empty mugs of hot chocolate. Slowly, in bits and pieces, the party was ending. Nick and Deirdre said their thank-yous to Jim and Laurel, and Deirdre was heartened by Laurel's invitation to come over for dinner any time.

"I'll go get our coats and your bag. You want to stay here?" Nick asked.

Deirdre nodded. She was happy to sit and watch the snow fall, to watch the partygoers amble out to their cars. She was sad because she was missing Anna, but the sadness felt necessary, like a wound healing. Although the thoughts that had plagued her were returning, the fears and doubts and the awful suspicion that what Sean Kincaid had told her might be true, she felt ready for it.

Not just ready for it. Ready for something else? To accept it as the truth? Perhaps not, but maybe she was ready to let go of the obsession. To let herself grieve. To accept that Anna was gone and that poisoning herself with anger was doing Anna's memory no favors, and only hurting herself. If she went on like that she could end up like Kincaid, with the same look of relief if someone put a gun to her head.

If what he'd told her wasn't true, she was no better off than she'd been. If it was true, well, now she knew. She could even see justice done, although Kincaid's remorse seemed a worse prison than any she could put him in. Perhaps she could just accept it for now, and give herself time to heal. Take up the search for truth when she had the strength to do it.

Making that decision felt the way her tears at Laurel's story had — like the easing of a cruelly heavy burden. Deirdre sighed with relief.

She was idly wondering when Nick would come back when her gaze fell on a group of men standing on the lawn not far away.

Save for Nick and Jim, Deirdre hadn't met any of the party guests before tonight. But she'd seen this man before. Walt Sorensen stood with a beer in his hand, looking not at his companions but at her. Like the last time he'd seen her, outside Richard and Anna's farm, there was recognition in his look, but of an entirely different kind. Then he'd been surprised and almost fearful. His look now was different. It seemed to change as their eyes met — nervousness and a certain shamefaced look, which turned to defiant arrogance. A look that said he knew something she didn't.

"Deirdre?"

Nick stood there with their coats and her purse. She blinked, looked at Walt again. He wasn't looking at her any more, he was laughing with his buddies. She might have imagined the whole thing. Might have.

"Deirdre?"

"Sorry. Spaced out there for a moment. Must be more tired than I thought." She smiled as if nothing was wrong and hoped it fooled Nick.

She was quiet on the drive back. Nick noticed, and she told him she was tired from the party, that's all. She wasn't tired at all. She was wide awake, her mind chattering and gnawing like a cooped-up rat. Walt, seen in photos with Richard and Sean and the rest of those guys. If she told Sean Walt's name, what would he say about it? *Never heard of him.* Or, *He was one of them.*

What if Walt had been one of them? What did it mean when Walt's brother was the sheriff who'd made no progress in the case of Anna's death, or in any of the recent deaths that had fallen on Du Lac?

Nick walked her to her door. She kissed him, but no lingering sweet high school kiss this time. She rushed through it, then followed it with a rib-bending embrace. She needed to know he was there, steady and sane. Because she had a terrible feeling that things weren't over, that knowing what had happened to Anna wasn't going to be enough.

Deirdre hoped Nick sensed nothing amiss. She didn't want him involved in this yet. The matter was between herself and Sean Kincaid. Perhaps Walt and Leo as well.

She waited until Nick was gone, until the sound of his car had faded away. The phone number was where she'd left it, in her wallet. Deirdre dialed, and after only one ring Sean's voice answered, "Yes?"

He sounded awake and alert, though it was nearly two in the morning and surely she'd roused him from sleep. "It's Deirdre," she said. "I have to talk to you."

Chapter Twenty-two

One of the keys to a successful marriage, Monique believed, was division of labor. After Michael parked the car, he played with the GPS and listened to the traffic reports on the radio while she went into the coffee house for caffeinated beverages.

She'd figured the place would be packed, and it was; full of people in comfortable travel clothes, getting the necessary fuel for holiday car trips to New York, to Boston, to Norfolk. She and Michael were on their way to his sister Angie's vacation rental in North Carolina, where they'd join assorted relatives for a holiday feast. The car was loaded up with presents for the nieces and nephews, and with gift baskets crammed full of foodie treats — English tea and biscuits, chocolate and biscotti, balsamic vinegar, smoked salmon, and French wine. Somewhere in the jumble of luggage and gifts was a wheel of Stilton Michael had bought on his last jaunt across the pond, and Monique had dusted off the fondue set they'd gotten as a wedding present, vowing that on this trip they'd finally use it.

In the past, Monique had never been much on holidaytime family get-togethers, mostly because her family was fractious enough for gatherings to be tense, tiresome affairs. All would be well for a few hours, then inevitably Brigitte, her San Francisco liberal sister, would accuse Monique of selling out, and the cousins would start arguing politics. Usually around dessert, her mother would start wringing her hands and complaining that neither of her daughters had produced children. The last time Monique had attended one of the Pavour holiday meals, it had been during the high-powered, high-stress time between Sean's departure from her life and Michael's entry into it — she'd finally snapped, stood on a dining room chair, and declared that she was not going to get knocked up just so her mother could go shopping at Baby Gap.

Michael's family, by contrast, didn't care about politics, or at least could discuss the subject in a civilized fashion. His parents had plenty of grandkids and never pestered Michael and Monique for more. Also, sister Angie was smart enough to rent a place big enough for everyone to stay out of each other's hair, with the beach a few sand dunes away and easily accessible for wandering. Monique was looking forward to pleasant conversation, abundant food, and plenty of time on the balcony listening to the surf and reading through the stack of Travis McGee novels she'd brought.

The line for coffee crept along. Just as Monique was regretting not bringing *Darker Than Amber* with her to read in line, it was her turn. She gave her order to the harried-looking barista, who showed visible relief that her order was simple — two medium cappuccinos. The order taken, the money paid, she inched her way over to the pickup station.

She was able to look out the window and see Michael. He seemed to have figured out the right route — at least, he wasn't fiddling with GPS any more. Now he was trying on hats — first the Santa hat, then the elf hat, trying to decide. As she watched Michael and waited for their drinks, she heard the barista, in an exasperated tone, call out: "Large decaf nonfat vanilla wet cappuccino for Frank!"

Monique giggled and tried to imagine what such a drink would taste like. Not like coffee, that was for certain. She couldn't wait to tell Michael; she knew just what he'd say: *Coffee should be cold and bitter! Like every woman I've dated!*

She caught a glimpse of an expensive trenchcoat covering sloping shoulders. Frank grabbed his drink without so much as a thank you to the barista, and as he turned away from the counter with his drink in hand, she recognized him.

It was Frank Halsey, the agency man who'd questioned her. There was no mistaking that rodential face. Monique felt her heart lurch and turned back toward the window, but it was too late. Halsey had stopped and was staring at her. "Ms. Pavour," he said. "What a surprise to find you here."

There was no sense pretending she didn't recognize him at all; even he wouldn't be fooled. "Hello, Mr..." she trailed off.

"Halsey."

"Hello, Mr. Halsey. Yes, this seems to be quite a popular place today."

She'd have to be more careful this time, because things had changed; now she had something to hide, and something was different about Halsey. He radiated an unhealthy tension and didn't seem to blink often enough as he looked at her. Time hadn't thawed the predatory chill of his gaze. Her dressed-down appearance — no makeup, her clothes battered old jeans and the Miskatonic University sweatshirt Michael had bought her for Halloween — didn't discourage his roving eyes either. She wished fervently her order would come up and she could get back into the shelter of her car.

"Going somewhere for the holidays?" he asked.

"Mmm, yes. Down the coast a ways."

"Visiting family?"

"Yes, my husband's relatives."

"Seeing any old friends?"

"No, just family."

"A long visit?"

She forced out a laugh, hoped it hit the right note of mild annoyance. "I just came here for coffee, I didn't expect the Spanish Inquisition."

Deliverance came in the guise of the barista calling, "Two medium cappuccinos for Monique."

"Excuse me," she said, and went to get her coffees. She smiled and thanked the barista and wished him a Merry Christmas, then turned and headed for the door. Monique could tell that Halsey wanted to talk to her, but she just gave him a nod and made for the exit. When she stepped out into the winter air, the cold breeze kissed the sweat that had broken out on her back and made her shiver.

Michael had settled on the Santa hat. "Pretty packed in there?" he asked as she handed him a coffee.

She nodded. "That's why I didn't get cinnamon on them. Too claustrophobic. You don't mind?"

"Yes, I do. I'm sure it's in the pre-nup that you have to get sprinkles on my coffee."

"We didn't have a pre-nup."

"We didn't? Bloody hell, I knew there was something I overlooked."

She could see Halsey looking out the window at them. "Forget about it already. Let's just go, OK?"

"Untwist your knickers, we're going," Michael said, and put the car in gear.

She hadn't mean to snap at Michael; it was the unexpectedness of seeing Halsey there. She was off her guard and off her game, because this time she knew where Sean might be. She just hoped Halsey hadn't guessed it.

Juliette's house was refreshingly free of Christmas decorations, though the holiday was just days away. Halsey appreciated that. He couldn't stand Christmas — the crowds, the insipid music, the God damned Salvation Army guys ringing those bells nonstop, and no decent shows on TV. As if all that wasn't bad enough, his ex-wives inevitably picked Christmas as their time to pester him. He'd sent presents but did that make them happy? Annette complained because the clothes he'd sent the kid were two sizes too small, Lisa had stopped drinking and was mad because he'd sent her a bottle of wine, and Trish had married a Jew and said he shouldn't have sent a Christmas present at all. There was no pleasing some people.

He sat down in the living room and told her about his encounter with Monique Pavour. Juliette leaned back on her sofa, stretched with a cat's lazy grace. "Kincaid's old flame, huh? What's she look like? Did Sean manage to snag himself a hottie?"

Halsey shrugged. "I suppose. If you like that sort of thing." He relayed the conversation, as best he could remember it, to Juliette. "What did she mean about the Spanish Inquisition? I didn't get that."

"I'll bet you didn't. What did she order?"

"Two cappuccinos, nothing special."

"Was she nice or nasty to the barista?"

"Nice," he said. Why people wasted time making nice-nice and saying thank you to baristas and waiters was beyond him.

"What was she wearing?"

"Jeans and a sweatshirt. Some place called Miskatonic University. I've never heard of it."

"I'll bet you haven't. What's she look like again?"

"I didn't notice."

Juliette threw her head back and cackled. She sounded like a witch. "So you noticed all those details but you don't know what she looks like? You are the worst liar, Francis. You not only noticed her, you want to jump her."

"Can we change the subject?"

"Francis loves Monique!" she sang in a schoolgirl taunt.

"It doesn't matter," he said in exasperation. "She didn't know anything about Kincaid."

Juliette sat up straight, her face serious now. "*Au contraire.* I think she knows something. In fact, I'm almost sure of it."

"But she didn't say anything."

"Exactly. Let's say that she doesn't know where Kincaid is or why he pulled that vanishing act. Wouldn't she have asked you if you'd heard anything? Perhaps she didn't ask because she doesn't want to risk letting on that she *does* know something."

Halsey frowned. "You can't know that. She told me back in September that she hadn't heard from him since she told him she was getting married. He probably got jealous and gave up on her."

"Of course that's possible, But perhaps he cut off contact with her when he knew he was going to turn rogue. Didn't want people like you bothering her."

"Why should he care?"

"Because he still has feelings for her. Besides, Kincaid's always had a soft spot for the womenfolk. You should know that."

He supposed he should, but he didn't. Halsey didn't know those sort of things about the agents — he didn't care to. It didn't matter. What mattered were the jobs and which agents were most likely to complete the jobs quickly and under budget. The agents' personal lives didn't interest him.

"So," said Juliette. "How's your homework assignment coming along?"

Halsey smiled. He'd been waiting for this moment, had his speech prepared. "Here's the thing, Juliette. I'm hiring you. I'm paying you. And I'll pay you some more if you figure out where Kincaid is."

"Really?" Her eyes lit up with what looked like greed.

"Really. You see, I didn't like that stuff you said about making people tell me what they knew. That's just not my specialty. It's yours. That's why I'm hiring you."

"You don't want to get your hands dirty."

"Exactly. When all this is done, I still have to go back to the agency and I don't want anything that's going to cause bad blood. It doesn't matter what you do to someone, you're retired and you won't get in trouble. Do you understand?"

She looked thoughtful. "Yes, I see."

He smiled. What was a little more money out of his pocket? No big deal, and he'd have her do the dirty work. She was used to it. Used to it? Hell, she liked it.

Juliette stood up. "I'm going to get a glass of water. You want anything?"

"No, thanks," he replied.

Juliette walked into the kitchen. "I understand your situation. Although personally I think a little first-hand experience would do you a world of good."

"I'll pass."

She came back to the doorway. "I'll get my hands dirty," she said and the smile he heard in her voice made him look up at her. She had a shark's grin on her face and a silvery pistol in one hand. "If you insist," she said, and shot him.

Chapter Twenty-three

She was already at the diner when he arrived; she sat at a booth in the middle of the room, in plain sight of everyone. Of course he knew why. When meeting with shady characters, it was standard procedure to have plenty of witnesses close by.

Deirdre sat with a cup of coffee and a blueberry muffin on the table in front of her. All around her were twinkling Christmas lights and decorations, but none of the glittery light seemed to touch her. Around her servers wished holiday greetings and couples argued and children bounced with excitement, but Deirdre was still, the eye of the storm. As Sean observed her, she touched the inside pocket of her jacket as if reassuring herself that something — what, he wondered — was still there. She hadn't said why she wanted to talk, only that it was important. He was the one who'd insisted it wait until morning, when she'd had some sleep and would be more clear-headed. She'd given in, albeit grudgingly. He wondered if his advice had mattered, if she'd slept at all. It seemed unlikely. Even for a redhead she was pale, her eyes dark-shadowed, the eyes themselves with a dry sparkle to them.

Sean walked over to her, purposely taking the route that would put him in her sight long before he sat down. Surprising her would be a bad idea. He sat down and as he did so, she eased herself toward the outer edge of the booth, putting more distance between them. He wasn't offended. It was a smart move on her part. Shakespeare had said it best: *He must have a long spoon that must eat with the devil.*

Deirdre stared at him, he stared back. They were sizing each other up. He'd been keeping an eye on her as much as he could these last few days, but since she'd mostly kept to her apartment he'd had little chance for observation. She sent the obviously smitten teenager who lived nearby out on errands, once for groceries, and once for a small Christmas tree in a pot. She drove somewhere with the Christmas tree and a bag full of ornaments; he hadn't followed. Last night she'd gone out with a guy he hadn't recognized at first. It wasn't until Sean saw the guy hold the car door open for Deirdre that Sean knew who he was — the deputy who'd come cruising by a few times, who had once even knocked on Deirdre's door. Sean hoped the deputy was a good sort. He seemed so, from a distance, but appearances could be deceiving.

Sean wished he knew what Deirdre had been like before Anna's death. How much damage had he done? How great was the debt to be paid?

Deirdre said, "I need you to tell me something." She reached into her pocket and pulled out several photographs, slightly worse for wear. She found the one she wanted and placed it on the table. "Tell me who they are."

Sean took the photo. Of course. The Labor Day party. He'd tried to avoid the camera as much as he could — they all had tried — but there was only so much they could do without raising suspicions. Here was the entire Rogue's Gallery. "Richard of course. And me. Doug MacReady. Steve Wickersham. His brother Eddie too, though you can't see his face. And Walt...I don't recall his last name."

"Walt Sorensen?"

"Yes, that's it." Walt had been low on the totem pole, a glorified errand boy. No doubt with Richard and Doug gone, Walt had slunk back into the woodwork.

"He was in the group?"

Did her question mean she believed him? "Yes."

"Oh shit. Oh fuck *me*." The words dashed any faint hopes he'd had that Deirdre was Anna's twin in not just looks but in spirit, and he didn't know whether to feel disappointed or relieved. She leaned close to him. "Walt's brother is Leo Sorensen. The county sheriff. He's been keeping it all buried, I'm sure. And there's more. They've been looking for you."

She told him how she'd found his picture, then found his apartment and sneaked in looking for a sign of him, to find out what he knew; told him how Leo and Walt had come in and nearly discovered her, how she'd run into them at the Christmas tree farm. Sean admired her ingenuity and was alarmed that she could have gotten herself in trouble.

"Leo's told you nothing?" Sean asked. "What about the media? You get any calls from reporters?"

Deirdre shook her head. "Maybe they just couldn't get hold of me."

"They're tenacious. They'd have found you if they wanted to. If Leo's trying to bury it all, that would make sense." After a moment he asked, "Do you believe...what I told you?"

She didn't answer. She studied him, fidgeted with her napkin, ripping little tears into the edges. "Something you should know," she said. "I look like Anna but I'm not nice like she was. I wish that was different. I always wanted to be like her. Maybe she could forgive you. But she's gone, and now there's just me. I can't forgive you. I won't. Ever.

"So now that you know that, is there anything about your story you want to change?"

She was right, of course. He'd gone to her apartment that night hoping she would grant forgiveness and he could fool himself into thinking it was Anna's absolution he was receiving. A fool's hope, now dashed — but if forgiveness was not possible, perhaps amends were.

"It's true," he said. "I wish it wasn't, but it is."

"I'm starting to believe you," she said. "Not just your story, but Leo hiding things. He and Walt sweeping all this under the rug. Last night I was at a party, and Walt was there. He gave me this look, like he knew something I didn't, and was happy about it, but ashamed of himself too."

"Do you think that deputy's part of it?"

The instant he said it he knew he'd made a mistake. Deirdre went paler than ever, and the light of trust he'd seen in her eyes was snuffed out. "How do…were you spying on me?"

"I was worried about you."

She pushed her uneaten breakfast away and got up out of the booth.

"I wanted to be sure you were all right," he said. He didn't move. If he approached her who knew what she might do. She might have the pepper spray or his gun with her, and never mind that they were in a public place, she might use them.

"Leave me alone," she snapped.

"You can trust me," he said, knowing it was ridiculous even as he said it.

"Yeah, right." She put on her jacket, hoisted her purse onto one shoulder. "The way Anna trusted you?" she said scornfully, and walked out.

"Yes. Yes, that sounds fine. Thanks."

Leo hung up the phone, then lit a fresh cigarette off the still-hot butt that topped the pile in his ashtray. By New Year's all of this would be over and he could finally relax and quit this wretched habit.

On the other side of the desk a bleary-eyed Walt sat, his condition clearly not helped by the fog of cigarette smoke in the room. "Too much eggnog last night?" Leo asked him. The prospect of an end to matters made him relatively jovial.

"I saw Deirdre Monahan last night," Walt said. "You sure she's out of the loop?"

"Positive. It's all fixed. You didn't say anything to her?"

"Not a word."

"Good. If she flies off the handle, send her to me. I'll take care of her." Leo noted that Walt still looked uneasy. "Second thoughts? Doesn't matter. It's too late for those."

"It was too late when I joined up with Richard Blaine," Walt said bitterly.

"Why did you fall for all that, anyway?" asked Leo.

Walt said nothing for a little while. "Because Richard made us believe. In him. In what he wanted to do. We believed in ourselves, we thought we could make a difference. You wanted to do things for him, not because he bullied you into it."

"Sounds like bullshit to me."

"He was better than you."

Leo stubbed out his cigarette. Only the knowledge that he had things under control kept him from breaking his brother's nose. "You owe me, Walt. Don't you ever forget it. I could have thrown you to the wolves, but I didn't."

"I know. But you didn't do it for me, you did it for yourself. Don't worry, after New Year's I'm heading out of here. Going some place to start over fresh. I'll send you a postcard." Walt stood up and walked out of Leo's office, the smoke swirling in the air behind him.

"You do that," Leo said, though Walt was gone. Then he smiled, lit another smoke, and strolled out into the main office, to Nick Eliot's desk. "Nick," he said with all the holiday *bonhomie* he could muster. "I've got some good news for you."

Chapter Twenty-four

It was the afternoon of Christmas eve, and Jason Lund's first attempt at wrapping a Christmas present wasn't going as well as he'd hoped. He knew he had only himself to blame. In years past he'd put the presents in gift bags, and no one complained. More recently he'd wheedled or bribed his kid sister Jewel into wrapping presents. He wasn't pleased with the results of his wrapping job so far — it was all mismatched patterns and heavy on the Scotch tape — but if he asked for Jewel's help (or God forbid, his mother's help) there would be questions about who this present was for. He would have to answer, and he'd never hear the end of it.

Jason was fifteen, gawky and scrawny, couldn't get a date to save his life, He was also in love, or at least in the throes of a crush, and he'd told no one. Least of all the object of his love — Deirdre. He didn't tell his friends or family because he knew they would laugh, and he didn't tell Deirdre because he couldn't stand it if she laughed. So he did the only thing he knew to prove his love — bought *Good Omens* by Neil Gaiman and Terry Pratchett, his favorite book ever, and was now wrapping it up for Deirdre. As he clumsily taped the wrapping together, he imagined how it might go, played it in his mind like a movie. He'd walk down to her door and knock. She'd have her hair down instead of wearing it in a ponytail like he usually did. He'd give her the present and she'd unwrap it right there, and her eyes would light up and she'd say *Oh! I've always wanted to read this!* He'd somehow stay home from the church social tonight and invite Deirdre over and they could watch one of the *Lord of the Rings* movies and maybe smoke some of that weed he'd scored, and maybe they'd kiss on the couch, and that's where the film jammed in the projector.

Mom and Dad were out somewhere doing last-minute errands. Jewel sat at the dining room table, reading the paper. She always did that, never missed a day. "Hey, Braniac," he said, sitting down at the table next to her. "What you reading that for?"

"Current events for school," she said, not looking up at him.

"Dummy, school's out until New Year's."

"Dummy, there might be something interesting going on. I don't want to miss out."

"It's Christmas eve. Take a break. *A Christmas Story*'s coming on, you want to watch it?"

Jewel stared at the newspaper, but he could tell she was caving in. "Maybe."

"I'll make Jiffy Pop."

"I'm there." She pushed the paper to one side. He was getting up from the table when a photo on the page made him stop and look at the paper closely.

His first thought was to wonder why Deirdre's picture was in the paper, and who was that guy she was with — but it wasn't her. Still, the woman looked so much like Deirdre he had to find out more.

Jason read, and overheard fragments of gossip and parental conversation came back to him. His mother remarking on how upset Deirdre looked and his father saying, *Well, who wouldn't look upset, considering.* Jewel and Jason asking why they weren't going to the tree farm like they always did at Christmas, and Mom hushing them. Jewel saying later that she didn't know why Mom was making a fuss, everyone knew something bad had happened at the farm and the people who owned it were dead but no one knew why. Jason kept reading. Was this why?

"Jason? Hello, Earth to Jason?" called out Jewel from the living room. "Where's the Jiffy Pop?"

"Chill, sis. Something I got to do first."

Jason ran to his room, got the wrapped present, then grabbed the newspaper and went out the front door. It was freezing and he'd forgotten his shoes — the cold soaked through his socks but he barely noticed. He wasn't sure if he wanted Deirdre to be home or not. *Merry Christmas*, he'd say. *Don't kill the messenger, but have you seen this?* He found himself hoping she wouldn't be home. He could leave the paper on her doorstep. That way she wouldn't get mad at him. He could leave the present too. That way she wouldn't laugh at him.

She was just getting home. She had her keys in one hand and a grocery bag in the other. "Hi Jason." She smiled even though she looked tired, and he fell in love with her all over again.

He gave her the present first. "This is for you," he said. "Merry Christmas."

She set down the groceries and took the present, looked as if she didn't know what to say. If she laughed, he would die, but she smiled again. God, she was pretty. "Thanks so much, You're the sweetest guy," she said, and then gave him a quick hug. Her hair smelled really nice.

"Something else." He didn't want to spoil it, but he had to tell her. He couldn't take the easy way out and leave the paper on her doorstep, the way he'd hoped. Jason gave her the paper.

She read it, and her face went white. Like Lars Bunsen's did, that time they were out skating and his foot went through the ice. *Adrenaline dump*, Lars said later. Jason saw Deirdre's hands hang on to the paper so tight her knuckles were white as her face; he thought she might tear the paper in half.

She looked up at him with eyes like a cat's. She was beautiful and scary and for the first time in years he prayed — he asked God to please not let it be him she was mad at.

"Is this today's paper?" she asked. When he nodded, she said, "Thanks for giving this to me. For letting me know." She ran a hand through her hair.

"Are you OK?"

"I have something to do." Deirdre put the present in her handbag and ran down the hall to the steps, holding the newspaper in one hand, leaving her groceries on the doormat. She leaped off the third step from the bottom and hit the ground running, then got into her truck and was out of the parking lot in no time.

He stood there for a bit, even though he couldn't see or hear her truck any more. Jason turned and started walking back to his apartment, when there was the roar of an engine and the crunch of tires on snow. He looked to see if it was Deirdre.

It wasn't Deirdre's green truck, but a gray van. A man got out of it and went up the stairs much the way Deirdre had gone down them — fast, taking them two at a time. At first Jason thought it might be the cop Nick, who he'd seen coming around to talk to Deirdre a few times. Jason didn't mind, Nick was pretty cool for a cop; he didn't give the kids shit without good reason. But it wasn't Nick, it was another guy, an older, balding guy. Looked like Jason's uncle Bob. Until he got close, and Jason saw his eyes — dark and angry. Scary eyes, like bullet holes. The guy had a newspaper in his hand — Jason couldn't tell for sure but he thought it might be the same one he'd given Deirdre.

"Is Deirdre here?" the man asked. He didn't yell, he didn't have a fancy voice like bad guys in the movies, but there was something freaky about him all the same.

"No, she's not." Jason hoped he sounded braver than he felt.

"Do you know where she is?"

Jason shook his head.

The man stopped and looked out at the streets, as if he hoped to find Deirdre's truck there. Then he turned and looked at Jason. It was the weirdest thing — the guy was so ordinary-looking except for his eyes. It wasn't hypnosis or anything. More like when Jason had seen a snake at the zoo and couldn't look away from those unblinking reptile eyes.

"Did she see this?" asked the guy, holding up the newspaper. His voice was softer now.

Jason didn't know what to say. He had no idea who this guy was, if he was a friend of Deirdre's or not. To be honest, the guy looked a bit crazy. Crazy in the same way Deirdre looked when Jason gave her the paper. "Yeah," Jason said. "Just a few minutes ago. She went that way," he said, pointing. "I don't know where."

The guy smiled. Jason thought the guy had an idea where Deirdre had gone. "If she gets back, can you tell her Sean wants to talk to her?"

Jason nodded.

"Thanks." The guy turned, and was heading down the hall and down the stairs, faster than Jason would have believed a guy older than his dad could move. Before he knew it, the guy was gone, heading in the same direction as Deirdre.

Jason shivered, although he was just now feeling how cold it was. He got back to his place in time to stop Jewel from burning the Jiffy Pop, and tried not to think about what was going on with Deirdre.

There wasn't a Christmas eve party going on at the Silas County Sheriff's Department, not in the strictest sense. But there was a relaxed atmosphere that went well with the decorations on the walls and the Christmas cards on desks and bulletin boards, and the only downside for Leo was Sharon's scented candles, which assaulted your nose with fake cinnamon, eggnog, or pine when you walked by, depending on which candle was lit.

As afternoon eased toward dusk, Leo did paperwork and smoked light cigarettes — his strategy until New Year's when he would go cold turkey. The cigarettes tasted like shit, but he didn't mind. He didn't mind anything — not Sharon's stinky candles, not that damn Nutcracker music that Rodriguez wouldn't stop playing. Everything was under control.

He plugged away at his computer, fingers tapping over the keys. The door to his office was ajar and distantly he could hear some sort of fuss from the front desk, but paid it no heed.

"You fucking rat bastard."

She didn't yell it. Deirdre's tone was almost conversational, as if commenting on the weather. Leo looked up from his computer and saw Deirdre standing there with today's newspaper in her hands. He suppressed a grimace — he'd hoped that when he gave Nick an extra day off yesterday that Nick would have taken Deirdre with him. It didn't matter where — to his parents', to the local Winterfest, to the fucking House on the Rock — as long as she was out of town when the story came out in the paper. He'd make sure Nick got all the shit jobs when he got back to work.

"Can I help you?" he asked, as neutrally as he could.

"How could you do this?" Her voice was cold. That coldness worried him more than if she'd been screaming and yelling. "How can you say this is what happened?"

"Because that's what I learned in my investigation."

"The hell it is!" Now she yelled it, now people were looking to see what was going on. He would have to shut her up soon. God, why couldn't this woman just let it go? "You can't do this, can't call Anna a whore."

"There are witnesses — "

"Did you bribe them or threaten them?"

Threats, mostly. Walt's buddies from the group were easy. Their desperation to save their own hides had outweighed any lingering sentimentality and they'd provided all the scandalous quotes he'd needed for his story of lust, jealousy, revenge, and remorse. Getting Rose Flynn to rule that Richard Blaine was a suicide was another matter — he'd had to dig up some good dirt on her. More specifically on her godson, who'd been a peeping tom a couple years ago. He'd never been charged, but he always could be, and there would go his college scholarship and his chance to do something besides flip burgers for a living.

Deirdre went on. "It doesn't matter. I *know* what happened."

"Do you now?" Did she? How? Had someone spilled the beans?

"And I'm sure this reporter will love to hear what I have to say."

Time to play his trump card. Leo smiled, and watched Deirdre recoil slightly. "She won't believe you. Why should she? You've had a history of — how shall I put it? — unstable behavior lately. Lost your job because you assaulted a customer. Not the most reliable witness, are you?"

Deirdre's fists clenched.

"Care to spend tonight in jail for assaulting a police officer?"

She said nothing, just looked at him. He looked back. Finally she turned and walked away. As she went out the front door he heard Sharon say to one of the deputies: "I told you that bitch was crazy."

Leo shut his door, picked up the phone and dialed Walt's cell. "She just left here," he said. "Follow her and tell me where she goes and who she sees."

He saw her fling the door open and come stomping down the steps. She had the newspaper clenched in one hand. The other hand wiped at her face, leaving newsprint smudges — against her fair skin, they looked like bruises. If only he'd gotten to her five minutes sooner, it would have been better for them both. Now he was sure she'd done something foolhardy, not that he blamed her. When he'd seen that newspaper story he'd known who was behind the lies and why, and would have happily murdered Sheriff Leo

Sorensen. There would have been no trip to the confessional to repent of that one.

Deirdre stalked over to her truck, and before she could unlock it he slid the van's door open and hauled her inside, then shut the door behind her.

"What the — " She stopped and recognized Sean. "Let me go."

Sean asked, "What happened in there?"

"I said let me go."

"What did you say to the sheriff?"

"Why do you care?"

"Because Anna doesn't deserve this," he said, holding up the paper, then tossing it aside. "And you can't fix things if that sheriff throws you in jail."

Deirdre sat down on the floor of the van, twisting the newspaper in her hands. He sat down in front of her. "I can help you," Sean said. "I can help clear her name and get the truth out there, but you have to trust me."

For the first time she looked at him without hatred or mistrust. After a moment she said, "You really did care for her." Her voice was soft with wonder. "But when people know what happened, won't you go to jail?"

Perhaps he would. More likely his former employers would find him and take him away to...who knew where? Or they'd just send someone like Juliette to take him out. If he did end up in jail, would that be so different from his life as it was now? In reply, he said only, "Probably."

She nodded. "OK. I trust you."

Chapter Twenty-five

The night glittered with Christmas lights of every hue and variety: simple icicle strands of white, flashing rainbow hues, large-bulb lights with chipped paint that had seen holiday duty for decades. Other drivers were scarce; for the most part everyone was where they needed to be. With friends, with family. Gathering at restaurants and churches. Occasionally there were groups, carolers mostly, or a family bringing home the tree. Most people were snug behind doors, safe in the comfort of hearty food and the company of family and friends.

Deirdre wondered if these people looked outside and saw the green truck driving through the night, and if so, did they pay any mind, or did they spare a kind thought or prayer for those out in the cold? If the revelers could see the cab of the truck, what would they make of what they saw? Deirdre and Sean, both heedless of the festive night, wanting only to get what they needed and avoid trouble with Leo.

They had gone to Sean's motel after they left the sheriff's station. There were things he needed, he'd said. She waited in her truck while he went inside; she wore no watch and couldn't tell if he was in there longer than he needed to be, or if her anxiety made time slow down. While she waited she glanced out the window, looking for cop cars or for Leo. Deirdre regretted her hasty words to Leo, for she hadn't missed the gleam in his eye when she'd said: *I know what happened.* The more she thought about it, the longer she waited for Sean, regret turned to anxiety and then to fear. For if Leo had gone to such lengths already to hide the truth, how much further might he be willing to go?

Sean finally emerged from his motel room. He paused, giving the parking lot a quick glance, then came down the steps and walked to her truck. At first she could see nothing different about his appearance, but then realized that the way he walked and moved had changed. There was a peculiar lightness to his step, and when he stopped, paused by the door of her truck to look around once more, she thought of a wolf sniffing the air for hints of prey.

"Let's go," he said.

"Where to?"

"The tree farm."

She put the truck in gear and started the drive. Dusk was nearly over, and the sky was a deep blue, as if the sea and the air had swapped places. Driving east to the tree farm was like diving into the water, going deeper with every mile, and who knew what they'd find as they dove.

"What will we do when we get there?" she asked.

"Richard kept most of the details about things in his head. He didn't write much down."

"That's why Leo and Walt couldn't find anything."

Sean nodded. "He did have some documentation, though. There's a safe hidden in his basement, and he only gave the location and combination to his number two guy, Doug MacReady, and to me."

"What's in the safe?"

He shook his head. "I don't know. I never actually opened it or saw what was in it. Richard just told me where it was and the combination, in case something happened to him."

Deirdre didn't look over at Sean. Something had happened to Richard, and Sean was the something. Not for the first time since they'd left the sheriff's station did she think she must be crazy to be alone with the man who'd admitted that he killed Anna and Richard, among others. That was why Deirdre had insisted on driving tonight; it gave her some control of the situation. The thought of being Sean's passenger was too frightening — what if he was really a crazy, cold-blooded killer? What would happen if he turned from Jekyll to Hyde? Too late, she knew that merely being the driver was no protection. She was at his mercy.

Deirdre felt a sudden longing to see Nick. She wished she'd taken him up on his offer to visit his parents for the holidays. They could be out eating Chinese food or looking at Christmas lights. Of course, if she'd done that she wouldn't have seen the newspaper. For a moment, she wished she hadn't, that she could have been ignorant of the slur on Anna's reputation and gotten on with her own life. Shame flooded through her, bitter and scalding. What was she thinking? That she would let people think the worst of Anna, just so she could spend Christmas with Nick? Was she that awful of a person?

A traffic signal was red, and she took advantage of the stop, covered her face with her hands. She wanted all this to be over. She wanted to somehow close her mind down for the next few days and wake up to find Anna's reputation restored, Sean Kincaid out of her life, Leo Sorensen disgraced and dismissed from his job. But her mind stayed awake; too awake, she could feel strain gnawing at her.

"Deirdre?"

She looked up to see Sean holding out a hip flask. "This might help you feel better."

She hesitated only a moment, then took the flask. Before drinking she looked at the flask itself: black leather with a monogram that looked like real silver. There were no words engraved, just initials: M-S. Deirdre briefly wondered who M was, then lifted the flask to her lips and drank. She was half expecting cheap whiskey or some high-grain stuff like Everclear. What she tasted was some liquor so smooth and rich-tasting she took no more than a small swallow. It was obviously precious, and not to be drunk lightly. "My God," she asked, "what is this?"

He smiled, and for the first time she understood why Anna had wanted her to meet him. "It's cognac. Courvoisier."

She made a mental note to remember that name — if everything worked out well, if she cleared Anna's name, when she got a job, she'd buy a bottle of this stuff and celebrate with Nick. Deirdre felt the warmth of the cognac spreading through her body. Her hands loosed their death-grip on the steering wheel. "Thank you," she said as she continued driving. "Who's M?"

His smile faded. "Someone I used to know."

"Kill the lights."

Walt obeyed. Leo cracked the window, tossed a butt out into the frigid night, lit another cigarette off the dashboard lighter. The taillights were tiny pinpoints, but Leo said, "Slow down."

"We're going to lose them," Walt said.

"Doesn't matter. I know where they're going."

Leo felt Walt's glance. He paid it no mind, let himself focus on those taillights. Despite everything he felt calm. The pieces were in place now. He had answers, could stop wondering. It had all been clear to him when Walt had called, saying that he'd seen Deirdre talking with Sam Lewis. Leo had half-listened while Walt yammered *Where's he been all this time* and *What's he talking to her for* and *Do you think he told her stuff?* He half-listened and made sure his gun was loaded, stuffed two extra clips into his jacket. He said, "Do I have to draw you a picture? He ratted you out. Never mind it. Just get here fast."

They were close now. Leo made sure he had everything: the gun of course, his nightstick, and a can of mace. That should be enough. Judging from the picture Walt had taken with his cell, he was up against a guy who looked like an accountant and a skinny little girl. He could handle them, and he would. Leo took out his gun, checked it once more, made sure there was a round in the chamber.

"Jesus, you're not going to — " Walt didn't finish.

"Think of it as some loose ends from that bomb you guys set," Leo said. "That's all. Does that make you feel better?"

While Deirdre drove, Sean checked the mirrors. He wouldn't put it past Leo to put a tail on Deirdre, and there was Leo's brother Walt to consider. Walt would recognize him, and though Walt was no genius even he would know something hinky was going on when "Sam," who'd been missing in action since the time Richard disappeared and Anna died, suddenly showed up in the company of Anna's cousin. It was impossible to tell if they were being followed. Occasionally he saw headlights behind them but that was all — it might have been anyone. The moon was full tonight and its light would have helped, but now it was behind clouds, and he could tell nothing about who the pursuer, if there was one, might be.

When they arrived at the farm, she asked if she should park some distance away. He hesitated, then decided it would be best to just get in and get out. Closer would be better. She nodded, and parked. After she set the brake she reached into the glove box and took out his gun. Wordlessly she handed it to him, and wordlessly he took it. He sighed as he holstered it; he'd felt almost naked without it, had not slept well without its reassuring bulk under his pillow.

The snow by the gate was unmarred by tire tracks or footprints. No one was here, unless they'd gone in the back way, which he knew was difficult at best with no easy access roads. First he climbed the fence, then she did, and they went at a fast walk down the road to the house, keeping close to the trees. It was slow going, for the road had not been plowed. The silence was complete save for their breathing and the crunch of their boots in the snow. The moon was visible now and its light on the snow was nearly bright enough for them to cast shadows. The light did not reassure him; it illuminated everything, took away comforting shadows. When they reached the house, the moonlight only served to make the house look even darker and more abandoned than it was. It might have been deserted for years, not just a few months.

And yet, if Deirdre hadn't been with him he might have enjoyed himself. It was like old times. Almost.

"The doors are locked, and I don't have a key," Deirdre said. " But I broke a window when I went looking in here. It might still be open."

They walked to the back of the house. Sean kept looking behind them to make sure they weren't being pursued, and to keep from looking at the house where he'd spent so much time. Where he'd plotted and deceived, and also been happy. His left hand began to burn again. The sensation intensified as they climbed in through the broken window. It was as cold inside the house as it was outside; perhaps even colder, though that couldn't be true, could it? Sean took a small flashlight from his jacket and his gun from its holster, and with the flashlight in his left hand and the gun in his right, and with Deirdre following close behind him, he went to the stairs that led down to the basement.

It was exactly as he remembered it. The big octagonal table that was ostensibly for poker and other card games, but really was the place where Richard and his friends plotted. So many nights he'd sat here with them, playing a game far more complicated than any variety of poker. It all seemed very far away and long ago to him now.

The bookshelf was on the far wall. He knelt down to look at the bottom shelf. Deirdre knelt beside him and he gave her the flashlight, holstered his gun. The bottom shelf was full of old encyclopedias, forestry textbooks, and a couple of outdated phone books — the sort of books a person might be reluctant to throw away, but that no one would want to borrow. Sean took the books off the shelf, stacked them on the floor. Deirdre shone the light into the back of the bookshelf. Nothing was obvious at a casual or even a careful glance. Sean took the flashlight and angled it back to look in the corners — there. A thin gap, narrow as a fingernail. He took his knife out of its leg sheath, tried to pry off the board, but the knife's point was too wide. He slipped the knife back into the sheath, then took his Swiss Army knife from his back pocket, unfolded one blade. He slipped the point into the groove and pulled back, gently and carefully. A rectangle of wood came away, and they were looking at the dial of a wall safe.

He spun the dial, wondering if the numbers had any significance to Richard. Probably not. Richard had been clever. Perhaps too clever. As Sean spun the dial one last time it occurred to him that it might be a trap. Richard might have put something nasty in here. But there was no other choice. He opened the safe door.

No surprises. Just two manila envelopes, one thick and one medium-size. Sean gave them to Deirdre, who started to open one. He shook his head at her. "Later," he said. She didn't protest but stuffed the envelopes inside her jacket, tucking them into the waistband of her jeans. He put the Swiss Army knife back in his pocket, then closed the safe but didn't replace the panel or the books. An uneasy feeling was on him, and he wanted to get out of here.

He kept the flashlight on only long enough for them to get to the stairs. When they started up he turned off the flashlight and put it away, then took out his gun. Sean crouched low as they reached the top of the stairs. Deirdre was beside him, also keeping low to the floor. Moonlight shone in through the window, the house was utterly still, and they both heard the noise from outside. Footsteps.

Sean motioned to Deirdre to stay where she was. Slowly he eased himself along the floor to the living room. The curtains were drawn, but he was able to peer through the crack between the curtain and the window sill. A man stood by the trees, obscured by the shadows. But there was enough moonlight to make out the letters on his cap: SCSD. Silas County Sheriff's Department. Leo Sorensen.

He waited for the man to move. Sheriff Sorensen remained still, making no sound. Sean slipped back over to Deirdre.

"Leo's out there," he murmured. "Go to the back door. I'll distract him and keep him occupied. When I do, you get out the back door and go as fast as you can to the truck. Don't stop for anything."

"What about you?"

"I'll find a way back."

"What will you do to Leo?"

He didn't answer.

Deirdre nodded, went slow and careful. Again he felt admiration. He watched as she made her way to the kitchen door — he could just see it from his position in the living room. She stood by the door, bounced on the balls of her feet to limber up her legs, then put her hand on the doorknob. She closed her eyes briefly, took in a deep breath, and looked over at him. She nodded. She was ready.

So was he. Sean picked up a marble bookend from the end table. With a silent apology to Anna for damaging her pretty house, he threw the bookend through the window at the far end of the living room, then opened the front door. Dimly he heard Deirdre open the back door and start running. He stepped out onto the front porch and saw Leo running toward the broken window. Sean fired at the running figure and missed, the man turned to face him. The man's cap had fallen off and the moonlight revealed not Leo but Walt, with a look of panic on his face and no gun in his hand.

Trap. Sean heard a footstep in the snow behind him, and as he turned and raised his gun to fire, two rounds hit him in the chest, like twin blows from a sledgehammer. The world spun and went black, and he toppled off the porch into the snow.

Walt stared, feeling snow-cold inside and out. Bad enough that Leo had used him for live bait, but Sam had shot at him and just barely missed — Walt had actually felt the bullet go by. Now Leo had shot Sam, who lay gasping, his eyes staring at nothing Walt could see.

A smiling Leo walked over to Sam, stooped and picked up the gun Sam had dropped. "Now let's just — " Leo stopped, turned and stared.

Walt followed the direction of Leo's look and saw Deirdre standing some distance away, arms crossed over her torso, staring at Walt, Leo, and the man who lay dying in the snow. She turned and ran.

Leo tossed Sam's gun to Walt. "Finish him off," Leo ordered and ran after Deirdre.

Walt held the gun, looked down at Sam, whose breaths were long and rasping now. A head shot would finish things but he couldn't bring himself to do it. Never mind that he'd participated in the killing of more than three hundred people — he had just helped plan it, he hadn't actually *done* it. Walt's was the squeamishness of a life-long meat eater who wouldn't be able to wring a chicken's neck if his life depended on it.

He walked a couple yards away, looked up at the moon, waiting for that rasping breathing to stop. He'd tell Leo that Sam had given up the ghost on his own. By then Leo would have dealt with Deirdre, and they could go home and forget all this.

The breathing went on. Couldn't the man just die already? Why was it taking so long? Finally it stopped. Walt sighed, but his relief was short-lived, interrupted by another sound — a wet cracking that seemed to come from behind him. Walt fell, dead before he hit the ground.

Sean tried to pull the knife out, but it was stuck fast in Walt's neck, its blade severing the spinal cord just below the brain stem. He looked quickly for his gun but couldn't find it. There was no time to search for it. He started in the direction Deirdre and Leo had gone, trying to run but achieving only a drunken-looking lurch.

The Kevlar vest had saved him from Leo's shots, but there was blunt force trauma to be reckoned with, and the pain was bad. Worse still was his heart, hammering wildly and erratically; he tried to breathe slowly, tried to make his heart resume a normal beat but it would not obey. *Not a heart attack, please.* If it was, he and Deirdre were done for.

Sean heard a yell and a curse from somewhere in the trees. He forced himself into a run, as fast as the pain and his skittering heart would let him.

He heard a scream, and ran faster.

From the moment she ran out the back door, Deirdre tried to think about one thing only — getting out of here as fast as she could. Somewhere her mistrust of Sean had become reliance on his obvious experience, and though she knew he was right that they split up, it was a terribly vulnerable feeling to be running through the snow, the envelopes taken from Richard's safe clutched against her body. The crunch of her boots in the snow seemed so loud; surely Leo could hear her blundering away, yet she dared not go more slowly and quietly. Get away from them, get to the truck, get the hell out of here.

Then the gunshots. First one, then another two in quick succession. She knew she should keep running but she stopped and looked, as helpless to resist as Lot's wife had been. Deirdre saw Sean stagger, drop his gun, topple into the snow. She made some small exhalation, a reverse gasp. Dead. Surely he was dead. She was on her own.

The thought froze her for a crucial second, and Leo saw her. Deirdre turned and ran, no more worries about the noise of her progress. Now she needed to not just reach the truck, but avoid Leo should he decide to shoot her as well.

Her first impulse was to flee up the road to the gate, but that would leave her an easy target. Too easy. If he had to catch her, let him work for it. She veered into the rows of trees, zigzagging as much as she dared but always heading toward the gate. Behind her she heard Leo blundering through the trees, could smell the used-cigarette reek of him. He called out something, some order for her to stop, then she heard the sound of cracking branches and an incoherent curse — he must have fallen or run into a tree. Deirdre tried to run faster; her legs were strong from all those nights dancing at the Stagger Inn, but the cold seared her lungs and the snow threatened to trip her up and the branches slapped at her face and body. Faster, she had to go faster. She stopped zigzagging and ran straight, ran fast.

Leo's tackle caught her around the legs and they both crashed to the ground. She twisted in the snow, trying to get away from him. He grabbed for her jacket and the files she carried; she flung a handful of snow and pine needles at his face. Leo let out an animal growl and now his hands were going around her throat. Deirdre felt their meaty grip and knew taking the files wasn't enough for him now — he was going to kill her. Something seized her; not terror so much as anger. Knowing she had one chance and vowing to make it count, she hooked her hands into stiff claws and went not for the hands starting their death grip on her neck — she'd never pry those huge hands loose — but went for his face.

She went hard and fast, dug her nails in. She felt her right thumb strike the orbit of his eye and did not pull back but instead shoved in, and down, and out. Leo's scream split the night's quiet as he let go of her neck and staggered away, hands clasped to his face. Deirdre dropped her prize into the snow, got to her feet, and started running again.

Her legs trembled and a stitch hurt her side but she ran, fueled by both her victory and the knowledge that if he caught her again he would tear her to pieces. Now the truck was visible in the distance, and she felt the beginnings of relief. Almost there, almost there.

A whooping sound, like a baseball bat swung through the air, but instead of the crack of the ball there was an explosion of pain in her right hip. Her leg went numb and she fell, then rolled over to see Leo standing above her, his left hand cupped over the bleeding hole in his face, his remaining eye blazing with rage, and the nightstick raised high in his right hand.

It was as if the numbness in her leg had spread to her mind. She was looking at death, and was afraid, but not much. Mostly she felt a sense of detached wonder that this was how it ended, and hoped that Leo would make it quick. She shut her eyes and waited for the blow.

It never came.

A soft thud as the nightstick fell into the snow. The sound of feet scuffling. Deirdre opened her eyes and saw Leo standing there, both hands flailing behind him, then scrabbling at his throat, where she saw something black, a cord or wire, tightening mercilessly.

Numb, Deirdre wondered who could be doing this. Leo fell to his knees and Deirdre saw Sean behind Leo. Impossible, but it was him. Sean didn't look at her. He was focused only on the job at hand. He ignored Leo's struggles and the look on his face was one of concentration, of a man performing a task that was difficult and somewhat tedious — and familiar. *Of course,* Deirdre thought. *He's done this before.*

She didn't want to see that look on Sean's face but even a peripheral glance at Leo was more than she wanted, his face turning red-purple and a look of naked terror in his eye. Then, thankfully, Leo pitched down into the snow. Still Sean kept the cord tight.

Deirdre tried to speak, let out a croak, then found her voice. "He's dead," she said. "You can stop, he's dead."

"It's best to be sure," he said, not looking up at her. As if to prove him right, Leo's limbs twitched, spasmed; his hands clutched at nothing. Then he was still. After another minute Sean released his hold. He backed away from Leo and sat down. He looked awful — his face was ice-white and his hands were shaking. Then he asked, "Are you all right?"

Deirdre wanted to laugh. Was *she* all right? *He* was the one who'd been shot, for God's sake. But she seemed to be all right; her hip hurt but feeling had come back into her leg. "I'm OK."

"What's wrong with your hand?"

"Nothing." What was he talking about? She held up her right hand, looked at it, and understood. "That's Leo's. How did... he shot you."

He laid a hand over his chest. "Vest. Kevlar vest." Sean tensed, seemed to be gathering his strength. Then he was up and on his feet, though none too steadily. "Go home," he said. "I'll take care of this."

Deirdre also got to her feet. Her right leg trembled, then decided it would hold her up for now. Her hip throbbed. "Where's Walt?" she asked.

"Dead." He stared down at Leo's body, and for the first time he saw what Deirdre had done to him. Sean seemed impressed. He nodded. "Good work."

Deirdre felt unreal. It was too much, the events of the last hour. A need to do something — laugh, scream — bubbled up. She caught sight of her right hand again, streaked with Leo's blood, and turning away from Sean she leaned against a tree and threw up. She was beyond embarrassment, just wanted this nightmare to be over. Still gagging, she thrust her hand into the snow, rubbing it into the snow until the blood — most of it, anyway — washed away. Her hand was numb, her midsection hurt, her hip still throbbed, and her throat burned but despite all this she felt better. Able to do things like walk, get to her truck, drive home.

"Go home," Sean said again. He put himself in motion, then began going through Leo's pockets. "Damn," he muttered.

"What are you doing?"

"Looking for his keys. I have to get these bodies hidden somewhere."

"Can't you…" She thought of the movies, with their vague talk of removals. "Can't you call someone?"

He shook his head. "I quit. They didn't want me to go after Richard. No one to call. Walt must have the keys." Sean started walking back to the house. Deirdre followed him. "Deirdre, please go home."

"I'll help you."

"No."

"You saved my life. I'll help you. And then we're done."

She could tell that he wanted to refuse. If he'd been up to it he would have scooped her up and carried her to the truck, tossed her in and ordered her to go home, but he wasn't up to it. Looking at his white face and shaking limbs, she wasn't sure he was up to much at all. He nodded, and they went to find Walt and search his pockets for the keys.

Deirdre watched as the car rolled down the road. At first it seemed slow, too slow, and she worried that it had been for nothing. But the car picked up speed, half rolling and half sliding down the icy road, until it smashed through the flimsy guardrail, sending pieces of rotten wood flying. It went over the ledge and landed on the frozen lake. The car's weight and impact punched a hole in the ice with a loud crack, and the car tilted and started sinking. For a moment it seemed it might get hung up on the ice, but then water poured into the driver-side window they'd left open, flooding the car.

She could see the figures in the car — Walt in the driver' seat, Leo in the passenger's seat. Though they were both dead already, it was hard not to be alarmed at the way the icy water enveloped them. The water filled the car's interior, and after that it went down quickly, slipping under the surface with no noise save for bubbles. The headlights shone still, ghostly and opaque under the ice.

Deirdre shuddered, thought she felt Sean shudder in tandem. It had been hard work these past two hours. They'd found Walt's keys and then his car, which Walt had thoughtfully driven onto the property — it seemed Leo had the key to the gate. Sean had driven the car close to the house and they'd somehow managed to get both bodies into the trunk of the car. That had been the worst part. Deirdre was still astonished at how heavy the two men had been; unresisting and yet difficult to move. After that she'd let Sean rest, for his color wasn't improving and she could tell he was in pain. She hunted down Sean's gun, and Leo's gun, which Leo had dropped while chasing her through the trees. She'd found those, and she'd also shut the front and back doors to the house.

They drove, she in her truck and he in Walt's car, to Deer's Head Lake, to one of the twisty roads that were ostensibly closed at this time of year but which always attracted daring truck drivers and snowmobilers. Not the best solution, probably, for what would Leo and Walt be doing out here? But it was all they could think of. Sean had said if luck was with them, the car and the bodies wouldn't be found until spring, by which time the bodies would be far gone enough to hide the real cause of death.

As she watched, the bubbles diminished and ceased. The headlights' glow did not fade but abruptly winked out. Sean, standing beside her, muttered something that sounded like, "Keep you company."

"What did you say?" she whispered.

He didn't answer. She didn't think he'd heard her. He was paler than ever, and as she looked at him he went to his knees in the snow. He was looking at the lake as if hypnotized. Then he closed his eyes, said something. It sounded like a name. Something like Mona. Still kneeling, he sat back on his heels, arms wrapped around himself. Deirdre reached out to him, realizing that she had to —

Leave him.

She stopped, unsure of where that idea had come from. Now that the notion was here, it seemed rather appealing. Yes, Sean had saved her life, but if it wasn't for him her life wouldn't have been in danger. If it wasn't for him she wouldn't have had to help hide bodies, had to gouge a man's eye out, had to worry about what would happen when Leo didn't show up for work.

If it wasn't for him, Anna would be alive.

All she had to do was run to her truck and drive away. Bulletproof vest or no, he was hurt already and she could almost see the cold sapping the life out of him. He might make it back. He might find a ride, somehow, even in the middle of nowhere. If he didn't, well, he wouldn't suffer much. They said freezing to death wasn't a bad way to go. You just went to sleep and didn't wake up, like in that Jack London story she'd read in school. His debt for Anna would be paid in full.

Deirdre felt herself move, but somehow couldn't tell which way her body was moving. Until she reached down and pulled Sean up by the arm. "Come on," she said. "Come on. Let's go."

When they were in the truck she cranked the heater up to full and drove back to Lakeside. With the heater's warmth and a couple shots from his hip flask he revived somewhat and was able to make it up the stairs to her apartment. She was glad, for there was no way she could have carried him up, not with her limbs shaking with exhaustion and her hip a steady drumbeat of pain.

They stepped over her forgotten groceries — it seemed like years ago that Jason had given her the newspaper — and got into the apartment. "Just rest," she said, and guided him to the couch.

He didn't lie down, but asked if she had anything for pain. She went to the medicine chest and got the bottle of Vicodin left over from a root canal six months ago. Sean dry-swallowed two and lay down, and either passed out or fell asleep in seconds.

Deirdre took one of the Vicodin herself, for her hip. Exhausted as she was, she would not sleep. She had to find out what was in those envelopes they'd fought so hard for. She'd wanted to know what had happened. Now she would.

While Sean Kincaid slept, she sat down at her tiny dining room table, the two manila envelopes in front of her. "Go on," she whispered to herself, and opened up the envelopes to see what was inside.

Chapter Twenty-six

He woke to pain. At first it was just that — pain. After a minute he could distinguish different kinds of pain. A sting in his neck, like an insect bite. Crampy aches in his shoulders. A migraine-like throb in his head. A heavy, grinding pain in his knees. A regular Whitman's Sampler of pain, except in his legs below the knees — they were numb.

He raised his head upright, moaning as his shoulders twinged and his neck made audible creaking sounds, as the throb in his head grew and lessened in erratic cycles. Darkness. Blind? No. A band of what felt like cloth over his eyes, snug and tight so no light — if there was any light where he was — came in. He tried to reach up to the blindfold, but his hands were tied behind him. He was on his knees — had been for some time, it seemed. Impossible to stand or to move to the side. He could move forward a bit, touched nothing but air. Scent gave no clue. Just a faint mustiness in the air, the smell of a room not often used.

How long had he been out of it? Halsey's last memory was of Juliette with a strange, silvery pistol in her hand. Had she shot him? He inventoried his pains again but none felt the way he imagined a bullet wound must feel. Halsey licked his lips with a dry tongue and said, experimentally, "Juliette?"

No answer.

"Juliette?"

Silence.

"Is anyone there?"

Nothing.

"Juliette, quit screwing around. This isn't funny!" He could hear panic edging into his voice but was helpless to stop it. He was thirsty and in pain and where the hell was he and what was going on. "Juliette!"

He waited, the silence in his ears getting louder, his mouth getting drier, the ache in his knees steadily gaining. He didn't think about why he was here or what was going to happen. To do so would bring on panic. Better to think this was just some prank of Juliette's. She wouldn't do anything serious to him, no matter how much she disliked him. He hadn't paid her yet.

"Juliette!"

"No need to shout." Her voice was close by and he'd heard no doors opening or footsteps approaching. She'd probably been there a while.

"What the hell is going on? You shot me!"

"It was just a tranquilizer dart."

"I don't care. Joke's over, now untie me."

"No."

Her voice was soft and cold, like a dead kitten. There was no mockery in her voice, none of that teasing quality which so infuriated him. He felt his bewilderment blooming into outright fear. For the first time in weeks he understood what Juliette was.

"What do you want?" he asked.

"What I asked you for earlier. Where is Sean Kincaid?"

"I don't know. Look, quit all this and untie me. I get it, I get it, I should have found out, and I'll do my —"

She grabbed him by the hair and shoved forward, his head was submerged in icy water. He gasped involuntarily and water went up his nose and into his throat. Halsey gagged and coughed, and then Juliette yanked his head back up into the air. Water dripped onto his shoulders and chest, and he realized that he'd been stripped naked. He coughed, sucked in air, and let it out in a croak: "What are you doing?"

"I need information from you, Francis. Where's Kincaid?"

"You don't have to —"

Her voice hadn't changed, was still remote, almost bored. "You wanted to learn how it's done. I said I'd demonstrate. Where is he?"

"I told you I don't —"

Into the water again. This time he was ready for it, and tried to fight her, push his head back up. It was impossible. Her hands held onto his neck, biting into his muscles and tendons, and he couldn't get enough leverage to push himself up.

When she yanked him up again he shouted, "Stop this!"

"Tell me where he is."

"You're insane!"

"You think?" She shoved his head under again.

After the third dunking he figured he'd play along until she got tired of it. After the fifth he realized that she was holding him under a little longer each time. After that he lost count. When she shoved his head under for so long his lungs burned with their demand for air, he understood that she could kill him like this if she chose to. Surely she wouldn't do that.

After a couple more times, he knew she very well might.

He tried to think of something that would make her stop, some bit of information that would pacify her. His mind was blank. He couldn't think at all, was just trying to tell when she would put him under again so he could get as deep a breath as he could.

"I'll be honest with you," she said. "I'm bored. And I have a previous engagement this evening. So here's the last time I'll ask you, Francis. Where is Sean Kincaid?"

She didn't mean it. She couldn't possibly. "Juliette, please. I'll pay you anything, do anything, just let me —"

"I take it you still don't know."

"For the love of God—"

"Oh well. *Je ne regrette rien.*"

He started to plead one last time but she shoved his head under. He struggled against her and still she kept him under. His lungs burned and still she kept him there. Soon it wasn't a burn but pressure that grew unbearable, a vise clamped around his chest, constantly tightening. Multicolored sparks danced before his blind eyes and he knew she meant to kill him. Mortal terror jostled with rage that he, Frank Halsey, would die at the hands of a crazy woman, tied up and naked with his head shoved in a bucket of water, drowned like an unwanted puppy. Impossible. It could not be happening this way, and yet it was. Fear and rage built in his mind as the agonizing pressure built in his chest; he screamed, not with his mouth — he dared not let out any air — but with his mind. The scream seared his mind like a white-hot flame, was so loud his head was full of nothing else, and his last thought was that he'd hear the echo of that scream forever.

He regained consciousness to find himself untied, slumped on the floor, a blanket wrapped around him. The blindfold was off. For a moment Halsey could only stare, bewildered, not remembering what had happened or why he was here.

He was in what looked like a basement room. The floor was concrete, a set of wooden steps led up. A furnace lurked at one end of the room, the rest of the place was empty save for a plastic bucket full of water and a chair. Astride the chair, her chin resting on the back, was Juliette.

She smiled, and it all came back to him. Shaking, shivering, unable to speak, Halsey stared at Juliette, who cocked her head to one side and asked, "Was that refreshing?"

His terror was forgotten; rage overtook it and spilled out of him. He screamed at her, called her every foul name he could think of. He'd forgotten her warning never to call her names, but it seemed she'd forgotten it as well. She merely sat there, indulgently nodding when he dredged up the vilest epithets he could and told her he hoped she'd spend her time in Hell being gang-raped by lepers.

When he paused to take a breath, she asked, "Are you quite finished?"

He wasn't. He unleashed another torrent of names and curses. She smiled, and after a while glanced at her watch.

"Well, that was educational. I didn't know such things *could* be done with a monkey wrench. But as I said, I do have a prior engagement so let me explain something before we call it a day.

"Part of this was practical. If you want to be like us, you have to know about all of it. Not just dishing it out, although now you see how it's done. But taking it. That's one of the risks you run. I could have skipped that, of course, but that would deprive you of the full experience, and I couldn't shortchange you like that."

Halsey spat out, "Screw that. As if anything like that's been done to you."

Her smile went away. "It has. My assignment was a Russian mafia bigwig. The handler screwed up and the contact betrayed me. Any of this sounding familiar? It should. You hired the handler, you arranged the contact, and they left me behind and that bigwig worked me over the same way I worked you over. Only he took longer about it. A lot longer. You've no idea how much I've wanted to repay you for that."

Halsey didn't care. That was her job, and if she got caught, that wasn't his problem. She knew the risks. "That doesn't mean you—"

"He worked me over that way and he didn't just make me pass out. I got to try breathing water, and let me assure you, that's just as much fun as you'd suspect. I could have done that to you," she said, her smile returning. "And believe me, I wanted to. But that could have made things dicey and I have somewhere to be tonight. I don't have time to dump you at the ER. So I didn't give you the full measure, but I gave you enough. Think of it as my little Christmas present to myself."

Juliette stood up. "Your clothes are over there," she said, pointing to the far end of the room. "Don't be too long about it." She went upstairs.

Halsey sat for a while. Not moving, for his body felt as though it had been emptied out and filled with sawdust. Not thinking, for in the aftermath of his rage his mind was blank. After an unknown time he got to his feet, slowly, for his legs were cramped and his knees sent out sharp jabs of pain when he moved. His limbs felt half-numb as he shoved them into his clothes. Only when he was halfway up the stairs did he realize his wallet was missing.

He wanted to run up the stairs, get his wallet and get away from this awful basement and from Juliette, but his legs were clumsy as a marionette's and he was a poor puppeteer, had to take the steps slowly. He opened the door at the top of the stairs and found himself in Juliette's kitchen. She was nowhere in sight. "Juliette," he called in a voice rough from all the coughing and his rage-fueled rants at her. "Where's my—"

Juliette appeared by the breakfast bar, looking through his wallet. "Oooh, American Express Platinum! I'll save that for later."

"Give me that!"

She danced away from him, kept going through his wallet. "Nice driver's license photo and what's this? Condoms? Ha! Like you'll get lucky any time soon."

"Give it!"

Juliette snapped the wallet closed and tossed it at him. As he caught it he noticed that she was dressed for an evening out: opals glittered at her ears and throat, an evening gown of dark crimson shimmered with the light's play over her body. She was lush and gorgeous, like a rose in human form, yet he was so numb that his desire was only theoretical.

It was night, he saw when they stepped outside. He'd been here all day. How much time had he lost? Surely it had only been one day. Yet it felt longer. It felt like a lifetime ago that he'd seen Monique Pavour in the coffeehouse. How excited he'd been at his chance to catch her off guard, find out what she knew. Or to make an impression on her. *Look at me, I have money, I have a family that can trace its line back to the Mayflower. Why settle for a loser like Kincaid or that goof you're married to when you could have me?* A pipe dream, like thinking he could ever get the best of Juliette.

The cold night air hit his wet hair and scalp, making his skin tingle unpleasantly. Still, it was a relief to feel something. He walked over to his car, wanting only to go home. "Happy holidays, Francis," Juliette called out to him, but he didn't answer. He only gave her a quick glance, saw her standing in her crimson dress with a sable wrap over one arm and a satisfied smile on her lips. She blew him a kiss, then got into her car and was gone, vanished into the December night.

Halsey didn't remember driving home. One moment he was getting into his car, the next he was sitting in his living room. Still wearing his coat, his keys clutched in one hand. The house was empty. Only a table lamp was lit, the rest of the house was in darkness. Vaguely he thought that he would like a drink — a very large, very strong drink — but the housekeeper had gone home and he couldn't summon the will to get the drink for himself.

Slowly, feeling began to come back into his body but his mind was numb. An empty room with bare walls and splintery floors, and the ozone smell of a burnt-out fuse. It was as if that mental scream had burned away his thoughts, left nothing but this emptiness in its wake.

He looked at the clock, looked away. When he looked back at the clock, three hours had gone by. It was after midnight now, and silent. There was no sound in the house, no cars passing by on the street. The carolers had all gone home. Silence inside and out.

Some time later he was in bed, trying to sleep. In the dark he fumbled in the drawer of the night table, looking for his sleeping pills. His hand closed not on the pill bottle but on something else, something strangely familiar. In the moonlight he saw what he'd picked up. Robert Dvorak's gun. After he'd stolen the gun he'd put it in the drawer, and had nearly forgotten he still had it.

It was not a very large gun, and it looked rather old, but it fit nicely into his hand. It felt right. As if it belonged there. Sensation traveled from the hand that held the pistol, down his arm, throughout his body. Watching the pistol's metal gleam in the moonlight, he recognized the empty room in his mind for what it was — a new room, ready for new ideas of all sorts. For possibilities he could not have thought of — would not have dared to think of — earlier. All that night he looked at the gun and considered possibilities.

Whether she'd meant to or not, Juliette had helped him. Before, revenge had just been a dream. Before the long night ended, he knew he had the power to make that dream a reality. A very pleasant reality.

Chapter Twenty-seven

Sean was just beginning to emerge from sleep when the phone's ring woke him. He tried to sit up and immediately regretted it as pain shot through his chest. Wincing, he remained as still as he could; when he was fully awake and focused, he saw Deirdre standing there, holding the phone, clearly dreading who might be on the line and what they might want to know. After another ring she answered.

"Hello?" Sean saw her dread change instantly to relief. "Merry Christmas to you too!"

He guessed the caller wasn't asking about Leo and Walt Sorensen and where Deirdre had been last night. Sean slowly maneuvered himself into a sitting position. Chest pain aside, his body ached dully and there was an unpleasant twinge in his back, probably from that fall he'd taken off the porch. It was manageable, as long as he didn't move suddenly.

You OK? Deirdre mouthed at him.

He nodded. He wasn't coughing blood, and if there had been internal bleeding or lung damage he'd either be dead or in far worse shape than he was. Yes, OK.

Bathroom? He mouthed back at her, and she pointed to a door on the far side of the living room.

Deirdre's bathroom had a bit more personality than her living room did, mostly thanks to the profusion of candles throughout the room and the stack of paperbacks by the tub. *Bathtub books, my favorite genre,* Monique had always said, as she settled into a bubble bath with a fat historical novel or one of her beloved Travis McGee stories. Sean used the facilities and splashed water on his face, glanced at his reflection just long enough to determine that he looked no worse for wear than usual. Then he took off his jacket, his shirt, and finally the Kevlar vest.

The force of the bullets had left large, black bruises on his chest. From the bruises' location it was clear that Leo had been no slouch with the pistol and that if Sean hadn't worn the vest he would be on a morgue slab. Or more likely, at the bottom of Deer's Head Lake in the cab of Deirdre's truck, with Deirdre keeping him company.

The bruises were ugly but nothing to be concerned about as long as they healed right. Sean put his shirt and jacket back on; he'd dispose of the vest later.

Deirdre was still on the phone when he came back into the living room. Her talk was cheery enough but she looked exhausted; when she said her goodbyes and hung up, she seemed relieved to be done with the conversation. She stared into space for a moment, then glanced at Sean. "Are you OK? Really?" she asked.

He nodded. "It'll heal. I've been through worse. How are you?"

She didn't answer, just gestured toward her kitchen table. "Have a seat. I'll make some coffee." Deirdre turned and went into the kitchen, busying herself with the coffee maker.

Unable to gauge her mood, he sat down in one of the two metal folding chairs. She'd opened the envelopes they'd taken from Richard's safe, and a small stack of papers lay on the table. Deirdre glanced over her shoulder at him. "Go ahead and look," she said. "I'm sure it'll be familiar to you."

The smaller, thicker envelope was on top of the pile of papers. He took the envelope and glanced inside. Money, a good deal of it. Cash in all denominations from $10 to $100. He remembered last summer, how the members of the group had been assigned IRS buildings in neighboring states. Richard had handed them the cash they'd needed for travel and other expenses, asked them to be frugal. Well, it had to come from somewhere.

Deirdre came in and sat down for a moment. "There's about $40,000. More than I've ever made in a year. All right there. And Anna told me they couldn't afford to get new air conditioning for their house." She smiled, a jagged thing that didn't come near her eyes, and went back into the kitchen.

Sean put the money aside, looked through the papers. Nothing he saw surprised him. Richard had been smart, putting as little as he could on paper, but even he hadn't been able to keep everything in his head. Here was the nuts and bolts of it all — the amount of the plastic explosives they'd used, the placement around the support columns in the Los Angeles federal building parking structure, the possible targets for the next attack. He was not surprised to see his name — or rather, his alias — in the papers. It seemed that he'd been Richard's choice to be the mole on the next target. Sean smiled his own bitter smile. Of course. Richard had trusted him. How much differently might things have gone if there had been a little less trust?

Deirdre asked him something he hadn't caught. "Pardon?"

"How do you take your coffee?"

"Hot and black is fine."

She placed a mug of coffee before him, sat down in the other chair with her own mug. Her eyes moved over the papers but he could tell she was not reading anything. She'd probably spent all last night reading them, probably knew their contents better than he did.

"I want to apologize to you," she said.

"You don't have to."

"I didn't believe you. I should have."

"You didn't have a reason to believe me."

Deirdre's eyes closed. "Please shut up. I don't have any more nice left in me, and I need to say some things now."

Her voice had a raggedy edge to it and he fell silent.

Deirdre said, "I was realizing that I don't know how Richard and Anna met. But I remember the first time I met him. Christmas Eve, about ten years ago. Or maybe eleven. I was visiting Anna's parents. Her mom's dead now — cancer — and her dad's in a home, Alzheimer's. She was a late child, like me. But they were sweet people, treated me better than my own family did. Just in case you were wondering how she came by it. I walked in the door and almost the first thing that happens is Nan comes over and tells me there's someone special I have to meet. And I didn't have to meet him to know she'd met the right guy. The one you're meant for. If you believe in that sort of thing. I could see it in her eyes.

"But she was right, he was someone special. Not just the way he looked, though that was pretty considerable. The sort of man who's only going to get better-looking as he gets older, you know? No, it was…they talk a lot about charisma, but you don't understand it until you meet someone who's got it. Only thing like it was once when I was watching some old movie with James Cagney — couldn't take my eyes off the man. Magnetic. That's what he was. And he was nuts about Anna, too. Like they say, head over heels."

She paused to take a swig of her coffee. "And it was all a God damned lie. No, don't say it. He loved her, of course. But not enough. Not as much as he loved this." She flicked her hand contemptuously at the papers. "Richard was a lot of things, but stupid wasn't one of them. There were too many ways for it to go wrong. They could have gotten caught. The bomb could have gone off at the wrong time and killed him. Or someone in the group could have got scared and tattled. Or someone like you could have come along.

"Don't you see? Nan's life was going to be ruined no matter what happened. If they got caught and Richard went to jail Nan would have lost everything. And for the rest of her life people would want to know what she knew and when she knew it and no one would really believe that all she did was marry the wrong guy. And how could she have known? Shit, *I* wanted to marry him. I did marry a guy who looked a bit like him, and he turned out to be a liar too. Smaller stuff, not about blowing up buildings, just about his drinking and the screwing around, but still a liar. And what about you, Sam? Oh, I'm sorry, Sean." Her voice was too bright, it trembled on the edge of hysteria, but he couldn't bring himself to interrupt. "I *know* you're a liar. How much of a liar are you? Did you ever tell Anna anything about yourself that wasn't fake? Do you have a wife tucked away somewhere? Some nice woman who thinks you travel a lot 'on business'?" She held her fingers up and made quote signs. "Well?"

Before he could reply she went on: "I opened up those envelopes and you don't know how bad I wanted there to be something else in them. But I guess I knew. Leo and Walt wouldn't have come after us if they didn't think there was something important there. But you were right, and here it all is. What's killing me is that it was always there, like some dead body buried behind the wall. And we never knew it. We never guessed. Poor Nan, lied to all this time by Mr. Wonderful.

"Nan was strong. Just because she was sweet doesn't mean she wasn't strong. She had to be, taking care of so many people, like her mom, like Laurel. Losing all those babies. I'm sitting here thinking of different ways this could have gone. But none of them end up good for her. Not with Richard being what he was. Not with what he did.

"I got to thinking, maybe it's good that she never really knew. Maybe what happened was for the best."

Deirdre's ragged voice fell silent. Sean could think of nothing to say. Deirdre snatched up her mug and flung it at the refrigerator. It exploded into fragments, spraying the kitchen with lukewarm coffee. She let out a long, low moan, a sound of mortal pain that Sean longed to shut out somehow. Deirdre slumped onto the table, her moan giving way to sobs as she wept for Anna. She cried for a long time, her sobs cresting into that bereaved moan from time to time, once into a keening wail that made him think of banshees crying in the night. Through it all he sat, a witness to and partial author of her grief, unable to offer so much as a comforting touch because his hands were sullied with Anna's blood. When her weeping tapered off, he gave her a dish towel to dry her face but dared not touch her — her grief and his guilt made him an easy target for any violence on her part, and though that did not trouble him, the thought that she would be alone facing any fallout from Leo and Walt did. She didn't look at him when her tears dried, just let out a deep sigh. Sean had heard a sigh like that before: from Robert, when the morphine had kicked in.

Deirdre got to her feet, unsteadily. Sean stood and offered her his arm. She took it, and said, "I should lie down. I'm tired." Her eyes were so swollen he doubted she could see very well. He guided her into her bedroom, and she stood swaying beside her bed, the way a jumper must sway before taking the plunge off the high ledge. She turned and regarded him with blind-looking eyes. "Stay a while if you can. We need to talk." Deirdre collapsed onto her bed.

He arranged a blanket over her. On his way out he bumped into the doorknob, but the sound didn't wake Deirdre. She was out.

Sean went into the kitchen, cleaned up the broken glass and spilled coffee. He wanted to take some of the Vicodin but didn't want to feel doped up; instead he took four ibuprofen tablets, and then settled on the couch to wait until she woke. When the pills started to work and the pain lessened somewhat, he turned on the TV. It was Christmas, and that meant he could always find one of the holiday movie chestnuts to keep him occupied. After a few minutes he found *It's a Wonderful Life*. It would do.

Deirdre slept through *It's a Wonderful Life* and *Miracle on 34th Street*. She slept through the Alistair Sim version of *A Christmas Carol*. She walked into the living room during the George C. Scott version, about the time Scrooge was unsuccessfully trying to write off Marley's visit as an underdone fragment of potato. Deirdre stood and looked at Sean quizzically, as though she'd forgotten why he was there, or despite her request for him to stay, she hadn't really expected he would. "You're still here." A slight upward intonation to her voice; not quite a question, not quite a statement.

"Do you want me to go?" he asked as he turned the TV off.

She regarded him. Despite her sleep she still looked exhausted. "Not yet. Are you hungry?"

He was famished. "I could eat."

She nodded. "Let's eat. Then we'll talk."

Deirdre didn't speak again until she put plates of food — English muffins topped with Canadian bacon and scrambled eggs — on the table. "Eggs McMonahan," she said with a crooked smile. "I'm not much of a cook, but this is my one specialty."

"I'm the same way," he said. "My specialty is corned beef hash."

The food was good. They were both done in less than five minutes. Deirdre made coffee and Sean asked if he could smoke. She nodded, gave him a saucer to use for an ashtray.

"That was Nick who called this morning," she said.

"Nick?"

"The deputy I went out with a few nights ago. He's off work for the holidays. He didn't say anything about Leo. So my guess is that no one's noticed Leo's missing yet, or if they did, no one told Nick. Or Nick knows and he's a better liar than I think." Deirdre fidgeted with her teaspoon, didn't look up at him. "Someone's going to notice Leo's gone, sooner or later. What do I say?"

It would be easier if she hadn't gone to the sheriff's station and confronted Leo — people would remember that. What worked in her favor was that she didn't look like a person who could kill. He knew otherwise, not just because Deirdre had put a gun to his head, but because he knew that a person's exterior appearance gave little indication of what was within. Look at Richard, look at Robert, look at himself or at most of the agents he'd known and rogues he'd worked against. Look at that *belle dame sans merci*, Juliette.

Yes, it would have been better if she hadn't confronted Leo, but they'd work with what they had. It was all they could do. He sat in thought for a moment, smoking, almost relishing the challenge. "What did you tell Nick? Anything?"

She shook her head. "Not much. I told him I spent last night driving around looking at Christmas lights."

"And so you did."

"But what about —"

"You saw the newspaper story and yes, you went to the sheriff's station. And after that you drove around looking at Christmas lights."

"I..." She stopped. "You're right, that's what I did. I thought it might cheer me up."

"How late did you get home?"

She shrugged. "Some time around eleven. Maybe a little before."

"You drive around that whole time?"

"No, I got some drive-through for dinner."

"Which drive-through?"

"McDonald's. I don't like Burger King's fries."

"And after you got home?"

"Channel-surfed and went to bed."

She was good. If she could keep up that naturalness and not get rattled if a cop asked her these questions, she'd do well. "Stick to that story and I think you'll be fine. The only ones who know it's not true are me and that kid down the hall."

"Jason."

"Yes. But he'd probably lie for you. He's got a crush on you. And besides, as far as he knows, driving around is what you did do last night."

She gazed at him for a moment. "How do you do it? Know what to do. Not panic."

Sean didn't know what to say. How did he do it? He'd done it for so long he'd forgotten a life when he didn't. "Practice," he said. "Lots of it. And that's what you have to do. Rehearse your story till it's natural. Think about the little details. But don't tell anyone unless they ask for it. You don't want anyone to catch you out on inconsistencies." They were Robert's words, spoken to Sean years ago, preparing him for one of his first undercover missions.

"OK," she said, then touched the pile of papers and the envelope full of money. "What about this?"

"We let it lie for now."

Her eyes narrowed, her jaw clenched. "The whole reason —"

"It's too soon to bring this out now. Deirdre, I know you don't want Anna's name dragged through the mud. I don't want that either. But if the truth comes out, so will the fact that Leo covered it up. People will ask more questions. They'll put you under a microscope instead of just looking you over."

"No one knows I was at the farm last night."

"And no one knows you were anywhere else. You don't have an alibi. All you have working for you is that you're an unlikely suspect."

Sean paused to let his words sink in. After a moment Deirdre nodded in unwilling agreement. "You're right. But how long do I wait? What do I say?"

"We'll work it out when things settle down."

"We?"

He couldn't tell if she was pleased or otherwise. "I'd like to stay around until this is all sorted out." Until he was sure she was safe. "Keep an eye on things." And on her.

She seemed relieved. "I didn't want to ask, but that would be good." Deirdre began abruptly clearing the plates. She went into the kitchen and with her back to him said, "No offense, but it's not that I like you. I can't forget what you've done. But you know what you're doing. And I know you'll look out for me. You're a necessary evil."

He supposed she was right, but he wished she hadn't said it.

They decided it was best that they not be seen together, so they waited until nightfall for her to drive him back to his motel. While they waited they watched *It's a Wonderful Life* again. Rather, they sat in front of the TV while it showed *It's a Wonderful Life*; Deirdre talked off and on the whole while. Her glances at Sean were few; most of that time she stared at the TV without looking at it. You couldn't call it a conversation, for he said very little. Deirdre did the talking, and she talked about Anna, about meeting her at a family reunion. How she'd saved all her money from paper routes and babysitting so she could get bus fare to visit Anna every summer. How Anna tried to tell her that Randy wasn't perfect husband material but never once said "told you so" when her predictions came true. About her last conversation with Anna, when Deirdre had suspected that Anna had good news, had finally been able to keep a pregnancy past the third month.

Deirdre spoke and with every word he could sense some of that poisonous brew of anger and grief leaving her. He knew he would stay as long as it took, do whatever it took, to make sure that Anna's name was cleared and that he'd helped Deirdre heal as much as he could, which would never be enough.

After nightfall, Deirdre drove him to his motel. She didn't say much as they parted; he didn't expect her to. She'd need a lot more time to deal with everything that had happened. Best to leave her alone, and check in on her after a couple days.

Cheerless as his motel room was, he was happy to get back to it. He ached in every muscle and his chest more than ached. Without bothering to turn on the lights, he went into the bathroom, took some painkillers from his kit, turned on the shower as hot as he could stand it, stripped off his clothes, and let the near-scalding water do its work. He rested his forehead on his arms, leaned against the shower wall. The water melted the tension out of his muscles, the heat numbed his nerve endings. His eyes closed. Darkness. White noise. Half-asleep standing in the hot shower, he drifted back in time to the funeral of Edwards, his first boss. Edwards had died a few years after Halsey had taken the reins, somewhere in those first few rounds of purges. Robert had just been retired, Sean was less than a year from getting the boot. Only Sean had attended the funeral itself, and he would have gladly avoided it — as he'd avoided all funerals since his mother's — but Edwards had been his first boss, and Sean respected and admired no man more, save for Robert. As for Robert, he hadn't attended the funeral — only actual employees of the agency were invited to do so. But he'd been there at the reception, along with a number of agents both retired and in practice. Sean and Robert sitting on the sidelines of the, sharing a bottle of cognac. "To Edwards," Robert said. "May he be in Heaven half an hour before the devil knows he's dead," Sean said. They drank to that, drank some more, and watched the crowd. The old guard stood in tight knots, drinks in their hands and sorrow in their faces. Around them swirled the new blood, the ones brought in after the Cold War — opportunists, not idealists. Sean and Robert watched as Halsey circulated through the crowd, attaching himself remora-like to those with greater position and power. "Edwards died too late," Robert said. "Sometimes I think it wasn't a stroke that killed him but having to watch this sort of thing." Sean had replied, "It's not all bad, yet. There's still good people." They both knew it would only get worse. Robert said, "Do good work as long as you can. Edwards would have wanted it that way. *Na zdraví*," he said as they raised their glasses again. "*Sláinte*," Sean replied. The cognac's warmth crept through him. "I found someone," Sean said. "New blood but old school. Her name's Deirdre." She smiled at them, pushed over a shot glass to them. Robert filled her glass with cognac. "Welcome, Deirdre," said Robert. "How did you find her, Sean?" Deirdre raised her glass high. "To absent friends," she said, and knocked back the liquor. She held the empty glass in a hand still stained with Leo Sorensen's blood. "He didn't find me, I found him. He killed my cousin."

Sean snapped his head back, nearly slipped. He'd fallen asleep standing under the shower, had drifted from memory into dream without even noticing. Christ, he was far gone if that was happening. He shut off the shower and a few minutes later was stretched out on the bed; he had been too exhausted to bother turning down the garish bedspread. He couldn't recall the last time he'd been so worn out. It wasn't surprising, really. He was out of condition, was probably not fully recovered from that bout of pneumonia. He could sleep all night and all day if he wanted. Deirdre was most likely safe for a couple days.

He closed his eyes and drifted. No sound from the neighboring motel rooms. His only companions on Christmas night the faint moan of the wind, the tick of snow blown against the windowpanes.

Chapter Twenty-eight

The neighbors upstairs were having a party, with either small children or a herd of ponies in attendance; Monique wasn't sure which. The party noise aside, it was a quiet New Year's Eve. It was particularly quiet in the Pavour-Banks apartment. One of Monique's work friends was having a party, and both Monique and Michael had been invited. But Michael had been called to do the red-eye flight from D.C. to London — the original pilot was ill and the backup had a family emergency. Monique didn't mind. The week in North Carolina with Michael's family had been fun, but she was rather glad of a little alone time before the holiday season ended and everyone grudgingly returned to the workaday world.

She supposed she could have gone to the party by herself, but she simply didn't have the energy for socializing and didn't fancy being the only partygoer not kissing someone at midnight. Far better to laze around in her pajamas and watch a movie. Monique rummaged through the refrigerator and gift baskets, making a ramshackle dinner from the last of the holiday goodies: a hunk of Stilton, a wedge of panettone, leftover puff pastry hors d'oeuvres, a couple slices of ham, and the last of the crab cakes, with peppermint bark for dessert and half a bottle of champagne to chase it all down. After a moment's consideration, she added a tangerine and a handful of pistachios to give the dinner something resembling nutritional value, and took it into the living room.

She decided to take advantage of the situation and watch *Gladiator*. It was her fate to be attracted to men who liked the movies as much as she did, but who had cinematic blind spots that conflicted with hers. Michael was something of a history buff, the older the history the better, and this would be her only chance to watch the movie without his sarcastic remarks every time there was an inaccuracy. She had no room to complain, for she was just as bad when it came to movies with courtroom settings. At least Michael wasn't as bad as Sean; she'd learned early on to never watch a James Bond movie with Sean, for he spent the whole time muttering about guns and ludicrous technology and his per diem and how he'd never gotten to wear a tux while on a mission. The only Bond movie he ever shut up while watching was *On Her Majesty's Secret Service*, and that was because he was in love with Diana Rigg. Monique had a bit of a girl-crush on Ms. Rigg herself, so again, she had no room to complain. Still, it would be nice to watch the movie in peace, eat her calorie-laden dinner, and wait for Michael's phone call from London.

Michael called, and from what she could tell he was having a decent New Year's Eve. Ironic, considering that he had to work, but it was his luck that the new flight attendant was, like Michael, a member of the Society for Creative Anachronism. "So Kristine and I are just hanging at the pub, talking about tournaments and Faire. Her partner — what's her name?"

From somewhere in the background Monique heard a female voice say, "Beth."

"Beth. They're going to the Fool's Twelfth Night later this month. Maybe we could go and if we all hit it off we can go to Faire some time."

"That sounds fine." It had taken some time for Michael to talk Monique into going to Renaissance Faire, but she'd found she rather liked it. The food and the music were good, the clothes surprisingly comfortable, and while there were a few who took it a bit too seriously, most of the participants were nice, funny people. Besides, it was good to have her Monty Python quotes be appreciated for a change. At work, the only responses to her quips about killer rabbits and the airspeed velocity of an unladen swallow were blank stares.

"Anything exciting going on there?" Michael asked.

"Not a thing. I'm in my PJs watching movies and I ate the last of the Stilton. I'm a wild woman out of control, me."

"Indeed you are. The proprietor's about ready to kick us out of the pub, so I'm off for some shut-eye and I'll be back tomorrow night."

"Have another round and charge it to the airline."

"That I shall do. Happy New Year, dollybird."

They exchanged love-yous and goodbyes. Monique made herself some hot chocolate and settled in to watch Russell Crowe kick some gladiatorial ass.

There was no reason for her to stay up until midnight, but she did. The old year went out, the new came in. There were a few cheers from the neighborhood, a car horn honked. Otherwise a midnight like any other.

It wasn't until she was in bed, waiting for sleep to come, that she knew why she'd stayed up. She'd been wondering if Sean would call.

New Year's was his favorite holiday — as far as she could tell, it was the only one he seemed to care about. As for Christmas and Thanksgiving, he was not a grinch, merely uninterested. "Why New Year's?" she'd asked once out of curiosity. She'd never cared much for the holiday herself; its main purpose was to delay the post-Christmas return to the real world.

He hadn't answered for a moment. Then he said, "My profession has a high rate of attrition. When New Year's comes around, it's like celebrating. Another year is here and so am I."

She'd started to ask if his birthday wouldn't be a better choice, then stopped. His job didn't get easier with age. Better to mark the passage of time some other way.

Now two New Year's Eves had come and gone with no call from Sean. No communication except that strange hang-up call back in October (if that had been him and not a confused telemarketer), and the letter. If it had only been the hang-up call, she could tell herself that Sean had for whatever reason decided to cut his ties to her, settle down, and maybe marry some cute divorcée who wouldn't mind his *tabula rasa* past. But there had been too many other things, and she worried. She had always worried about him, though she'd tried not to. How could she not worry, when she never knew when she would see him again? Or in what shape he'd return, assuming he did return? Some might have thought it was the same with Michael, but it wasn't. Lots of her friends couldn't believe she'd married a pilot. *He's gone so often. How do you handle it?* She always replied that in the right amounts, absence made the heart grow fonder, and besides, reunions could be fun. Michael's absences were a cakewalk compared to Sean's. If the worst did happen — she instinctively clutched her Saint Christopher's medal — she would know. There'd be no waiting, no uncertainty, no mystery. If Sean had died on the job, no one would have told her. He'd have just disappeared.

She'd thought it over during those beach walks down in North Carolina, and had made a pact with herself. By New Year's Eve, she would hear from Sean. Or she wouldn't. Either way, she would not worry any more. He had been her lover, and she'd cared for him more than she had for any other man except Michael, but that was years gone now. He needed help — his letter proved that — but what he needed was nothing she could give him. She had already given him everything that she could, everything that he could accept from her. It was not enough for either of them.

Her New Year's resolution: She would not worry where he was or what he might be doing, or who might be looking for him and what they might want. She would forget about that letter from Sean, and about the rat-faced man who'd questioned her. It was out of her hands.

Chapter Twenty-nine

Halsey would never admit, even to himself, that he was afraid to see Juliette again. Several times during that week between Christmas and New Year's he'd started to call her, then hung up before he'd dialed more than three digits. She had tortured him, nearly killed him, and just laughed about it. She'd have done worse if she hadn't wanted to inconvenience herself. He'd always known on a theoretical level that she was crazy and capable of anything — now he knew it from experience.

He shoved the thoughts out of his head the only ways he knew how. During the day, he went to the gun range and practiced, at first with the .22 and the .38 Juliette had given him. After a while he began to practice with the .32 he'd stolen from Robert Dvorak. He wasn't sure why: the gun was old, probably had some sort of sentimental value for Dvorak. It wasn't all that reliable, and had a tendency to jam, but it felt right in his hand. Sometimes he thought that with every shot he fired from it, the weapon was becoming his, would serve him better than any other gun would. Halsey took to carrying the gun with him. Some of the time he wore it in a shoulder holster, but often he preferred to carry it in a pocket of his coat. When it was in his pocket, he could touch it, feel the polished smoothness of the grip, the cold surface of the metal. Could feel the reassuring weight of it, so unlike that .22 Juliette had so condescendingly given him. The .32 was a real gun — a man's gun.

At night, he found that sleeping pills and gin not only put him under, but in the right combination they kept the dreams away. Still, sometimes the dreams crept through. When he woke from those dreams, only by holding on to Dvorak's .32 could he get back to sleep; he often dozed off still clutching the gun, and before long took to sleeping with it under his pillow.

Just in case.

He didn't hear from her until the second of January. He came home from the gun range to hear a message on his answering machine. "Hello, Francis. I'll be expecting you tomorrow at ten." Nothing about where she'd been or what she'd been doing. No apologies for what she'd done to him. Just the summons.

Halsey considered not going, but he still needed her help to find Kincaid and besides, he owed her the payment for the training. If he didn't pay up, he knew she'd come after him and the best he could hope for was that she killed him quickly. He arrived on her doorstep feeling not at all well — he'd needed quite a bit of gin to get to sleep the night before, and last night's dream had been particularly unpleasant. He stood on Juliette's doorstep for several minutes before ringing the bell, his mind and gut roiling with fear, hatred, and shame. Finally he pressed the button.

Juliette flung open the door. "Happy New Year, Francis," she sang out. Halsey could only stare at her, as desire overwhelmed all his other emotions. He'd tried to forget Juliette's loveliness, but if possible she was more beautiful than ever: she was tanned, nearly glowing, obviously having spent the last week someplace sunny. She wore a white blouse, a red plaid skirt, on her head was a black fedora. Juliette smiled, obviously relishing the effect of her appearance, and he wanted her and hated her in equal measure, longed to kiss her and bite her at the same time.

"You look like hell," she said. "What's wrong? Didn't Santa bring you what you wanted for Christmas?" She turned and walked into her living room, and he followed, noticing that she was wearing white knee socks and no shoes. Knee socks. Jesus H. Christ.

He didn't answer her question. Christmas had been a washout. Neither his brother nor his sister had invited him anywhere, and he'd have refused any invitations anyway, as he couldn't stand his siblings or the fools who'd married them, and never mind their annoying spawn. His disgrace at the agency meant no invitations were forthcoming on that front either, but Juliette didn't need to know any of that. He said, "Where were you?"

She sat down, crossed her legs — good Lord, that skirt was short — and twirled a lock of hair around one finger. "Bora Bora. Have you ever been? Lovely place. Just lazed around on the beach, went swimming. Very relaxing."

"How nice," he said through gritted teeth.

"Good food there. Lots of handsome young men there, too. Almost a shame to have to come back but," she said with a lazy shrug, "duty calls. Do anything fun while I was away?"

"Not really."

"Pity. Well, let's be off. I want to see how your shooting skills are faring." She plucked a pair of black shoes off the floor and put them on.

Halsey breathed a sigh of relief. She hadn't brought up their last encounter, nor asked him about Kincaid's whereabouts. Maybe he'd never have to think about it again. His relief was short-lived, for as they stepped out of her house Juliette seized him by the hair, the way she had when she was torturing him. He cringed, he couldn't help it, and didn't know what was worse, acting like a kicked dog or Juliette's pleasure at his reaction. Although he impressed her at the range — she actually praised his performance — he could take no satisfaction from that. It was tainted by the memory of his debasement at her hands. He longed to see her humiliated as he had been. Preferably even more than he had been. If he had anything to say about it, that would happen.

Halsey didn't know what to think. Since her return, Juliette had treated him differently, though not with what you'd call respect. There was something restrained about her. She still teased him, but at times it seemed more a habit than something borne of malice. She didn't bring up her interrogation of him, nor did she ask him if he knew Kincaid's whereabouts. He was afraid to broach the subject, so it didn't come up. They kept up the firearms training, and she showed him the tranquilizer gun and how it worked. She gave him some basics on surveillance — "You have to get close enough to him to shoot him," she said — and seemed more interested in giving him information than in mocking his lack of skills. He wanted to think that she finally had some respect for him, told himself that so often that he came to believe it. He believed she was ashamed of her earlier behavior, which was why she seemed preoccupied much of the time. He believed he had learned everything he needed to from her, which was why she sometimes took several days off from their training, or spent gun range sessions looking over papers or making phone calls, her side of the conversation maddeningly cryptic.

Despite this apparent change of heart — or perhaps because of it — he found himself on edge in her presence. He'd hated and feared her before this, but at least he'd had an idea of what to expect from her. Halsey had no idea what this quieter Juliette was thinking, or what she wanted from him. He waited to find out and in the meantime took to bringing Robert Dvorak's gun with him.

Just in case.

Early February, and he was on edge from the drive to Juliette's house, for the sleety rain made the roads treacherous. After he rang the doorbell he heard her call out, "Door's open, come in."

That was odd. Usually she greeted him at the door, while she made some supposedly witty remark. Halsey opened the door, stepped inside. Juliette sat at her dining room table, papers in front of her. "Come sit down," she said without looking up. "I just made some coffee."

Halsey walked over to the table, not bothering to take off his trenchcoat; he was too uneasy. Something was different about her. Not just her appearance, although she was dressing conservatively today: a long dark skirt, boots, and a pale gray sweater. It was her manner, distant and almost polite.

He didn't bother with the coffee, just sat down at the table. He waited for her to speak. To say, *I'm sorry for the way I've treated you.* Or admit that she had not given him the respect he was due.

"Good news. It looks like I've found where Kincaid might be. Now, we know that he went after the people who did the Los Angeles federal building. Intelligence had it as being a domestic group in the upper Midwest. Minnesota, Michigan, that sort of thing. A lot of territory there. But it turns out it was a good thing that Beatty took the job. His body was found here —" She took a map out of the small pile of papers in front of her and laid it on the table. It was a map of Silas County, Wisconsin, with a number of red circles drawn on it. "Deer's Head Lake. And that's not the only body to turn up in that area recently. Last October there were five suspicious deaths. Doug MacReady, Steve Wickersham, Eddie Wickersham, Richard Blaine, and Anna Blaine. Five killings in one month. Someone's been busy."

Halsey had trouble following this. "How do you know it's him?"

For a moment her eyes flickered with the familiar contempt. "I don't *know.* This is educated guesswork. Now, the medical examiner's reports on all these people were rather interesting. MacReady got it with a single knife wound to the heart. The killer knew what he was doing. Ditto for one of these Wickersham guys… Steve, that's it. Crushed trachea. Easy to do *if* you know how. The other Wickersham and Richard Blaine both got it with a 9-millimeter pistol."

She paused, evidently expecting him to understand the significance.

He didn't. "So?"

"Kincaid's weapon of choice, according to his file, was a Sig Sauer P210, which fires a 9-millimeter round. Excellent gun, by the way. And here's something interesting. Most of the bodies were found close to home. But

Richard Blaine's was found in Canada. Not just over the border but all the way in British Columbia, about ten yards from property owned by the agency. There's a safe house there. It's not used much any more but it's there. A search of the house turned up Kincaid's fingerprints, blood matching Richard Blaine's type, and evidence of a third party."

"Who's the third party?"

"Tell me, when you think about that Los Angeles bombing, what's the first thing you see in your mind?"

The blonde whose picture was on the cover of every magazine in those weeks after the bombing. The last person to make it out. "That girl. The one the firefighter saved. What's she got to do with this?"

Juliette sighed. "Did you ever wonder why Kincaid wanted to come back in for Los Angeles? Why that job in particular?"

He shrugged. "Got fed up with retirement, I guess."

"He was fed up with retirement before he got on the plane to Florida, and if you'd had any sense you'd have kept him on in an advisory capacity." Juliette took out a copy of *People* magazine out and laid it before him. It was a follow-up on the Los Angeles bombing, and the blonde girl's picture was prominent on the cover. "This is why. She's why he wanted back in."

"You can't know that."

"Like I said, educated guesswork," she said, tapping Kincaid's file. "Look. Three times during the last few years of his career Kincaid was reprimanded for not completing missions within the time frame or budget, and all three times his justification was that it would have put civilians at risk. All three times the civilians were women. Remember what I told you about Kincaid holding doors open for me? He's got a soft spot for women. Why do you think he never mentioned his ladyfriend to any of the other agents, even though they had a steady thing for years? He didn't want her involved. I'd bet my life savings that if this picture," she tapped the magazine cover, "had been of some businessman Kincaid would still be down in Florida. But this got to him. And besides, this girl moved to British Columbia last year. To a town not very far from the safe house. She may even have been at the safe house — they found blonde hairs there and those don't match Kincaid or Blaine."

He wondered where Juliette was heading with all this. "That's all well and good, but that doesn't tell us where Kincaid is now."

"It does, more than you think. Let's go back to these bodies in Wisconsin. All professionally killed, except one. All more or less dumped, except one. Here's our exception. Richard Blaine's wife Anna. Died from a skull fracture, apparently from hitting her head on the fireplace mantel. Manslaughter or misadventure. Certainly not Kincaid's usual work. But there's O positive blood under a couple of her fingernails, which matches Kincaid's type. Here's the interesting thing: she was the only body that wasn't dumped. She was moved to a couch and a blanket was put over her."

"He was trying to hide the body?"

"No. It's respectful to cover the face of the dead. Notice none of these other bodies got that." Juliette regarded the papers before her for a moment. "Here's my theory. Kincaid goes after the Los Angeles guys. He gets most of them, but the Blaines are special. My guess is that Richard was the big kahuna; he's the one Kincaid dragged all the way to Canada. I think Anna Blaine got mixed up in it somehow — probably got in the way accidentally, and that wasn't at all how Kincaid intended it to go."

"I still don't — "

She went on as if she hadn't heard him. "So, Kincaid finds who he's looking for, takes Blaine to Canada, executes him there." She paused. "I wonder if he executed Blaine in front of the girl? If so, that's rather fucked up. Huh. Anyway, he dumps Blaine's body. Then he goes to Maine, to Robert Dvorak's house. Speaking of Dvorak, he sent a note to Kincaid's old ladyfriend telling her that people would come around asking about him."

"How did you find that out?"

"I talked to Dvorak's hospice worker."

Talked to him? Or…

She read his thoughts, smiled. "Oh no, I didn't harm him at all. Just paid him a visit, rattled off the names of his patients, and said I'd pull out their fingernails if he didn't help out. I didn't have to actually do anything. It's always so much easier with people who care. Just threaten who they care about. But you wouldn't know about that, would you, Francis? You don't care about anyone but yourself."

"I could say the same about you."

"Of course. Now, here's where we have to do some conjecture. Kincaid goes to see Dvorak. The hospice guy said Kincaid looked very strung out. Had obviously been doing some hard traveling, and his neck was all bruised up like someone had tried to throttle him. Kincaid and Dvorak were talking when he left, and when he came back the next morning Kincaid was gone and Dvorak was dead."

"Where did Kincaid go?"

Juliette was silent for a little while. She had a focused yet detached look on her face. "I think he's gone back to Wisconsin."

"That's insane. Why would he do that?"

"Look at this." She pulled out a sheet of paper — a news story printout. "Same county where all the deaths have happened. The local sheriff and his brother are missing, have been since right around Christmas."

"Coincidence."

"I don't think so. Nothing much happens in this place, remember. I think Kincaid's got some sort of unfinished business in Wisconsin. I think something didn't go according to plan, which is why he showed up in Maine looking like death on toast. I think that Blaine woman has a lot to do with it. And I bet if you go to Wisconsin, you can pick up Kincaid's trail."

Wait a minute. "If *I* go?"

"You've still got a while before your suspension's up?"

He did, but that wasn't the point.

Juliette continued: "You're good with the gun. Better than I'd ever thought you would be. You know the basics of surveillance. If you time it right, he's yours." She spread her hands out. "Here ends the lesson."

"You mean…that's it?" He'd loathed nearly every moment of her lessons but it could not be over, just like that.

Juliette rolled her eyes. "Yes, that's bloody well it. I trained you on weapons. I trained you on surveillance. I showed you how to do an interrogation that won't leave marks. I did all the legwork in finding out where Kincaid might be. What else do you want?" She smiled teasingly. "Were you hoping I'd throw in a mercy fuck?"

His face aflame at her last words, he gathered up the papers she'd put together, the background on Kincaid's whereabouts. So that was it. He'd expected something else. Something more. "I couldn't persuade you to come with me, could I?" he asked as he got up from the table.

She stood up, started walking to the living room. "No. Remember, I always liked Kincaid. I still don't like you, though our lessons have helped pass the time."

"How much do I owe you?"

"Nothing."

He was dumbfounded. "Was this for free?"

"Charity is for suckers. You've paid. You've been paying me all along." Juliette laughed. "Don't you get it?"

He did. She'd never wanted his money. All she'd wanted was to tease him, taunt him, belittle him, humiliate him, torture him. And she'd enjoyed every minute of it.

Juliette's back was to him, as she poked at the fire in the living room fireplace. "And now that you get it, you can go. It's been fun, Francis. Give my regards to Kincaid if you find him."

Halsey turned to go. He reached into his trenchcoat pocket for his keys, and as he did his hand brushed Dvorak's .32. Something happened in his mind: a key turned, tumblers fell, a door opened.

Juliette was still facing the fireplace. He raised the .32 and shot her twice in the back. She let out a cry and fell forward, caught on to the mantel and kept herself from falling. She turned her head to look at him and he saw animal rage in her face but he wasn't afraid and shot her in the side. In the abdomen. Still she didn't fall; she was trying to get to the kitchen counter where the knives were kept. He shot her twice more, in the chest, and still she would not fall. Halsey pulled the trigger again but the gun's magazine was empty. No matter. He walked over and pistol-whipped her in the face; finally she dropped to the floor and lay there, breathing raggedly, dark bloodstains blooming on her clothes.

Halsey set the gun down on the kitchen counter. He felt more alive than he ever had, every nerve and muscle singing with energy. It was power in its purest form. The power to do what she'd never thought he had the will to do. She stared at him with disbelief and fury that he could have done such a thing; ah, the power to make that look appear on her face. The power to do that and much more.

He dropped to the floor, pinned her body down with his. She clawed at him but he caught her wrists before she could do much damage. Juliette snarled, tried to bite him but was too weakened by her injuries. Halsey pinned her wrists down with his left hand. With his right hand he ripped at her clothing.

"So, Juliette," he said, "how about that mercy fuck?"

He waited until dusk to leave. Halsey was not particularly worried — no cops had arrived, no neighbor seemed to have heard the shots — but it wouldn't do to be seen leaving her house with his clothes bloodsoaked and his face and neck scratched. For a while he passed the time by going through the case where Juliette had kept her weapons, taking the tranquilizer gun and a dozen darts, bullets for his .32. It was his lucky gun now, and he'd never use anything else.

Mostly he sat in the living room, looking at Juliette's body, smiling to himself, basking in the afterglow. Many had tried to do what he'd done to Juliette; many more had longed to do it. But only he'd had the guts and the will to do it.

And the luck, a dissenting voice said in his head. He frowned, and against his will remembered the last thing Juliette had said to him. He'd heard a rasping, raw sound and had looked down to see Juliette staring up at him, blood leaking from the corners of her mouth. Again the sound, and he'd realized she was laughing. That laugh and the mad glitter in her eyes had made him almost afraid. Almost. In between rattling gasps she'd said *Is that the best you can do?* He'd clamped a hand over her mouth to silence her, but there was no need for it. Those had been her last words on that or any subject.

Never mind it. The bitch was dead, and he had everything he wanted from her. When the afternoon light had dimmed sufficiently he got up and walked over to her. He prodded her with his foot; she was stone cold, already beginning to stiffen. Even her beauty was gone now.

Halsey was elated once more. As he left Juliette's house, he decided the voice wasn't dissenting at all, just stating a fact. Yes, he'd had the luck. Juliette's had run out, as she said luck would.

His luck was just beginning.

Chapter Thirty

Voice mail picked up after the fourth ring. Deirdre listened to the message, and after the beep said, "Good afternoon, this is Dr. Foley's office calling to remind you that you have a cleaning appointment at 3 p.m. tomorrow. If you need to cancel the appointment or have any questions, please call us. Thank you very much, and we'll see you tomorrow."

She hung up, glanced at the clock. In ten minutes the office would reopen after the lunch break. Deirdre could hear the staff getting ready for the afternoon shift: the two hygienists, Larry and Terry, were reviewing the appointments and arguing over who got Mr. Wyler, who never flossed; Dr. Foley was sneaking in a few minutes of listening to his iPod before rest of the day's work; the woman in charge of insurance and billing, Elise, was coming Deirdre's way with a stack of envelopes in her hand. "Hi Deirdre," Elise said. "Would you be able to get some postage on these and send them out today?"

"Sure thing." Deirdre took the envelopes, then picked up some pink "While you were out" memos off her desk, handed them to Elise. "Delta Dental and Blue Cross both called while you were at lunch."

Elise took the notes, scanned them, smiled. "This is a relief." She leaned down conspiratorially, whispered, "Our last admin was nice but her phone messages were in hieroglyphics. Thanks!" Elise winked and walked down the hall, past Larry and Terry who were playing rock-paper-scissors to settle the Mr. Wyler issue.

Deirdre smiled to herself. It was a little thing, Elise's praise, but in her time at Dr. Foley's office there had been many little things like this, and they added up nicely.

The dental office wasn't large, but it was by far the most pleasant place Deirdre had ever worked in. Years ago it had been converted from a house, and had many homey touches that would not have been in a strip mall or office building. Dr. Foley's wife did most of the decorating, and her style often made Deirdre think of Anna's house. What had been the living room was now the waiting room, and Dr. Foley had kept the gas fireplace, which was now lit and very welcome on this cold winter day. On Fridays, all the staff members took turns bringing in a snack (last Friday had been Deirdre's turn, and she'd brought in Anna's deviled eggs).

The people were all pleasant to work with as well. Dr. Foley was silver-haired, and tanned from being outdoors. Every time he came into the office he looked like he'd just come from camping, or from a hike out in the woods. He seemed more at home in jeans, boots, and a flannel shirt than he did in his dentist's scrubs. He also understood that for most people, going to the dentist was not something to look forward to: he regaled his patients with fish stories or a tale of waking up to find a badger sleeping in his tent, and was particularly good at soothing the fears of children (and a few grownups). Terry, the female hygienist, was a tiny brunette barely five feet tall; the male hygienist, Larry, was a huge blond fellow who looked more like Haystack Calhoun than a dental professional. As for Elise, Deirdre thought of her as the office's Jekyll-and-Hyde. When she was on the phone with insurers, depending on how the conversation was going spoke in a voice smooth and delicious as butter, or in tones that took no nonsense and would not back down until she could speak with a supervisor, now. A good crew to work for, and they seemed to like her well enough. Larry had invited her to join his softball team when practice started up in the spring. Terry, like Deirdre, was a reader and they had already swapped some books back and forth.

Deirdre still wasn't sure how she'd managed to get the job. The interview had been two days after Christmas, and she'd never felt less prepared for anything in her life. She was shaken from the events of Christmas eve, still limping from the blow to her hip. Sleep didn't help much, not when she kept dreaming of her flight from Leo Sorensen, only the snow sucked onto her legs like tar and when Leo caught up, her screams went unheard; not when during her waking hours she kept waiting for the police to come hammering on her door. If she didn't get this job she would have to dip into that money of Richard's. She supposed she could have done that, but the money felt dirty to her. Besides, she could only use so much before someone wondered how she was paying the rent while unemployed.

The morning of the job interview she'd got up, showered, put on her nicest outfit, and drunk a cup of coffee, which she'd promptly thrown up. She'd had an office job before, and liked it, but that was years ago. The Deirdre who'd had that job was a different person. Back then Anna had been alive and happy. Back then Deirdre hadn't known the truth about Richard. It was before Deirdre's world was overturned, before she'd had to fight a man off with her bare hands and help dispose of bodies.

She'd expected that last thought to make things worse, but it had the opposite effect. Yes, that had happened, but she'd handled it. Done so quite well — there had been no mistaking the look of respect in Sean's eyes, and surely he was in a position to know. If she'd managed that, surely she could go into a job interview and give coherent answers.

On the drive to Dr. Foley's office, she'd felt her mind start to run in circles of panic again. She'd parked outside the dental office, and had sat in her truck looking at the pleasant little place. As she'd watched, a minivan pulled up, and the hulking blond fellow who was Larry jumped out and trotted up to the office door. He was singing as he did so: a spectacularly off-key rendition of "Jingle Bell Rock."

The office looked like a nice, normal place. Why shouldn't it be? Nick was a patient here, and he was a nice, normal guy. This job wasn't just about the money: it was a chance to get some niceness and normalcy back into her life. She needed that more than anything.

The interview had gone well enough for them to hire her on the spot. That night she called Nick to let him know; he wouldn't be back until the next day but promised he'd take her out to celebrate as soon as he returned.

She'd thrown all her dedication into the job, determined to reward both Dr. Foley's and Nick's faith in her. Deirdre not only did her job — managing appointments, pulling files, calling for referrals — but she did other things as well. She created a system for the day's patient files that made it easier for Dr. Foley and the two hygienists to know which type of appointment they had next; she started a purge of files for patients who had died or moved away; she even made daily runs to the coffee house across the street. It was a way to prove that she could handle a nice, normal job. It was a way to keep from thinking too much about Leo and Walt. And about everything else.

At half-past-five she said her goodbyes to Dr. Foley and to Terry (Elise and Larry had left earlier). Deirdre put on her coat, wrapped her scarf around her neck, got her purse, and stepped outside.

It was cold, but at least there was no breeze. You could stand the chill if you put your mind to it. She walked along the brick walkway and down the steps to the sidewalk, past the sign for Stan Foley, DDS, open Saturdays, walk-ins welcome. As she walked to her truck she happened to glance at the coffee house across the street.

He was there. Sitting at one of the outdoor tables along with a few other hardy souls. He had a large mug in front of him and a book open before him. As she glanced his way he looked up, quite casually, and happened to look across the street at her. Their eyes met for a second; then he went back to his book, and she continued on to her truck.

Deirdre didn't always see Sean after work. Sometimes she saw him near her apartment. Once she'd seen him at the farmer's market where she bought potatoes and home-made preserves. She wasn't sure if her infrequent sightings meant that he didn't always shadow her, or that he only let himself be seen when it suited him. Probably a little of both, but tending toward the latter. She had noticed that she never saw him when she was out with Nick: either he didn't shadow her then, or he was very good at keeping himself concealed.

It didn't bother her. She recalled being angry when she learned he'd been following her, before Christmas, and now wondered why it had upset her so. She was still angry over what he'd done and wasn't sure she liked anything about him, but she felt safer knowing he was around. She needed the shelter of his competence and ruthlessness, for a while. Until it was all over, and then she could send him out of her life.

When Deirdre arrived at her apartment, as always she looked for police cars in the parking lot. As always, she waited for someone to step from the shadows as she entered her apartment and tell her she was suspected of being involved in the disappearances of Leo and Walt.

As always, nothing of the kind happened.

She had been questioned by the police. Just before New Year's, when the Silas County Sheriff's Department could no longer pretend that Leo was somewhere sleeping off an eggnog bender. Two cops, officers Rodriguez and Nykvist, had talked to her, and she'd known right away from their methodical, slightly bored manner that it was routine. She was just one of many names on a list; anyone Leo had seen or talked to in the last few weeks was on that list. Sean had been right: they didn't think she would be capable of anything like murder. She'd told the police exactly what she'd rehearsed, and as far as she could tell they were satisfied with it. There had been no other visits, not even a phone call.

At first she wondered if the cops' disinterest had been a diversion. For a while she was even on edge during her dates with Nick. When would the penny drop, when would he ask her what she knew about Leo and Walt? That moment never came. One January night, after they had gone ice skating (Nick not so much skating as shuffling wobbly-ankled across the ice, Deirdre executing a reasonably acceptable figure eight) they went out for something to eat afterward — he talked about Leo's disappearance and how the retired sheriff was going to come back and fill in for a while. Knowing that Sean would call her a damned fool for doing so, but unable to stand the wait any longer, she asked Nick if he thought Leo's disappearance had anything to do with the deaths of Anna and the others.

He'd thought it over, then said, "I honestly don't know. It's like trying to put together a puzzle with only a few of the pieces. I don't have enough to go on. No one does, until they can get a court order to search Leo's house and see if he left any information there."

Nick reached out and took her hand. Deirdre knew hers was cold and damp from her nerves. Surely he'd notice that and realize something was amiss, but when he spoke, he smiled. "Make sure you're careful, Dee. Just in case Leo has anything to do with the other. Tell me if you see anything funny. Suspicious funny, I mean, not 'ha ha' funny." He'd rubbed her hand between his palms. "Have some hot chocolate or something, you're still freezing."

Of course. It never would occur to him that she might have had anything to do with it. Knowing this made it easier to lie to him, but the lies weighed heavy on her heart. He deserved honesty, but she could not be truthful with him. Yet.

Tonight, he called between 6 and 6:30, as usual. She found the consistency comforting. Randy had never called at the same time for more than two days running, and she should have known early on what a sign of flaky behavior that was. Nick called, at his usual time. "I'm free," he said. These days Nick never knew from one day to the next if he'd have to work late. "Sweet Christmas, but I'll be glad when we're back on a regular schedule." Leo's disappearance had thrown the department into some disarray, despite the return of former Sheriff John Grayson, and all the deputies were working longer hours these days.

"You get paid overtime, don't you?"

"Yeah, but overtime pay only makes up for so much. I'd rather spend that time with you."

Deirdre felt a grin spreading over her face. She saw Nick several times a week. Sometimes she and Nick went out — to the movies mostly, sometimes bowling. On occasion they went to the Stagger Inn, where Nick proved himself to be a rather good dancer — a better dancer than an ice skater, at least. They'd spent New Year's Eve at Jim and Laurel's house: that gathering was a much smaller affair than the Christmas party, about five couples there to eat lasagna and garlic bread while waiting for midnight. Mostly, though, Nick and Deirdre had stuck close to home; usually his home, where they'd snuggle on the couch and watch a movie or a few *Twilight Zone* episodes (Nick had gotten the complete series on DVD for Christmas).

They took things slow. She said it was because of her divorce from Randy, and Nick was fine with that. That was another lie. Deirdre would have jumped headlong into a romance with Nick if she had her way. But there was too much else going on, too many things she needed to be wary of. She couldn't afford to lose her bearings now.

There were no good movies showing tonight; Nick asked if she liked to play pool. She did, although she wasn't terribly good at it. No matter, he said, neither was he. He'd pick her up in twenty minutes and they'd go to the Billiard Room over in Du Lac.

Deirdre hung up. She did not immediately go to change and brush her hair but stood gazing at her phone. All she had to do was wait for things to blow over with Leo and Walt. For herself to summon the nerve to call that reporter and say what really had happened with Anna and Richard. For Sean Kincaid to go ... wherever he was bound. For life to get back to something like normal. Wait for all that, and then she'd give herself permission to fall in love with Nick.

The weekend before Valentine's Day. Saturday night and Deirdre was on her own because Nick was in Green Bay on business for the weekend. She'd planned to sit around and watch movies in her pajamas, perhaps be decadent and eat popcorn *and* ice cream. Instead, she found herself pacing restlessly; she looked through her books but nothing called her name. Her apartment seemed too small.

She ended up at the Stagger Inn. Deirdre hadn't been there on her own since before Christmas. The few times she'd been back, Nick had been with her.

Nothing had changed. The same smell of alcohol and sweat, a faint whiff of pot, the lingering scent of bar food. The same bass vibration underscored by dancer's footfalls. She blinked, adjusting her eyes to the light, and looked to see if Jim was DJ tonight; if he was, Laurel might be with him. It would be good to see them again. But the DJ wasn't Jim. Deirdre shrugged, ordered a Sprite from the bar, and after a while went to join the dance floor.

It wasn't the same. Before, she'd come here to work out those overpowering feelings of sadness and rage. Both emotions were still there, but they were tempered by time and knowledge. Now she knew how Anna had died and why. Now she knew what Richard's part in it had been. It was bitter knowledge, but she had to admit that it was better to know than to go on wondering and driving herself mad.

She danced for a while, enjoying it in a different way than she had before — enjoying the physicality of it, the chance to stretch her legs a bit. (Her new job was on the sedentary side, and if she didn't watch out she'd end up with a case of Desk Job Ass.) Before she could get a good dancing groove on, the

DJ cued up a ballad. Couples joined the floor to slow dance. Of course —
Valentine's Day was coming. She'd forgotten.

Deirdre took her Sprite and started to head outside. Before she reached
the door, she saw Sean. Sitting at a table by himself, looking at the menu with
an abstracted frown. She wondered how long he'd been there.

They had spoken once or twice since Christmas, but only on the phone,
and only to talk about the Sorensen brothers' disappearance: what she'd told
the cops, and what the cops had said. All the times they'd seen each other, not
a word had been exchanged. Deirdre had been fine with that.

She wasn't sure why she found herself walking over to his table. Perhaps
because she was restless and lonely. Perhaps because she knew she could tell
Sean anything. The irony was although she could tell him anything, he didn't
always understand her. She'd asked if it was OK to keep the money that had
been Richard's fund for his group. *Of course,* he'd said. *As long as you're careful
and don't make big purchases. Buy gas and groceries with the cash.*

That was good to know, but it hadn't been what she meant. She'd tried
again, wanted to know if it was right to use the money at all. Was it dirty
money? Blood money? Would using it put her on Richard's level? (Strange to
think that being like Richard was now a bad thing, when once she'd have
given anything to have a man like him in her life.)

There had been a silence from Sean, and she could sense his puzzlement.
Does it matter, he'd finally said, *as long as you don't use it for anything bad?* She
supposed it didn't matter. If only she could talk to Nick about these things.
Nick would have known what she meant.

Deirdre walked over to Sean's table. He looked up at her, and she caught
a flicker of genuine surprise in his eyes. "Hi," she said awkwardly.

"Hello."

"OK if I sit down?"

"Of course." He pulled out the other chair and she sat.

"Anything look good?" she asked, nodding at the menu.

He looked at the menu, squinting at it in the dim light. "Well, there's regular fries, garlic fries, cheese fries, chili fries, a fried onion flower thing, fried chicken, fried clams, fried mozzarella sticks, and fried zucchini."

"I sense a theme here."

He chuckled, smiled in an oddly charming way. "And buffalo wings, which I suspect are fried. And mini-burgers."

"The mini-burgers are good. And the fried onion flower thing, too. But stay away from the clams if you know what's good for you."

"Thanks." Sean put the menu down. "You've been here before?"

"I came here a lot last year. To dance. That's how I blew off steam. I'd get so … angry sometimes. I had to let it out or I'd explode. Do something crazy."

He nodded. "I understand." The waitress came by and he ordered mini-burgers and the onion flower. "Need anything to drink?" he asked.

"I'm fine."

Sean ordered a beer with his food. When the waitress left the two of them sat in a strangely comfortable silence for a while. "How are you doing?" he asked.

"Isn't that why you're here? To see how I'm doing?" What she'd said sounded too harsh. "I'm fine with it, really I am. But I thought…"

"I want to be sure no one's following you. The police, I mean. But you have a hard face to read sometimes, and I can't tell how you're feeling. Especially when I just see you from a distance."

She was surprised by what he'd said about her face being hard to read. She'd never thought herself much of a liar. Maybe it wasn't about lying but about not letting anyone see what she really thought. Letting her mother or brothers see would have given them more ways to get past her armor. Her father had never cared what Deirdre thought. And there had been all those years in school, pretending she wasn't bothered by the girls teasing her and the boys ignoring her, and then the years of fooling herself and everyone else that things were just fine with Randy. Only Anna had been able to see past the mask, but then, only Anna had really loved her. "I'm all right," she replied. "The job is good. It keeps me busy. And I've been seeing Nick. He's very nice." She wondered just how much Sean had shadowed her when Nick was around, remembered a few nights ago when she and Nick had spent a good while necking in his car. Deirdre felt a blush creeping up her face; she cursed her fair skin and hoped the dim lights of the Stagger Inn concealed her embarrassment. Hurriedly she went on: "It's better than it was. With Anna, I mean. Knowing what happened helps."

She looked up from her drink and saw that he was regarding her with a curious expression. Looking for something. Probably hoping she'd forgive him. That would never happen. She no longer felt that killing rage at him; much of her anger now went to Richard, who was to blame for his crazy murderous group and for putting Anna in danger. But Sean was the one who'd done the deed, and grateful as she was to him for his help and for saving her life, nothing could change that.

The instant he registered that she was looking at him his face changed. Became a mask — like one of those translucent ones they'd sold at Wal-Mart last Halloween that subtly altered the wearer's face, an effect more unsettling than any rubber fright mask. His eyes lost that questioning gleam and showed nothing more than polite interest. How did he do that? She remembered that detached look in his eyes when he'd killed Leo, just minutes after he'd been shot. No emotion in those eyes. Did he simply not let it show, or did he shut it off completely?

"Were always a …"

"A spook?"

She nodded.

"Always." If he was surprised by her question, he didn't show it.

"Did you like it?"

"I was good at it."

"But did you like it?"

He hesitated. "Of course. It was my life." Sean took a long drink of his beer. "When they retired us…well, it was hard. I never stopped hoping they'd call me back again."

"You didn't have anything else?"

He shook his head.

She vaguely recalled asking him on Christmas if he had a wife somewhere, and that she'd never given him a chance to answer. Before she could ask again, he answered: "My folks are long gone. No other family. I don't have a wife."

"What about Mona?" She remembered the initials engraved on his hip flask.

A quick spark of surprise. "Monique," he said in a way that made her think he hadn't meant to let that name slip.

"You said her name. Out by the lake. You were pretty out of it."

After a moment he said, "An old girlfriend. But that's been over for years and besides, she's married now."

"But you care."

"Yes."

For some reason she was relieved to know that he wasn't completely dead inside. At times she'd thought how much easier it would be if she'd never cared for Anna, never had to lose someone she loved. Every time she'd thought this she'd feared it might come true, that she would forget Anna and never let anyone come near her. No matter how things ended with Nick she'd be grateful to him for letting her know she could care for someone again.

She asked, "That night...how did you do it? How come you weren't afraid?"

He didn't answer for a while. The food arrived and they ate, and abruptly he put pushed his plate aside and said: "You learn how to push the fear down. You don't let it take you over. You know there's danger and you're alert to that, you have to be. But it's not fear, really. Sometimes, you can let yourself feel it later. When you're back at the safe house. But a lot of times, you're so busy and on alert that you don't have time to let yourself feel it. Or if you do feel it, it's like the memory of fear instead of the real thing."

"That doesn't sound so bad. Not feeling afraid."

Sean gave a strange smile. Not his charming smile at all; this one was twisted, the smile of a man who'd just downed a very expensive and very bitter drink. "Except you don't feel much else, either."

She had nothing to say to that. Eventually she asked, "What happens next?"

Sean said, "I'd like to wait until spring to see what happens and what they find. See what the evidence points to. Then we can come up with some way to get the truth about Anna and Richard out. I think maybe a confession letter with the papers we have ought to do the job. You'll have to be ready, though. You'll get a lot of scrutiny."

"I can handle it," she said, hoping she sounded more confident than she felt.

He gave her an appraising look. "Yes, you can."

Deirdre started to push her chair back, and then wondered something. Strange that she should wonder this — why should she care? "After that, after we're through, where will you go?"

"To Canada. British Columbia, a town called Haven Cove. The girl I did all this for, Jennifer Thomson, lives there. I want to be sure she's all right."

Deirdre had nearly forgotten the reason behind Sean's mission. What a shock that must have been for some ordinary woman, to find out she'd been the object of obsession. The reason for a quest that had gone wrong for so many people. Deirdre felt sorry for Jennifer. She might have been the catalyst for Sean but she wasn't to blame for any of it. She'd even let Richard go. Deirdre didn't think she could have done that.

But then, she'd let Sean go, hadn't she?

"After that, where?"

He shrugged.

Deirdre felt a chill. He didn't know, probably didn't care. What was left for him after that? She remembered the way he'd looked relieved when she put the gun to his head, and shuddered.

To her surprise, Sean gave her a little smile. He reached out as if he wanted to touch her hand, then drew back. "We'll work things out. No one's been following you. We just need to wait a bit longer. Do what you've been doing. And stick with that Nick fellow. He loves you."

Deirdre felt the blush rise into her face again. "He hasn't said it."

"Doesn't have to. He's easy to read. I don't know if he's much of a cop, but he seems like a good man."

She almost laughed, because many times she'd thought that Nick was in the wrong profession. Maybe when she told him everything else she'd tell him that as well, but she'd break it gently.

"I'm going to dance for a bit more," Deirdre said. "You'll be around?"

He nodded.

"OK," she said. She danced, and when she looked back at the little table, Sean was gone.

That night, drifting toward sleep, Deirdre remembered a summer with Anna. Not the summer of the family reunion. The year after that, when she took the money she'd saved and bought a Greyhound ticket for Minnesota. When she spent a month at Anna's house: running around the woods, going to the movies, baking cookies. Traipsing through the woods, they'd come to a small river. There was nothing like a real bridge, just a narrow plank no wider than the balance beam at Deirdre's school gym. Deirdre, who'd never liked heights, had watched fascinated as Anna blithely stretched out her arms and walked along the beam without looking down. "Come on, Dee!" she'd called from the other side, and she'd watched patiently as Deirdre inched her way across.

"How did you do that?" Deirdre had asked when she finally reached the riverbank.

"Put your arms out," Nan had said. "Yes, like that. Now imagine that someone is holding you up. One person on each side."

"Guardian angels?"

Anna had laughed. "Maybe. You know what they say. God looks out for drunks and little children. Imagine they're there. They won't let you fall. That's how you do it."

Half-asleep, Deirdre thought that these days she did have guardian angels — a good angel and a bad angel — holding her up. They wouldn't let her fall. She hoped.

Part Three

Chapter Thirty-one

The motel's walls were thin, and the cold crept in under the door. Sean didn't feel the cold; some time ago he had set up a metal bar in the doorway to the bathroom, and was well into a set of chin-ups, had already worked up a sweat. He didn't count repetitions. He never did. This wasn't about numbers, it was about making sure he was strong when he needed to be.

He'd fallen out of the habit until recently, and it felt good to be getting back into shape. He was a long way from being in top condition, for he couldn't run in the snow, and walking was a poor substitute. This would do for now. It soothed his body and his mind, and though he didn't think he would need to be in fighting shape again, the workout was a habit that died hard.

Besides, he had little else to do these days. He shadowed Deirdre, but not as much as in the past. The dangerous time had been right after Christmas, when the police were asking about Leo and Walt. Sean hadn't been sure she would be able to handle things if she fell under suspicion. She'd proved her mettle at the Christmas tree farm, but she was new at this, and still dealing with the loss of Anna and the revelations about Richard. It might take only a small matter to make her crack. He'd seen that sort of thing happen before.

She hadn't cracked. She'd gotten the job at the dental office, and was having a fine time with that deputy sheriff who was so sweet on her. Good for Deirdre. She deserved a little happiness — God knew she'd been through enough the last few months. He shadowed her not so much out of worry for her but to make sure that she kept healing. That the wounds he and Richard had given her did not scar her too deeply.

All they had to do was wait a little longer. Until spring, and the inevitable discovery of Leo and Walt. If no signs of foul play remained and the deaths were ruled an accident, it would be simple. He'd already written up an anonymous letter from a member of Richard's group, stating what had happened. That, along with the evidence Deirdre already had, would set things straight and clear Anna's name.

If the elements had not done their work and a coroner ruled that Leo and Walt were murdered…Sean would take the fall to keep Deirdre out of trouble. The thought of prison did not trouble him, as long as he restored Anna's reputation and ensured that Deirdre was left out of it. One qualm remained: he would have no chance to go to Canada and look in on Jennifer Thomson. Make sure she, like Deirdre, was healing.

Sean paused in his workout as Deirdre's voice spoke in his memory. That night at the roadhouse when she'd talked with him. *After that, where?* she'd asked. He hadn't answered. How could he? After Deirdre was safe, after he saw how Jennifer was recovering from the damage he'd done, there really was nowhere for him to go. Unless he went to Robert's house, in Maine. Perhaps by then he'd have earned the right to claim it.

His workout finished, he showered and dressed, feeling the chill now as the early March wind found the cracks in the windows and walls. Outside the ground was still snowy but the snow had lost its beauty long ago, had a flat, dingy look. Spring could arrive any time now, as far as he was concerned. It would be nice to be warm again, nice to walk without sliding in the snow and slush.

The knock at the door startled him. Housekeeping had already come and gone. Deirdre, perhaps? But she'd never once visited him here, only called when she needed to talk. Probably it was the motel manager, who cut Sean a good deal on the rates in return for small fix-it jobs and shoveling snow off the walkways.

The doors were cheap, like the rest of the place, and had no peepholes. Sean went to the door and opened it. Any greeting he'd prepared died in his throat; his heart gave an unsteady lurch and then hammered double-time at the walls of his chest, like the victim of a premature burial banging on the coffin lid.

He hadn't seen her in more than five years but it might have been five days, she was so familiar to him. The only change was a white streak in her hair, by the left temple, and the laugh lines around her eyes etched a little deeper. He already knew her voice was the same bittersweet honey tone; from when he'd called her last October and she'd said, *Flint, is that you?* Everything else — her dark eyes, the little tilt of her head when something intrigued her — the same.

In a way, seeing her was a greater shock than when he'd mistaken Deirdre for Anna. He'd always known Anna would come to haunt him, one way or another, but he'd never expected to see Monique again.

She stood looking at him, perplexed, as if what she saw did not jibe with what she had expected. Why had she come, what was she doing here, and how in hell had she found him? His heart sent out its steady drumbeat of *Danger*. He caught Monique by the arm, pulled her inside, and slammed the door closed.

They stared at each other, Monique and Sean. Both spoke at the same time: "How did — " "I thought you — "

Silence. Sean broke it first, and right away Monique knew things were amiss. In other circumstances Sean would have invited her to speak first, in that gentlemanly way of his. "How did you find me?" he asked. His voice was low and fast, not angry but with an urgency that could be mistaken for anger. For the first time she was hearing the voice of the other Sean, the one who went away for weeks or months at a time.

"I got a note," she said. "It said you needed me."

"Who sent it?"

She shook her head. "I don't know. It came from Maine. Same as the one from last year, the one that said people would come asking about you." Monique felt a queasy sinking sensation in her belly; she'd been duped. "They're not from the same person? How do you know?"

"My friend Robert sent you the note last year."

"Maybe — " she began.

He shook his head. "Robert's dead. Since October." Sean ran a hand through his hair. "Christ, what a cock-up. What did the note say?"

Monique shifted on her feet. "That you were sick, maybe dying. That you kept calling for me. But you wouldn't ask me to come."

"Why did you come?" He was angry now, but not at her, she knew.

"What should I have done?"

"Stayed away."

"And how would I have known that? You disappear without telling me anything. Leave it to your friends to tell me someone might come around to give me the third degree. You call me from Montana in the middle of the night and hang up on me. You send me this letter telling me you've gone off the rails. Do you know how bad off you sounded in that letter?" Monique flung her purse down, kicked at the floor. "When I got this last note, it was almost a relief. I finally knew. And I thought, 'Well, at least he's not a suicide'."

A shadow crossed his face and Monique knew that this last had struck home. If nothing else, she vowed to get some answers from Sean. While she waited for him to speak, she studied him. He looked older than when she'd last seen him, but not much. Sean had one of those faces that made him look older than his years in his youth but carried him well out of middle age without showing the passage of time; he'd joked once that he'd looked like a middle-aged man since he was thirty and would look the same until he was seventy. It was his eyes that told the truth; before, his eyes had never given anything away. There had always been thoughts locked behind them, never for her to see.

All that was different now. Everything had been so plain to see when he'd opened that door. Shock, pleasure. Fear for her. What had happened to change him so?

"Why did you come?" he asked. "I'm not worth it."

She shook her head. Why had she come? Because she had cared, once. Still cared, in a way. Because she sensed he was alone in the world save for her. "I was afraid if I didn't you'd die alone."

"That could have happened any time when I was in the agency."

"That was different. You're on your own now."

Mention of his former employers seemed to bring the professional side of him back. "Who talked to you?"

"Frank Halsey."

"Anyone else?"

She shook her head. "Just him, and just once. His interrogation skills weren't much but there was something creepy about him. Kept checking me out. He seemed to have some kind of fixation on you. You think he sent the note?"

"I don't know. He'd never have found me on his own, which means he's had some help. We're getting you back home ASAP." He turned abruptly and went to the room's closet, opened the door, and turned back with something she couldn't identify in his hands. Sean handed it to her. "Put that on."

She took it from him. A vest. Heavy, but supple. She felt that queasy sensation again as she knew what it must be.

Sean took her silence for puzzlement. "It's a bulletproof vest. Put it on under your sweater."

Monique didn't ask if it was necessary. Of course it was. Whoever sent the note knew where Sean was. If they'd wanted to kill him they could have done it, but there was more at work if they'd lured her here as well. She clenched the vest in her hands and cursed Sean for being flirty with her the night they met and for being such a simpatico partner during that time in her life. She cursed herself for letting it go on so long when she knew it would never last; for not writing him off when he disappeared from her life.

She sat down on the floor with the vest still clutched in her hands. In her peripheral vision she saw him checking to make sure his gun was loaded, then putting it into the holster; saw him pull up his right pants cuff to strap a sheathed knife on to his leg. Once she'd thought it might be interesting, and possibly even a turn-on, to see Sean go into his professional mode. Now she just felt ill-prepared for whatever lay ahead.

She'd gotten the note a couple days ago. As soon as she'd finished reading it, she'd packed a carry-on bag with a change of clothes, called to see what flights were available out of National. Then she waited for Michael to call.

He was in the air when she got the note and she'd had no way to reach him. She had to wait for his call, and she didn't know how long she waited. Time stretched out and she finally turned the clock away so she didn't have to watch the minute hand's slow creep. At first she worried that she'd arrive too late to help Sean. But as she waited her thoughts took a different turn: that Michael would not understand, would think she was running off to have a fling. She knew many men would not take well to the idea of their wives dropping everything to visit a former lover. There weren't many ways to justify it, but if she didn't go, the thought that Sean might die completely alone and without comfort would haunt her for the rest of her days. If he had been on the job, that would have been different. But he was on his own, in trouble, and she could not in good conscience leave him to that fate.

When Michael called she didn't immediately pick up the phone. She let the answering machine pick up — she often did, because the messages he left always made her laugh. Monique listened as Michael's voice, tired but cheerful, said: "Good evening, ladies and gentlemen, and welcome to London. If you enjoyed the flight, this has been Air Atlantic and I'm Captain Michael Banks. If you did not enjoy the flight, this has been Ozark Airways and I'm Captain Billy Earl Ray Bob McGillicuddy..."

Monique picked up the receiver then. "Hi, Michael, I'm here," she said, hoping her voice sounded normal.

It didn't. "What's wrong?" he asked. "What is it, dollybird?"

Her eyes closed at the endearment. She remembered the first time he'd called her *dollybird*. They'd been dating for a couple months, and after getting back from one of his London jaunts, he'd given her a shawl, Irish wool in a gorgeous forest-green color, soft like no other wool she'd worn before. *The instant I saw this I knew I had to get it for you, dollybird*, he'd said. "Something's come up," she said. "That friend I told you about, who's in trouble. Things are worse, and I need to go see him."

Silence on the other end.

"So, I may be away for a few days."

More silence.

"Michael?"

"I'm here, I'm here. I'm just worried, that's all."

"It's not..." She wasn't sure how to finish.

"Monique, dollybird, it's all right. I trust you. Why wouldn't I?"

Her sense of relief was so great she almost didn't hear his next words.

"Your friend, it's not that spook, is it? The guy from Department 56 or whatever it was?"

"Yes, it's him."

Michael sighed. "I know you will anyway, but let me say it: Be careful. I've known some people in that field and they never *really* retire. If things look weird, get out and come home. Be safe. He'd want you to do that."

"I know. I'll be careful. And I'll be home before the weekend." Regaining her calm, she said, "I'll make dinner reservations at Citronelle for Saturday. You know I won't miss that."

"I know. I love you."

"I love you, too. I'll see you in a few days."

At the time, Monique had been too relieved to fully appreciate Michael's reasons for concern, but now it made perfect sense. She'd walked right into it, when she should have known better. Now she was sitting in a ratty motel room holding on to a bulletproof vest.

"Moni?" Sean's voice was gentler than it had been since her arrival. He sat down next to her.

She looked at him. Again she noticed that change in him, in the way she was able to read his eyes. "Tell me what's been going on," she said. "I'll get on the first plane back to D.C., but first just tell me what happened."

"Put on the vest first."

She took off her jacket and sweater and put on the vest over her turtleneck, hating the way it felt and the necessity of it, but taking comfort in the protection it gave her. Monique put her sweater and jacket back on and felt oddly comforted to know the vest was out of sight. She looked at Sean. "No his-and-hers vests?"

"That's my only one. No arguments."

"I wasn't going to argue. Tell me what's happened."

Sean looked away from her, looked down at his hands. As he spoke he never took his eyes off his hands, as his story went on she saw that he began to rub his left hand back and forth against his right hand, as if some maddening itch lay below the skin, or as if the hand had gone numb and he was trying to massage feeling back into it.

She listened and felt a curious mix of emotions wash over her, turning her hot and cold, making her want to give him comfort and slap him at the same time. Monique thought of the woman he'd killed and those whose lives he'd turned over, and she would have hated him and walked away forever if his remorse was not genuine.

"You have a lot to answer for," she said.

He nodded. He still hadn't looked back at her. Probably he was afraid that she'd hate him now, but she couldn't hate him, not when he was trying to make amends. How many of his kind would have simply written it all off as a botched mission and not bothered to right the wrongs? Many, she suspected.

"I know. And now you've been brought into it." He shook his head. "I don't have any right to ask anything from you, but can you tell me how you're doing? I mean, are you happy?"

"Yes. I'm very happy."

"Your husband, is he good to you? Because if he isn't, I'll give him a thrashing."

"I'd like to see you try. He's into Ren Faire and has a real broadsword."

He laughed, and looked at her for the first time since he'd started telling her what had happened. He had been smiling, but now his smile faded. "I'm sorry you got dragged into it. I never thought… I was so busy looking after Deirdre, I forgot anyone might still be looking for me. You need to know, I always tried to keep you safe. I guess it would have been best if we'd ended it after that first night. But I wanted to be with you."

Monique put her arms around him. No passion, not even the echo of it, but consolation. She felt him try to pull away from her, then he gave in and returned the embrace. Only for a moment — then he withdrew. The man was gone, the agent was back.

Sean stood up, glanced at the window. "It'll be dusk soon. That'll give us some cover. Once you get in your car, don't stop until you get to Green Bay. Don't take the vest off until you're about to go through security at the airport.

Get the first flight out of there, worry about a connection later — do you need money?"

"I've got plenty."

"Good. I don't think —"

Monique's cell phone rang, startling them both. She reached for the phone; caller ID listed a 202 area code, but the number wasn't one she recognized. "Hello?"

A moment of silence, then a woman's voice. "I need to speak with Sean. Tell him it's Deirdre."

Deirdre? The Deirdre he was trying to help? Monique told Sean; he blanched and she suspected she didn't look much better. He took the phone. "It's Sean." Monique leaned in close and was able to hear.

"Frank Halsey's here. He's got me at Anna and Richard's house. You have to come here now." The caller hung up.

Sean stood for a moment with the cell phone in his hand, looked as if he might crush it or throw it against the wall. He did neither. With a calmness she found more unnerving than any display of rage, he gave her back the phone and put on his jacket. "I'm getting you to your car now."

Monique grabbed her purse, stood up. As they headed out the door and went at a trot through the parking lot, he said, "Remember, don't stop for anything, just get h-"

A popping sound from somewhere, she wasn't sure where. Sean had been holding on to her arm; his grip suddenly slackened, he stopped walking. Monique turned and saw Sean standing in the snowy parking lot. One hand groped at his neck, the other reached for his gun. His eyes were open but unfocused. "Run," he said in a low, slurry voice, then his eyes rolled back to whites and he fell to the ground.

Run, he'd said, but she froze, looking to see if he'd been shot. He had, but there was no bullet hole; in his neck she saw a silvery dart.

She felt the trap's jaws closing; she turned and ran for her car, almost made it. Less than a yard from the car, she felt a sharp pain in her leg, like a bee sting, and the curtain came down.

Chapter Thirty-two

Deirdre swam up out of the dark. She wanted to get to the bright surface of consciousness yet was in no hurry to see what would be there when she woke. Even half-conscious, she couldn't fool herself into thinking that she had dreamed this day's events, and that she'd wake up and find life had returned back to normal in time for her to go bowling with Nick.

That morning, she'd woken and showered as usual on a Monday, when the dental office was closed. As she was making the coffee she found that the half-and-half had gone bad; Deirdre was willing to have coffee without sugar, but coffee without cream was simply unacceptable. She put on her jacket, stuck a five-spot into the pocket of her jeans, grabbed her keys, and went out the door, on her way to the convenience store.

When she reached the bottom of the stairs, a hand seized her by the arm and pulled her into the alcove under the stairs. She let out a gasp, and whirled around, ready to give Sean a dressing-down for scaring her like that.

It wasn't Sean. The man was younger than Sean, and taller, with a pointed face and beady eyes that gave him a distinctly ratlike appearance. Before she could try to break free or even say anything, he was pointing a gun at her face. "Keep quiet," he said, "and come with me."

He tugged on her arm but she resisted. "What's this about?"

The man's eyes had a scary glitter to them. He tried for a reassuring smile but it didn't match up with his eyes, and the effect was ghoulish. "This is government business. I need your help finding Sean Kincaid."

At first she'd thought he might be a straggler from Richard's group, but when he said government business she guessed he was from the agency Sean used to belong to. Deirdre sensed right off this wasn't business at all, but personal. It was in the way the glitter in his eyes intensified when he said

Sean's name, the way his upper lip sheened with sweat as he pointed the gun at her. Deirdre felt an adrenaline jolt run through her, making her limbs shaky and her fingers tingle; she was more afraid than she'd been when Sean pointed his gun at her in the cemetery, or when Leo had chased her through the trees. They seemed paragons of sanity next to this man.

"Come along, Deirdre," he said, and she felt another queasy thump inside as he said her name. He pushed her along, not to her truck but to a swanky SUV. She'd seen it before, parked near Dr. Foley's office the other evening. He must have been shadowing her. Or shadowing Sean. Deirdre wanted to run but didn't dare. She could feel the muzzle of his gun against her back, and if she tried to flee he could pull the trigger before she got three steps.

He motioned her to get in the SUV. When she did, he sat down in the driver's seat, took out a pair of handcuffs, and locked them around her wrists. Then he smiled and pointed the gun at her.

"Now here's what we're going to do. Tell me a place we can go that's out of the way. I need to have a private talk with our mutual friend Sean, and I don't want any interruptions."

She tried to think, and the only place that came to her was Anna's house. It had what this man wanted, but Sean knew the territory. She remembered, feeling something like hope, there was a shotgun in the bedroom that Anna had kept around for home protection. There was nothing else to save her — she thought of Nick but knew he would be gone all day in Green Bay and not back until evening at the earliest.

"Come on, girlie. Time's a-wasting. I've got a schedule to keep," he said, waggling the gun in her face.

She gave him the address, and he plugged it into the GPS. He put the car in gear, then looked at her. "By the way, my name's Frank Halsey. Sean might have mentioned me."

"He didn't," she replied.

He scowled at her, then put the pistol on his seat, out of her reach, and started to drive.

Deirdre sat quietly. To an observer she looked bewildered, vacant even, but her mind was ticking carefully through her options. Nick was out of town and out of reach. So were the police — she didn't have her cell and the phones were out at Anna's house. As were the electricity and heat — it would be cold there. Dr. Foley's office was closed and she'd made no plans — there was no one to wonder where she was. She was on her own.

Deirdre rested her cuffed hands in her lap, and felt the pepper spray canister through her jacket. It was in her right pocket. Slowly she began inching her hands over to that pocket, hoping she could work her hand in despite the cuffs and get the canister. If she could get one good shot at him, she could buy herself enough time to get out of the car and out of his range. She worked at it slowly, resisting the urge to hurry, although if she didn't do this soon they'd be out of town and her only place to run would be the woods. Still, she'd run the risk of frostbite rather than take any chances with this lunatic.

She kept working. He didn't notice, seemed content to glance at her now and then. He wore an infuriatingly smug expression, like a cat licking the cream off its whiskers. Her hand closed around the canister; perhaps she could do something about that smug look.

At a stop sign, he paused to consult the GPS. She eased the canister out of her pocket, put her finger on the trigger, and said, "I know a short cut."

As he looked up at her, she brought up the pepper spray canister. Her sweaty finger slipped on the trigger, and in the second it took to regain her grip and pull the trigger, he got a hand up in front of his face. The spray hit not his face but his hand, turning it a bright red and making him howl.

She wouldn't get a better chance. Deirdre lunged over to the door, unlocked it, opened the door and was halfway out when Halsey seized her by the hair and yanked back. The pain was huge, as if the top of her head were coming off, and she screamed as he hauled her back into the car. Her cry echoed on the empty road, no one to hear her, and she knew her chance was gone.

Halsey glared at her with a hatred out of all proportion to his injury or her escape attempt. He pointed a gun at her — a different one, silver-colored, but she scarcely noticed. Halsey looked at his inflamed, painful hand and then back at her. "Women. Bitches. *All of them!*" he snarled, and then pointed the pistol downward and shot her in the leg. She had just enough time to register that it was not a bullet but a dart, like the tranquilizer darts they used on nature shows, and then darkness swallowed her.

She woke to find herself lying on the floor of Anna's bedroom. The handcuffs' chain had been looped around the leg of the bedframe. After a woozy few moments, Deirdre got to her knees and tried to lift the bed enough to get the handcuffs free, but it was impossible. The bed was a solid oak four-poster, she'd never lift it high enough. She tried pulling her hands out of the handcuffs, but they were closed snugly on her wrists.

There was nothing to do but wait.

After a while, Halsey came into the room carrying a portable space heater. She was relieved, though she didn't say so — it was bitterly cold in the room. He set it up, turned it on. Then he stood and stared at her. "You're welcome," he finally said.

When she didn't answer, he said, "You should be happy I got this, especially after that stunt you pulled." He flexed his hand, which seemed to be fine now. "Still, you're no good to me if you turn into a popsicle." His cell phone rang, playing Kenny G's "Songbird." Now she *knew* he was insane.

"Yes?" he barked into the phone. After a pause: "Perfect. We'll talk when I'm back in D.C."

Halsey hung up. "Relax for a bit. In a little while we'll go for a drive."

They drove to Sean's motel, and once there they parked in the lot and waited. Halsey spent some time fiddling with the radio, looking for music, but nothing pleased him and he turned the radio off. He glanced over at her, looked her up and down.

"You don't look like I expected," he said. "You're not Kincaid's usual type. You're a feisty little thing, though. Maybe that's the appeal. You've got something that he likes. That's how I found him. Following you. Old Sean's gone soft, following you around like a puppy dog. Let me guess, he was in love with your cousin. Thought if he came back you'd give him a tumble like she did. Am I right?"

She lowered her face, didn't answer him. His fingers went under her chin, pushed her face up to look at him. "Am I right?"

Deirdre jerked away from him. He smiled, and for the first time in weeks her rage got the better of her. She bit his fingers as hard as she could. He let out a girlish scream that almost made her laugh, and yanked his hand back. She spat on the car floor — it was tinged with his blood.

"You bit me. You fucking bit me!"

"Talk trash about Anna again and I'll bite you worse."

Halsey brought the tranquilizer pistol up, very close to her face. "How'd you like one of these darts in your eye?"

"You won't. You need me to be the bait."

He let out a disgusted snort, lowered the pistol. "Wait a while. You'll see I'm no one to trifle with. You'll all see."

He kept quiet after that, went back to staring out the windshield and drumming his fingers on the dashboard. Finally a blue coupe pulled up: a rental car. A dark-haired woman, fortyish and attractive, got out. She looked at a piece of paper in her hand, then went up to Sean's room. Deirdre was able to see the look of surprise on Sean's face, saw it change to alarm as he brought the woman inside and closed the door. *That must be Monique,* Deirdre thought. *Does Sean know he still loves her? As much as he's able to love anyone?*

"He's not going to come out here," Deirdre said in a last-ditch attempt at reasoning with Halsey. "He knows by now it's a trap and so does she."

"He will," Halsey said. "He cares. It's his weakness."

Still they waited. Finally Halsey sighed. "What's taking them? Are they having coffee?" He took out his cell phone and dialed a number, told her what to say and held the phone to her.

Deirdre did what he said. She couldn't see any other choice. All she could hope for was that Sean figured out it was a trap and outsmarted this Halsey fellow. How was this going to end? Was she going to make it out of this? She'd thought after surviving the night at the tree farm that she'd made it through the worst life could throw at her, but who could have predicted this man with his insane need for revenge? She thought it might be a complete surprise even to Sean.

Surprise or no, she was going to make it. She'd been through too much in the last few months just to be the toy hostage of a psycho. Her mind groped for something comforting; she focused on Nick. His smile. Before the picture could come into focus completely, there was the sting of the tranquilizer dart again, in her leg. *I'm getting used to it,* she thought, as the world went dark.

Now she drifted back up to consciousness. She heard the hum of the space heater and knew she was back at Anna's house. She opened her eyes, stirred. Winced as her muscles protested, for she was sitting on Anna's bed, slumped against one of the posts. Deirdre sat up straight; she tried to lean forward, but could not. Her wrists were cuffed behind her now, the chain around one of the bedposts. On the bureau stood a Coleman gas lantern, lighting up the room with its shivery brightness.

Hearing the sound of breathing, she turned and saw Monique. Unconscious still. Like Deirdre, propped against a bedpost with her hands cuffed behind her. As far as Deirdre could tell she seemed fine — there was a quarter-size bloodstain on Monique's trousers, probably from being shot with the dart, but no other injuries that Deirdre could see. No one else was in the room.

Deirdre was wondering where Sean and Halsey were when Monique stirred. Her head went forward, then she jerked back. Monique's eyes opened; she shook her head and looked around the room, then at Deirdre. "You're...?"

"Deirdre."

"Yes. Sean told me, but I'm still foggy." She shook her head again, winced as her stiff neck muscles creaked. "I'm Monique."

Deirdre nodded. She thought she could hear male voices from another room.

"Where's Sean?" asked Monique.

"I think I hear him. Listen."

Chapter Thirty-three

The space heaters didn't warm the room much; they made the cold tolerable and that was it. Halsey didn't mind. He was happier than he had been in years, and his happiness warmed him inside and out. It was a Christmas eve feeling — that sense of anticipation for what the next day would bring. He hadn't needed sleep on those childhood Christmas eves, had preferred to lie awake and bask in anticipation. On those nights he had never let himself remember that inevitably Christmas day itself was a disappointment in one way or another, that usually the day ended with his father drinking too much of whatever liquor he'd been gifted and giving his mother a tongue-lashing — one year, he had given her a black eye and a broken nose — while the relatives pretended nothing was amiss and his siblings and cousins ignored him. The anticipation was the best part, and he reveled in it.

Just as he reveled in it now. It had been hard work, this last month, and at times he'd been tempted to settle for less than he wanted, or give it up altogether. Then he'd think of what he'd done to Juliette, and reassurance swept away any doubts. She'd underestimated him, and paid for it — and he'd gotten away with it. As far as he knew, he wasn't a suspect in her death. No one had questioned him. He was even able to laugh off that last taunt of hers: *Is that the best you can do?* No, it was all going to work out the way he wanted it to.

Not that it had been easy. For days he'd locked himself in his house, not answering the phone, living off coffee and the take-out the housekeeper brought in, going without sleep as he looked over the evidence Juliette had collected for him. For hours he'd sat staring at the documents, jotting things down, and at the end of the day he usually threw a bunch of wadded-up paper, discarded ideas, into the fireplace. (His fireplace was getting quite the workout these days; it was where he'd disposed of his bloodstained clothes after leaving Juliette's house that last time.)

There were two problems he faced: the first was knowing where exactly to look for Kincaid. If he drove around aimlessly looking for the man, chances were good Kincaid would spot him first. Halsey couldn't fool himself into thinking otherwise. The second was getting Monique Pavour to the same location. Before, he might have never tried to solve that second problem, but killing Juliette made him believe anything was possible. If he was going to do this, he would go all the way.

He got a break when he called the weekly paper in Silas County and asked them to send a copy of every issue that had come out since the beginning of October last year; to sweeten the deal and speed things along, he'd wired them the money for overnight delivery. Halsey had spent the next two days going through the papers looking for something — anything — that would give him a clue. For a long time he found nothing, just an endless catalog of small-town provincial life that was so deadly dull to read about, he couldn't imagine actually living it. Kincaid had done this town a favor; the killings were the most action this place had seen since the nineteenth century. What he found wasn't much — a puff piece about the Christmas tree farm the Blaines had owned — but it mentioned a cousin of Anna Blaine. Deirdre Monahan was the name, and Halsey thought that if Juliette was right and Kincaid had unfinished business in Silas County, that cousin might be a good place to start. He'd sat there holding the newspaper, laughing softly to himself, his unwashed hair askew and his hands smudged black with newsprint, and that was when the housekeeper got spooked and quit.

He got a second break from an unexpected phone call. Agent Larson — make that former agent Larson — whom Halsey had gotten fired on the day he was demoted. Former agent Larson was jobless and broke, his wife *this* close to leaving him and taking the kids with her. Former agent Larson was desperate to save his marriage, knew Halsey was due to go back to the agency in a couple months, and would do anything if Halsey could get him a job, any job, with the agency again. It had been perfect — the extra set of hands Halsey needed. Once Halsey had been to Wisconsin, found the Monahan girl, and tracked down both her and Kincaid, he put Larson in charge of sending the note to Monique Pavour, and then relaying to Halsey which flight she got on and when she was due to arrive in Green Bay.

Everything had gone just the way he'd planned it. He wasn't thrilled about that Monahan girl trying to zap him with her pepper spray and biting him — he hadn't expected her to be such a scrapper — but it was nothing his tranquilizer gun couldn't fix. Now he had all three of them, right where he wanted them.

While he waited for his three captives to come around, Halsey paused to take three Excedrin, chasing them down with a shot of Tanqueray. His whole body ached outrageously. He hadn't realized how much work it would be to manhandle three unconscious people. Thank God none of them were very big or heavy. (If he had permitted himself to remember how Juliette had knocked him out and tortured him, he would have respected her ability to drag him downstairs and truss him up; that couldn't have been easy.) The women had been easiest; all he'd had to do was haul them onto the bed, prop them up against posts, and cuff their hands behind their backs. Kincaid had been the hardest. Halsey only had two sets of cuffs, and those were on the women, but he found some rope in the tree farm's shed and used that to tie Kincaid's ankles and legs to the chair, his hands behind his back. By the time he was done his muscles were trembling with exhaustion, and he was happy to sit and rest for a while.

While he waited, he thought of Juliette. *So, what do you think? Nicely done, I'd say. Got Kincaid, got his old flame, even got that red-haired girl Kincaid's been following around.* These last few weeks he'd often found himself having these one-sided mental conversations with Juliette; sometimes, when he'd been without sleep or proper food, wired on caffeine and plotting his strategy, he got the feeling that Juliette was there, looking over his shoulder. On those infrequent occasions he went out, he sometimes caught what he thought was a glimpse of her. It was always some other woman with a similar hair color or way of walking, never Juliette of course.

Kincaid was starting to come around. Halsey smiled. He pulled one of the straight-backed chairs closer, turned it around and sat astride it. While he waited he observed Kincaid, whom he hadn't seen up close since their meeting after the Los Angeles bombing. He was disappointed to see Kincaid not looking as haggard as he'd apparently been when he dropped in on Robert Dvorak. After everything Kincaid had put Halsey through, Kincaid ought to look worse for wear.

Kincaid took in a deep breath, let it out. Was very still for a couple minutes, and Halsey had decided that he wasn't coming out of it after all when Kincaid opened his eyes, raised his head. He gave Halsey a cursory glance before craning his head to look at his bonds. He shifted in his chair, either testing the bonds or making himself more comfortable, and only then gave his full attention to his captor. "Halsey. Been a while." Kincaid glanced around the room, and Halsey knew what he was doing. Looking for another person. He didn't think Halsey could have done this on his own, and Halsey pushed down his anger. Save it for later. There would be plenty of time for it.

"Surprised to see me?" Halsey asked.

"Yes and no. Robert said you were looking for me. Who helped you?"

Halsey was about to say that it had been all his own work, but decided it might demoralize Kincaid to know a former colleague had helped track him down. "Juliette."

Kincaid didn't seem bothered. "Comradeship was never her strong suit. What did you have to pay her?"

Halsey tried without much success to keep his ears from turning red. "Nothing."

"How nice." Kincaid shifted in the chair. "Where are Monique and Deirdre?"

"Somewhere safe."

"Show me."

"Don't you trust me?"

Kincaid said nothing. His face didn't change but there was a chilly look in his eyes that made Halsey wonder just how good a job he'd done tying up Kincaid.

Halsey took his cell phone out of his pocket and found the picture he'd taken of the women once he'd cuffed them to the bedposts. He held it up to Kincaid. "See anything you like?"

"Let them go."

"Not a chance."

"They're nothing to you."

"True, but they're something to you. Besides, Monique gave me the run-around when I was looking for you and that redhead gave me a lot of trouble." Unconsciously he fidgeted with the bandages he'd put around the fingers Deirdre had bitten.

Kincaid looked calm. Halsey glared at him, anger rising, for he'd always hated that placid mask of Kincaid's. He'd seen it in countless meetings and debriefings, that smug look that said *I'm better than you.* Even now, tied up, his women hostage, all three of them at Halsey's mercy, he was calm.

Well, perhaps Halsey could do something about that.

"It wasn't any picnic trying to find you, I'll say that. Top brass wasn't interested, for some reason. So I went to see Robert. I thought maybe he might know." As he spoke, Halsey took out Dvorak's .32, let it rest casually in one hand. He was gratified to see a look of recognition on Kincaid's face, the calm look gone. "This look familiar? Robert had it stashed under his mattress in case he decided to make an early exit. I was looking for correspondence from you and I found this. Took it along with me."

That got to Kincaid, he could tell. The poker face wasn't quite what it used to be.

"You know," Halsey continued, "Robert looked just awful when I saw him. I was surprised he hadn't used this already. I can't imagine how bad it must have gotten by the time you finally showed up."

Kincaid's eyes were beyond chilly now — they were subzero. Halsey heard the ropes creak as Kincaid strained against them, and knew that if those knots didn't hold and Kincaid got free, Halsey would be dead inside of thirty seconds. For a moment he regretted the whole thing. No. He'd gotten the best of Robert and the best of Juliette. He could handle Kincaid too.

"That's what impressed Juliette, you know. Oh, she liked you, and Robert too, for some reason. But she thought taking that gun showed some style. I asked her to help me find you and take care of things once I did. She taught me plenty of things. And now," Halsey said with a wave of his hands, "here we are. You didn't see this coming, I know. You underestimated me. You always did. So did Robert, and so did Juliette, and they've both paid for it, and now so will you."

"Where is Juliette? I'm surprised she didn't tag along to enjoy the show." Kincaid's voice was steadier than Halsey would have thought possible; he could see how tense the man's whole body was, his arms straining at the ropes.

"She's taking a dirt nap. Courtesy of yours truly." Kincaid took this news calmly, seeming almost bored, and Halsey's temper flared. By God, he was tired of people underestimating him. "I shot her, six times. I shot her, and then I fucked her."

No boredom in Kincaid's face anymore, and none of the respect Halsey expected either. Just revulsion too strong to be hidden behind any mask. "You raped Juliette?"

"She had it coming. I thought you'd be impressed."

"By what? That you have to shoot a woman before she'll lie still for you? Yes, I *am* impressed."

"Don't get sarcastic with me, Kincaid. I've seen your file, I know how many people you've killed. And don't say it was part of the job, because not all of it was. Like this half-assed noble quest of yours. That didn't go according to plan, now did it? You killed Beatty, and you killed that Blaine woman. You don't exactly walk on water."

Kincaid said, "Just tell me why you're doing all this."

Wasn't it obvious? "Because you have been a thorn in my side for too long. All those years I would complain to the top brass about you, and Dvorak, and the rest of them. Taking so long on every mission, always whining for more time, more guns, more this, more that. And when I turned you down, you just walked away from me. Like that! Do you know what a laughingstock that made me? Every time I talked to an agent, all they'd say was, 'Wow, I heard Kincaid really gave you what for.' Drove me crazy. And then that stupid fuckhead Beatty botched the job and his wife started asking around and making a big stink, and then your girlfriend wouldn't cave in and I *know* she knew what you were up to but I couldn't crack her. Freeman and Yates and Peters called me on the carpet, suspended me and demoted me, all because of you. And Juliette, Juliette, oh, she said she'd show me what to do and she did but she showed herself off and worked me over and *mocked* me. All of this because you had to go off half-cocked and I will not have it any more! Do you understand!" Halsey's voice had risen to a shout. It was the memory of every humiliation, every setback, every taunt, every injury physical and emotional.

"This is all your fault," he said, his voice lower now. "And now it's time to pay."

Kincaid was silent. Halsey had expected protests, justifications, but Kincaid just looked tired and a bit sad. "You disgust me," Kincaid said. "I'm sick of all this."

"Good. So am I," Halsey said. "And seeing as how you've got the reputation for being a gentleman, I'm sure you'll be glad to know that ladies go first. You're not the only one who has to pay. Your old fuck-buddy Monique gave me the run-around on your whereabouts, and I don't appreciate that. I might have let that redhead go, but she put up a real fight. Hit me with pepper spray and then bit me. *Bit* me. I don't have to take that shit from anyone ever again."

"What are you going to do?" Kincaid asked, his voice strangely flat, his body shifting about in the chair.

Halsey thought it over. "There'll be a slight change of plans. My first idea was to show you a neat little trick I learned from Juliette. I even brought a bucket along. But I think now that they'll get the same treatment Juliette did."

Halsey got up, started to walk down the hall to the room where the women were. He stopped and looked back over his shoulder. "And you'll get to watch."

Chapter Thirty-four

"Listen," said Monique. "If we can get off this —" She pulled the cuffs against the bedpost. "We can get some help."

"We'll still have the cuffs on," said Deirdre. Even if they got off the bed, they could do precious little with their hands behind their backs.

"I know how to get the cuffs around to the front. Sean taught me. See if we can get that canopy off, reach up and get the cuffs off the post. Ready?"

Deirdre nodded. Even if it didn't work, it was better than sitting here waiting for nothing good to happen. From the other room she could hear the men talking; not their words, just the voices. *Keep talking, Sean. Give us a chance to make this work.*

It was soon clear that only Monique was tall enough to reach the top of the bedpost, and even she was shy by a couple inches. She stood as tall as she was able to, legs trembling as she stood tiptoe on the mattress, but she had to lean forward to get her wrists up behind her. She reached as high as she could, grimacing with the strain, then relaxed and dropped her arms. "Just a few more inches," she said with a gasp.

"Wait." Deirdre lay down, stretched out as far as she could. She scissored her legs and caught hold of a pillow from the head of the bed; she swung her body around and brought the pillow over to Monique.

Monique stood on the pillow, gaining a little height but not quite enough. "Get a couple more."

Deirdre did, reaching all the pillows that she was able to. Thank God Anna had plenty of those bolsters and decorative pillows that Deirdre herself would never have bothered with.

When they had all the pillows they could get, Monique stood on top of the pile. Deirdre watched as Monique reached as high as she could, reaching back behind her, shoulders creaking in protest. She reached the top of the bedpost, pushed at the canopy to lift it off. At first it wouldn't budge. Deirdre winced — Monique wouldn't be able to maintain that posture much longer. Then the canopy came loose with a small rip and a pop; with one last effort Monique got the cuffs over the top of the bedpost. She lost her balance and pitched forward, bouncing off the mattress, and then onto the floor with a loud thud.

Deirdre heard a hiss of pain, a muttered "Son of a bitch!" Then: "I hope he didn't hear that."

Deirdre cocked her head toward the bedroom door. "I don't think so. He was yelling something. You OK?"

Monique stood up. "Yes. Any ideas?"

"Anna said she had a shotgun. I can't remember where, try under the bed or in the closet." Deirdre tried to recall if Anna had said anything more, but nothing came. What she did remember was being full of disbelief at the idea. Anna, who made her own pie crust and wore holiday sweaters, wielding a shotgun. Yeah, right. *Would you use it, Nan?* she'd asked. Anna had gotten a strange, somber look on her face. *To protect me and mine, I would.*

Monique dropped to the floor, came back up a few moments later. "I can't see anything. Let me get these around front and I'll try the closet."

The door opened and in walked Frank Halsey. He stopped, caught off guard by Monique's escape, but only for a moment. She tried to run, he went after her, and there was a struggle behind Deirdre; she couldn't see what was happening but she could hear Monique putting up a considerable fight despite her bound hands. It was short-lived, though, and soon they were back in Deirdre's sight. "No you don't," said Halsey. "Not yet. I'm saving the best for last." He glanced around, looking for a place to keep Monique where she couldn't escape. He looked at the closet, and Monique let out a whimper and tried to back away. Halsey smiled, started to drag her over in the direction of the closet, and Monique whimpered louder.

"Scared of the dark, little girl?" he asked.

She didn't answer, just let out a chilling moan, making Deirdre wonder if this really was a don't-throw-me-in-that-briar-patch act. Monique put up a fight as Halsey opened the closet and manhandled her into it, closed the door behind her. He didn't bar it with anything, trusting in handcuffs and Monique's terror to keep her captive. Halsey turned back to Deirdre, who pleased as she was by Monique's clever thinking, had no trouble keeping her hope hidden and her fear in plain sight. There was too much that could go wrong, too many *ifs*. *If* there was indeed a shotgun in the room, *if* it was loaded, *if* Monique could get her handcuffed hands back to front, *if* she arrived in time to stop Halsey from whatever he had planned for Deirdre and Sean, which was surely nothing pleasant.

Halsey reached into his pocket and took out the handcuff keys. He unlocked the cuff around her right wrist. "Get up," he said, and when she didn't immediately move he seized her by the arm and pulled her off the bed, then took the other cuff off, put the handcuffs in his pocket. She stood, putting all the contempt into her stare that she could. Whatever he wanted from her, he wasn't going to get it easily. She was going to go out fighting.

He regarded her for a moment. "You're just like him, aren't you? Not afraid of anything."

What had Sean said about fear? *Push it down.* She would do that. Would try to do that.

Halsey moved behind her and put the gun's muzzle against her back. "Down the hall, to the living room. Now."

She cast one glance at the closet with faint whimpering and scuffling sounds coming from behind the door. The gun nudged into her back, Halsey gave her a little shove, and she started walking.

Monique breathed a sigh of relief when they left the room; making those noises to keep up the pretense of claustrophobia only made a hard job harder. She took a precious second to rest, try to relax her already strained muscles, then went again.

It's easy if you know how, and if you're lucky, Sean said so long ago. *You can't do it at all if the chain's been shortened.* She could do this; she'd done it before. Lie on her back, draw her knees up as far as she could, slip first one foot, then the other, in between her hands and then bring her hands around to the front. Like a yoga exercise.

Except when she'd done this before she'd been several years younger, hadn't worn a coat and bulletproof vest that impaired her movements, and the only price for failure was that she got stuck and had to ask Sean to unlock her. Things were always harder when the cost was higher. She breathed in deeply, let her muscles relax for another second, and then focused on nothing else but getting her feet through the cuffs.

She was nearly there when one of her shoes caught on the handcuffs' chain. Her legs started to cramp and for an awful moment she thought she would be stuck here, cramped and unable to breathe; her pretend fear of the dark closet became real. One foot slipped through, then the other. She had done it.

Monique didn't stop to savor the victory. She got to her feet, opened the closet door, and snatched up the lantern. She saw clothes, a laundry basket, galoshes and there — leaning against the wall. The shotgun.

When he'd first come out of the tranquilizer haze, Sean had remained still, assessing the situation. His gun was taken, so was the knife in the leg sheath. He was tied with rope around the ankles, just above the knees, and around the wrists. Given enough time he might be able to work free of the knots around his wrists, and he might have tried it, but he could hear Halsey in the room. He couldn't hear Monique and Deirdre, didn't know where they were. They were in danger, because of him. Well, he'd put them in danger, and he could get them out of it. There had to be a way.

There was. In his back pocket he could feel the reassuring weight of his Swiss army knife. He always carried one; Robert had given him his first one, a present for his acceptance into the agency. *Don't laugh*, Robert had said. *You might be surprised at what you can do with one of these. Always have one and take good care of it.* He'd followed that advice and never regretted it. He raised his head and looked at Halsey, guessing that Halsey would be too busy gloating and doing his Talking Movie Villain act to notice much else. He shifted in his chair, and managed to reach into his pocket and very slowly — if he dropped it, all was lost — retrieve the knife. With infinite patience he found the serrated blade, positioned the blade on the rope, and began to cut.

It was slow going, made worse by some of the things Halsey told him. What he said about Robert hurt deepest, brought back the memory of that awful night when he'd seen the pain-wracked living corpse his friend had become.

The news about Juliette appalled him. Sean was under no illusions about Juliette — after all, she had gladly helped Halsey track Sean down, probably just for her own amusement. That did not justify Halsey's actions. Killing Juliette in self-defense would be one thing — Sean would have done that, had the situation arisen. But to shoot her and then rape her while she was dying was beyond repulsive. Sean had seen things nearly as bad in his day, and had heard of things far worse, but it had been the other side that did those things — not his side, not his people. Until now. Probably his side had been just as bad all along and he'd been blissfully ignorant. *And I used to work for these people. I must have been as crazy as they are.*

When Halsey announced his plans for Monique and Deirdre, Sean knew time was running out. As soon as the man's back was turned Sean sawed fiercely at the ropes, never mind if the blade slipped and gashed him; there would be time to deal with that later. As he heard the sounds of struggle from the bedroom the cursed rope finally gave way. He sawed at the ropes around his ankles and then his knees, and as the last rope parted he saw that he was too late.

Halsey and Deirdre were already halfway down the hall. They couldn't see him yet, but he could see them in the hallway mirror. Sean had a second to assess the situation. He only had the knife. Halsey had the gun. If the gun had been just held in his hand Sean would have chanced attacking Halsey, but the gun was trained on Deirdre's back. One move on Sean's part and the gun would go off, leaving Deirdre a cripple if not dead. Even then he might have chanced it, except that Halsey was a good shot, as his expertise with the tranquilizer gun had shown.

Sean remained still, hoping Halsey didn't notice the loose ropes. He watched them approach, and saw that Deirdre was white-faced but calm. Refusing to let her fear show. She reminded him of someone. Not Anna. She no longer looked like Anna to him, for she was too different from Anna. She reminded him of himself.

Halsey stopped. Considered for a moment, then smiled the same sick grin he'd worn when telling what he'd done to Juliette. "Stand next to Sean," he told her. "Put your hand on his shoulder. Like that, yes." He backed away about a dozen paces, always keeping the gun trained on Deirdre. She laid her hand on Sean's shoulder; though her touch was light, he could feel the faint tremor of her fear. "I want you to feel it when I shoot her, Sean."

Sean did not look up at Deirdre. He kept his eyes trained on Halsey, not sure what he was looking for but obeying instinct, as he always had. Then he saw it.

The safety was on. Halsey must have forgotten it during the struggle in the bedroom. He would need a second to thumb the safety off. Robert's gun was old, an inheritance from his father, and the safety took a second or two.

It was all the time Sean needed.

As Halsey took the safety off, Sean moved. Up, out of the chair, putting himself between Halsey and Deirdre. Halsey pulled the trigger, too far gone to stop even as he saw his target had changed. Sean put his arms around Deirdre, shielding her, and the bullets hit one two three in his back, short sharp shocks; he heard Deirdre scream and then no scream as his arms tightened around her and squeezed the breath out of her. No more shots, just the sound of Halsey howling with rage. No pain, just a terrible weakness and the knowledge that damage had been done, no guess as to how bad it might be. No spine injury, he could feel his legs though they didn't want to hold him up, he had to lie down and rest but wouldn't, not yet, wouldn't let go of Deirdre. Strange that this should be the worst he'd been shot. Strange that it should happen like this. He didn't feel himself falling but he was on the floor, still holding on to Deirdre, the two of them facing each other and very close, almost as if they were lovers, and so strange that it should be this way.

She had stood, her hand on Sean's shoulder, and it was like the time Leo Sorensen had been ready to beat her to death with his nightstick. That eerie calm fell on her, but this time Sean wouldn't be able to save her. He was bound, unable to move, wouldn't even look at her. But as Halsey raised the gun and started to fire there was a blur of movement, and Sean was there, she was crushed against him and felt the bullets hit him. She screamed but he didn't. He was shot but he'd be all right, like that time at the tree farm, because of the vest. Except that as he held her tight, so tight she could scarcely breathe, she felt no extra bulk of a vest. He trembled, staggered and fell to the floor, taking her with him.

They lay on the floor, facing each other, and though her hand touched his back, felt the rips in his jacket and the blood trickling out, all she needed to do was look at his eyes. They seemed darker and yet filled with an odd light that waxed and waned like a campfire ember. He asked in a monotone whisper, "Are you all right?"

She nodded. He almost smiled but it turned to a grimace. The light in his eyes was flickering. Deirdre put a hand on his shoulder. She spoke, but did not know what the words would be until they were said. "I forgive you."

Halsey dragged her away from Sean, roughly shoved her to one side. He kicked Sean hard and Sean let out a groan. "You and your God damned chivalry! These bitches are still dead. Stay alive a little while, you'll see."

While Halsey was yelling, Deirdre looked around for a weapon — something, anything. A Swiss army knife lay open on the floor; she grabbed it and went after Halsey. He saw her coming and caught hold of her arm. Her still-shaky legs betrayed her and she fell to the floor. He squeezed her wrist but she wouldn't drop the knife; he yanked hard on her arm and pain exploded in her shoulder, pain so huge she couldn't scream it out, could just lie there gasping and wondering where her arm had gone, she couldn't feel it.

Monique held the shotgun. It was a huge, heavy thing, double-barrelled. It felt like holding death in her hands. She had no idea how many shells were in it nor any way to look for more shells. She hefted it, hoisted it, turned off the safety, and with a cold numbness in her gut saw that with the handcuffs on it would be damned hard to hold the barrel and squeeze the triggers. One chance, with no opportunity to reload. One chance to save an innocent woman, to save a man trying to make amends. One chance to get herself back home to Michael.

Those were odds she didn't like but they were the only ones she had.

As she reached for the bedroom doorknob she heard the shots, a scream, and a thud, and she was too late. Monique wasted no time, kept her anguish inside. Instead, she moved. Put down the shotgun, open the door, pick up the shotgun again, run down the hallway.

No one saw her. Sean was farthest away, lying on the floor. Halsey and Deirdre were closer, struggling for a knife that Deirdre held. Monique held the shotgun braced against her body but dared not fire, not with Deirdre so close. Halsey yanked on Deirdre's arm, and Monique heard Deirdre's arm pop out of its socket. The knife clattered to the floor. Deirdre lay writhing. Monique started to aim but Halsey was faster; he saw her and fired his pistol. Monique felt a sucker punch in her left side and dropped to the floor. It hurt like a bastard but the vest had kept her safe — which Halsey didn't know.

As Halsey laughed and walked over to Sean, Monique looked at Deirdre. The haze of pain had lifted from Deirdre's eyes, her gaze was clear. They looked at each other and understood what to do. Monique inched her way toward Deirdre, dragging the shotgun with her.

Halsey stood over Kincaid, aimed another kick at the man, who lay on his side. "Look at me," Halsey said. Kincaid didn't, instead he kept looking at the women. Well, let him look. Let him look long and hard. First Halsey would shoot that redhead — she was like a rabid dog, he had to put her down. Then he'd put another round in Monique and take her like he'd taken Juliette. Let *that* be the last thing Kincaid saw before he croaked. "I wish I had a camera. The folks back home wouldn't be so impressed with you if they could see you like this. I'm going to have my hands full in the next few minutes. Any last words? I was going to just toss you in a dumpster but if they're good enough I'll get you a tombstone. Well?"

Kincaid still didn't look up. He said something that made no sense. "Higher." Then he nodded.

Then he smiled.

It reminded Halsey of the way Juliette had smiled, at the end. He looked up to see Monique and Deirdre on the floor: Monique bracing the shotgun, her finger on the triggers. Deirdre with a look of ghastly determination, holding the barrel up with her uninjured arm. Holding it higher.

"Please d— " A deafening roar filled the room and something hit him, but there was no pain. They must have missed. Ten feet away and they still missed, the stupid bitches.

He tried to raise his gun to shoot but it had fallen out of his hand. Halsey tried to speak but couldn't. Something was wrong. Couldn't move, couldn't talk. Someone laughing. *Juliette?* Couldn't breathe. The room was filling up with black water. Endless fathoms below. Couldn't scream. He tried to keep his head above the black water but he sank and it closed over his head. He sank and went on sinking.

The shotgun's recoil jolted Deirdre, and the pain was like the shotgun's roar, huge and deafening. She felt herself slumping to the floor, gray fog rolling over her. Dimly she heard the wet thud of Halsey's body hitting the floor, and a shaken-sounding "Oh dear God!" from Monique.

Then everything went away for a while.

She thought she heard urgent whispering, thought she heard Monique cry out, "No!" But it was all lost in the fog.

The fog turned cold. Monique calling her name. "Deirdre. Deirdre. Wake up."

She didn't want to.

"Just a little way. Just to the car. I can't carry you and if I try I'll hurt you worse. That's good. Just a few more steps. I'm going to get you to a doctor, they'll fix you up. Here we go. I'm opening the car door. Here we go. Just sit down, nice and easy."

The engine turned on, and after a moment blessedly warm air began to fill the car. "I'll be right back," Monique said, and Deirdre opened her eyes just long enough to see Monique run back into the house.

Some unknown time later Monique was back, with a fuzzy quilt she wrapped around Deirdre as best she could. Monique got into the driver's seat, began fiddling with the GPS. "Hospital, hospital, where is a fucking hospital?" A raw edge in Monique's voice, combined with the warmth of the car, roused Deirdre to full awareness. "There we go," Monique said, and put the car into reverse.

Something wrong. Something missing.

Not something. Someone.

Deirdre turned her head, looking. The back seat was empty. "Where's Sean?"

Monique hit the brakes. She didn't look at Deirdre but stared straight ahead, and in the dashboard's dim glow Deirdre could see shiny teartracks on her face.

"He's not coming," Monique said.

Deirdre's insides felt numb, missing, like her arm. She heard Monique let out a single sound, a choked half-sob, then Monique began to drive again.

Deirdre closed her eyes so she wouldn't have to see Monique. Her eyes stung and her throat hurt. "He saved my life," she said.

"I know," Monique replied.

"I told him I forgave him,"

"It's all right. We'll be all right."

"Monique, I —"

"Shhh. Shhh," Monique repeated as if she was a mother soothing a baby.

The gray fog was back, wrapping itself around Deirdre's mind the way the quilt was wrapped around her body. Both soothed her, and she drifted off until they reached the hospital.

Chapter Thirty-five

It was after dark when Nick got back to the sheriff's station. He parked, and sat behind the wheel for a few minutes, rubbing his forehead, where he could feel a headache coming on. Driving all the way to Green Bay to spend the day in court, getting held up in traffic leaving the city, and then driving all the way back home was not his ideal way to spend a day. He'd planned to go bowling with Deirdre tonight, but sitting here half-listening to the crackle of the police radio — technically he was off duty and didn't have to pay attention — he thought he might ask her if they couldn't just stay in and watch a movie.

He was reaching to turn off the radio when there was the urgent sound of the 911 dispatcher. Nick stopped in mid-reach, listening. Gunshots, the dispatcher said. The caller said people were getting hurt. The dispatcher gave the address: the Evergreen Christmas Tree Farm, 430 Hidden Forest Drive.

The Evergreen Tree Farm. "Deirdre," Nick whispered, and laid ten feet of rubber as he drove out of the parking lot.

As he drove, sirens and lights on, it occurred to him that Leo Sorensen would be pleased with him tonight. Leo had always chided him about his driving speed, or lack of it. *You're a sheriff, not a chauffeur, so move a little faster.* Now he redlined it to the farm, weaving past cars and disregarding semi trucks' honks as he dodged them. It also occurred to him that if he hit a patch of black ice he could wipe out, but his fear for Deirdre overrode his caution.

Nick made the right into the farm's driveway a little too hard; his car spun in the snow and hit a fencepost, mashing his rear fender. No matter. He straightened out, drove as fast as he could down the unplowed driveway. It was easier than he'd thought it would be, there were fresh tire tracks. Remembering that he might be destroying evidence, he steered as far as he dared off the driveway, fearful of hitting a tree. The snow slowed his progress and he hit the steering wheel in frustration. It was irrational, there was no reason to think that Deirdre was involved.

But he knew she was.

Finally he reached the house. Though it had been empty for months now, there was light coming from the front windows. Not electric light, though. From the light's white, watery quality he guessed it was a Coleman gas lantern or something like it. Nick looked around. No other cars, not a sign of anyone nearby. Not a sound from anywhere, save for his breathing and heart, both too fast for his liking, and the crunch of his boots on the snow.

The walkway was a mess of footprints and furrows. He dodged them as best he could, then listened at the door. No sound. "Police, open the door," he said, then hammered on the door. Still no sound. He tried the knob — to his surprise the door was unlocked. He drew his gun and went inside.

Two bodies on the floor. One, a tall man, had been blasted at close range by a shotgun. The weapon was on the floor but even if it hadn't been, Nick knew nothing else could have caused damage like this. Blood on the floor, on the wall. Sweet Christmas, it was on the ceiling. Nick's gorge rose and he turned away for a moment to spare himself the sight, but it did no good. He could smell the blood, a warm, metallic scent. He didn't want to look closer but did, saw that the man had nearly been cut in two by the blast. No point checking for a pulse. Nick went to look at the other body.

It was mostly covered by a wool blanket, dark crimson stains just beginning to seep through. Everything was so fresh, this must have all happened just a little while ago. Shaking, Nick dropped to his knees beside the covered body and pulled back the blanket to see who the victim was.

Nick looked, and eyes looked back at him. The man was still alive. There was also something distantly familiar about him; Nick was good with faces and knew he'd seen this man somewhere before. But there was no time to worry about that. Nick snatched up his radio and yelled that he needed an ambulance fast, he had a gunshot victim who was probably going to need the trauma unit in Green Bay.

Nick knew he should go investigate the rest of the house, make sure whoever had shot these two wasn't still around, ready to bust a cap on Nick himself. But he couldn't leave this man who was lying here so still. Nick would have not believed he was alive if it hadn't been for those eyes, so intense they almost seemed to be burning, as if what life left in the man was concentrated there.

He felt for a pulse. It was there. Unsteady but there. "You're going to be all right," he told the man. "Help's on the way. Just hang on, OK?"

Silence, and then the man spoke. "Deirdre."

Nick felt his heart lurch. "Where is she?" he asked, restraining himself from shouting questions into the man's face.

A whisper he could barely hear. "Gone." A pause. "Doctor."

"Is she hurt?" Nick was afraid of the answer. How could someone have escaped this bloodbath without injury?

A hint of a nod. "But not bad."

Nick wanted desperately to find out what had happened, but the effort of talking had clearly cost the man. In the distance, Nick could hear the howl of sheriff's cars and medical emergency vehicles. "I hear them. They'll be here soon," Nick said in as reassuring a tone as he could. "Tell me your name."

The man said nothing. Nick looked closely at him — something was wrong. His breathing was labored, his face pale, a blue tint starting on his lips. The breathing became harsh gasps, his eyes lost their focus, and when Nick felt for a pulse it was not a beat but an uneven thrum, like a guitar string after a chord had been strummed. In the middle of a gasp the breathing stopped. And the paramedics still weren't here.

Nick sent up a quick prayer, rolled the man onto his back, and started CPR. Though he knew it wasn't logical, he had the idea that saving this man was the only way to make sure Deirdre was safe as well.

After Monique had pulled the trigger of the shotgun, bare seconds after Halsey went to the floor — *that's for Robert, you rat bastard, and when you get to Hell give the Devil my regards* — she dropped the gun and ran over to Sean. He'd had to say her name several times to get her to listen. There wasn't any pain yet, just that terrible weakness, but it was hard to speak, and harder to make her understand.

That she was to leave him here. Take Deirdre and get her to a doctor. Leave him here.

She refused. If she left him he'd die and she wouldn't let that happen.

He didn't *want* her to leave him. She was the last good thing in his life, and that was why she *needed* to leave. So her life and Deirdre's would not be damaged by him any more. So that they were never again in danger because of him. So that Deirdre had no reason to regret her forgiveness. So that it was over, for good and all.

How had he finally convinced her? Sean didn't know, never would know. He remembered saying *Please* and finally she agreed. *God forgive me but I'll do it. If that's what you want,* she'd said.

Once she made her decision she did not hesitate. She got Halsey's handcuff keys and car keys, showing no squeamishness as she went through the dead man's pockets. She freed her hands from the cuffs, then got Deirdre semiconscious and walking out the door. She came back, rifled again through Halsey's pockets, found his cell phone and called 911. The call made, she left the room and came back with a quilt and a wool blanket in her arms. She knelt, laid the wool blanket over Sean. Monique looked in his eyes for a moment, then leaned forward and kissed his forehead. "Goodbye, Flint," she said, and he knew it was the last time he would hear her bittersweet honey voice.

She left, and Deirdre with her. Only when he was sure she was gone did Sean whisper, "Love you, Moni." He'd never said it before, didn't know if it was true, but it seemed the right thing to say.

He waited. Even though there was pain now — a pulsing ache in his midsection, a sharp jab at every inhalation — waiting was not half as hard as trying to speak to Monique had been. There was nothing else to do but wait, and there was a certain peace that came with that knowledge. He would live, or he wouldn't. A rescuer would be in time, or they wouldn't. If he died, he'd die alone, but he'd always known that's how it would be. He had the look in Monique's eyes when she said goodbye; he could still hear Deirdre saying *I forgive you*. It was enough.

Sean was cold despite the blanket, and the pain was getting worse. The floor didn't feel steady beneath him. He drifted in the current of a dark, silent river, but was still moored to the shore. He couldn't move, could only drift, and someone would arrive in time and pull him from the river. Or they would not arrive, or be too late; the mooring line would let go, and the river's current would take him wherever it would go.

He heard a siren, getting steadily closer and when the cop looked at him, Sean was not at all surprised to see it was Deirdre's boyfriend Nick. He wasn't sure if he could talk but Nick looked so worried for Deirdre that Sean told him what he could.

Something went wrong then; some damaged part of his body gave way. Hard to breathe, so very hard, and he was so tired. He saw Nick's look of alarm and wanted to reassure him: *Nothing to be worried about. It's all right now, Deirdre forgave me, and nothing hurts any more.* But he couldn't breathe, couldn't speak, and he couldn't see Nick any longer. The line tethering him to shore broke, and he drifted on the river of dark silence. No more cold, no more pain. He wondered why he had feared this for so long; wondered why it was different than it had been when Richard Blaine had choked him.

After a time he stopped drifting. Darkness faded, became light of a strange muted sort, like the sun behind thick fog. Sean felt coarse sand beneath him, heard the sound of waves. He knew where he was now. On the beach in Maine. That fellow Pete would be there. He'd have another chance. This time he would do a better job of making amends. This time he would keep Monique and Deirdre safe from harm. This time he would make sure Jennifer was all right.

Sean saw not Pete but Robert sitting there. His old friend was no longer disease-ravaged and in pain; he merely looked the way Robert always used to look. Robert regarded him with pleasure and some surprise. "I didn't expect you so soon," Robert said.

Sean looked around. The fog was not cold. He could not determine where the sun hid behind the fog, the muted light seemed to be its own source of illumination.

"Is Anna here?" he asked.

"No," said Robert. "Not here."

Of course. He was still a long way from where Anna would be.

The fog thickened, swirled around him. The dark river swept over him. He wasn't afraid, only saddened at leaving his friend. Robert said, "Be seeing you," and Sean managed to reply in kind before he drifted away again.

Nick had never done CPR on a real person. What seemed so easy on a first aid training mannequin was much different when faced with a barely living, not-breathing person. *Clear the airway. Two rescue breaths, thirty compressions. Two, thirty.* It was hard work and he didn't flag, although he wished the paramedics would hurry the fuck up. The man's heart was still going but it was wildly uneven and he gave the occasional hitching gasp but wouldn't come back all the way yet.

Nick wanted to weep with relief when the paramedics came in. He let the experts take over; though other deputies had arrived and Sheriff Grayson was there as well, Nick couldn't make himself look away from the rescue efforts. It wasn't like the TV shows. There was a cool professionalism that Nick admired, even as he wondered if *tension pneumothorax* was as bad as it sounded.

After what seemed forever he heard one of the paramedics say, "Got him back." The man breathed again and so did Nick. He turned away, found himself facing Sheriff Grayson. "Hi, son," Grayson said. He called all the male deputies *son*. "Weren't you in Green Bay today? How'd you get here so fast?"

"Heard the dispatch come through just as I got back," Nick said. He didn't want to mention his fears for Deirdre. There was no sign of her here, the man said she had gone to a doctor. Nick had to talk to Deirdre first before he said anything beyond describing the scene.

Grayson looked around. "There's no one else in the house. No other bodies." Grayson walked over to the shotgun victim; Nick reluctantly tagged along. After putting on his gloves, Grayson picked up the cell phone lying next to the corpse. "The 911 call was made on this phone. The caller was a woman. Huh. I can't believe I came back to this shit. If I want puzzles, I'll do the crosswords."

Nick looked away at the news about the 911 caller, wondering if the woman had been Deirdre. His gaze landed on the dead man's face, which was a mistake; he turned away from that bloodless face and its vague look of horror. The blood smell was worse here, there were too many people in the room, and Nick quickly made his way out the door.

The air was cold but it was fresh, and he breathed in deeply, gratefully. Not far away the paramedics were loading the injured man into the ambulance. One of the paramedics paused, looked at Nick. "Good job," the paramedic said. "Nice work keeping this guy going."

"He going to be all right?"

"It could go either way. He's got three bullets in him and God knows what internal damage along with that collapsed lung and some major internal bleeding. I've already called the Green Bay trauma unit, they'll be sending a copter over."

Nick walked over to the gurney and leaned down. "You'll be all right," he said with more conviction than he felt.

Incredibly, there was a reply. A barely audible whisper: "Don't tell her."

Did he mean Deirdre? What shouldn't he tell her? But there was no chance to ask. The man was loaded in, the ambulance doors closed, and the sirens screamed away into the night.

Nick knew he should go back into the house. But he couldn't just yet. He was remembering the first time he'd come to this house, when Deirdre had found her cousin's body. Ugly sights he'd never be able to erase from his mind, and he didn't want any of it. All he wanted was to find Deirdre. Everything else could wait.

He became aware of Sheriff Grayson next to him. Grayson clapped him on the shoulder, not unkindly, and said, "Son, you look beaten all to hell, and you did a great job keeping that guy alive. Go write up your report and go home, get some rest."

Nick nodded, but there would be no rest until he had Deirdre home and safe with him.

Chapter Thirty-six

Monique disliked hospitals.

The dislike didn't come from experience; no friends or relatives had died in hospitals, she herself had never stayed overnight in one, but she had always found them enervating. Every time she went into one, even on a happy occasion like the birth of a friend's baby, the harsh fluorescent lights, the cold linoleum, and the ever-present smell of disinfectant worked on her nerves — and her admiration for those who worked there and saved lives increased.

If she disliked hospitals in general, she hated emergency rooms. The atmosphere of distress, physical and emotional, made everything harsher.

Shortly after they arrived, after they'd filled out the initial forms and had Deirdre sitting as comfortably as possible, Monique went into the restroom, where she took off her jacket and sweater and stripped off the bulletproof vest. She stared at the rip in it, at the bit of lead lodged in the material. Amazing that such a small thing could do so much damage. It seemed unlikely. She thought of Sean and the three bullets he'd taken, no vest to shield him.

Monique stuffed the vest in a trashcan, then pulled up her turtleneck to see if the bullet had done any damage. There was a bruise that was bound to look unpleasant for a while, but nothing else. For a long while she stared at the bruise, and then at her reflection in the mirror. She felt the same sense of unreality she had when they arrived at the emergency room and saw that it was not yet 8 p.m. Surely this hellish day had been going on longer than that? Surely she couldn't have escaped with nothing more than a few bruises and the puncture wound from the tranquilizer dart? Not when Deirdre had a dislocated shoulder and Sean...

Monique did not permit herself to think about Sean. Later she could, once Deirdre was all right. She pulled the turtleneck back down over the bruise and went back to the emergency room.

This emergency room was better than most. Saint Eustace was a newer hospital; the linoleum was less grubby than usual, the chairs padded vinyl instead of hard plastic. They sat and waited. At least they were comfortable. The nurses had wrapped Deirdre up to keep her warm and given her a hit of something to ease the pain. Now they just had to wait for a doctor to fix up her arm.

The room wasn't crowded. A few sheepish-looking teenagers, banged up from some minor auto accident, huddled in one corner. Across the room, a pale young mother held a toddler who alternately coughed, fretted, and slumped feverishly against the woman. Monique had already gone over to the woman and asked if she could get her something to drink or eat, but the woman just shook her head and went back to stroking the child's hair.

"Do you have any kids?" Deirdre asked when Monique sat down afterward.

"No. I'm the classic career girl, didn't even get married until year before last. You?"

Deirdre started to shake her head, then winced slightly and said, "No. My ex was a flake and I knew that it wouldn't be fair to kids if we had them. Besides, I always hoped Anna would have some, and I could be an auntie, and that would be enough."

It didn't occur to Monique until they were finally ushered into a treatment room that they had no explanation for Deirdre's injury. Ordinarily Monique would not have worried — like any lawyer, she was good at thinking on her feet — but her mind felt numb and the task of coming up with a plausible explanation was one she didn't want.

Deirdre was the one who came through. "It was my ex-husband," she said, lowering her face as if ashamed. "He gets crazy, and when he drinks it's worse. It's my fault, really, we'd been fighting about stuff..." She didn't say more but she didn't have to. The doctor was nodding his head mechanically. Still a young fellow and he'd heard this song-and-dance a hundred times. When he stepped out to get the materials for a sling — and, no doubt, some references to the local women's shelter — Monique asked, "Is your ex really like that?"

Deirdre shook her head. "He was a liar and a cheat but he didn't hit. It was all I could think of and it's not like I'm going to press charges."

"Good thinking," Monique said.

When the doctor came back, Deirdre held out her good hand, looked inquiringly at Monique, who nodded. She let Deirdre hold on to her hand while the doctor, as gently as he could, maneuvered Deirdre's arm back into place, then put the arm in a sling. It was good news, the doctor said. A simple dislocation, no surgery needed. Just rest and physical therapy and a prescription for pain medication.

Deirdre stood, somewhat shakily, and held on to Monique's arm as they made their way to the pharmacy. Once Deirdre sat down, Monique, noticing how pale and exhausted the other woman looked, asked if she could get her a coffee or something while they waited. "Yes," Deirdre said in a wondering tone that was partly the painkillers and partly the fallout of this awful day. "I haven't eaten a thing all day. I was going out to buy half-and-half when that..." She struggled to find an epithet worthy for Frank Halsey and could not. "When he caught me." Deirdre took a breath and said, "I'm so sorry, Monique. I should have tried to warn you or do something ..."

Monique leaned close to Deirdre, wanted to put an arm around her but dared not jostle the injured woman. She settled for putting a hand on Deirdre's back. "You don't have to be sorry for anything. That Halsey guy was crazy; I met him months ago and I knew there was something wrong with him. He had a grudge against Sean and you and I got caught in the middle."

Deirdre sighed harshly, stared at the far wall with the fixed look of someone trying not to cry. Grateful for a chance to let the younger woman have time to compose herself, Monique went and got coffee from a vending machine. Deirdre took the drink wordlessly, nodding her thanks, and after a while, in a voice so low that Monique had to strain to hear it, told how it had happened, how Sean had been Deirdre's shield.

Monique was about to say that Sean had been alive when she left, that she had called 911 and for all she knew he was going to make it. But something stopped her.

She put down her coffee. "I have to step out for a few minutes. Will you be OK?"

Deirdre leaned her head back, nodded. "I'll stay right here."

Monique followed the signs and found the hospital's chapel. It was tiny, no larger than a good-size living room, and deserted. The stained-glass windows were dark and their images muted; in the daytime they might have been lovely. Something of a believer but very little of a churchgoer, Monique found the place soothing. She picked a seat in the middle and sat down.

For a while she did not think at all, simply let her tired mind rest. Let her thoughts become a still pool of water, and waited to see what would swim up to the surface. It was interesting to see what did not surface: there was no horror at pulling the shotgun's triggers, just a wish that she'd never had to. What did come to the surface: a longing to be home and safe with Michael; worry for what this would do to Deirdre after all she'd been through; wondering if she'd done the right thing leaving Sean behind.

Leaving Sean preyed on her mind, no matter that he had asked her to leave him. He'd said it was for Deirdre — he'd tried to pay his debt to her and

342

having done so, it was right that he vanish from her life. And from Monique's as well? Perhaps that was what he'd meant, when he'd said, *Either way...out of her life,* and then pointed a trembling finger at Monique.

In the distance she heard a siren. Far away, fading. It had occurred to her more than once that she could try to find out what had happened. Call hospitals, the police, even the local papers and find out if anyone knew anything. It had also occurred to her that once Halsey's body was identified, people from Sean's agency would come for it, and they would have questions.

That gave her pause, but what she understood now was that Sean's request had not just been for Deirdre, or for Monique. It had for himself as well. If he died, he would do so with honor; if he lived, he would gracefully exit from Deirdre's and Monique's life. She remembered the look that had been in Sean's eyes when she kissed him and said goodbye and knew she had done the right thing. It felt the opposite of how it been when he was retired and packed off to Florida; it felt right.

Monique bowed her head and said a prayer. Nothing formal, no rosary beads. Just wishing for a safe journey home to Michael. Healing to Deirdre. And peace to Sean wherever he was.

Deirdre was still sitting in the chair by the pharmacy when she returned. "We're ready," Deirdre said, holding up a bottle of pills. As they walked to the parking lot Deirdre asked in a small, shy voice, "Can we go get something to eat? That coffee just made me hungry."

Anxious as Monique was to get Deirdre home and herself on the road to Green Bay airport, she couldn't refuse Deirdre's request. As she stopped to think about it she became aware of her trembly limbs and the way the acid burned in her stomach. There was still a long way to go; it was a few hours' drive to Green Bay and God knew when she'd get a flight out or how bad any layovers might be. Yes, rest and food would do them both some good.

The restaurant was called the Hot Plate. It was decorated in a style that was not to Monique's usual taste — very country, with knickknacks everywhere, but somehow not too kitschy. Their hostess was friendly and all the food Monique could see looked good. "Nice place," she said.

Deirdre nodded. "Nick and I come here a lot. I like it. It's about the only thing I do like about this town any more."

"Why so?"

"Too much has happened. Too many ghosts. I came here to be near Anna and now..." She tried to shrug, winced, and began looking through her menu.

Monique studied her own menu, and put it down to see Deirdre holding not a menu but a dog-eared photograph, looking at it intently. Monique was startled to see Sean in the picture. "May I see that?" she asked.

Deirdre handed her the picture. Monique was further taken aback to see Deirdre in the picture with Sean, at some sort of party. It didn't connect with what Sean had told her. On closer examination, Monique realized the woman wasn't Deirdre.

"That's Anna," Deirdre said. She was about to say something else when the waitress arrived with their beverages.

Monique looked at the picture. The affection between the two was clear, and Monique began to feel the first pains of grief, not just for Sean but for the woman in the picture, even though they'd never met, and for Deirdre, who had lost her cousin and learned what her cousin's husband had really been.

She gave the picture back to Deirdre, who looked at it again with an expression Monique couldn't put a name to. Monique took a sip of water to ease her suddenly dry throat and mouth, and asked what she'd been wanting to know since they left the tree farm. "When you told Sean you forgave him, did you mean it?" Or had it just been something said to comfort a dying man?

Deirdre was silent for so long Monique thought there would be no answer. Then she said: "Anna was everything to me. My family never wanted much to do with me, and Anna was the first person to love me. She always did. She was sweet and kind, and I never heard her talk trash about anyone. She liked helping people. Not because it would make her look better but because she wanted people to be happy. She wanted to set me up with Sean, can you believe that?" Deirdre looked abashed, apparently thinking she might have offended Monique. "What I mean is, he wasn't my type."

"Don't worry," Monique said with a wry smile. "You weren't his."

Deirdre smiled, then her smile faded. "I was going crazy, trying to find out what had happened to Anna. And when Sean told me that he ... I hated him more than I thought it was possible to hate a person. I had a chance to kill him and I didn't. Because I could tell he was suffering over what he'd done. I wanted him to suffer, because I was suffering too. And later, I wasn't so angry at him, but I thought that if I forgave him, it would be like betraying Anna. I could never do that."

Monique looked away. It was what she had expected, and she didn't blame Deirdre.

"But I think I did mean it," Deirdre said. "I was afraid that forgiving him meant that what he'd done was all right. It's not all right, it can't be. But I didn't hate him or want him dead any more. I wanted him to try to ... I don't know. Get rid of the bad and find the good that was left in him." She sighed. "I guess now it's too late."

Monique was about to say, *Maybe not*, about to tell Deirdre that Sean might have made it. But behind the shock and exhaustion and sorrow in Deirdre's eyes she could see something else. Relief. Not just relief that they'd survived relatively unscathed, but relief that Sean was gone from her life. Monique couldn't deny Deirdre that relief, and made no reply.

"Do you want me to wait until you get inside?" Monique asked.

"No, that's all right," Deirdre said. She opened the SUV's door but did not immediately get out. "I'm sorry we had to meet like this. You seem like a nice person. And I'm so sorry about Sean. I know you cared about him."

"Thank you," Monique said. On impulse, she reached into her purse and took out a business card. "If you ever need anything, let me know. Even just to talk."

Deirdre looked at the card, then at Monique. "Will you be all right?"

Monique nodded.

They said goodbye and Monique watched as Deirdre went up the stairs. She sighed, and then drove away.

She parked Halsey's rental a block from Sean's motel. After making sure she and Deirdre had left nothing behind, she left the keys in the ignition but locked the door. What happened to the SUV wasn't her problem.

Monique walked to the motel's parking lot. Her own rental car was still there, and the keys were in her purse. As she went to her car she averted her eyes from the door to what had been Sean's room; she half expected the sting of a tranquilizer dart or to hear Frank Halsey's voice. But there was nothing, only the quiet Wisconsin night.

The car started with no problem; all was as she'd left it. Monique felt a weight slide off her. It was almost over. She left the motel without looking back and drove to the highway. Only when she was on the highway heading to Green Bay did she take the cell phone out of her purse and dial her home number. Michael answered on the first ring.

"It's me," she said, "I'm coming home."

Deirdre stood in the hallway leading to Nick's apartment for a while before she summoned the nerve to knock. She'd been torn between longing to see Nick and fear of having to tell him not just about tonight, but about everything. At first she'd tried coming up with halfway plausible lies, but then she'd asked Monique, "What are you going to tell your husband?"

Monique had looked at her as if she didn't quite understand the question. "The truth."

Well then. Deirdre supposed that if Monique could do that, so could she. Just as long as Nick wasn't angry with her for keeping so much from him. As long as he didn't hate her for what she was capable of.

She raised her good hand and knocked on his door. It flew open almost immediately and there was Nick, disheveled, his face collapsing into relief that quickly turned to concern as he saw her arm in its sling. "My God, Dee, are you all right?"

"They fixed me up, I'm OK," she said as he led her over to his sofa. She could tell he wanted to hug her but didn't dare with her injury. Instead he took her good hand in his, kissed her palm and laid her hand against his cheek. She wanted to weep at the tenderness of it, but kept her tears in check. Later, she could cry.

"What on earth happened?" he asked

"I'll tell you everything. Including some things I should have told you a long time ago. Can you get me a Coke or some water? I have a lot of talking to do."

Early on, she lowered her face while she talked. Afraid to meet his gaze, instead she spoke to her fingers as they fidgeted with a loose thread on her jeans. He said nothing throughout: once, when she told him Sean was dead, she thought he was about to speak, but afraid of what he might say, she went on before he could talk.

At the end of it she took a long swig of water, and said, "So you're probably pissed that I didn't tell you any of this, and that's OK, I understand. And you probably have to arrest me, and I understand that too. Just maybe if

you could wait a month or so because there's something I need to do first."
She was alarmed at how much her voice wobbled.

"Deirdre."

She didn't look up.

"Deirdre, look at me. Please." His fingers brushed one side of her face
lightly, then touched her chin. Like the way Halsey had touched her earlier
that day, but not at all like that. She looked up at him, ready for the worst.

He wasn't angry; he looked more sad than anything. "Why didn't you tell
me this sooner?"

"I was scared," she said, and her voice did more than wobble, it cracked.
She tried to explain more but couldn't, any more than she could hold back her
tears.

Deftly he scooped her up in his arms and held her close. Her arm and
shoulder sent out a few twinges but she ignored them. They didn't matter.
What mattered was the feel of Nick's arms around her as she cried, the sound
of his steady murmur. "It's all right now. Let it out. Brave girl."

Much later she fell asleep, and when she woke the next morning, Nick
was, even in his sleep, still holding her. Deirdre cherished the feeling of his
arms around her. It was the safest she had felt in a very long time.

Part Four

Chapter Thirty-seven

"No, nothing serious," Monique said to Lucy. "Just a bad headache. I'll go home and sleep it off."

Lucy nodded sympathetically. "Feel better, then."

"I will."

Monique wasn't lying, not entirely. She did have a headache but it was nothing two Aleve tablets couldn't have handled. She just didn't want to face the whole day here — she needed to get outside and think.

On the way home she reflected that she'd done a lot of thinking already. And a lot of remembering: that was easy, for everything was so clear. If someone had asked, she'd have said that day in Wisconsin seemed like something from a dream. That's what people said in the movies — it was what you were supposed to say — but it wasn't dreamlike at all to Monique. She remembered every detail with harsh clarity. The way she'd fallen into unconsciousness as if it was a great dark feather bed, after the tranquilizer dart hit her. That struggle to get her handcuffed hands back to front and noticing even in such dire circumstances the pleasant, cedar-sweet scent of the dark closet. The grim triumph she'd felt as she pulled the shotgun triggers, thinking, *This is for Sean, you nasty little shit*. Those last moments with Sean, the skin of his forehead cool under her lips as she kissed him, a metallic smell of blood and adrenaline coming off him. Watching Deirdre head up the stairs to her boyfriend's apartment, walking carefully to spare her injured shoulder any pain. That seemingly endless journey home: driving to Green Bay airport, catching the first flight she could, enduring the layover in Cincinnati and the agony of waiting for the plane to touch down in Washington. How she'd gotten off the plane and run through the airport, dodging people as best she could, until she saw Michael waiting for her just past security. How she'd flung herself into his arms and how they had sunk to the floor, ignoring the admonitions of the TSA official, so overjoyed to see each other again. How only then she'd known it was over, that she was safely home. She remembered it clearly and always would.

"You did the right thing," Michael had told her. "You helped that girl. You got yourself out in one piece. And you did what your friend asked." He'd told her that, and she believed him. She told herself all that, and believed it. It wasn't the memory of that day, or of the choice she'd made, that made her leave work early. It wasn't what she believed or what she knew, but what she didn't know.

Had Sean made it or not?

Monique had heard nothing since returning to Washington. No one from the government had come to visit. There hadn't been so much as a phone call. She had no way to interpret the silence, and at first was grateful just to be left in peace. She was still grateful, and would have been perfectly at ease — if she could just know for certain.

Once she got home, she changed into casual clothes and took a walk; after a time she wandered past the local coffee house, then turned and went in. She ordered the biggest latte they offered and a blueberry scone — screw the diet, she wanted some comfort food. When her order was ready she sat at one of the small tables; the place was not empty but not packed either. A mix of professionals on coffee break and soccer moms back from late-morning errands, with a few senior citizens thrown in. Monique sat, sipping her coffee and nibbling at her scone, half listening to the chatter of the other patrons and the music playing over the speaker system.

A song she didn't know faded out, a song she did know came on. The Platters: "Smoke Gets In Your Eyes." *Oh yes,* she thought before she could stop herself. *Sean loves this song. Loved this song.*

A little thing to cause her pain, such a stupid thing. What tense to use? She could wonder that for the rest of her life. She had no difficulty accepting either outcome, Sean alive or dead, she just wanted to know what the outcome was. Such a small matter shouldn't mean so much, but it did. That knowledge shouldn't be so hard to come by, but apparently it was.

"Ms. Pavour-Banks?"

Monique looked up. In front of her stood a woman, probably around Monique's age, wearing a standard-issue Washington suit and holding an attaché case. She was well-maintained, her hair in a simple pageboy cut. "May I speak with you for a moment?" Her voice was polite but there was an air of authority that turned her question into something more like a request.

Caught off guard, Monique nodded, swallowed a half-chewed lump of scone — it went down hard, for her mouth was dry. She dusted sugar off her fingers and shook the hand the woman offered.

The woman sat, holding the attaché case on her lap. "My name is Donna Hamilton," she said. "I'm here on behalf of the agency that employed Sean Kincaid."

Of course. Donna Hamilton hadn't had to say where she was from. Monique could have guessed it from the woman's eyes. That assessing quality. Well, she should have known the silence couldn't last forever. They knew about her, probably had her in a file as a known acquaintance of Sean's. They might even know she was the one who'd blasted a hole the size of a salad plate in Frank Halsey. At least this was a public meeting and Monique hadn't been hauled off to some interrogation room. Nothing too awful could happen in a busy coffee house, could it? Monique suppressed the urge to edge her chair away from the table.

Agent Hamilton said, "The agency offers its apologies for recent events. We want you to know that Mr. Halsey's actions were not in any way authorized, and in fact, he was on a six-month suspension at the time. To be blunt, it seems he was quite mentally unbalanced."

Any number of responses jostled in Monique's head, most of the *Really? The hell you say!* variety. But she knew that no matter how tempting it was, you didn't get sassy with government people. Most of them had no sense of humor. She replied, "Yes, well," and left it at that.

Agent Hamilton opened her attaché case. "The agency would like to compensate you for the recent unpleasantness." She took a greenish slip of paper out of the case and extended it to Monique.

She recognized it as a check. A substantial check. And she recognized it as a reward for her silence, the price of ensuring that she didn't talk about the psycho they'd had running things or about the truth of the Los Angeles bombing. Yes, quite a substantial check. All those zeroes.

"No, thank you," Monique said.

The agent's face didn't change but she blinked once, like the shutter of a camera.

"I appreciate the offer, Ms. Hamilton, but I don't want or need it." It was true. If she'd needed the money she'd have taken it; she hoped Deirdre would take any money she was offered. But she didn't need it, and her next words were truthful.

"Please understand I have no intention of telling anyone about what happened, now or ever. All I want to do is get back to my life and forget the whole thing ever happened. That seems to be the wisest course of action."

"Are you certain?" the agent asked.

"Quite certain."

Agent Hamilton's gaze lingered a beat longer. Monique felt she'd been weighed, assessed. Had she been found wanting? Impossible to say. Probably the woman thought she was a fool for not taking the check. Most likely she *was* a fool.

"Very well." Agent Hamilton withdrew the check and put it in her case.

Ask. Now. Before she leaves. Monique found herself artlessly saying, "Can you tell me if Sean survived?"

The agent didn't even look up from her case. "I'm afraid that's classified information, Ms. Pavour-Banks."

Of course. Monique had felt remarkably little anger over the ordeal in Wisconsin, but she was angry now. *You'll wave around a big fat check but you won't tell me one thing. You can say it. Just one word. Yes or no. Can't you do that one thing? Or are you just their wind-up robot? Was Sean the only one of you who still had some humanity left? He'd have found a way to tell someone. At least he'd have tried.*

Agent Hamilton stood up. "Once again, please accept our apologies," she said, and extended her hand.

Monique didn't want to take it. Manners won out, and she stood, shook the offered hand. The agent's handshake was firm as it had been earlier, but now her hand held a small object that she transferred to Monique.

Monique, her heart pounding, did not look down at her hand or the object, which felt like a piece of paper. Agent Hamilton gave her a fleeting glimmer of a smile, and then turned and walked away, her efficient stride carrying her out of the coffee house in seconds.

After sitting down, after the sound system played three more songs, after she'd sipped more of her coffee, Monique finally looked down at what the agent had given her.

A slip of paper, no bigger than one from a Chinese fortune cookie, folded in half. She opened the paper. Two words, that was all, but that was all she needed: *He's alive.*

Chapter Thirty-eight

Despite the dangerous nature of his profession Sean had spent remarkably little time in hospitals. This one wasn't bad. The food was edible, if bland, and he had his own room with a good view of the bay. He appreciated the view, for he didn't have the energy for more than looking out the window, and was grateful for that much.

He'd been lucky. None of the three rounds had been immediately fatal. One had lodged in his ribs, one had hit his lung, and the third had taken out part of his liver; this last injury had lost him a good deal of blood. Much of what had happened right after Nick had found him was lost in haze. He remembered fragments: doctors' faces behind surgical masks and unpleasant-looking medical equipment, mostly. Time passed but seemed to stay still also, and it wasn't until a day or two after the surgeons were done repairing him and the doctors pronounced him out of immediate danger that time began to mean something again.

Sean sometimes wondered what the nurses made of him. Surely it wasn't usual for patients to receive no visitors or so much as a phone call. No doctor or nurse had asked him why he had three bullets in his back, and no police had come to ask about the dead man who'd been found nearby.

He wondered, but not much. For now he was content to look out the window, watch TV, and rest.

Not long after time resumed its meaning, Camille poked her head in, smiled at him.

He smiled back. Camille was his favorite nurse. She was young, her looks either on the plain side of pretty or the pretty side of plain, depending on how tiring the day had been. But she had wondrously gentle hands. He'd noticed she always had a paperback in her pocket, and they often talked about books. Just yesterday she'd brought in some for him to read, and he was touched and grateful.

"You have visitors," she said, her voice chirping like a bird's, and ducked back into the hallway.

Sean was very still, the book open before him but forgotten. Visitors? Who even knew he was here? He heard footsteps on the hallway linoleum and a prickling sensation went down his spine.

The man came in first. An off-the-rack suit, medium height and build, a face so ordinary — except for the eyes — the mind almost didn't register it. The man looked Sean over briefly, then turned to the doorway and nodded.

The woman who walked in wore no badge of rank. All the authority she needed was in her demeanor. Sean put down the book and tried to sit up straighter despite the pain it caused.

The head of the agency looked Sean over. "You've led us a merry chase, Kincaid," Freeman said. As always her face was unreadable, masklike. "They tell me you're on the mend and well enough to hold a conversation. You certainly look better than I would have expected."

"Thank you," said Sean. It was all he could think of to say. He'd only spoken to Freeman twice before in his entire career, which had been a good thing rather than a bad. When she or Yates or Peters wanted to talk to you, it was rarely because they were pleased with you. Stalling for time, he asked, "How did you find me?"

Freeman waved the question away as if it was no matter of importance. Truth be told, it wasn't. They might have known where he was months ago, or they might have only learned when Halsey turned up on the morgue slab. Something to consider — how badly they wanted payback for Halsey, and how he'd deflect blame for Halsey from Deirdre and Monique onto himself.

In the agency, Freeman was famous for being direct about the matters that interested her. Nothing had changed. "Have the people behind the Los Angeles bombing been terminated?"

"Most of them, yes. There are a few stragglers left."

"Anyone who could carry out another attack?"

"No. They're lower-echelon. Too disorganized and too scared to do anything."

"What about that sheriff and his brother?"

They must know everything. They had Halsey's belongings and all the intelligence Juliette had collected for him. They had probably been to Sean's motel and taken everything he had — including all the documents from Richard's safe, which Deirdre had given to him for safekeeping. They probably knew about Deirdre, and Monique, and Jennifer Thomson.

"The brother had been involved. The sheriff was trying to cover it up. The brother figured out I had been a double and they came after me." He shrugged with trademark nonchalance.

"I see. Good work, then. I'd have preferred it if you hadn't had to turn rogue, but I don't lay the blame for that at *your* door." Freeman took several steps closer. "I'd like to make you an offer. When you're recovered, a position with the agency. Not field work, mind you, but training."

Sean was dumbfounded. He'd turned rogue, helped kill his former boss, and Freeman was asking if he wanted a job? "This seems a bit odd."

"Recent events are shaking things up a bit. It's time to reinstate some of the old ways. We could use some of your style again, Kincaid. There's been precious little style lately."

"What about Halsey?" he asked.

"What about him?"

"Won't there be some trouble if you hire on the person who killed him?" It only now occurred to Sean that his fingerprints weren't on the shotgun that killed Halsey, and he wondered if Freeman knew...or cared.

"As I said, things are changing. Halsey's ... departure actually helps us a great deal. A nonpolitical solution to a very political problem," she said. "Your role in his death won't cause any problems."

Something about the way she said this told Sean she knew he hadn't been the triggerman. She was willing to pretend he had been, as long as he was kept in line one way or another. As for her offer, if it had been made a year ago he would have leapt at the chance, but now it held no allure for him. If he took it he would lose everything he had gained these last few months. He would lose what had brought Monique to his aid and what had compelled Deirdre to offer her forgiveness.

"I'm sorry, but I'm retired now. For good."

To his relief, Freeman nodded. "I thought that would be your response. Very well. Full retirement with your pension reinstated, and increased to allow for your success terminating the group. Now hear my conditions. You are never to go back into the field. This time you *stay* retired. Is that understood?"

"Yes."

"Good. Now, when you're a bit more healed up we'll do a debriefing. But once that's over you will not tell anyone about who was behind the Los Angeles bombing or about any of the events from the aftermath of your mission."

He thought of Jennifer, whom he had wanted to check in on. He thought of Deirdre, unable to restore Anna's reputation without his documentation about Richard's group.

Freeman saw his hesitation and shook her head. "No, Kincaid. There has already been entirely too much difficulty surrounding this matter. You would do well to agree to my terms. If you do not, the repercussions will be unpleasant and you will not be the only person to suffer them."

That made it simple. "I accept."

"Good." The strangest expression flickered across Freeman's face, and Sean realized that she was pleased. "Expect a debriefing within a week. When you're ready to leave here we'll make all the arrangements." She began to walk away. Before she reached the door she turned and said, "Get well soon. I'm told Maine is lovely in the spring."

Freeman walked out of the room. The anonymous-looking agent, who had been standing nearby in silence the whole time, followed her. On his way out he stopped for a moment, smiled, and gave Sean a thumb's up.

Sean sat for a long time after they had left, looking out the window but not seeing a thing. He was free: chained and muzzled, but free. He had only one regret and one concern. Regret that he would never find out how Jennifer Thomson fared. Concern for Deirdre. He felt certain that Monique and Jennifer would keep quiet — they'd tell the truth to a spouse or friend, but not to the media. But he knew Deirdre wanted to clear Anna's name, and without the truth there was no way to do that effectively. Even without Freeman's conditions, he would not contact Deirdre. She needed to be shut of him forever. He could rest easy, if he knew she'd be all right.

Help came with his second and last visitor. Two days after Freeman's visit, a man knocked briefly at Sean's door and walked into the room.

It took a moment for Sean to recognize Nick out of his deputy's uniform. Nick stood for a moment, regarding Sean with a solemn look. "You're going to be OK, they say," Nick said awkwardly.

Of all Sean's fragmented memories from the shooting and its aftermath, the clearest was hearing one EMT tell another that Nick's CPR had kept Sean going until their arrival, and if not for that, it probably would have been too late for the EMTs to do much good. "All thanks to you," Sean said.

"You're welcome. But the paramedics, they did the real work." Nick sat down, then almost immediately got to his feet again. "I'd have come sooner but it's been chaos. Those government guys were here the next day, taking over. Most people have no idea what's going on." Nick took a breath. "I don't know a nice way to say this. Deirdre thinks you're dead. I haven't told her otherwise. That's what you wanted, right?"

"Yes. I think that's best."

"She's told me everything. Don't worry, she won't get in trouble for Leo and Walt. That's all getting swept under the rug. I just wish I'd known about all this sooner, so I could have helped her."

"You have helped," Sean said. "And you can help her heal. Just love her, and be good to her."

Nick smiled. "That I can do. It'll be like falling off a log."

"One thing, though. Maybe you know this already, but the whole truth isn't going to come out. Not any time soon. Maybe not ever. What I mean is that your old boss said some things about Anna Blaine that weren't true. Deirdre and I were hoping to set that right. But that's not going to happen now. You need to make Deirdre let it go."

Nick was quiet for while. "I think I can do that."

"Do whatever you can. None of this has to touch her again, but she has to let it go." Sean paused, and then said, "I think it would be best if she moved away. There's going to be nothing but ghosts and bad memories for her if she stays."

"I don't want to lose her."

"Then go with her. You're the best things in each others' lives now. Don't let that slip through your fingers." Sean tried to find a diplomatic way to say this next. "And you'll forgive me for saying so, but it would be a good way for you to find another line of work. You weren't meant to be a cop."

Nick sighed. "I've felt that way for a while now. But if I left it would be like saying I was a coward."

"You're not. Not at all. But you're not a cop either. And if you stay it'll take away what Deirdre loves about you."

"Is that what happened to you?"

The truth was more complex; Sean had never been the good-hearted man Nick was. If he had been, he would not have chosen the path he had. But it was simpler to nod in reply.

"What happens once you're well?"

"I'm retired. Gone far away from here."

"There's something you should know. Deirdre...once her arm's better, she wants to go to Canada. To see the girl you wanted to help, the one who was in the bombing. Make sure she's OK. I told her she doesn't have to do that, but she's insisting. Says that since you can't go, it's the only way to be sure that it's all over. She says that you and she will be even. 'Paid in full' she said."

Sean felt tears sting his eyes. Let that be how it ended. Let Deirdre make sure Jennifer was OK, then go back to her life. Whether she stayed in Wisconsin or went elsewhere, as long as she had Nick with her. And Sean would be gone, to Maine. Far away from all of them. For everyone's sake.

"I know you can't tell her this," said Sean. "But understand that I'm very grateful to her for doing that. She's a wonderful woman and I wish I could have known her under other circumstances."

"Should I tell you what she finds out?"

He longed to know. "No. Best to not know where I am."

"I understand." Nick stood up. "Thank you for saving Deirdre's life. Although I wish you hadn't needed to." He seemed about to say something else, then abruptly turned and left the hospital room.

Sean listened to the footsteps fade away. It was over. Now all he had to do was wait, and heal.

Chapter Thirty-nine

Deirdre was awake quite some time before the alarm went off. She never slept well the night before traveling, was always worried that she'd oversleep and miss her ride or her flight. This morning she didn't mind waking early. She was content to lie here and bask in the pleasure of this snug bed. To listen to the sound of Nick's breathing and his occasional murmur — he talked in his sleep. To feel his arm, warm and heavy with sleep, draped across her hip.

She shifted a bit, not because she was uncomfortable but because it was a relief to move without pain. So good to sleep on her side again and not worry if she might turn the wrong way or that Nick would accidentally jostle her. Deirdre's arm wasn't back to its full strength and motion yet, but she never complained; things could have ended much worse.

She wouldn't think about it. Instead she snuggled closer to Nick. He sighed in his sleep and she could no longer stand being the only one awake. After all, they would be apart for a few days. Deirdre fanned her long red hair out over the pillows, for she knew he liked that, and kissed him awake.

Deirdre missed the old days at airports, when people could tag along to the gate and it was almost fun to put your bags through the X-ray machine. She wished Nick could come. If he was still a deputy he might have been able to flash his badge and go through, but he'd quit in April and now worked on a friend's construction crew. The pay was lower but the work pleased him; he came home smiling and with the scent of sawdust clinging to him. What he really wanted — one of the reasons he wasn't coming with her — was a ranger job at a national or state park. He had an interview tomorrow.

This morning, Nick drove her to the airport. Outside the terminal, he asked again, "Are you sure you want to do this?"

"I'm sure."

"I can still come with you."

"I'll be fine. I just want to look in on her, and then I'll come back." She didn't add that Sean had taken three bullets for her — she owed him this much.

Besides, it was the sort of thing Anna would have done. In a way she was doing this for Anna, because it was all she could do. There was no way of clearing Anna's name from Leo Sorensen's slander now, not with the government folks sweeping in and hushing everything up. They hadn't threatened her, they hadn't needed to. There had been two meetings. The first with two men in dark suits who asked her to tell her tale. She had, and the way they calmly accepted it made her sure they knew most of it already. They asked for her silence and she gave it. She hadn't asked for a chance to clear Anna's name and while she was ashamed of that, she was more frightened of the agents' efficiency and coldness. It reminded her of the look in Sean's eyes when he'd strangled Leo.

Nick, as always, reassured her. "It's bigger than both of us," he'd said. "And we need to lie low and keep quiet." When she'd started to protest he'd said, "We're small stuff to them. Loose ends. What Leo did wasn't right but Anna wouldn't want you to get hurt for her. You've been through enough. Take what they give you and let it go."

She had. When that other agent had come with her check Deirdre had understood it was a reward for keeping quiet. She also understood it was the means not just to go to Canada and make sure it was all over, but to perhaps create a new life for herself now that the old one seemed gone beyond recall. And now, as she felt the plane leave the ground, she felt some burden fall off her spirit.

366

Deirdre had never been to Canada, not even to Niagara Falls, and she had not guessed it would be so lovely. Green and lush in a way Wisconsin never could be. Even the airport was beautiful with its soaring ceiling and its fountains. Why couldn't she have had a two-hour layover here instead of at O'Hare?

The airport people were kind and patient, cheerfully answering her questions and helping her change her money into Canadian dollars. She rented a car and was soon heading north on the coastal highway. Deirdre had never been close to the ocean before and she found its tangy scent intoxicating. She rolled down the window so she could breathe in more of that clean salty air.

It was late afternoon and when she rounded the turn to Haven Cove; the sun cast a golden glow on the town, glittered on the water in the harbor. She couldn't tell if the town itself was lovely, or if that golden light lent beauty to everything it touched. She checked into her hotel, a pretty little place overlooking the sea. After dinner that night — the best salmon she'd ever tasted — she sat on the tiny balcony of her hotel room, listening to the soothing sound of the sea. The waves had been here for millennia before her and would be here after her, until the end of time. Theirs was the sound of eternity.

Thanks to Nick, she knew where Jennifer Thomson lived. Before he left the department he'd pulled some strings and, he'd never explained how, found her address.

Deirdre sat in her rental car with an orange juice and a bear claw snatched from the hotel's continental breakfast. She sat a few doors down from 314 Douglas, waiting. No sunlight golden glow today — the sky was gray, the clouds turning ominously dark.

The door opened and a blonde woman around Deirdre's age came out. She walked down her steps awkwardly, and Deirdre wondered if the woman was hurt until she saw the reason — Jennifer wore rollerskates. Jennifer stopped, looked up at the sky, and apparently realized that skates would not be the ideal form of transportation today; she went back inside. She came back out a few minutes later wearing regular shoes and a raincoat. Again she stopped, again went back into her house, and came back outside holding an umbrella. This last time, an orange tabby cat ran between her feet, streaked across the yard and out of sight. Jennifer, looking exasperated, yelled a name that sounded like, "Pete!"

A minivan pulled up to the house next door to Jennifer's. A red-haired woman came out of the house, opened the minivan's side door, and hoisted out a toddler. She waved goodbye to the minvan's driver, and then stopped to talk to Jennifer. Deirdre couldn't make out much of their conversation, but it seemed they were agreed that Jennifer's cat was crazy to dash out in such weather. A few fat raindrops began to fall, and the redhead went inside with the toddler while Jennifer ran to her car, a blue VW.

Deirdre had never followed anyone while trying not to be obvious, and her unfamiliarity with the town made things difficult. Luckily Jennifer didn't go far; she drove to the town's library, where she worked. After a while Deirdre went into the library where she idled about the stacks like any normal patron. Jennifer spent most of the morning behind the library's desk, answering questions, checking out books, wagging her finger at people who'd racked up impressive fines. Some of the time an older fellow, short and bearded and looking to Deirdre like a minor character in a Tolkien book, joined her in conversation. They seemed fond of each other.

Deirdre spent the day pretending to do research but really looking after Jennifer, trying to see if the woman was genuinely content or if she was wearing the sort of mask Deirdre had worn during those hellish days at Wal-Mart. Deirdre left her post only once, to get a quick lunch.

Jennifer herself stayed at the library until three. Deirdre didn't follow, and twenty minutes later Jennifer was back, this time with a young boy who looked to be eight or nine years old. Jennifer and the boy ducked into the library's office for few minutes, then the boy went into the children's section, carrying a pile of books. They stayed at the library until a little after five, then went back to Jennifer's house. Deirdre parked outside, trying to peer through the rain to see what was going on. She couldn't see much, but after a while a pickup truck drove up and a blond, balding fellow got out and dashed through the rain to Jennifer's house — the boy opened the door and he and the man hugged. It was clear from their physical resemblance that they were father and son. Deirdre was fairly certain she saw the blond man and Jennifer kiss. Shortly thereafter, the next-door neighbor came over, carrying Jennifer's cat in one arm and with the other holding hands with a large, bearded fellow Deirdre assumed was the redhead's husband.

She felt lonely and a little sad sitting here. Outside, in the rain, alone, while inside Jennifer's house was warmth and companionship, and probably dinner. Deirdre's stomach let out a growl, and she decided to call it a day. She went back to her hotel, had another fine meal, and after calling Nick — his interview had gone very well, he said — she lay listening to the waves again.

Jennifer Thomson seemed fine. She seemed to have built a nice life for herself, seemed content, seemed undamaged. *Seemed* all of these things, but Deirdre had spent much time putting up a good front, and wondered if Jennifer too wore a mask. She'd give it another day, perhaps get a closer look at Jennifer when she wasn't with her friends and see if there was darkness hiding behind her eyes.

The next day's routine was the same, except that the weather cleared around mid-morning. Deirdre was not the only one staring longingly out the library windows at the sunshine; by noon the place was empty. Instead of going into the library office to have her lunch, as she'd done yesterday, Jennifer took her lunch, a book, and an old quilt outside to the grassy lawn.

Deirdre followed a few minutes later, strolling onto the grass in what she hoped was a casual way, seeing Jennifer sitting on the quilt with her lunch and her book. There was a plaque commemorating something or other not far from Jennifer, and Deirdre went over to take a look and to observe Jennifer while she was at it.

"You can say hello. I won't bite."

Deirdre stopped. She'd just given herself away. She turned and saw Jennifer looking at her calmly, curiosity in her gaze but no distress.

"I saw you yesterday at the library," Jennifer said. "And Matthew saw you follow us home."

"I'm sorry," Deirdre said. She felt herself blushing. So much for being stealthy. If Sean were alive she could have asked him if anything embarrassing like this had ever happened to him. "I should just — I'll be going. I didn't mean to bother you."

She was walking backwards as she spoke, and though her words stumbled out of her mouth, her eyes were going over Jennifer, trying to take the measure of Jennifer so she could say for certain if the woman was doing all right.

Jennifer met her gaze, then frowned slightly and cocked her head to one side. "Did Sean Kincaid send you?"

Deirdre knew she should say *Who?* and go on her way. But she stopped, so unexpected was Jennifer's question. "No. He didn't send me."

Jennifer gestured to the quilt. "Sit down. There's room. I've got an extra Coke if you want one. I'm Jennifer, but I guess you knew that."

Deirdre sat down, feeling unreal. This was the last thing she'd expected. "I'm Deirdre."

Jennifer popped the top on both Cokes and handed one to Deirdre. "I thought you might be a reporter at first," Jennifer said. "It's not so bad now, but around the first anniversary I had to change my number, I got so many calls.

"Today, though, I saw the way you were looking at me. It reminded me of Kincaid. I thought, no, that couldn't be. Figured it was just me being paranoid. But just now, when you were walking away, you looked at me kind of like he did."

"How did he look at you?"

"Like I was the answer to a question."

Deirdre couldn't quite gauge Jennifer's mood or her feelings toward Kincaid. "He didn't send me. I came as a favor to him. Something I owed him."

Jennifer was quiet for a while. "He's dead, isn't he?"

Deirdre nodded. She watched emotions flicker across the blonde woman's face. Relief. Pity. Anger. Pity again.

"Was it suicide?" Jennifer asked. "He seemed so… I shouldn't have said that. You must have been a friend of his."

"No, not a friend. It's hard to explain." Deirdre didn't want to burden this woman with the whole story. To her relief, Jennifer let her take a while to find the right words. "He was trying to make amends to me, for some things he'd done. He ended up saving my life. Two times. The second time it cost him his. He knew that what he'd done to you was wrong, and he told me he wanted to find out if you were doing all right. But now that he can't, I thought I owed him that much. I shouldn't have come, I was hoping you wouldn't see me, but I wanted to know…"

To Deirdre's relief, Jennifer was calm. She took Deirdre's hand. "It's all right. I won't lie, I always thought he'd come back and it's a relief to know that he won't. He scared me and he put me in a terrible position but at the same time I knew he was trying to help me.

"The only person I told about that night was my boss. I know, it's weird, but if you knew him you'd understand. He used to be a priest and in a way he still is. You can tell him anything. I told him I wasn't sure I'd done the right thing by letting that Blaine fellow go, and that I didn't understand why I felt sorry for Kincaid more than I hated him. He said that it was what forgiveness was about — hating what they'd done but at the same time hoping they could get past that and..."

"And find the good that was still left in him," Deirdre said.

Jennifer smiled. Her smile was like the golden glow of the sun that day Deirdre had arrived in Haven Cove. "Yes. That's it. You do understand. I never thought anyone would, except Mr. Bradbury and he's a priest, of course *he* gets it."

"Harder for us mere mortals, though," said Deirdre.

Jennifer nodded. "That's true."

"So are you all right?" Deirdre asked.

"I am. I'm even getting married this summer," she said.

Deirdre now spotted the ring on Jennifer's left hand: a thin white gold band with a tiny sapphire. Jennifer continued: "I've got good people who care about me, and that makes all the difference."

"I know," said Deirdre, thinking of Nick.

"So you'll be all right?" Jennifer asked.

"Yes." She would. Accounts in balance, scores settled. It was time to leave, to let Jennifer go her way and Deirdre would go hers. She stood, held out her hand to Jennifer, and they shook. Deirdre knew that for the rest of her days she'd keep Jennifer in her thoughts, hope she was doing well. She knew Jennifer would do the same for her.

"Thank you for coming here," Jennifer said.

"I hope I didn't upset you."

"No. It's good to know what happened. I can stop looking over my shoulder," Jennifer said. "*Pax vobiscum*."

Deirdre looked at her quizzically.

"Sorry. It's something my boss says. It means 'peace be with you'."

That seemed the right sentiment. "*Pax vobiscum*, then. And thank you." Deirdre left Jennifer to her lunch on the sunny lawn. She did not return to follow Jennifer again. Deirdre spent the rest of that day strolling on the beach, finding pretty shells to take back home with her. One last fine seafood dinner, one last night listening to the waves. The next morning she checked out early and began the journey home.

Chapter Forty

Freeman had been right. Maine was beautiful in the spring.

The day's warmth was very welcome after the long Wisconsin winter. The sky was so blue it seemed unreal, until he looked at the ocean and saw an even more brilliant blue. The first blooms of spring were fading, he'd arrived just a little too late, but the roses were in their glory. It was a weekday and the streets were quiet; the occasional sound of a car's passage and the noises from the other houses could not drown out the sigh of the wind in the trees, or the distant sound of the ocean.

Sean stood to one side while the estate lawyer found the key and unlocked the gate to Robert's house. The lawyer was a cheerful, chatty fellow. Sean wasn't sure if this was the man's natural temperament or if he was just happy to have a break from relatives waging war over who got to inherit Aunt Tillie's doily collection.

"...so pleased when you called. I wanted to reach you the moment the will was read but I couldn't find any contact information for you. I apologize for the delay."

"It's all right," said Sean. "I was traveling on business."

"I understand completely. I was just worried because estates can drag on, and sometimes the property has already depreciated — oh, you've no idea how much — before things get sorted out."

Sean nodded as they walked to the house's front door. He was only half-listening. Part of him was patiently waiting for the lawyer to leave so he could have the house to himself, and part of him was convinced that this all was a pleasant illusion, a morphine daydream that he'd wake from to find himself back in the Green Bay hospital.

"...had to stop the landscaping service in the meantime, but I've got their number if you'd like to reinstate it. Oh, and the house is almost entirely as Mr. Dvorak left it. The hospice and medical care equipment was removed, of course, and a few other nonessentials. But all other arrangements have been left up to you."

"That's fine." Would the man never leave?

They were inside the house now. Indeed, just as he remembered it. The books, the bric-a-brac collected during Robert's travels.

"...set up the utilities as soon as I heard from you. So it's all ready for you to move in. Do you have a moving service? If not, I can refer you to one."

"I've got it all arranged." In truth, everything he owned was in the trunk of the nondescript sedan the agency had given him.

"Excellent. Now, if you will just sign and initial in the places I've indicated." Once that was done, the lawyer's demeanor changed, became much more businesslike. He opened his briefcase and took out a set of keys and a manila envelope. He handed the keys to Sean, then said, "Part of Mr. Dvorak's will was that I give this envelope only to you, and only when you took possession of the house." He gave the envelope to Sean, then held out his hand. They shook, and the lawyer smiled. "Thank you, Mr. Kincaid. And let me know if you have any questions or need anything."

As the lawyer was leaving, Sean saw another car turn onto the street. Intuition spoke and he obeyed, casually walked inside and tucked the manila envelope onto a bookshelf, in between *Bartlett's Familiar Quotations* and *Roget's Thesaurus*. Not five minutes later, two agents were on his doorstep. Sean was surprised to recognize one.

"You look well," said Donna Hamilton as she handed him paperwork to sign. "All back in one piece?"

"More or less," he said. "What doesn't kill me makes me stronger and all that."

Briskly, Hamilton took the papers and handed them to the other agent. "Go send those in, would you? Thanks."

As the agent headed out the door, Sean asked, "Have you been back in long?"

"Last year, about a month after Halsey got demoted. A lot of us are back now. Are you sure you don't want to reconsider?"

Sean smiled, shook his head. "I'm sure."

"By the way, we're all glad you made it." She glanced to make sure the other agent was in the car, scanning the papers. Pitching her voice low, she said, "The women are fine. Monahan and Pavour. I took them checks and agency regrets." Hamilton smiled and Sean knew she'd enjoyed that errand; she'd always detested Halsey. "Monahan took her check."

"Good for her."

"Pavour didn't take hers. Said she didn't need it."

"Good for her."

Hamilton hesitated a moment, glanced outside once more. "Pavour asked if you made it. I let her know you did. I hope I wasn't out of line."

"You weren't." For a moment Sean had trouble speaking. "Thank you."

Hamilton shrugged. "It seemed the right thing to do."

"It was." For him and Monique. He could see the other agent heading down the walk and knew he and Hamilton had little time left. "Say hello to the old crowd for me and ... tell them I'm sorry about Beatty."

"I will. We know it wasn't what you wanted to do."

All business now, she handed him back his papers, and in another minute both she and the other agent were gone.

After the agents left, Sean retrieved the envelope from the bookcase and sat down in one of the leather wing chairs. The same one he'd sat in two years ago when he'd first had the notion of helping Jennifer Thomson, and had come to Robert for advice. He sat holding the envelope, not opening it yet.

He wished Robert was here, if for no other reason than to tell him how things had gone. Perhaps, though, Robert knew. Sean remembered with dreamlike clarity that interlude when he'd come so close to dying from Halsey's gunshots. Robert looking at him and saying *I didn't expect you so soon.*

He opened the envelope. It contained two sheets of paper, with Robert's handwriting only a little shaky. He must have written these before things got too bad. The first sheet was a letter to him.

If you're reading this it means that you're back. I'm presuming that it also means you've stopped running. But preparedness has always been our watchword, so in case you have need, on the other paper you'll find the location of some things that may be of use to you. They're hidden well; no one else knows about them. Use them or not as you deem fit.

At the time I'm writing this, I've just gotten the word that nothing more can be done, and this battle is one I won't win. It's not as terrible as I'd feared. To be honest, I'm more worried about you. I fear that my greatest regret will be that I did not dissuade you from your mission. I knew something was wrong from the moment you told me your plans, and I'm dreading that whatever has gone wrong will destroy not your life but your humanity. And no matter what you've done over the years, you've never lost that, which is more than most in our profession can say.

All I can ask is that you not hate me for not doing more to discourage you. And that you not let whatever may have happened ruin you.

I've reached the end of my life and I don't know any longer what I believe in. Only that I believe you a true friend. And I believe, as the old song says, we'll meet again. Some sunny day, perhaps?

Be seeing you,

Robert

P.S. I nearly forgot. Down in the wine cellar you'll find a bottle of Bordeaux. 1924 Chateau Lafite Rothschild. It's the last of the family's wine (we smuggled some bottles out when we left Prague). Open it, let it breathe, and drink to your health and my memory.

Sean sat reading the letter over several times. He gave the other sheet a cursory glance. Hidden caches of money, papers, weapons. It was good to know about, but he felt certain he would need none of it. Why would he? He was home now. Sean had lived in countless places over the years but he'd called none home since his childhood. But home he was, and here he'd stay.

That evening he opened the Bordeaux, let it breathe, poured a glass. He did not drink right away, but instead carried the glass with him out into the small yard. The night, cool and quiet, wrapped around him like sheltering arms. He stood in the moonlit night and his sight blurred with tears. For Anna and Robert, who he still missed so much. For Monique, who he'd pushed away to keep safe. For Deirdre and Jennifer, both wronged by him, and whom he hoped would be all right. For himself. He wasn't sure what the future held for him, only that his old life was gone, and he was glad of that.

Sean raised the glass up into the moonlight. "To absent friends."

Sitting in her corner office on a day when the sultry Washington summer was beginning to make its presence felt, Monique looked through her mail; the letter caught her attention immediately, its handwritten address standing out from the usual laserjet-printed labels. She did not open it immediately, but took a moment to buzz Lucy and ask to put her calls into voicemail for the next ten minutes. Monique was surprised and yet not surprised to receive the letter. It was the first she'd had from Deirdre.

Dear Monique,

I'm sorry I haven't written to you sooner. I've been meaning to, but at times it's been hard to believe everything that's happened, especially that day. Sometimes I'm glad my arm got hurt (don't worry, it's all better now). That made me know it wasn't some crazy dream I'd had.

I went to Canada to look in on the girl S was trying to help, and she's doing fine. It looks like she has a good life. She and I talked a bit, and I told her that S is gone. I think she was relieved. She said she always thought he'd come back.

But like I said, she seems like she's going to be all right. I thought you'd want to know that.

And just so you know, Nick (my boyfriend) and I aren't going to be in WI much longer. We're moving to Minnesota, not too far from the Twin Cities. Nick's got a job as a ranger at one of the national parks there, and we'll be close to his family — I met some of them at Easter and they're nice people.

I'm not going to start working right away. Instead I've registered at the University of Minnesota for this fall. I haven't decided on a major yet but I've got some ideas — and perhaps you could tell me if their law school is a good one? Thanks in advance.

I'll let you know my address when we finish moving. Again, I'm sorry I haven't written sooner. I think about you a lot. How smart and brave you were that day. And I think about S a lot too.

Yours,

Deirdre

Monique put the letter down, sat looking out her window. She was not so much surprised by Deirdre's letter as she was touched by it. It would have been easy for Deirdre to put everything that had happened behind her, to will herself to forget any of it had happened. But she'd made sure the woman in Canada was doing all right, and she'd thought to let Monique know that things were well.

Monique often thought of Deirdre, and her thoughts had always ended with the worry that Deirdre would be poisoned by what she'd been through. She no longer had to worry.

Her reverie was interrupted by her iPhone beeping at her. Time to get back to work. She was taking Friday off, so she and Michael could have a belated anniversary getaway weekend in Boston. *That's the trouble with being a pilot,* Michael had grumbled, *you never get to travel where or when you want to.* Yes, time to get back to work, but first she'd write back to Deirdre, thank her and wish her well, tell her that University of Minnesota had a fine law school, and ask her to keep in touch.

Deirdre navigated her way through the maze of boxes that the apartment had become. Nick and Jim had gone to get the moving van, and tonight Laurel would cook them a farewell dinner. Glad as she was to be going to Minnesota, Deirdre was sorry to be leaving Jim and Laurel; they were good people. Nick and Deirdre had made sure the house they were renting had a guest room and access for Laurel's wheelchair so she and Jim could visit.

It never failed to amaze her, whenever she moved, how the boxes stacked up. Nick's things, of course. Those she'd brought when she moved in, which didn't really amount to a lot. But there were boxes of Anna's things too. The estate had been settled; the farm and the house would be sold, to pay off the mortgage. The contents of the house were willed to Anna's and Richard's families. Deirdre didn't know exactly what was to become of Richard's possessions, and in fact she did not care. But it brought her both pleasure and sadness to learn that Anna had decreed her relatives could take whatever of her possessions they wanted, and that Deirdre got first pick.

She'd gone to the house a month ago. Nick had been with her, and though they never spoke of it she knew they'd both been remembering the last time they'd been there. As they approached the driveway Deirdre had felt her arm send out a phantom throb of pain, felt her throat tighten. She had once loved this house. She had once sat at the kitchen table with Anna, the two of them drinking tea and talking of happy times and inconsequential things. Now she wanted only to take a few mementoes and never see the place again. Her memories of it would be mixed up with grief, betrayal, and fear.

She'd braced herself for walking into the front room; she'd never seen the aftermath of what the shotgun blast had done to Frank Halsey, and judging by Nick's pale look she was exceedingly glad of it. But the room was clean. Too clean. The government agents had swept it all away, just as they'd swept away the whole story of Richard and Sean and Leo and God knew what else.

After that it was easier. Deirdre didn't want much. She took a few photo albums — not the more recent ones, but older albums with pictures of she and Anna, taken during those magical summers. She took a number of books, even some cookbooks and gardening books, in case she ever decided to get serious about cooking or have a garden. She took Anna's rolltop desk, and a patchwork quilt. A framed picture of she and Anna, taken a couple years ago. The last thing she took was a knickknack — a glass unicorn. Nothing remarkable, just that it had been her first Christmas present to Anna, and had somehow survived all these years without so much as a chip.

All these things save the desk were in boxes now, ready for the drive up to Minnesota. She was ready too, once she'd attended to one last matter.

The day was hot, but a strong breeze took the edge off the heat. Deirdre's skirt fluttered and the breeze lifted the scent of the daisies she carried into the air. As she drew closer, she saw that her small Christmas tree was still here and doing fine, though the ornaments were sadly faded. Flowers were here as well. As Deirdre knelt and placed her daisies on Anna's grave she realized that every time she'd come, there had been a token placed here. Always, flowers: today there were some Icelandic poppies that looked remarkably like the ones in Laurel's flowerbeds. Around Eastertime, someone had left a beautifully painted egg. And small stones had been put on the headstone (this last had puzzled Deirdre until Terry from the dental office had explained it to her).

"Hello, Nan," she said. Deirdre was careful not to look at Richard's grave nearby. Her visit was for Anna, not Richard.

"Nick and I are going tomorrow. I hope you don't mind it. I thought for a while I shouldn't go, but when Nick said Minnesota, well, I remembered that summer. Did you understand how much that meant to me? You probably did. I could sit here for a year and never say enough thanks for that.

"I wish we could have had more time. I wish it had all ended better." She drew a ragged breath. "I wish I knew if I'd done right." Words failed her, but she was wondering, as she sometimes did, if she had been right to forgive Sean instead of taking revenge. But then, revenge was why Sean had come to Du Lac in the first place. Deirdre's desire for revenge had put her on a collision course with Leo Sorensen. Of course there was Frank Halsey and his grudge.

She still wasn't sure if she'd done right, but it was what Anna would have done, and that was enough for Deirdre.

I'm sorry, she started to say, meaning to apologize for not clearing Anna's name of Leo's slander. She looked again at the tokens left here by those whose lives had been touched by Anna. There was no need to apologize, because those who had loved Anna knew better than to believe such things. What were Leo's petty lies against the love she saw in these tokens? Nothing to be concerned about.

She had regrets, and grief. She had anger and was sometimes afraid of the things she was capable of. She had love — Anna's and Nick's — and most of all, she had the capacity to love. For if Anna had not taken the time to befriend Deirdre so many years ago, what might have happened to Deirdre? She did not like to think of it. Anna had saved her, and Nick would help keep her safe.

"I love you, Nan," she said as she stood and prepared to leave. On impulse, she picked up the Christmas tree. It would come with her to

Minnesota, she decided, and when she and Nick were settled she would plant it. Every Christmas she would decorate it, and remember her cousin.

Deirdre left the cemetery, carrying the Christmas tree. She no longer felt that she was leaving Anna behind. She was leaving the bad times, her own rage and guilt. She was taking the best of things — her memories, her love, the capacity to forgive — none of which she would have had if not for Anna. So she could be more like the person whom she had loved best.

The end

HOW THE STORY BEGAN... IN *ASHES*

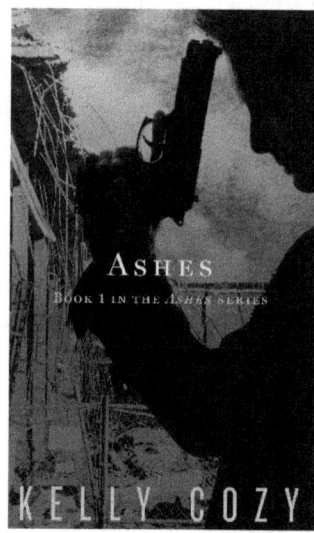

Anonymous. That was Jennifer's life. But when she survived a domestic terrorist attack and her last-minute escape became the iconic image of the event, that life was over. Wanting only to disappear, she cashed in on her unwanted fame and moved to a small town.

Retired. That was Sean's life. A former covert operative, he'd been pushed unwillingly into a life of suburban peace and quiet. But his retirement ended when he saw Jennifer's rescue; from then on he only wanted to find those responsible for the attack, even if it meant turning rogue.

"From the mind-set of a survivor of a terror attack, as well as a well-meaning retired government operative bent on revenge, it flows effortlessly between the two while also drawing a vivid picture of both characters' emotional state.... It will resonate long past the last page, and leave you longing for the sequel.." - *Literary R&R*

"Had me glued by the first few pages... the most suspenseful story that I have read in a long time." - *The Reading Cafe*

"Ms. Cozy has a remarkable way with words and has made *Ashes* a definite must-read novel." - *The Bibliophilic Book Blog*

"Will draw the reader in and unable to tear themselves away from the ending."
- Erica Moulton, *POD People*

Available in print and ebook.
For more information, contact smitepublications@gmail.com

PRAISE FOR KELLY COZY'S DEBUT NOVEL
THE DAY AFTER YESTERDAY

The events of a single night can change a life forever, as musician Daniel Whitman discovers when he loses his family and home.

Overwhelmed by grief, unable to find solace in his music or accept comfort from his friends, he flees up the California coast. Daniel thinks he's leaving everything behind, but his journey will take him to the places and people that will help him find his way back.

The Day After Yesterday is a story of hope, friendship, and the redemptive power of music.

"This book has touched me in a way I didn't expect and will never forget. ... It's breathtaking, heartbreaking, and just plain beautiful. I can't recommend it enough."
- Tia Silverthorne Bach, author of *Chasing Memories*

"Ms. Cozy has a definite gift for writing that allows the reader to intimately know her characters... A beautiful story by a talented writer." - *Literary R&R*

"I found myself stopping and setting it aside - I didn't want it to end. By putting it down, I could enjoy it longer, savor it more." - *The Book Bag*

"This novel captured both my attention and my heart. The characters are realistic, multi-faceted, and endearing. I shared in both their laughter and their tears, and was saddened to reach the end of their tale. I highly recommend this book."
- Mary Smith-Fuller, *Flurries of Words*

Available in print and ebook.
For more information, contact smitepublications@gmail.com

ABOUT THE AUTHOR

Photo © Loa Allebach

Kelly Cozy is the author of *The Day After Yesterday* and *Ashes*. She is currently at work on her next novel.

Her first nonfiction work, *A Nerd Girl's Guide to Cinema*, will be available in 2014 from Smite Publications.

She lives in California with her husband, son, and cats. Visit her online at:

Blog: kellycozy.blogspot.com

Twitter: @Kelly_Cozy

Facebook: Kelly Cozy, Author